MW01256306

HEMLOCK
&SILVER

HEMLOCK & SILVER

T. KINGFISHER

TOR

TOR PUBLISHING GROUP

NEW YORK

This is a work of fiction. All of the characters, organizations,
and events portrayed in this novel are either products of the author's
imagination or are used fictitiously.

HEMLOCK & SILVER

Copyright © 2025 by Ursula Vernon

All rights reserved.

A Tor Book
Published by Tom Doherty Associates / Tor Publishing Group
120 Broadway
New York, NY 10271

Tor® is a registered trademark of Macmillan Publishing Group, LLC.

ISBN 978-1-250-34203-4

Printed in the United States of America

For Sergei

HEMLOCK
&SILVER

CHAPTER 1

I had just taken poison when the king arrived to inform me that
he had murdered his wife.

The poison was a distillate of chime-adder venom, which
burned my sinuses when I took it off my wrist the way some
people take snuff. The king was a tired man of medium height,
with sandy hair and deep grooves worn into the sides of his face. I
hadn't recognized him at first when he stepped through the door
of the stillroom. Well, why would I? The king was someone that I
had seen far off, at the head of a long table or perched on a throne.
Without context, he was simply a well-dressed man who had come
in without even knocking.

Still, he *had* looked naggingly familiar, and I thought perhaps
he was one of my father's friends, so I simply said, "Wait a moment, please," and turned back to stripping rosemary leaves off
thin wooden stems. (I always process rosemary after snorting adder venom. The fragrance of the rosemary helps to clear out the
awful burnt smell of the venom.)

Then the little voice in my head whispered, *One moment please,
Your Majesty,* and recognition crashed over me like cold water.

I spun back toward the man in the doorway. He wasn't standing
in profile, so I couldn't see if his face was the same one that was
stamped on coins, but Saints help me, he was wearing a circlet, a
thin little silver thing, and surely no one would wear that except
royalty. Which meant he really was the king after all, except that
he was standing in my workroom, where he had no business being. And I had just ordered him to wait.

I panicked and tried to curtsy, but when I clutched my skirts,

I dropped the rosemary, and the leaves went spilling down over my skirt and clung to the fabric, sticky with sap.

"Your Majesty," I croaked. My mouth was so dry that I half expected to hear my tongue rasp against the roof of my mouth. "I'm sorry. I didn't recognize . . . That is, I didn't expect . . ." Could I ask him to turn sideways so that I could check his profile? No, probably not.

He did not look angry. He smiled faintly while I brushed futilely at my skirt. "Mistress Anja?" he asked.

I nodded. That was my name, although I won't swear that I wouldn't have nodded no matter what he'd said.

"You have doubtless heard that I killed my wife," the widowed king said. "It's true. I did."

The words made no sense to me. They might have been a mouse's squeak or a beetle's click. I stared at the king with my sinuses full of venom and my mind full of nothing at all.

Why is he here? Father was part of a council of leading merchants who sometimes advised the king on economic matters, but he always went to the king, not the other way around. *Am I supposed to entertain him until Father returns?*

No, that was absurd, my father wasn't due back for nearly a week. And this didn't seem like a man who would be entertained by a treatise on the dangerous properties of powdered lead. Regardless, the housekeeper should have settled him in the best room and brought him wine and come to fetch me, not brought the king here as if I were his equal. And the staff knew that—at least theoretically, I couldn't imagine they had any more practical experience with kings than I did—so either he had snuck in or he had demanded to see me, and neither scenario made any sense at all.

Perhaps he wants an antidote or some prevention against poison? That was the only thing that might make sense, but why would he come himself instead of sending a messenger? Kings had people to run errands for them. It was one of the few reasons I could imagine wanting to be king.

"Well?" he said.

I blinked at him. "Well what, Your Majesty?"

He made a quick, impatient gesture. "The rumors that I killed my wife. I told you, they're true."

It is very hard to respond to a statement like that. Even if I had been at my best, even if he *hadn't* been a king, what could you say? Besides, I hadn't heard any such thing. I knew that the queen had died a few months ago, that was all. Gossip found its way into my workroom only slightly more often than kings.

If I were the person that I should be, I would have been angry. It wasn't right that someone could just announce that he was a murderer and expect everyone to smile and nod along, simply because he was the king. A good and decent person would have been filled with righteous outrage. But my heart was starting to race from the venom and my mind was cloudy, and it was simply all so baffling that I heard myself say, "Ah?" as if he had just said something mildly interesting at a party, and part of my brain said, *That should be "Ah, Your Majesty?"* and the rest ran in little gibbering circles inside my skull, wondering if I was about to be executed for sheer foolishness. I had never heard that the king was prone to executions, but until a moment ago, I had also never heard that he had killed his wife.

He didn't look as if he was about to have me executed. He looked tired and worn, and the deep lines carved on either side of his mouth did not appear on the coins. He didn't fidget, but he shifted his weight, anxious in the way of men who are not used to being anxious and aren't very good at it. "I wanted to get that out of the way," he said. "In case you could not see past it."

He's expecting me to see past a murder? *How? And why would he care? He could have just not said anything about it, and I would have been just as confused and awkward as I am now.*

"Ah," I said again, searching his face in hopes that everything would become clear. It didn't.

Surely a murderer would look different? Not so tired? At thirty-five,

I was more than old enough to know that evil could present a fair face, but I had never heard that it got tired. Quite the opposite, really. Evil is relentlessly energetic.

For that matter, did *he actually kill her? Or did she die in childbirth or of a broken heart and now he blames himself?* That seemed much more plausible. Gossip was one thing, but the king murdering the queen was the sort of scandal that would have rocked the entire city.

Nevertheless, he had brought it up, and clearly that was the topic of conversation. "How did she die, Your Majesty?" I asked politely.

If the question surprised him, the king gave no sign. "I ran her through with my sword."

Well. So much for that theory. I clenched sticky fingers in the folds of my gown, feeling the first stirrings of outrage. *And he expects me to see past it? Does he think I'll just overlook murdering his wife? Some sins are unforgivable, even for kings!*

"She was cutting our daughter's heart out," he added.

. . . or not.

Dust motes floated between us, suspended in the beam of sunlight from the windows. Glass alembics glinted, and the chimeadder moved restlessly in her cage, accompanied by the thin sound of bells. My heart thudded in my chest, hard and fast, as the venom did its work.

"Forgive me, Your Majesty," I said, forming each word carefully. "I think I need to sit down."

The widowed king took my arm, all courtesy, and helped me to the chair. He was shorter than I was, which didn't seem right at all. I'm a big woman, granted, but kings are supposed to be taller than ordinary mortals, even if only by the height of a crown. That extra half inch seemed somehow anti-monarchist.

There was only one chair in the stillroom, and I knew that you weren't supposed to sit when a king was standing, but you *definitely* weren't supposed to faint when a king was standing, so my options were limited. I sat.

The king hitched one hip up on the table and faced me, which was enough like sitting that it probably counted. I tried to smooth my skirt and succeeded only in dislodging more rosemary leaves. The smell rose, cleansing and pungent, and chased away any possibility of fainting. I was *here*. In the workroom. There were bundles of dried herbs hanging from the rafters and distilling equipment arranged along the table, and also there was a king.

My nose itched dreadfully. It always does after snorting venom. I tried to wipe it in a dainty and ladylike fashion, with minimal success.

"I am very sorry, Your Majesty," I said finally. "That sounds dreadful."

That startled him, I could tell. His eyes had been on the floor and rose sharply to my face. "Yes," he said. "Yes, it was. Very . . . very dreadful. I've never had to . . . That is . . . killing someone in battle isn't like that."

I suspected that this was the first time he had spoken those words. Had no one offered him sympathy? Perhaps it had simply been the wrong sort of sympathy. I could imagine everyone telling him that he had done the right thing, the needful thing, and no one actually suggesting how terrible the right thing must have been.

I didn't want to feel bad for him, not when I was still angry at him for coming into my workroom and being the king. But it was hard not to feel some kind of sympathy.

"Your daughter—" I began.

"She died."

I wasn't surprised to hear it. Cutting someone's heart out is a very specific process, after all. You'd have to get quite far along before it was distinguishable from mere stabbing. "Shit," I said, and then slapped my hand over my mouth in horror.

Shit, Your Majesty, my brain informed me. I clamped my fingers down to prevent the sudden hysterical laughter from rising. *Ah yes, laugh at his daughter dying. That's sure to endear you to him.*

The king snorted. There wasn't much humor in it, but there was a little, and I liked him better for it. *Not that I have any place to be liking or disliking a king.*

"Don't," he said, gesturing to my hand. "That's possibly the first honest thing anyone's said to me about it."

"I'm sorry for that, too, then."

He nodded. "You're probably wondering why I'm here," he said.

This was such an absurd understatement that I choked back another hysterical laugh. "Yes, Your Majesty."

He glanced around the workroom, as if seeing it for the first time. "Your father says you know much of poisons."

Had I thought my mouth was dry before? Now it felt like my tongue was swaddled in wool. I could not believe that my father had been so indiscreet as to speak of such a thing to the king. Of course, he was proud of me, I knew that, but still. People had been put to death for knowing too much about poison. Granted, the Temple of Saint Adder had extended me the title of *Healer* for my work, but that was a thin protection against slander. Physicians could get away with knowing too much about poison. Middle-aged spinsters could not.

"Antidotes," I said, a bit feebly. "My interest is in antidotes, not poisons." Granted, one of those poisons was currently coursing through my veins, but it didn't seem like the time to mention it.

"Of course." The king inclined his head. "But they are two sides of the same coin, are they not?"

I picked at the rosemary on my skirt and looked around the workroom, trying to buy a little time. The room was full of herbs and glassware and a sharp clean smell, but I had not realized until that moment how worn all the furnishings were and how many cobwebs had gathered in the distant corners, as if the king's presence threw all the stains into sharp relief.

A little resentment pushed back the bafflement then, a thin thread that said how *dare* a king come here, into my own space, where he did not belong, and make it seem so shabby by comparison?

The absurdity of the thought struck me before it even finished forming. Kings went where they chose in their own kingdoms, and merchants' daughters smiled and agreed. Even if they were agreeing to something that might get them burned or hanged or stoned to death.

"I have learned a few small things about treating poison," I admitted. (Which was false modesty, but I was hardly about to brag to a king. There are wonder tales about what happens when you brag to royalty. Many of them involve getting your head chopped off if you fail to deliver.)

"I am hoping that you can help me," the king said.

"Err," I said. *Err, Your Majesty.* "How so?"

Thud, thud, thud went my heart, so loudly that I was surprised the king couldn't hear it.

"My daughter Snow is sick." He spread his hands. "It is slow, whatever it is, but it is killing her. None of the physicians I have consulted have the least idea what is wrong. Most of them say it is simply shock at losing her mother and her sister, but I know that it is more than that." He put a hand over his heart. "I *know*. But I do not know what to do."

Now I was on firmer ground. "Ah. What are her symptoms?"

He shook his head. "I don't know. I don't know what is a symptom and what is simply being a grieving twelve-year-old girl. She eats little, she is very pale, her moods are erratic—but which of those is significant? And what am I overlooking?"

"I see." He wasn't wrong. Family members were forever trying to tell you what the symptoms were, in my experience, and half the time, they'd fixated on entirely the wrong thing. The other half of the time, they were convinced that they knew exactly what had poisoned the victim and were pointing fingers at each other over the sickbed.

How much worse would that be when the sickbed belongs to a king's daughter?

"I have had what feels like every doctor in the kingdom attend my daughter," the king said. "They have bled her and sweated her and accomplished nothing. They tell me that it is not consumption, nor ague, nor any one of a hundred ailments. But they cannot tell me what it *is*. And she gets no better."

I doubt that I'd get better if I was being sweated and bled and having my feet blistered and the saints know what else, I thought, but I certainly wasn't going to say that out loud. "So now you're wondering if someone is poisoning her."

It was a statement of fact, but he answered anyway. "I do. And I hoped that you would come to the palace and tell me what you find."

I rubbed my temples. "Your Majesty," I said wearily, knowing that I should just agree to whatever he wanted but fearing the consequences if I did. "I am at your disposal, but I must warn you that very few ailments are actually the result of poison."

"No?" A half smile crossed his lined face. "To hear gossip tell it, no royalty has ever died of natural causes."

I could not hide my exasperation. "Because it is a much better story to be poisoned than to have eaten a bad bit of fish, or contracted choleric fever, or drunk oneself into a stupor. People reach for poison as an excuse because they want something to blame. Most of the cases that I see have nothing to do with malice at all, and much more to do with drinking fouled water or eating the wrong thing by accident."

My hammering heart palpitations gave the lie to what I was saying, but I reminded myself that the king couldn't possibly know about them.

"You say *most* cases," the king said. "Not all, then?"

I bit my lip. "No," I admitted. "Not all."

It occurred to me belatedly that I was talking to a man who had inherited his throne because of poison. The old king had been convinced that his enemies were trying to murder him. He had been quite mad but not, as it turned out, incorrect.

The king nodded slowly. "I sent Snow away from the palace early on, away from courtiers," he said. "When we still thought it was grief. She improved for a time, but then it worsened again. My fear is that the poisoner has followed her."

I picked at my skirt again. It was old and stained, the fabric long overdue for the rag bin, and I resented him a little more for seeing me in it. *But it's not as if I can wear a ball gown to process herbs, on the off chance a king stops by.*

Probably there were noblewomen who did wear ornate gowns all the time, for just such an eventuality. But I presumed that they spent less time around open flame than I did.

"Do you have any idea who might want to poison your daughter?" I asked finally.

"That's the maddening thing," he said, rubbing his hands over his face. "I don't. I have an heir already, and Snow is nowhere in the line of succession. At best, she *might* marry and have a child that *might* someday be in line for the throne, if my son Gunther's line dies out."

It seemed to me that this meant the most logical poisoner was the king's heir, seeking to remove a possible future rival, but I didn't want to say that. I'd never heard any ill of the prince, though, and in any case, he was currently several hundred miles away, courting the eligible ladies of the kingdom of Tohni.

"Will you come with me?" asked the king abruptly.

I lifted my head, startled. "Come with you?"

"To Witherleaf. To see Snow for yourself. To see what the others have missed." Whatever my expression, he mistook it, because he gestured at the workroom, the sweep of his hand taking in the glass alembics and the jars and the chime-adder drowsing in her cage. "Bring your equipment. A workroom will be prepared for you. Anything you require. Witherleaf is only three days' ride from here."

Three *days*?

I swallowed around my first instinctive protest. One did not say no to a king, and one certainly did not shout *no!* in a king's face.

"But . . . surely if you suspect poison, there are others better equipped . . ." I tried, while part of me panicked about how I would continue my work so far from the city, and the other part panicked about what would happen if I failed to cure the king's daughter of whatever mysterious ailment had taken hold of her, and a third, largely insignificant part noted that this batch of chime-adder distillate was the strongest one I'd cooked up yet, and I should probably back the dosage down if I didn't want to give my patients heart failure. (This is why I test each batch on myself.)

"If it *is* poison, who can I trust?" the king asked. "My advisors have suggested a dozen physicians, for all the good it has done. So now I must ask *why* they put those names forward and whom they might have served in doing so." He shook his head. "But you . . . well, your father mentioned you to me a year ago, long before Snow became ill."

"I'd saved his horse from snakebite," I said wearily. "I think he told everyone in the city."

"He told me, certainly." Another faint smile from the king. "When I began to suspect poison, I remembered the story. And I have come to you alone to ask for help."

"I did wonder where Your Majesty's . . . err . . . entourage was."

"Doubtless drinking the excellent wine your servants have provided and wondering what on earth I am doing. Meanwhile, you have no ties to any of my advisors, no one has put your name forward, and you stand to gain nothing if my daughter dies."

And neither of us will mention what I stand to lose. I wound my fingers in the folds of my skirt, feeling something duller than fear sink into my bones. It was not good to brag to a king, but it was much, much worse to fail one. "I . . . Your Majesty, you realize . . . I cannot promise anything."

He met my eyes steadily. I thought again of how tired he looked, and part of me wanted to help him and part of me wanted to hide under the bed until the world went away and left me alone. "I'm not unreasonable, even if I am a king. If you cannot cure her, at least I will be no worse off for having you try."

It was no use. My course had been set as soon as the stillroom door had opened to admit a king.

I tried one last time to change it. "I don't want to give you false hope, Your Majesty."

"And you are afraid of what may happen to your father and yourself, if you cannot cure my daughter," the king said. "Aren't you?"

I felt my lips twist. He knew, then.

Of course he knows, he's the king, he's been playing games with nobility all his life. And everyone remembers what his uncle was like. "The thought had crossed my mind."

The king nodded. "I promise that no stain will attach to either of you," he said. "I am grasping at straws. Don't think I don't know it."

You say *that, but it will happen anyway. But what choice do I have?* I blew out my breath in a long sigh. "Then, Your Majesty, I would be honored to grasp at them alongside you."

CHAPTER 2

My interest in poisons began when I was eleven years old.

My sisters and I had been sent to the countryside to avoid the foul air that was said to permeate the city that summer, bringing typhus and glandular fever with it. My father had an estate there with orchards and olive trees and a small vineyard, all of it capably managed by our aunt. It was startlingly lush to my eyes—Four Saints is on the edge of the desert, and while you can grow plenty of things there, few of them come in such shocking shades of green.

On the first day, our cousin Anthony was given charge of his cousins and told to show us around the estate. Anthony was nearly thirteen and clearly resented being saddled with three younger children—my sister Catherine was only seven and inclined to be weepy—so he dedicated himself to showing just how ignorant the town-based cousins were.

"Bet you don't know what this is," he said, about the olive trees and the presses where the oil was made. "Bet you don't know what this is," about the killdeer pretending to have a broken wing and the great fields of ripening wheat and the ant lions hidden in their funnels of sand. "Bet you don't know what this is," he said, of the purple and yellow flowers of nightshade, which, he assured us, would kill us dead if we so much as touched a petal to our tongues.

And "Bet you don't know what this is," about a tall plant with a lacy mop of white flowers, which he pulled up from the ground, displaying a pale, knobbly root crusted with dirt.

"What is it?" asked Catherine, as she had asked for the last four hours.

"It's a carrot, stupid," said Anthony. "Don't you know anything?"

"Really?" asked my sister Isobel, as she had also asked for the last four hours.

"It doesn't look like a carrot," I said. Carrots, in my experience, were purple or yellow, not cream-colored, although it was carrot-shaped and had the same little leggy roots.

"It's a *wild* carrot," said Anthony. "Bet you didn't know they could grow wild. Bet you thought they only came from a market cart."

I shrugged. I had never given much thought to the origin of carrots.

Anthony laughed at me, chopped the root off with his knife, wiped off the worst of the dirt, and popped it into his mouth.

Two hours later he was dead.

The next day, while the whole estate was plunged into mourning and Anthony's mother had taken to her bed, I slipped away to the field where the poison hemlock that looked so much like wild carrots grew. I looked for the knot of lacy white flowers, pulled one up, then laid it out on the ground and crouched over the pale root, studying it.

I knew that death existed, of course. I had lost two grandparents and one baby sister in the crib. I had not particularly liked Anthony, though I felt very bad for his mother, so I could not say that I was mourning him. But it struck me as deeply bizarre that Anthony had been alive and then his path had intersected with this quiet little root and now he wasn't alive any longer.

I sniffed cautiously at the carrot-like shape. It smelled like mouse nests. I wondered if Anthony had noticed that and simply kept chewing because he didn't want to spit it out in front of his cousins after making such a big deal about it. Bravado and a little root no thicker than my own small thumb had killed him.

I could pick the root up now and bite into it, and I, too, would be dead. The thought gave me a strange queasy feeling, as if I was looking down from a very high place.

It had all happened so *fast*. Two hours! It seemed wrong that something so large and irrevocable as death could happen so fast. The sun hadn't even gone down. Anthony had died in daylight, and no one had been able to say, *Wait, stop, this shouldn't happen*, and change it.

But when the horse threw the stable boy last year and his head hit the stones and he died, it took less than a minute. Two hours is much, much longer than that.

Two hours should have been long enough to do *something.*

I jammed my chin onto my fist, my mind twisting and turning over those two hours. My aunt had tried to make Anthony vomit, but it had been too late. They poured medicines down his throat and rubbed oil under his nostrils, hoping to stave off the creeping effects of the poison, but nothing worked. In the end, they prayed desperately to Saint Adder, but it seemed that not even a saint could help.

"There's no antidote," one of the servants had said softly to another, not realizing that there was a young girl listening. "Oh, poor boy. There's no cure for hemlock. Better they should let him go peacefully."

I sat back on my heels beside the root that was stronger than a saint, thinking. Overhead, the sky was a perfect shade of blue, and the wind rustled in the grass, and a killdeer called, crying over its not-broken wing. I cataloged all those things absently, but the thought that kept coming back to me was a simple question.

Why isn't *there a cure?*

I was a child with a child's attention span. Many adults think this is no more than a butterfly's, flittering from thought to thought, but they have forgotten how, in some children, it is as sharp and pointed as a stiletto. Mine was focused now.

The victim I chose for my stiletto was the herbwoman who made up possets and tinctures for the estate. I walked into the stillroom, smelling the rich array of scents, pungent and sweet and acrid by turns, went up to the herbwoman, and asked, without preamble, "Why is there no cure for hemlock poisoning?"

The herbwoman was good with herbs and awkward with people, particularly children. She was so awkward, in fact, that she did not answer with a story that would impose order on the world, as my nurse would, nor a parable placing it in the hands of the saints, as the family priest would. Instead she told me the exact truth.

"I don't know."

My eyes narrowed. An adult telling me that they didn't know something was both novel and unwelcome. "There *should* be a cure," I said.

"There may be one," the herbwoman offered, inching away slightly, "but no one knows what it is."

This opened up new possibilities, and I didn't like any of them. If there *was* a cure, then Anthony had died because of ignorance. (The weary young woman who attempted to teach languages and deportment to me and my sisters was very fond of the word *ignorance* and used it often.)

I stood in the quiet of the stillroom, thinking. The herbwoman, with many sidelong glances, went back to grinding dried borage with a mortar and pestle. Soft crunching sounds drifted through the room, while I worked through the ramifications of ignorance.

Some poisons *did* have cures . . . No, that was wrong. Some poisons had cures that people *knew about.* I had seen people hawking such things on the streets of the city, promising antidotes for arsenic and the bites of mad dogs and *overindulgence in lead,* whatever that meant. But not hemlock.

"How many poisons don't have cures?" I demanded, startling the herbwoman so badly that she dropped her pestle.

"Saints!" the woman said, getting down on her knees to retrieve the wayward implement, which had, of course, rolled under the table. "I don't know," she said again. "Lots, I suppose. Beetleblister

and cherry laurel water. Autumn crocus. Distillate of cyclamen."
She scrabbled for the pestle, which had rolled too far back for her
to reach.

"I'll get it." I flattened myself, slid half-under the table, and
emerged with the pestle, which I handed over. The herbwoman
wiped it off on her skirt and went back to work.

"Could those other poisons have cures, too?" I asked. "Except
nobody knows what they are?"

"Very likely," the herbwoman said, clearly wondering when this
alarming child would go away.

I folded my arms. "How did people find the cures we *do* have,
then?"

The herbwoman rubbed a hand over her face and again told
the truth, which, in this case, many adults would not have. "In
ancient times, they'd poison prisoners and then give them an antidote. If the prisoner lived, they'd know it was a cure. If he died,
they'd know they hadn't gotten it right yet."

If she was hoping that this gruesome information would cause
me to flee, she was disappointed. I lifted my head like a warhorse
hearing battle. "*Really?*" I breathed, appalled and fascinated,
imagining the poisoned prisoners and the desperate hope that
they would be the lucky one who got an antidote that worked.

"They don't do that now," the herbwoman said hastily, doubtless
wondering what idea she'd put in my head. "Only a long time ago."

"What do they do now?"

"Err . . . test it on dogs, mostly. Or doves sometimes, or rabbits."

I made a pained noise. I was fond of dogs, and this seemed
much more real and immediate than a prisoner from ancient times
who would've been long dead anyway.

"At *any* rate," said the herbwoman, in a desperate attempt to
wrestle back control of the conversation, "doctors know all sorts of
cures these days. But there are lots of poisons, so be careful what
you eat. Not like poor young Anthony."

She turned her attention firmly to the table in front of her. When she finally looked up, I can only assume that she was enormously relieved to see that the merchant's daughter and her questions had gone away.

My sisters and I returned to the city as soon as it was safe to do so, leaving the olive trees and the poison hemlock and the grieving mother behind. I, who had never particularly cared for my lessons or my tutors, went into the library and ran my fingers across the tooled bindings of the books, then pulled one down and began to read.

No one bothered me for two days, and then I heard footsteps and looked up to see my tutor standing in the entrance to the library.

"Anja? What are you doing here? It's late . . ." He trailed off, looking at the stacks of books that lay open around me, stacked in teetering piles, which made it fairly obvious what I was doing.

His name was Scand, and like most tutors, he was a scholar who needed money for his research and had consented to teach children languages and natural history and the rudiments of classical scholarship to get it. I knew that he was an old friend of my father's, but I'd never given him much thought beyond that. He was an indifferent teacher, and his students were indifferent pupils, and of all of them, I suspect I was not the one that he would expect to break the mold.

But he saw me sitting there, surrounded by open books, and he recognized at once what he was seeing—someone digging through every volume they could lay hands on, trying to find a specific piece of knowledge that they *knew* must be written down somewhere, if only they could find it.

I looked up at Scand and I didn't see the mediocre teacher—I saw an adult who often knew things that I didn't. I said, "Anthony died of eating poison hemlock. There must be a cure. *How do I find it?*"

It was late, and by rights he should have told me to go up to bed. The woman who taught us deportment would have taken one look at the books I was reading and been thoroughly appalled. Medical textbooks with anatomical drawings were not considered appropriate for eleven-year-olds, and the fact that I wasn't particularly interested in the pages with genitals and was instead puzzling over the digestive system would not have soothed her. (Besides, my sisters and I had found the drawings of genitals years earlier and giggled over them then.)

Scand, however, pulled out a chair of his own and said, "What have you found so far?"

"I can't find anything," I said miserably. "There must be a cure. Everything has a cure. Why isn't anyone looking for this one?" I slapped the table, which I think startled me more than it did Scand. I was half-drunk on frustration. Here was a problem that *could* be solved, and solving it would make the world better, *so why wasn't it solved yet*? "Why isn't *everyone* looking for it?"

"Someone may be," Scand said. "Or they started to and then got distracted trying to find a cure for mercury poisoning or lead or scorpion stings. Or they may be looking, but they still can't find the answer. You can't *force* a medical breakthrough."

He was talking to me like I was an adult, so I was determined not to burst into tears, which is what I wanted to do. I wanted very much to force a medical breakthrough. It wasn't *right* that your life could intersect with a little white root and then you were simply dead, without possibility of appeal. I was eleven and still believed in the fundamental justice of the world. It seemed as if I should be able to bring poison hemlock to the attention of someone—a saint or scholar or doctor or priest—and they would agree that this was a terrible oversight and *fix* it.

"Most of these books don't even mention hemlock," I said. "They spend whole chapters on arsenic and then mention in passing that there are 'various unwholesome herbs.' None of them even know how hemlock *works*."

"We'll have to find other books, then," Scand said, and that *we* warmed a place in my chest that had been cold since Anthony died.

"Here," I said. "I did find this one thing." I pulled one of the books toward me, running my finger over a passage that I could practically recite by now. "For as the Key fits unto the Lock, because the Lock is its mirror image, so the Antidote fits unto the Poison as its own mirror image. Look then unto the Poison's mirror, and so unlock the Curative to match it, each to each." I swept my hands across the stacks of books. "It makes sense. But how do I find the mirror image? What is the *opposite* of hemlock?"

My tutor shrugged. "I don't know," he said. "But I'll help you look."

I was extremely lucky to have Scand, even though I didn't realize it at the time. With the self-centeredness of youth and wealth, I never questioned that a tutor might spend dozens of hours a week helping their student learn about poison. I had simply assumed that it was part of his job. When I finally realized how unusual it was—mostly by listening to my cousins complain about *their* tutors—I was intensely embarrassed by how long it had taken.

When I asked him about it, many years later, he laughed. "I was bored," he said. "I couldn't pursue my own work any longer, and I was adrift with nothing to occupy me. And then you turned up in the library, hunched over a book as big as you were, and it interested me. I hadn't been interested in a question in quite a long time."

Regardless of why he'd helped me, he had. Not by pointing me in the right directions, but simply by being there. There is a crazy-wild delight that comes over you when you discover something new, something extraordinary. If you try to share that and people look at you blankly, it's crushing. But if there's someone else there to say *really?!* and take fire with enthusiasm alongside you—well, that will keep you going for a long time. Even though his great passion was optics and light and refraction, he had a good scholar's joy in discovery, and he gave it to me unstintingly.

Scand also championed my cause, such as it was, to my family.

Because of that, I was allowed to keep going. I overheard him talking to my father—

Well, no. I *shamelessly eavesdropped* on him talking to my father. He'd prepared a list of books that our library didn't have, which might help pursue our study of antidotes, and brought them to my father to ask if he might purchase them. I slunk along after him and waited outside Father's study, hoping that none of the servants would happen to walk by and see me with my ear pressed against the door.

"Upset over her cousin, is she?" Father asked. I could practically hear his raised eyebrow.

"I think it's more than that," Scand said. "Anja wants to *know*. It's as much about finding an answer as anything else."

"Still. All these treatises on poisons . . . Seems a bit morbid for a young girl, eh?"

I wanted to burst in and argue that it *wasn't* morbid, it was the *opposite* of morbid, it was about medicine and saving lives. I bit my tongue hard and listened for Scand's reply.

"I can't speak to that," Scand said, sounding much more casual than I felt, "but as her tutor, I can tell you that her reading's improved more in a month than in three years of my teaching. And half the books are in Tohalish, and she's going through them with a dictionary in hand." (Which was true so far as it went. My everyday Tohalish was still abysmal, but I could now carry on quite a good conversation about the effects of arsenic. Cook, who was from Tohal originally and normally helped me practice, had banned all such discussion from the kitchen the day that I learned to conjugate the word *vomit*.)

"Ah, well," Father said. "Whatever keeps her occupied, I suppose. I'm sure she'll get bored with it soon enough."

My father was a gifted merchant but a poor prophet. My interest did not wane, but only grew deeper and more intense. For my twelfth birthday, instead of a pony, I requested the six-volume *Materia Botanica*. "I could have bought three or four ponies for that price," he grumbled, but he bought it, and I lost myself in hundreds of drawings of herbs, each with painstakingly hand-tinted plates. Most of them didn't even grow out in the desert, but I memorized them anyway. My mind filled up with leaves and roots and symptoms of poisoning, though most of them ended the same way.

Aconite: vomiting, burning sensation, sweating, confusion, and finally death . . .
Belladonna: blurred vision, scarlet rash, delirium, convulsions, death . . .
Foxglove: confusion, vomiting, irregular heartbeat, difficulty breathing, death . . .
Hellebore: vertigo, thirst, swollen tongue, collapse, death . . .

It turned out that the sort of adults who were willing to listen to children prattle on about puppies and kitties and ponies and parties got a bit twitchy when a small girl began lecturing on toxicology. My father began sending me out of the house when new business associates came to visit.

Despite this, I still had not found the cure for hemlock poisoning.

"This is infuriating," I said. (Much like *ignorance, infuriating* was one of my deportment teacher's favorite words.) "It's been three months, and we still don't know what the opposite of hemlock is. In fact, I think I'm even more confused than when we started!"

"It happens that way sometimes," Scand said mildly, sliding a bookmark into the volume before him. "Learning just makes you aware of how much there is to learn."

I groaned and flung my legs over the arm of the chair, sliding down until my head rested on the opposite arm. I stared up at the ceiling with its peeled-log supports, as if the answers to my questions were written in the lightly polished wood. "Hemlock is green," I said, "and the opposite of green is red. And the root is poisonous, and the opposite of roots is probably flowers? Except that the root is sort of whitish, so the opposite might be black, and the whole thing is a vegetable, so the opposite is an animal, unless it's a mineral. It has the cold, watery aspect of the phlegmatic humor and thus is associated with Saint Trout. So I'm looking for a red or black flower . . . or mineral or animal . . . with a hot, dry aspect, of the choleric humor, which would be associated with Saint Lizard or Saint Adder. But that means it could be anything from torch flower to charcoal to . . . I don't know, a reptile of some sort. There are red-and-black lizards, aren't there?"

"There are," Scand agreed.

"An infusion of torch flower is good for sore eyes," I said, "but once you've eaten hemlock, I don't think you're worried about your eyes. Charcoal is good for some poisons, but not this one." I stared broodingly at the ceiling. "I don't know about the lizard."

"As I recall, the passage you found also said 'mirror image,' did it not?"

"I thought of that, too," I said. "But if I hold up a mirror to a hemlock root, it doesn't matter if the reflection would be an antidote, because I don't have any way of getting it out of the mirror." Scand was silent for so long that I sat up. "What is it?"

"Nothing," he said. "I thought once . . . but that was a long time ago." He hastily moved to distract me, which wasn't terribly hard. "Perhaps we're going about this the wrong way. Maybe an antidote *isn't* an opposite."

"But the book said it was."

"Who wrote the book?"

"It was translated from Harkelion the Physician."

Scand leaned back in his chair and steepled his fingers. "What if he was wrong?"

I stared at him in alarm. "What? But he's—he was one of the classical scholars! You know? He wrote half the books on medicine!"

"That doesn't mean he was *right*," Scand said.

"But physicians still use his books!" I tapped the cover of a book next to me. "They quote him all the time." Practically every book I'd read had at least an epigraph attributed to Harkelion, and most of them had much more.

"I'm sure they do," said Scand. "But that doesn't mean he was right. It just means that everyone has learned to repeat his errors."

I felt as if he had kicked one of the legs out from under my chair and set everything wobbling. "But he lived in ancient times! They were more enlightened—they knew things that we forgot—"

"In some ways, yes," he said. "But just because someone lived a thousand years ago doesn't make them correct."

I put my head in my hands. "But everybody says they were so *wise*."

"Some of them were," Scand said gently. "And there's a reason we go back to so many of their manuscripts. But they were still just people, like you and me. If someone found your notes in a thousand years, would that make you right?"

I glared at him through my spread fingers. "But you're the one who taught us the classics! You made me read that entire essay on geometry!"

Scand laughed, which did nothing to mollify me. "And if you had any interest in geometry, it would have been a very useful foundation, too. But it doesn't mean that all the classical scholars were right about everything they wrote. Some of them were very egregiously wrong, in fact. I think it was Marthian who advised cutting open a pigeon and placing it on the forehead of someone who was feverish in order to draw out the sickness."

"Eww." I thought of my last fever and how sweaty and miserable I'd felt, then tried to imagine how much worse everything would have been if there was a vivisected pigeon on my forehead.

"Exactly. We discard the writings that don't work for us and keep the ones that do." Scand shook his head ruefully. "One of my teachers had this exact conversation with me when I was studying. But I was nineteen at the time, so you're doing better than I am."

This was not much consolation. "But if Harkelion was wrong, then we're back where we started," I said, waving to the books that I had gone through with such care and the piles of notes in my crabbed handwriting. I had gotten painful hand cramps writing all those notes, and I'd cut myself twice sharpening quills. "And all this will have been *wasted*."

"Not at all. You've learned a great deal. You know the precise effects of hemlock on the body. You know a dozen common antidotes and why none of them work on hemlock, but why they may work on other poisons. And you've read the *Materia Botanica* twice. You probably know more about poisoning than most physicians. You don't have to redo any of that." One corner of his mouth twisted up in a smile. "That's the thing about learning. You get to keep it."

"I would rather have the answer," I muttered.

"Maybe you'll find the answer to a different question. If you never find the antidote for hemlock, but you do find one for . . . oh . . . colchicum, say . . . would you still consider your time wasted?"

I considered that for a few minutes. Colchicum is our autumn crocus, which is beautiful and grows in many gardens. Every now and again, someone takes it in their head to eat some. It can take up to a week to die, and it's not nearly as painless as poison hemlock. "That *would* be pretty useful," I admitted grudgingly. "But I'd rather find an antidote for both. And *anyway*"—I thumped the book again—"if Harkelion was wrong, then I don't know how to go about finding either one." According to the herbwife, I would probably need to poison either dogs or prisoners, and I had moral objections on both counts. (Also, I was twelve and unlikely to be given access to the palace prisons for scientific purposes.)

Scand reached out and tugged the offending book toward his side of the desk. "Even if he *was* right, this is a translation. Translation isn't always precise. It may be that someone used the wrong word and set us off on the wrong track."

I scowled. "So what do we do about *that*?"

"Well," said Scand, "you *could* learn a dead language . . ."

I let out a wail of despair.

". . . or I could translate it for you, if we can find something closer to the original."

I stared at the book. Then I stared at the ceiling. A little voice whispered to me that I could just give up now. I'd taken this as far as I could go, and I *had* learned a lot. As Scand said, I got to keep that. I could admit defeat and put the books away.

Surely if there was an answer, someone would have found it by now. Harkelion had lived a thousand years ago. You could still see the ruins of the city he'd lived in, all weathered stone and tumbledown walls. If he'd just been translated wrong, someone would have figured that out in the centuries it had taken for those walls to come down.

It was ridiculous to think that a twelve-year-old girl might find an answer that a thousand years of physicians had overlooked.

There was a hot, headachy feeling behind my eyes, like suppressed tears.

"I'll never find it, will I?" I said out loud. "This is pointless."

"*No,*" said Scand, and I stopped looking at the ceiling and looked at him instead, because he didn't sound the way he normally did, all calm and measured. He sounded raw and angry, the way that I felt. "Anja, you may or may not find the cure for poison hemlock, but I promise you, if you keep studying, you will find *something*. Something that will make all the work you've done worthwhile."

"I'm twelve," I said, in a very small voice.

"Then you've gotten started early." He reached out and squeezed my hand, which came as a surprise. Scand never touched anyone, so far as I could tell. His fingers were dry and warm, and his grip was tight, as if I'd slid over the edge of a cliff and he needed to haul me back up. "If you keep asking questions, you *will* find answers. I promise you."

It took me more than twenty years, but in the end, I proved him right.

CHAPTER 3

"*Of course* you've heard the rumors about his wife's death," my sister Isobel said, clearly exasperated. "I *told* you about them."

"What? No." I was packing straw around my distilling equipment, but paused and straightened up. My lower back did not appreciate the angle I'd been leaning at, and made its displeasure known. I rubbed it, which didn't really help. "You did?"

"Yes," Isobel said. "I did. I was standing here and you were standing over there"—she gestured in the general direction of the worktable—"and you said, 'Oh, hmm, interesting.' And I asked if you thought it was true, and you said that you hadn't any idea, and then something caught fire."

"Oh, *that* day," I said, relieved. "Yes, I remember that. And it was only a small fire."

"But you forgot about the king's wife."

". . . It wasn't *that* small a fire."

Isobel rolled her eyes. Both of us take after our father, dark-haired and dark-eyed, but Isobel was scaled down in every dimension, neither absurdly tall nor excessively wide. I, on the other hand, am a female copy of him: broad shoulders, barrel curve of a stomach, thighs like pillars, heavy muscle generously smoothed with fat. Being tall has its advantages, especially in reaching high shelves, but I still often felt like a water ox next to my sister.

"Still, the king! Think of it!" She spread her arms wide. "Perhaps if you cure his daughter, he will fall madly in love with you and marry you and make you the queen!"

"Given the fate of the last two queens, I'm not certain I'd want that."

"Oh, poo. You can't count Queen Maevis—she died of purpureal fever."

"I'd rather not die of *that* either, thank you very much." I shut the lid on the trunk and tightened the straps to hold it closed. I had very little hope of my distilling equipment arriving in the same number of pieces that it left, but I was going to do my damnedest anyway. Perhaps the king had access to wagons that didn't rattle like the bones of the dead.

Isobel sat up straighter, clearly struck by a sudden thought. "Wait, what are you going to wear?"

"I *had* planned on wearing clothes, but I am open to suggestions."

My sister groaned. "No, no. You don't *have* any clothes. Not any that you can wear in public."

"He's already seen me in my worst gown. I don't think he cares."

"*He* probably doesn't, but everyone else will."

I sighed. "I have a perfectly respectable wardrobe. I go out in public in it all the time."

"Yes, but you look like a nun."

"Isobel, I'm going to try to cure the king's daughter. If I succeed, no one will *care* what I'm wearing."

Her expression was unexpectedly grave. "You know that half the nobles won't care if you succeed or not, if you're wearing the wrong thing when you do it."

"That's not true," I said, more because I didn't want it to be true than because she was wrong. I slammed another trunk shut. "Anyway, it doesn't matter what *they* think. The king's the one who matters."

"The nobles are the ones most likely to buy Father's stock," Isobel said. Which was also true, so far as it went. *And if I fail, we will lose buyers. Possibly a lot of buyers. And backers on future projects will pull out, and without backers, there will be nothing for anyone to buy anyway.*

Nor would my sisters escape unscathed. Isobel was married to a man who had invested heavily in his father-in-law's business, and while Catherine's husband was in the military, who could say what promotions might go to other, less worthy men, if his family was in disgrace?

I braced my arms on the lid of the trunk and stared at it, though I didn't see it. I was seeing my sisters and their families and my nieces and nephews and my father, who was no longer young.

And behind them, faceless, the others. The ones I didn't know yet. The ones that I could sometimes save, but not if I was three days away.

"I'm sorry," I said. The edges of the rattan trunk bit into my fingers, stamping wave patterns into my skin. "I never meant for this to happen."

In the silence that followed, I heard the rustle of Isobel's skirts as she rose. Then my sister's arms went around me, and she said, "Dear heart. No one could have predicted this. Not even you."

I made a little choked sound that might have been a laugh or a sob. I couldn't tell and was afraid to find out. "No," I said, straightening up. "No, I don't think anyone could have."

"Besides," Isobel said, "I feel sorry for the girl, don't you? Losing her sister and her mother like that, and being poisoned as well."

"Assuming it's poison at all." I sighed. Of course, I felt a pang of sympathy for the girl. I wasn't a monster. *But a king's daughter has a whole kingdom to rely on, and some of the people I'm trying to help can't even rely on themselves . . .* "I don't even know how long I'll be gone," I said.

"As long as it takes," said Isobel. "Perhaps you'll walk in, recognize it immediately, and be back home within the week."

"Your faith in me is touching. More likely I'll be stuck there for months. And what do I tell the king if I can't figure it out? 'I'm sorry, I'm stumped, can I please go home now?'"

"You always say that it's probably *not* poison. Just tell him that." Isobel had been subjected to a great many of my lectures about how rarely people are actually deliberately poisoned, and I was gratified to see that apparently she'd listened to at least one of them.

"I tried," I said. "But royalty is . . . different."

That was something of an understatement. Up until the time I was six years old, our king had been a man called Bastian the Demon. It was not a title given out of affection. He had been powerful, violent, and paranoid, convinced that his courtiers were part of a grand conspiracy to poison him. No one, from the low-liest servant to the highest noble, was safe. Those around him said that Bastian would be calm, even charming, for days at a time, then would suddenly shift, almost in midsentence, and lash out. The king's guard would appear on people's doorsteps in the night and take them away for their role in imagined conspiracies. Rumor had it that he'd once stabbed his own poison taster in the middle of a royal feast, rolled the man's body onto the table, and proceeded to eat the rest of the courses off the dead man's back.

(*But Anja,* you ask me, *why didn't the nobles just overthrow the Demon?* Good question. My guess is that no one wanted to be the first one to step up, because if no one stepped up behind you, you were dead. Monarchy, as the ancient philosopher Margay the Younger wrote, is a terrible form of government, but at least there's always someone around to blame.)

The king—our current king, the one who appeared in my workroom two days ago—was the Demon's nephew. He had been kept at the palace as something between an heir and a hostage, since the Demon could never quite decide if his nephew was in danger from the conspiracy or a leading figure in it.

Before he came to a final judgment on the matter, Bastian died, much to the relief of everyone in the kingdom, with the possi-ble exception of his mistress. Ironically, the autopsy showed that he *had* been poisoned, which led to questions that no one really wanted answered. The Demon was buried quickly, his nephew took the throne, people stopped disappearing, and that was that.

So now here we were, thirty years later, with the king's daughter maybe going the same way as her uncle. At least, I couldn't rule it out.

"I'll do my best. You know I will. But if the physicians couldn't figure it out, how will I? And in the meantime, how many people *here* that I *could* help will . . ." I trailed off. If I didn't say the word *die* out loud, maybe it wouldn't happen. Which was completely irrational, of course, and unworthy of a scholar, but I still didn't say the word out loud.

"Is there someone else they can go to?" Isobel asked.

I grunted. After a minute I said, somewhat grudgingly, "Healer Michael can handle most things, I suppose." This was ungracious even for me. Michael lacked my encyclopedic knowledge of poison, but he was the better healer in every way that counted. "Except for the lotus-smoke cases. No one else does those."

No one else even tries. Everyone knows it's hopeless, except me.

Isobel knew better than to say anything. I squeezed her hand instead. We sat together in the emptied workroom, the sun shining on bare wood and tile instead of glass. In her cage, the chime-adder shifted with a jingle of miniature bells.

"Enough grim thoughts," Isobel said finally, standing up. "Let's go out. I know a dressmaker who can work miracles in a day and a half."

"Well, since it apparently takes twice that for the king's retinue to actually go anywhere . . ." I stepped away from my glassware. "I'm still going to dress like a nun. It's safer than sending me out in gowns that will catch fire or fall down when I least expect it." It was also safer, as a spinster-scholar, to look like a nun. People did not bother nuns, and sometimes they even listened to them.

"Fiiiiine," said Isobel, drawing the word out in mock despair. "At least you can look like a nun with good taste." She threaded her arm through mine. "And we'll take one of those guards with us to carry the packages."

The guards were named Aaron and Javier. Aaron was short and tanned, with curly black hair and a ready smile. Javier was tall and rawboned, with an impressively hawk-like nose and skin the color of walnut wood.

Their presence had been a surprise, although I realized that it probably shouldn't have been. Having made it clear that he did not want anyone influencing me, the king would of course take steps to enforce it. When he left, the pair of them were already stationed at the door, challenging anyone who approached, including the boy who delivered the milk. The cook still remembered the old days when the king's guard on the doorstep meant that you were about to be executed for conspiracy, so I'd had to spend twenty minutes soothing her nerves; meanwhile, the housekeeper had gone into strong hysterics and threatened to relocate to the country at once. (She did this about once a week, so I wasn't *that* worried. I took up a cup of peppermint tea and a plate of honey cakes and explained that I had been called away and that she would have to manage everything until Father returned. The prospect of being essential—and more important than the cook—revived her remarkably.)

The guards had relaxed their vigilance once it became clear that this was not precisely a hotbed of intrigue. The sprawling adobe house where I had grown up had been handed over to Isobel and her growing family years ago, and my father and I had relocated to a house better sized to an elderly merchant and a scholarly spinster. The courtyard was narrow but elegant, the rooms were tall and full of light, and neither contained any significant number of courtiers determined to suborn anyone.

I *had* been required to vouch for Isobel, and the guards had exchanged a significant look, but apparently sisters were allowed inside and not considered automatically seditious.

Aaron agreed to come with us on our jaunt. He was the more talkative of the pair. (Javier seemed to communicate primarily in monosyllables or, if possible, grunts.) It felt strange to set out with a guard behind us, and not merely a city guardsman but an actual king's guard with a sword and a breastplate stamped with the rising moon. I felt as if people must be staring at us, and I didn't like it. I wondered if they thought that I was being arrested.

The streets of our city—Four Saints Mountain, more commonly just Four Saints—are lined with white stucco walls. In richer neighborhoods, there are decorative tiles, and in poorer neighborhoods, there is graffiti, but the walls themselves are the same everywhere.

Set into the walls, every few yards, is a gate, and on the other side of that gate is a courtyard. The gates stand open during the day, and you can catch glimpses of the courtyards beyond. At the moment, anyone looking through the gate at our two-story house would see Javier standing guard, and they'd probably wonder what we had done to bring the king's guard down on our heads.

The wealthier houses have their own courtyards, but in most of the city, three homes will share, one to each side, with the courtyard as a communal space in between. It's the place where you put anything that wants to live almost-but-not-quite outdoors—clotheslines and potted plants and the sturdier sort of children's toys. (And the rain barrels, of course. In the desert, everyone has rain barrels.) Our courtyard held potted citrus trees and herbs and a row of pepper plants that our cook guarded jealously. The house I'd grown up in had a fig tree, which meant that we were overrun with pigeons when the fruit ripened, and the ground underneath became a treacherous landscape of overripe fruit and bird crap.

Most of Four Saints follows the courtyard design in one way or another. Houses are built around courtyards, shops are built around plazas, temples are built around cloisters, and the entire city is built around the palace, which stands on a hill and shines savagely down at the rest of us.

Isobel, Aaron, and I made our way down the street Father and I lived on, hugging the wall to one side. A member of the street sweeper's circle was pushing his broom along the ground, attempting to corral the pale dust that blows in from the desert. Depending on who you ask, either the street sweepers do nothing or the city would be buried without them. (I tend to lean toward the latter, myself, just because of all the time I spend chasing dust out of my workroom.)

It was a little after noon when we left, and the sky was a hard blue bowl overhead. The walls and the adobe buildings behind them shone so brilliantly that it hurt the eyes. It was a relief to reach the plaza where Isobel's seamstress worked, and to step into the shaded walkway that surrounded it. Green-trunked palo verde trees dotted the plaza, throwing complicated patterns of shadow across the ground. Someone was cooking fry bread, and my mouth started to water involuntarily.

Isobel's seamstress had a storefront between a bookseller and a haberdasher. I glanced over the books on display, mostly out of habit. The sort of volumes that I seek out are far too specialized to be found in such a fashionable place. Books on poisons are generally considered rather disreputable, and most sellers won't carry them at all.

(They did have the latest volume of the Red Feather Saga, though, which was an improbable story of swashbuckling romance imported from the eastern continent. In the last one, our heroine was being held prisoner by a pirate who, unbeknownst to him, was her long-lost older brother. She had just finished sawing through her ropes with a nail file when the sounds of battle filled the ship, whereupon it ended "until next time." I bought a copy of the new one immediately. It's not great literature, but after the fifteenth installment, you start to get invested.)

The dress shop itself was the sort that carried a range of styles and tailored them to your frame. There was a shrine to Saint Bird beside the door. (Technically clothing falls in the domain of Saint Sheep, patron of cloth and weaving, but I assume they were attempting to invoke the brightness of bird feathers.)

The proprietress wore the sort of extremely simple clothing that requires extremely elaborate sewing. She was all smiles and nods until Isobel explained that she wanted me to have a dress suitable for court functions within three days, whereupon her smile became a bit more frozen. I made frantic *no* gestures behind my sister's head. Isobel has never quite fathomed that when you reach a certain size, ruffles and petticoats make you look more like a parade float than a person.

Once my sister had exhausted her store of plans, the proprietress explained that madame's taste was exquisite, but there were simply not enough hours remaining to make such an outfit as madame required. I blessed the woman silently, and all her children unto the tenth generation.

Isobel sagged tragically. "Can't you do something?" she asked, gesturing at me. "Everything she owns looks like . . . *that*."

I glanced down at my current belted tunic and trousers. The tunic was earth brown, embroidered at the cuffs and hem, and the trousers were sand colored, which didn't show dust so badly.

The proprietress looked me up and down, taking in both what I wore and, I suspect, what I could be convinced to wear. "Perhaps Mistress Anja would consider a more formal over-robe?"

Mistress Anja was dubious but consented. I think that someone had to run across the plaza to the shop that sold men's clothing to find a size that would work, but the seamstress produced three robes, heavy with embroidery, that could be altered to fit me in the next two days.

"They're awfully dark," Isobel said doubtfully. "You still look like a nun."

"I like looking like a nun."

"But look at this! This is a marvelous color on you," said Isobel, holding a swatch of pale green silk against my arm.

"That is a *dreadful* color on me. I would look like a walking shrubbery."

"Saints forbid that you wear something other than brown and black."

"I like brown. It doesn't show dirt."

"Here," Isobel said, turning to our guard, who had been standing, relaxed but watchful, by the door. "Don't you think this is a lovely color?"

Aaron looked startled to be consulted, then slightly panicked. "I . . . err . . . yes, Mistress Isobel?"

"You see?" Isobel waved the green fabric at me menacingly. "Tell her, Aaron."

"Uh . . ." The guard's spine hit the wall beside the door as he attempted to retreat. My sister sometimes has this effect on people. "I'm not really a judge of such things, I fear?"

"Nonsense. You've seen plenty of women in your life. Surely you must have formed some opinions."

Judging by Aaron's face, he was ready to disavow having ever heard of women, let alone seeing one.

"It's a lovely color," I said, trying to come to his rescue. "Just not on *me*."

"Lovely!" Aaron said, seizing on this as a lifeline. "A marvelous color! Like—um—melon rinds?" Isobel's eyebrows went up, and he tried again. "New grass?"

Isobel frowned at the swatch. "More celadon than grass, I would have said."

"Yes. That, too. Absolutely."

"Perhaps," said the proprietress, "a compromise? A scarf of this color would go beautifully with the right shade of brown."

Isobel pursed her lips thoughtfully. Aaron gazed at the proprietress with naked hope blazing on his face.

"I'll take a scarf in that color, then," I said.

"But will you *wear* it?"

My sister has known me too long. *No.* "Yes." She narrowed her eyes. I attempted to look like a person who wore decorative scarves. (Honestly, I would like to be that sort of person. I simply never learned the knack.)

"If Mistress Anja would prefer, I have a new line of scarves that are quite subtle," the proprietress said, and draped something more like a priest's stole around my neck.

Isobel groaned. "Now you *really* look like a nun."

"I rather like it," I said, checking my reflection in the mirror. It did have an ecclesiastical quality to it, granted, but it looked more like a badge of office than decoration. (Also, Aaron had been right—it was exactly the pale green shade of a honeydew melon rind.)

"It lends you a certain authority," the proprietress said. "These are very popular among some of my clientele."

I suspected, as I paid for the scarf—and several others that Isobel had picked out, muttering—that what she meant was her older and more boring clientele. But I also suspected that I would shortly be in need of all the authority that I could get.

CHAPTER 4

When we arrived home, Javier was still standing inside the gate, guarding the courtyard, but there was a boy waiting there, too. He kept shifting from foot to foot and looking around, as if hoping to spot someone. I took in his clothes—too large, frayed hems, sandal straps broken and inexpertly mended—and knew at once who he was looking for.

"I'm Anja," I said. "How can I help?"

The boy looked up at me gravely. His eyes were too large for his face, and there were blue shadows smudging the lower lids. "Healer Michael sent me," he said. "It's my brother. He's . . . uh . . ." He slid a worried look at Javier.

Afraid of guardsmen. That doesn't bode well. "You can tell me," I said, turning to place myself between Javier and the boy. "No one will get in trouble."

The boy swallowed. "He, uh, was in a lotus-smoke den. For too long." He swallowed again. "He's at the temple. He won't wake up."

"Oh *hell,*" I said. "Wait right here." I bolted for the house, nearly trampling the startled Javier. Most of my equipment was packed, but I always left a bag by the front door for emergencies. I snatched it up and was back out the door before it had finished swinging shut. "Saint Adder's temple?" I asked. "Not the hospital?"

"The temple."

That wasn't good news, but I didn't stop to say so. "Come on, then," I said, and took off down the street.

Behind me I heard Isobel say, "No, give *me* the packages—*you* go after her!" Hopefully that meant Aaron was following, but if he wasn't, I didn't have time to wait.

Women my size generally don't run if we can avoid it. There are, let us say, certain structural concerns in the chest region, and I hadn't had time to put on the sort of binder that would keep things tamped down. But I could still manage a pretty good trot, and the Temple of Saint Adder wasn't that far away as the crow flies, at least if you're willing to dash across a main thoroughfare or two.

"How long has he been unconscious?" I asked.

The boy was keeping pace with me easily. He moved with the jerky whipcrack speed that most street kids seem to develop before they hit their teens. "He was like that when I found him. Couple hours, maybe?"

Worse and worse. No telling how long he'd been in the smoke den before they rolled him out. I tried not to let my alarm show on my face, but I picked up my pace even more.

Flint Way runs through the heart of Four Saints and serves as the main artery for carts and wagons entering the city. From there, smaller roads peel off to the various markets and plazas where goods are unloaded and sold. For our purposes, all you really need to know is that there are four lanes—I use the word loosely—on Flint Way, and at any given time, a lot of people and their horses are in a big hurry to get somewhere on it.

There are multiple pedestrian crossings that go under Flint Way. Unfortunately, they were all a couple of blocks away, and the temple was right across the road. If we went to a crossing, we'd lose a good ten or fifteen minutes, or, with steady nerves and a burst of speed, we could be there in under two.

I stood on the curb, waiting for a gap. The smell of manure assailed my nostrils. The street sweepers will only work on Flint Way after midnight, on the grounds that they are not paid enough to try cleaning the road while wild-eyed horses careen toward them. It is also extremely loud during the day: cartwheels on cobblestones, horseshoes on cobblestones, drivers yelling, drovers yelling, the

contents of the wagons squawking or oinking or rattling—all of it
blending into an overwhelming din.

I saw my opening at last and plunged forward. The trick was to
go in front of oxen instead of horses. Oxen are slower and rather
more phlegmatic about humans suddenly turning up under their
noses.

It worked, mostly. I made it across three lanes without incident.
The boy outdistanced me and was up on the far sidewalk before I
was even halfway across. That didn't surprise me. Street kids were
always darting across Flint Way and snatching things off the wagons, secure in the knowledge that the drivers couldn't stop or turn
around to catch them.

Unfortunately for me, a driver decided he was tired of waiting
behind the oxcart in the third lane and cut around him at high
speed into the fourth. I heard a shout and looked up, practically
into the nostrils of a horse that was trying to stop but being pushed
forward by the momentum of the cart behind him. Someone was
screaming, probably the driver.

I flung myself at the sidewalk and got a foot up just as a pair of
hands grabbed my arm and hauled. Between the two of us, I got
out of the way about a second and a half before the horse and I
became dangerously close acquaintances.

"Are you trying to get *killed*?" Aaron snarled, not quite yelling
but not far off. He was the one who had pulled me up.

"No," I panted. "It's fine."

"It is *not* fine! You could have been trampled! You know they
don't slow down—"

The street kid was suddenly between us. "Leave her alone!"
he said. His voice cracked. It was ridiculous, given that he didn't
come up to either of our collarbones, but I didn't laugh. Neither
did Aaron.

Instead my guard exhaled in a whoosh and said, "Sorry, Mistress Anja." He didn't sound particularly sorry, but I accepted it

anyway. It probably looked bad on a guard's record if your charge got trampled.

"It's fine," I said again, starting for the temple again. "The horse didn't want to step on me, I didn't want him to step on me, we were both in agreement. Come on, we don't have much time."

The Temple of Saint Adder is a busy one, as He is considered to hold sway over medicine and healing. The sanctuary is large and airy and beautiful, lined with bells, and full of pilgrims praying for blessings of health. It is a place of harmony and earnest calm.

Having someone charge through, sweating and cursing under her breath, trailing a guard and a street urchin, would tend to disrupt the mood. Fortunately there are multiple entrances. I passed the main one, veered down a side street, and found the gate that led to the temple infirmary.

The main hospital is a good distance away from the temple, and most of the healers work there. But a few patients always come to the temple, usually at night. The ones who can't make it to the hospital under their own power or can't be carried any farther. They're generally transferred to the hospital in the morning, unless they aren't expected to survive the trip. I could guess which category my patient fit into.

Healer Michael saw us as soon as we came in and hurried over. He was a round man with a gentle voice and gentler hands, clad in the indigo robes of a healer. He gave the boy a smile. "Jonas. I see you found Healer Anja."

Healer is a courtesy title at best when applied to me. For anything other than poison, I'm useless. A hangnail might as well be a broken leg. Still, it was hardly the time to argue.

Healer Michael—who deserves the title a dozen times over—ushered us to one of the small side rooms. I opened the door and saw a man on a pallet. Twenty, maybe, though illness made him look older. His cheeks were sunken, and he had a scruffy three-day growth of beard, but the resemblance to the boy Jonas was stamped clearly on his face.

I knelt down and took his hand, laying my fingers on his pulse. There was muscle along his forearm, so his addiction to lotus smoke was likely not far advanced. But I knew immediately that it was too late, even so. The patient's heartbeat was so weak that, if not for the shallow rise and fall of his chest, I would have thought he was already dead. He likely had minutes left, not hours.

Still, what else could I do? I had to try. Sometimes you get a miracle. Mostly you don't, but you still have to make space for the miracle to happen, just in case. I began unpacking my bag.

I didn't require much equipment for this. A vial of tiny crystals and another vial containing an inch of boiled water. A waxed paper tube about three inches long. I fished out three crystals and let them dissolve in the water, making a milky solution, and sucked it up into the tube, then popped my thumb over the end.

"Come on," said Healer Michael. "Let's let her work." He took the boy by the hand and led him from the room. I heard the door close behind me. It was for the best. This next bit wasn't pretty.

Sliding a tube as far as you can up someone's nose is difficult at the best of times, let alone when you have to keep your thumb firmly pressed over one end. I wiggled it in, then wiggled it in even farther, wincing. The patient couldn't feel it, but my nose itched sympathetically anyway.

I took a deep breath, bent over, and blew the solution up into the patient's nose.

"What in Saint Sheep's name are you *doing*?" Aaron asked behind me.

I jumped and nearly put my eye out on the end of the straw. "Don't *do* that!" I said, sitting back. I hadn't even realized he was still in the room.

"Sorry," he said. "But what was that?"

"Distillate of chime-adder venom," I said, pulling the straw back out. "It speeds the heart and forces it to beat more strongly. At least that's the hope." I looked down at my patient glumly. He hadn't moved at all. Usually they at least mumble a little when I blow the venom into their sinuses. Even the little bit I take to test the strength stings like hell. I can't imagine this feels any better.

"*Venom?*" He looked at me like I'd lost my mind. (Saints know he wasn't the first.)

"The heart is the organ sacred to Saint Adder," I said, sounding pompous in my own ears. "His children's bite therefore works strongly upon it. The venom is of the sanguine humor, and that is the humor being overwhelmed by the lotus, which is of the phlegmatic humor, so we must strengthen it."

"But won't the venom kill him?"

I sighed and glanced at the door to make certain it was closed. "He's probably already dead. Lotus smoke is a combination of opium and white thorn apple. Both of those relax the muscles. If you're not careful, they relax your heart until it stops beating."

Aaron digested this. "I see. So the venom keeps the heart beating?"

I curled my fingers around the patient's wrist, trying to find his pulse. "Sometimes. If I get there soon enough. If they're very lucky. If the saints are feeling generous."

"And the nose . . . ?"

People always make a big deal about that. I don't know why, since you have to get medicine into the body somehow, and it's not like the other options are that much better. "The most efficient way to administer the venom," I said. "At least to do it quickly. The stomach breaks it down, and we didn't have time for an enema." Was that a heartbeat against my fingers? I shifted my grip, feeling for something that might not be there, then gave up and pressed my ear against the man's chest.

Yes . . . there . . . a heartbeat. Then much too long a pause, and then another one.

Oh, I knew better than to hope, I knew that this was almost

certainly just the final rallying before the end, but I could fool myself that the beat was a little stronger, that maybe *this* time . . .

Aaron knelt next to me, not asking any more questions. I was surprised that he'd spoken at all. I'd thought all guards were supposed to be the strong, silent type. Maybe pushing me out of the way of the horse had opened the floodgates. Probably, it was seeing me blow something up someone's nose, though.

Ironically, now that I would have welcomed conversation, he'd fallen silent. There was a statue of Saint Adder in a niche in the wall. It was carved out of wood by an artisan with more enthusiasm than skill. The tail bells were blobs, and the head was too small. I prayed anyway, a little, but mostly I just waited for the inevitable.

It didn't take long. The man's pulse quickened as the venom took effect, faster but still thready, still much too weak, a thin little mouse of a sound, tapping inside his chest—and then, between one beat and the next, it stopped. I waited, not quite hoping, but the mouse had fled and left only silence. When I lifted my head from his chest, I saw that it no longer rose and fell at all.

We sat beside the body a little while longer. I had to be sure. It's so hard to tell when someone is dead, not just deeply asleep. I took the mirror out of my medical bag and held it in front of his lips. The surface stayed unclouded.

"Right," I said, sighing deeply, and began repacking my bag.

"I'm sorry," Aaron said quietly.

"So am I."

My guard offered the next statement cautiously, as if it—or I—were made of porcelain. "He was a criminal."

"He was," I said, my voice coming out clipped. This was an argument I'd had too many times with too many people. One that I still had sometimes, in my head. "But smoking lotus isn't a capital crime. The people who run the dens are the criminals, and they never end up here."

I don't know if Aaron reacted to my words or to the tone of my voice. I can't imagine it was kind. "You're right," he said. "I'm sorry."

Even though he'd apologized, it was hard to shed the anger. I would have liked to ignore the hand he held out to me, but it wasn't as easy to get to my feet as it used to be. I let him help me up, and we both stood looking down at the dead man.

My anger faded. Death has a way of clarifying these things. I turned away and blotted at my eyes with my sleeve. I wasn't grieving, exactly—I hadn't known the man, and I won't pretend that I'm the sort of kind soul who cries for every stranger—but I had listened to his last heartbeats, and they'd left some fragile, nameless emotion in their wake.

I took a deep breath and let it out. "I knew it was too late," I said, to Aaron or the statue or the body on the pallet. "But I had to try."

He gripped my shoulder for a moment, the way people do when they want to offer comfort but don't know how.

I opened the door. Healer Michael looked up as I stepped out, and I met his eyes and shook my head.

Jonas was sitting on a little bench against the wall. He looked up at me, and I said, "I'm sorry," which I would have said to an adult. Probably it was the wrong thing to say to a child, but damned if I knew what I was supposed to say. People had said all sorts of things to me when my mother died, and half of them had been insulting and the other half simply inane. And I had been younger than Jonas and far more sheltered at that. I'd bite my own tongue off before telling a street kid like Jonas that his brother was with the angels now.

He nodded once and looked away. I took myself and my guard away, leaving Healer Michael to deal with the aftermath of my failure.

⁎

Listening to all this, you may think that my work is all dead bodies. Dead cousins, dead addicts, dead dead dead.

It isn't, though. The vast majority of the people I see live. I don't descend like one of Saint Vulture's children and hang around while they expire. Most of the time, it's a child who's gotten into something they shouldn't, and I can fix it with either charcoal or vomiting. The hardest part is the loved ones trying to thank me. If I were a good person, I'd take it in the spirit that it was intended, but me being me, it's just excruciating. I want to yell, *It's just charcoal! I'm not superhuman! You don't have to swear that you'll do anything I ask, anything at all, for all eternity!*

(I don't say this, obviously. Healer Michael had explained it to me once, and his explanation made as much sense as anything. "Fear is like a balloon," he said, "and it blows up bigger and bigger. When it finally pops, relief comes rushing in to fill the space. The larger the fear, the larger the relief afterward. Then they have to find a way to let off that relief, and one of those ways is by dumping it all over the healer." Which is fine, and I've gotten better at smiling and nodding and even having people weep all over me. Still don't enjoy it, though.)

Adults tend to have more complicated problems. Some of them I can fix, some I can't—things like long-term lead poisoning are beyond the skill of any physician—but they still don't usually *die*. The human body is a strange combination of incredibly fragile and unspeakably tough. I've seen patients dosed with enough arsenic to kill any three normal people, patients with so much lead in their systems that there are blue lines in their gums, patients who've downed so many peach pits that prussic acid ought to be leaking out of their pores. Half the time they get up and walk out under their own power.

Hell, I've even managed to save three lotus addicts with my cobbled-together venom treatments.

(The corollary to this is that there are probably people who drop dead of such minuscule doses of poison that they never even make it to see me, and their deaths get written off as a heart attack or a thunderclap coronary. Which is terrible, of course, but there's not much I can do about it.)

Regardless, my point is that most of my patients leave on their feet and not feetfirst. And patients aren't even the majority of my work, come to that. I actually spend far more time at home, puttering around my workroom and distilling things into other things. The temple sends me the occasional jar of stomach contents to poke through and test for common poisons, and I have my own research to pursue, trying to find better treatments than charcoal and vomiting.

It's not the most exciting life, but it was mine and I enjoyed it. Until the king turned up in my workroom and turned everything upside down.

CHAPTER 5

Three days passed before the king was ready to leave. I had been a bit surprised to learn that when the king said *come with me,* he didn't mean within the hour, but Javier assured me that this was actually extremely fast as such things went.

Apparently a king could not go anywhere, even one of his own estates, in less than three days. Immense numbers of people had to ride ahead to every stop, to deliver food and bedding and other necessities, presumably so that the immense number of people had something to eat when they got there. And there were servants and guards and horses and grooms, and also a strangely large number of people who were going simply because the king was going and who seemed to fulfill no function whatsoever.

I'd had everything packed by the end of the first day and began to fret myself into near madness. I consulted every book in my library about poisons, running over the signs and symptoms—loose teeth, blue lines on the gums, garlic-scented breath, vomiting, vomiting, vomiting. When the human body is poisoned, vomiting is almost always the first line of defense. (This is another reason that I usually wear brown.) I knew all these things, and I knew that I knew, but I had a horrible fear that when I finally confronted Snow, I would panic and forget everything that I had ever learned.

Eventually I decided to go for a walk. Javier fell into step behind me. They switched off on who was the going-out guard and who was the staying-at-home guard. I wondered which job they preferred.

I meandered aimlessly around the streets, trying to think of something useful to do. There was nothing left to prepare. I had packed everything I could imagine needing, and a few things that

I couldn't. Lacking the princess's symptoms yet, I could not consult with another scholar in my field. I had written a note for my father and had dinner with Isobel and made all the arrangements with the housekeeper that you make when you are going out of town for an unspecified length of time.

At last I turned a corner, and there was the Temple of Saint Adder again. Scand used to say that prayer was what you did when you had done everything else you could possibly do. Apparently I was at that point now. I turned my steps toward the temple, listening to the echo of Javier's booted feet behind my own.

The great statue in the center of the sanctuary portrayed Him as a rearing chime-adder with his tail carved into dozens of bells. The sculptor had somehow made the serpent's eyes look both wise and kind. It was an impressive feat. I have seen a chime-adder rear that way on occasion, and never when the snake was feeling benevolent.

I made my way along one wing of the sanctuary, running my hand along the metal bells set into the wall. Dozens of bells ran the length of each wall, set at waist height, so that anyone walking past could send up a chorus in their wake. Other pilgrims were doing the same, so the bells formed a liquid backdrop to the sound of prayer.

My destination was not the main sanctuary but a small shrine, set down a flight of stairs and behind an unmarked door, as if the temple were slightly embarrassed by it. *Saint Adder may be the patron of poisons, but we prefer not to dwell on the matter.*

I started to kneel to crawl into the tiny entryway, but Javier stepped in front of me, ducked down, and looked inside. I rolled my eyes behind his back. Did he really think that someone was going to be hiding in there, ready to collude with me? Lurking behind the candles, perhaps?

Finding no suspicious characters, he nodded and stepped back, gesturing that I could enter.

The sound of bells faded behind me as I crawled inside. I heard the scuff of boots on stone as Javier took up a place beside the entrance.

The shrine of Saint Adder the Poisoner was old, older by far than the rest of the building, but they had not removed it when they built the great sanctuary overhead. It still had the original walls, made of dry stone laid without mortar, though surrounded on the outside by sandstone brick. On the wall opposite the door was an ancient painting in red ochre, a headless man with the coils of an adder set above his shoulders. The paint had worn over the centuries, and smoke had stained the ceiling, but the adder's tail bells were still clearly visible.

I took a deep breath and let it out, trying to organize my thoughts.

I'm not actually good at praying. Not when I have time to think about it, anyway. In the moment, of course, when there's someone in front of me who's accidentally eaten rat poison, I pray as much as anyone. But formal prayer, something beyond *oh Saints, let this work,* is another matter.

The problem is ramifications. If I convinced a saint to save a life, what might happen? I don't mean the stupid questions, like, *What if they go on to kill thousands of people?,* because in real life, that almost never happens. The number of people who go on to start wars or spread plagues is vanishingly small. But take my cousin Anthony, for example. I'm sure his mother prayed for him to survive. But if he had, I wouldn't have become obsessed with poisons.

There were sixteen lives that I was absolutely positive I had saved. Maybe more, but never mind—I was *sure* about those sixteen. Would all those people have died if my cousin had lived? I don't know. Maybe they would have, or maybe the temple would have realized they needed a poison specialist and trained someone, and maybe some of them would have lived. Maybe this hypothetical specialist would be better at their job than I am and more people would have been saved. How can you know?

And even if you could know, what gives you the right to say that

Anthony's life was worth trading away? One for sixteen sounds like a bargain, sure, but turn it the other way, and you're saying that a child should've died simply because it was *inspirational*. I'm pretty sure that's monstrous.

Maybe the point of gods and saints is that they can make the monstrous choices that people can't. Or maybe Anthony's life was always going to end when it intersected with that little root that smelled of mouse nests, and the best the saints could do was to bend his cousin's mind to an obsession that would someday save others, and pry some good out of tragedy. All I know is that when I think about these things, I wind up afraid to pray for anything too specific, as if I'd be joggling the elbow of someone who is trying to run the universe.

My sister says that I think too much. Scand said that I had too much of the melancholic humor of earth and needed to eat more red meat.

"I don't know if I'll be able to help this girl," I told the saint finally, as I sat there with my knees aching from the rough stone floor. "Just . . . please send me wherever I can do the most good. That's all."

I leaned forward and rang the handbell that stood in front of the painting, then sat while the echoes rang around me. When the last one had died, I felt . . . not better, exactly. Emptier, the way that you feel after a good cry. A little more peaceful. Some of the bitterness at having to leave my work in the city had faded with the echoes. Wherever I was going, if the saints were kind, maybe I could do some good.

I backed out of the shrine. Javier didn't say anything. I wondered if he'd heard me praying, and if so, what he thought of it, but I didn't ask, and unlike Aaron, he really was the strong, silent type. I'd heard perhaps a dozen words out of him in the last two days.

My knees were unhappy after I stood up, and I leaned against the wall, trying not to rub them too obviously, while Javier waited.

"You don't have to check every single room I go into," I said, still annoyed. "I swear I'm not colluding with anyone."

He actually looked startled. "Ah . . . Mistress Anja . . . we're here for your protection."

"Sure you are."

Javier cleared his throat and said, very carefully, "The king is concerned that if your mission becomes widely known, those responsible might seek to prevent you from carrying it out."

I stared at him. "Wait . . . *really?*"

"If someone is conspiring to poison the king's daughter, you can only be seen as a threat." His voice was deep and faintly hoarse, as if rusty with disuse.

"But . . ." My mouth felt suddenly dry. "But . . . it probably isn't even poison!"

His shrug was apologetic, but still a shrug.

I felt as if I'd been struck with a board. It hadn't even occurred to me that I might be in danger from anything except the king's displeasure. That was so large a thought that I couldn't quite see around it. It squatted in the middle of my head like a piece of furniture too heavy to move. I poked at it from different angles, but it didn't go away.

Those responsible might seek to prevent you from carrying it out.

No. Surely I'd misunderstood. "Are you actually saying that someone might try to *kill* me?"

He grunted, then apparently decided that wasn't enough, and added, "Possibly."

It was as if the world had picked itself up, turned ninety degrees, and dropped back down over me. Everything had shifted and nothing had changed. I stared up the steps to the sanctuary as if assassins might be hiding under every step.

At the top of the steps, I froze. Were all these pilgrims who they seemed to be? Was that woman who prostrated herself in front of the altar hiding a weapon? Was that old man as frail as he looked, or was he trying to divert suspicion?

Javier's hand landed on my shoulder. He waited politely while I tried to pretend that I hadn't yelped and jumped sideways, then said, "I do not think there is much cause for concern now. The danger will not truly begin until we are traveling."

Did that make me feel better? I wasn't sure. I took a step, then another. My guard was behind me. I wasn't in danger yet. I would be in danger later, but not yet.

Very well. I'd deal with *later* when it arrived.

We took a more direct route home, passing through several wide plazas, including the Plaza of the Quail's Fountain, which features an enormous bronze quail with water trickling out of its topknot. It's not good art. The quail has big goggling eyes, and the water runs down its back and over its tail and, by an unfortunate coincidence, makes it look as if the bird is peeing endlessly on the floor. You'd think that people would laugh when they saw it, but in fact, the first reaction is usually fascinated horror.

Over the years, the plaza has become home to a rather seedy open-air market. My theory is that if the residents complained enough to get it shut down, they'd be stuck looking at the fountain again. My guard and I passed by blankets covered in old books, much-mended pans, and jewelry of questionable authenticity and even more questionable provenance. Cobblers selling cheap sandals rubbed jowls with pawnbrokers and merchants hawking spices and soup mixes that were at least half sawdust.

You'd think that being among so many strangers would be nerve-wracking now that I had to worry one would kill me, but in fact, it was the opposite. I knew this place. I had been here a thousand times. It was normal and familiar, and I understood it, the way I would never quite understand assassins and kings.

And then, of course, there were the patent medicine people, selling cures and antidotes, hope and lies. The edge of a dozen pitches assailed my ears as we threaded our way through the stalls.

"Infallible remedy for . . ."

". . . a recipe handed down from the time of the ancients . . ."

". . . powdered from the horn of . . ."

"Just a sprinkle of this powder on a mad dog's bite . . ."

Indignation chased away fear. My hands had curled into fists by the time we were out of earshot of that last one. It wasn't so much the man's patter as the look on the faces of the crowd, the desperation and the hope. "I suppose if I broke that man's knee-caps, you'd have to arrest me," I muttered to Javier.

He snorted, which was the first expression I'd seen from him that wasn't apology or mild surprise. "Not effective, I take it?"

"There's no antidote for a mad dog's bite."

"Ah." We passed a half dozen gates, then he asked, "So what would you do if you were bitten?"

"Amputate immediately."

He considered this. "Seems extreme."

I shrugged. "People survive amputation. The only people who survive hydrophobia have had a limb so mangled that it was taken off immediately." There had been a time when I'd thought to study hydrophobia, but it had proved even more intractable than hemlock. "There's nothing *there*," I tried to explain. "You can *find* the venom in a snake's fangs or a scorpion's tail, but a mad dog doesn't have venom glands. And if you harvest their saliva—*not* an easy job—and dose a fowl with it, nothing happens. Some scholars don't think it's a poison at all." I leaned toward that view myself, but I wasn't confident enough to argue for it. It was possible that I just *wanted* it not to be a poison, since I'd been unable to isolate it.

"Maybe it's evil magic," Javier said. I couldn't tell if he was joking or not, so it was my turn to grunt. I didn't believe in magic. Any number of "magical" cures—usually obtained from markets like the last one—had proved worse than useless when I tested them. And in scholarly work, it seemed like magic was the last resort of an author who had a pet theory that he couldn't get to work any other way.

On the other hand, if there was ever a condition that seemed like malign magic, it was hydrophobia. Though it would say a lot about the world, if magical cures were useless, but a malign curse lived and thrived in the mouths of unfortunate dogs.

"Maybe," I said finally. "Saints know I can't prove otherwise."

Javier didn't reply. I wondered if either guard would be coming with me to the king's estate or if they would hand me off to a new set of minders.

I didn't know how to feel about that, so I put it on the pile of all the other things that I didn't know how to feel about, and let it go.

Both guards were still with me when it was finally time to leave. Two men with a wagon had come for my trunks the night before, and I watched them go, wondering if I would have a single unbroken piece of glassware remaining. Then I slept badly—I always do, the night before I know I have to be somewhere early—and was already awake when the maid came to roust me before dawn.

The cook had made a large mess of eggs scrambled with goat cheese, onions, and peppers. I ate at the kitchen table, alongside Aaron and Javier. If they thought it was odd eating breakfast alongside their charge, they didn't show it. The cook also pressed baskets of food on all three of us, apparently concerned that we would starve to death while traveling in the king's retinue.

Then I mounted my large, placid gelding, and my guards mounted horses that had been brought for them that morning, and we rode to the edge of the city where the procession was waiting.

A week ago, I might have thought that we'd be leaving immediately. Now I figured it would be a miracle if we were moving by noon. In fairness, it's hard to get that many people pointed in the same direction with any speed. (Maybe the army, but I think they train for it.)

I did not feel like being fair. I sat in the saddle and chafed at the delay. Dawn scraped its thin light over the ground, and people were still running back and forth, all of them looking as if they had Very Important Business to conduct, none of which seemed to get us any closer to moving. Knots of people in glittering clothes stood around, looking completely unsuited for a ride in the desert. I couldn't see the king anywhere.

The city of Four Saints doesn't have city walls, except that this part of it does, but they're to keep out the desert, not invaders. The wind blows from the south more often than not and carries dust with it, so the wall was put up to keep it out as much as possible. On the desert side of the wall was the large open space that cara- vans left from. It was called Snake's Hearth—don't ask me why.

The sun rose over white ground and the intricate little puzzle of desert shrubs, which grow almost-but-not-quite touching each other. As color leached into the landscape, I could make out the bright paint of the spirit houses on their poles, dotted all through the shrubs.

Spirit houses, in case you don't know them, are how we dispose of our dead in Four Saints. There just isn't enough good farmland to spend any of it on the dead, and if you chop holes in the desert, it takes a hundred years for things to grow back. The saints don't like that. The story goes that Saint Rabbit, in particular, doesn't like it, and was enraged by humans cutting up the desert for the dead, so Saint Bird intervened before Rabbit sent His thousand children to eat up our crops. In Her guise as Saint Wren, Bird taught hu- mans to burn their dead, and the ashes were placed in spirit houses, which, not coincidentally, resemble birdhouses. A spirit house is a little box on a pole, with holes drilled in the sides and a roof over the top. You place the ashes of the deceased in the box, and as the wind blows, they sift out of the holes and across the desert. When the ashes have been completely scattered, the period of mourning is considered done. (This does mean that if your loved ones die during the rainy season, you will probably be mourning them for a lot longer than if they die in the windy season.)

Occasionally a bird will take up residence in a spirit house. It's a sign of favor from Saint Bird, since She is the one who carries souls to the afterlife. Some spirit houses are designed specifically to encourage bird nests, but that's considered rather tacky.

Saint Bird has dominion over the lungs and the breath, the way that Saint Adder has dominion over the heart. There are lots of folk remedies for pneumonia that involve burning old bird's nests. Healer Michael despairs of it, because the last thing you need when you have pneumonia is smoke, but people still do it. I had looked for ways to empower struggling lungs, the way that chime-adder venom empowers a struggling heart, but had never turned up anything much. If you burn a feather and capture the smoke, then cool it, you get a tar-like substance so nasty that I hadn't even tried to test it. There's no point to a cure that no one can get down.

The nearest spirit house was painted bright turquoise with slashes of yellow. The shadows under it gradually darkened, then grew shorter and shorter as the sun rose overhead, until, by the time we were finally ready to ride out, its shadow was barely wider than my hand.

"We could have slept in," I muttered to my guards.

Aaron snorted. Javier gave a minuscule exhale that might have been a sigh.

And then, without any real signal, part of the crowd began moving. I wasn't entirely sure if that movement applied to us, but Javier pushed his horse into a trot, and I followed, with Aaron bringing up the rear. He found us a position in the column, about a third of the way back, behind a line of coaches, and there we settled. The initial trot didn't last long, probably because it was already getting hot, and soon we were just walking and eating the dust kicked up by the coaches ahead of us.

Snake's Hearth fell away behind us. I stopped worrying about my glassware and began worrying about the chime-adder, who had her own little cage among my saddlebags. The sides were tight wire mesh, large enough to let air in but keep fangs out, and I had draped a cloth over it to provide some shade, but no matter how you slice it, snakes do not appreciate being on horseback. I would have left her at home if I could have, but it is very hard to find people to watch a venomous snake for an unknown length of time. And this particular adder was the best I'd ever had in terms of venom production, and releasing her back into the desert seemed like a waste.

I fussed with the cloth for the third or fourth time, worried that she might not be getting enough air.

"You have a very odd pet, Mistress Anja," Javier said, eyeing the cage.

"She's not a pet," I said. "More like a, um, colleague."

His eyebrows were eloquent. I glanced over at Aaron, who already knew and was controlling a smirk.

"I harvest her venom and distill it into an antidote," I said.

"An antidote for adder bites?"

"I *wish*." I'd actually tried that for about six months but hadn't gotten anywhere. The principles seemed sound—like to combat like—but in practice, all I ever wound up with was dead roosters. (I test my work on roosters before I test it on myself. I don't particularly enjoy it, but every farm on earth has excess roosters that are slated for either the dogs or the stewpot. Also, the majority of them are absolute bastards. The ratio of good rooster to violent hen rapist seems to be about one in ten, I don't know why. This has two effects—one, that I know things about the inside of a chicken that chicken-kind never dreamed of, and two, there are currently three roosters at the house who weren't bastards and thus I couldn't bring myself to kill them. The cook complains that feeding them the kitchen scraps is a waste since we don't get eggs and we're never going to eat them, but I just can't. Sometimes I go and sit with them in the morning and feed them treats by hand. Octavian, the biggest one, likes to sit on my knees and make happy little burbling noises. I'm not made of stone.)

(Also, if you've heard that two roosters put together will always kill each other, you've heard wrong. As long as one rooster has space to run away, they'll establish a pecking order and settle down. Things only get tricky if there are hens to fight over. Probably there's a moral in that somewhere.)

"No," I said to Javier, "it's a treatment for lotus-smoke overdose."

"Really!" That was the most emotion I'd ever seen from Javier, who hewed closely to the silent-guardsman image I'd had in my head. "And it works?"

I grimaced. "Sometimes. If I get called in soon enough, and I'm lucky. One out of three or four times, say."

I waited for him to say something about lotus addicts being criminals, but instead he said, "That's still a great deal better than nothing."

"Thank you," I said, and meant it.

The road curved to the left, and I found myself looking back in the direction of the city. From this distance, it was dwarfed by the pale stone of the mesas that rose around it and by the three enormous figures painted across the cliff face above. Greatly elongated but still recognizably human, the paintings stretched several hundred feet before being abruptly truncated at the shoulder. In place of heads were the profiles of animals—a fish, a snake, a leaping hare. Saint Fish, Saint Adder, Saint Rabbit. And around the side of the mesa, hidden from view, was the last of the city's four guardians, Saint Bird. They had been painted long ago, in ancient times, and their old names had been lost, but the saints themselves endured.

There were other saints etched in other places, though none so dramatic as the Four. Saint Toad could be found a day's travel to the west, looming over his own town, and there were dozens of representations of Saint Lizard scattered across the region, often stained on rocks no taller than I was. Saint Toad's shrines popped up wherever water seeped to the surface. And, of course, three of the Four also appeared in other places, though Saint Fish was rare and found only on permanent waterways. It was only Saint Adder who was unique to our city, the great serpent, arbiter of life and death, sickness and health, poison and antidote.

I murmured a prayer under my breath, then set my gaze resolutely forward. Before long, we reached the first switchback and began to descend into the low desert.

If you look at the Kingdom of Saints on a map, it resembles an elongated hand making a rude gesture with its middle finger at the ocean. The wrist begins in a tangle of mountains, and the heel of the hand is a set of valleys sheltered by those same mountains. (This is where much of our food and all of our wine comes from.) Mesas and canyons carve up the base of the thumb, and everything slopes downward from there, so that much of the palm lies in the low desert.

Eventually you reach the sea and the rude peninsula. Cholla Bay is the largest city there, mostly warehouses and fishing trawlers. We don't have a deep enough port for really big ships, unfortunately, so about half our trade comes through our neighbor to the west, which charges us the sort of tariffs that make my father stomp up and down and snort obscenities. On the upside, between the mountains and the shallow ports, we're quite hard to invade. Every few years, some warlord sets themselves up in the waste past the thumb and the army has to be called out, and there was one winter when flint-wolves came out of the mountains and started eating buildings, but for the most part, we're fairly peaceful.

Witherleaf lay between the map's first two knuckles, in the low desert. We followed switchback after switchback downward, the slope growing gradually gentler, until they were less switchbacks than curves, and then not even that. The vegetation changed around us, some shrubs giving way to cactus and grasses giving way to bare ground. The soil of the road bleached from cream to bone.

We continued down the white road through the desert for an hour or so, breathing in white dust and coughing and (in my case) cursing. I was wearing sensible riding clothes—trousers, a tunic, a light over-robe, and a broad-brimmed hat—all in sand colors so that the dust didn't show, but I could feel it in my teeth and the inside of my nose. I pulled my scarf up over my face, which helped a little, but not much. It was hot. You get used to heat when you live in the desert, mostly by inventing ways to stay out of it. I checked on the chime-adder again worriedly. She seemed fine, but snakes always seem fine right up until they aren't. I reminded myself that she was bred for the desert and I wasn't.

Twice, Javier rode down the column of travelers and returned with water. Aaron and I traded the dripping waterskin back and forth gratefully. My guards were wearing long padded jackets that fell nearly to their knees, dark blue with a line of decorative silver closures. The jackets had half sleeves, with ordinary linen shirts underneath, and plain, loose brown trousers. I could hear Isobel in my head yelling that my guards were better dressed than I was. I took some comfort that the dust was showing up much more dramatically on the blue jackets than it did on mine. (Despite what you may have heard, black is just as cool in a desert as white, so long as you wear your clothing loose enough to let air circulate a bit.)

The third time Javier came back, it was to say that the king had requested my presence at the head of the column.

I said, "Uh?"

He repeated himself.

"Oh," I said. "Err . . . sure?"

Both guards accompanied me along the side of the road, past the coaches and a knot of riders who had to be nobility. Half of them were dressed the same way that I was, and the other half were wearing clothes that had probably been quite attractive before the ride. Hats decked with enormous plumes drooped over the wearers, and gems sparkled in settings covered in white dust.

I was more than a little surprised to find the king alone at the head of the column. Insomuch as I had thought about it at all, I had assumed that he would be surrounded by attendants, perhaps conducting what matters of state could be conducted from the saddle. He was dressed much the same as my guards were, except that the jacket was so stiff with embroidery that it probably functioned as another layer of armor.

What in Saint Adder's name am I doing here? I can't possibly have impressed him with my conversation earlier . . .

"Your Majesty," I said, wondering how on earth one was supposed to curtsy on the back of a horse. I settled for an awkward dip of the shoulders. He lifted a hand in what was either an acknowledgment or a gesture not to bother.

I didn't regret my choice of clothing, having just seen how the road treated gems and cloth of gold, but I did feel a brief pang that I didn't have a fancier horse. The king was mounted on an elegant gray mare, and I was riding Ironwood, who was basically a sofa with hooves. I felt immediately guilty at the thought and patted his neck. Ironwood was a good animal, damn it. Horses weren't like ball gowns you swapped out as the mood suited you.

"And how are you faring today, Mistress Anja?" the king asked.

"Oh . . . uh . . . fine, Your Majesty." I cast around for some observation to make, and settled on, "It's very dusty, though."

"Yes," he said, even though at the head of the column, he had much less dust to contend with. "Do you ride often?"

"Now and again. Mostly when I need to visit the hospital. It's a long way to walk." Oh, this was excruciating. I wasn't good at small talk at the best of times. "Do you ride often, Your Majesty?"

"Not as often as I'd like," he said ruefully. "When I was younger, it seemed like I was in the saddle every day, going somewhere to oversee something vital. Now everything vital comes to the palace, and by the time I think, 'I wanted to go riding today,' it's already dark."

"It's easy to get caught up in work," I agreed.

"I imagine you see patients regularly."

I shrugged. Then it occurred to me that one did not simply shrug off inquiries from the ruler of the country, so I cleared my throat. "Not regularly, no. The temple only sends for me when they suspect a poisoning. Sometimes I'll go months without seeing any at all."

"How many patients have you seen, then?" the king asked.

"Eighty or ninety," I said. "Perhaps as many as a hundred. I would have to consult my notes."

"And how many of those have you saved?"

(The last thing Isobel had said to me before I left was "Try to be tactful."

"I always *try*," I protested.

She gave me a Look. "Try harder.")

Tact. Yes. *Don't you think you should have asked me this before you hired me, Your Majesty?* I thought, but did not say. I studied my hands on the reins instead, admiring how calm they looked, how they failed to clutch nervously at the leather. "Sixteen."

"Sixteen?" The king's voice did not quite go shrill at the end, but it came close. His mare sidled a little in surprise. "Out of a *hundred?"*

Tempting as it might be to teach the king a lesson about checking one's credentials in advance, I had no desire to be known as the woman who had killed eighty-odd patients. "You misunderstand me, Your Majesty. The vast majority lived—but they would have done so anyway. At best I helped speed their recovery a little, but I can hardly be said to have saved lives that were never in danger."

"Oh." The king relaxed. So did Aaron. I wondered at myself, daring to alarm a king. Perhaps it was revenge, however petty, for how he had alarmed me in my workroom.

"Your modesty is becoming," the king said. "Most physicians would simply claim credit for all of them."

I shrugged. "I'm not really a physician. I'm a scholar who has studied antidotes at great length. As I told you the other day, most of what people think is poison really isn't. If I took credit for every bellyache that got better, I'd be no better than a charlatan."

Aaron cleared his throat, glanced at the king for permission, and said, "You said the vast majority got better. I assume some didn't?"

Clever Aaron. Of course, he'd seen one of them. "Nineteen," I said. Now my fingers did tighten on the reins, the knuckles going white. I watched them from a little distance, then loosened each one individually until they lay easy again.

The king had learned something, it seemed. When I looked up, I saw his gaze intent on me. "And how many of those *could* have been saved?"

I sighed. "With what knowledge we have? Perhaps none of them. There are still too many poisons that have no cure." I could feel my shoulders hunching, and I lowered them as consciously as I had relaxed my hands. "Mushrooms . . . prussic acid . . . poison hemlock. There's little enough that can be done for any of them, except to ease the victim's passing."

"But you have been able to save a few," the king said.

I nodded, feeling curiously reluctant to admit even that much, as if saving lives was a moral failing instead of a victory.

We rode for a little way. Despite the awkwardness, I was very pleased not to be breathing dust.

"What poison do you see most often?" the king asked after a time.

I had to think about that. "In children, probably arsenic. Toddlers getting into flypaper or rat poison. Adults vary more. Mushrooms are rare but tend to get whole families at a time. They don't grow around here, they come in dried, so it's impossible to tell what they are. Someone buys a package that includes a dried Saint's Tear and makes soup, and forty-eight hours later, you can practically pour the liver out of the bodies."

The king swallowed.

It occurred to me that was possibly a little more graphic than he'd been expecting. "Err . . . sorry, Your Majesty." *Really, I don't know why that would bother him. He's killed people in battle, hasn't he? Probably stabbed a fair number of people through the liver. Possibly including his wife.*

"Does that happen often?" he asked. "The mushrooms."

"I've seen it twice. Nine people total." I spread my hands. "When you think about how much dried mushroom is shipped into the city, I'm surprised it doesn't happen more often."

"Ah. Not something that requires royal action, do you think?"

I blinked. Somehow it hadn't occurred to me that I might, with a word, influence policy throughout the kingdom. "Um. No, I don't think so. I'm not sure what could be done anyway." What *did* require royal action? "If Your Majesty really wanted to cut down on poisonings, banning using honey or sugar water to coat flypaper would do a lot more good. Then toddlers wouldn't lick it so much."

He gave me a terrifyingly thoughtful look. "I'll keep that in mind."

We stopped that night at a shrine to Saint Toad. It wasn't a large shrine, but it boasted a spring that would let us water the horses, which was important. Saint Toad has dominion over the melancholic humor and the bowels, and laxative bottles often have toads stamped on the labels. People make pilgrimages to the big Toad shrine to the west of Four Saints mostly to ask for wealth, which is also His domain, but more than a few go to ask for regularity. (I am not here to judge. In the course of testing things on myself, I've had more than one occasion to beg for Saint Toad's intervention.)

I was surprised to discover that the king's entourage had been here already and erected dozens of tents. My guards showed me to one that was practically a pavilion, a two-room construction in a startling shade of red. There was a basin and a brazier and a chest, presumably in case I wanted to unpack one of my travel chests, then repack it in the morning. This seemed excessive, given that all I was going to do was sleep here for one night, but I didn't complain. Javier and Aaron had cots in the front room. I started to complain about that, then remembered what Javier had said about things not becoming truly dangerous until we were traveling. The guards were sleeping there so that they were between me and anyone who wanted me dead.

I had succeeded in pushing off my fears until later. Now *later* had arrived, and I wasn't somehow magically equipped to deal with it. Poor planning on my part, clearly.

I stared at the ceiling of the tent for about five minutes. There was dark purple trim layered over the red walls. It looked expensive. *Someone might try to kill me. Maybe being royalty means you have fancy tents as a matter of course. Also, someone might try to kill me.*

Stop that, I told myself. *You're not going to do any good if you stand there panicking. Do something useful.*

Useful. Yes. Someone might try to kill me, but I could still be useful until they succeeded. I unwrapped the chime-adder's cage and fetched a dish of water. This was actually quite centering, because you cannot be distracted while working with a venomous snake. I slid a thin piece of board in to wall off half the cage, set the dish in, pulled the board out, and snapped the lid down. It took about a minute, during which time I did not think about people trying to kill me. Unfortunately, after the minute passed, the thought came back again, and I still had no idea what to do with it.

I watched the chime-adder slowly uncurl, all blunt head and flickering tongue. A living saint, small enough to keep in a cage, the cold, dry melancholic humor made flesh. She wore the same colors that I did, browns and earth tones, with a pattern of pale chevrons along her back. Young chime-adders were an elegant little deadliness, all nerves and whiplash speed, but mine was old and thick-bodied and, insomuch as a venomous snake can be, even-tempered. She was in a bad mood today, though, probably because of all the jostling around on horseback. She'd struck at the board twice, her tail ringing a carillon, and now eyed the water dish as if it were personally responsible.

I felt a pang of sympathy. I, too, would have liked to bite something, and I didn't know who was responsible. No one had ever wanted me dead before. How was I supposed to feel?

I still hadn't figured that out when Aaron put his head through the flap and told me, almost apologetically, that I had been summoned to dine with the king.

CHAPTER 6

I was glad of the over-robes that Isobel's seamstress had prepared for me. Pulling one on over my traveling clothes didn't make me look like a courtier, but at least I looked like the better sort of eccentric scholar. I splashed water on my face and only thought, a moment too late, that if someone wanted to take me out of the picture, they could easily have changed the water out for something like lye or oil of vitriol. Well, my face didn't melt off, so apparently they hadn't. That was a relief.

I hastily re-braided my hair, wondering how exactly I'd be assassinated. A knife? Would I be walking along and suddenly feel a piece of cold metal actually *inside* me, down among my organs? An arrow? That felt like being struck, I'd read, a sudden hard blow, and only later did you realize that there was a piece of wood sticking out of you.

Better than oil of vitriol, I suppose.

Arrows seemed unlikely. People would notice that you were carrying a bow, wouldn't they? Compared to a knife, anyway. Or maybe the assassin would just shove me off a cliff. There weren't really any cliffs around here, as long as I avoided climbing a mesa, but for all I knew, Witherleaf was made of cliffs stacked on top of each other.

"Are there any cliffs near Witherleaf?" I asked Aaron, emerging from my side of the tent.

He looked puzzled. "I don't know. I've never been there."

"It's fairly flat," said Javier. "Why?"

"Nothing." I didn't want to have to explain my catastrophizing to my guards. It would probably sound like I didn't trust them to protect me. For all I knew, one had gone in and checked the water before I even arrived. "Let's not keep His Majesty waiting."

I hadn't really expected an intimate dinner with the king, but it must be said that I hadn't expected a pavilion full of courtiers either. The king ate at a table on a raised dais. It was quite an elegant table, made of polished rosewood. I wondered how they'd transported it here. I had plenty of time to observe it, because I was seated at the same table, along with about ten other people. I didn't know any of them, of course. I wondered if any of them knew who I was. Then I wondered if one of them might want me dead. My palms began sweating, and I rubbed them on my knees.

I was sitting on the king's left, a far more honorable position than I'd expected. I had a feeling that a great many people in the tent were looking at me and speculating on who or what I was.

The woman to my left was small and definitely older than she looked. Her skin was smooth, but the corners of her eyes and the very slight creases in her lips gave it away. I put her somewhere in her sixties and hiding it well. She introduced herself to me, but I forgot her name immediately. Fortunately she was busy conversing with the gentleman on her other side, so I didn't have to pretend I remembered it.

The servants brought out plate after plate. There were chickens stuffed with almonds and dates, dishes of thin rattail radishes pickled in sweet vinegar, and a magnificent slab of beef. Beef is expensive stuff compared to goat or lamb. *Perks of being king, I suppose.*

The dishes themselves were glazed a beautiful green, with an almost glassy sheen. Lead glaze. I looked at the cup in front of me, also green, and stifled a sigh. It would probably be rude to ask for a cup in a different color. *Oh well, one meal's worth of lead won't do much.* I wiped my sweating palms again.

"You need not fear poison, Mistress Anja," said the king, perhaps mistaking the cause of my nerves. "The food comes from the kitchen under guard."

"That is certainly one method, Your Majesty," I said, because

Isobel had told me to be tactful. *It's cute that you think that will work* would not have been tactful.

I wasn't particularly worried about poison in the food, truth be told. Everyone was served from the same dishes on the table, so anyone trying to poison those would have to be willing to kill all the other diners in hopes of getting me. And as for the guard . . . well, it would be even more difficult to poison a dish by sprinkling poison on top while it was being carried from the kitchen to the table. Even if you were sure that you'd gotten enough onto the food to have an effect, even if it didn't have a distinctive taste or appearance, you'd still have no way of being sure that your target would eat enough of the substance to be fatal.

Poisoning food on the spot is tricky, too, honestly. One of the servants might palm something and slide it onto the meat, say, as they handed me my plateful, but I'd probably notice a lump of strange powder sitting in the middle of the food. It is a sorrow to poisoners everywhere that very few substances dissolve on contact with meat.

You could probably get away with poisoning a sauce or a gravy, but it was far more likely that one of the servants would slip something into my cup of watered wine. Hmm. I could swap cups with the woman on my left when she wasn't paying attention, but then I'd possibly be dooming Lady . . . Lady . . . whatever her name was. Or if someone was trying to murder her, I'd doom myself. Hmm.

I was just wondering which was more likely when she turned to me with a smile. "Mistress Anja," she said warmly. "I am so glad to have a chance to speak with you."

"You are?" I said, then realized a moment too late that I should probably have said something less blunt.

She laughed, a practiced trilling sound that had undoubtedly taken years to perfect. The rest of her had probably also taken years to perfect. Every inch was carefully polished, and she had the absolute confidence that can only be achieved by people who never have to glance in a mirror to see if they are immaculate. Just looking at her made me feel like there was something stuck in my teeth.

"I am," she said. "You are a woman of great mystery, you know."

This time I managed to catch myself before blurting, *Who, me?* Instead I dabbed my lips with a napkin and said, "There's no great mystery about me, I'm sure."

"No?" She raised her eyebrows. "What takes you to Witherleaf?"

My mind went blank. I couldn't tell her that I was going there to investigate a poisoning, could I? But then why would I go to Witherleaf at all? And why would the king have singled me out to sit at his left hand, as if I was important?

Damnation. We should have worked a cover story out in advance.

"I . . . err . . ."

"Mistress Anja will be tutoring Snow," said the king smoothly, leaning forward to meet Lady Anonymous's gaze. "She is a scholar of some renown."

This was news to me, but I flashed him a grateful look. He smiled slightly and went back to speaking to the man on his right. I wondered if there was some skill that you learned as king that let you listen to multiple conversations at once and break into one at the exact right time.

"A scholar?" Lady Anonymous smiled warmly. "How interesting! What is your field?"

"Natural history," I said, which wasn't exactly a lie. I do study a great many plants, animals, and minerals.

"What fascinating work. And teaching young minds! I admire that."

"Mmm," I said.

"Children are such a blessing."

"Mmm," I said again. The problem with being plump, middle-aged, and a woman was that people expected you to be motherly, as if that was your default state. I am not. I am actually terrible with children. On the other hand, I have saved the lives of multiple toddlers who licked flypaper, which I feel should count for something.

"Do you have any children of your own?" Lady Anonymous asked.

I bet she wouldn't have asked Scand that. "No."

That must have come out a little too abrupt, because she pursed her lips sympathetically. "Oh, my dear, I'm sorry." She patted my arm.

I looked at her blankly, wondering what on earth I was supposed to say next. "I keep venomous snakes instead?" I offered.

That was probably not the right thing to say. Lady Anonymous paused for just a fraction of a moment, then carefully took her hand away from my arm. "How . . . interesting."

"It can be." I wondered idly how many poisons went into her cosmetics. *Antimony for the eyelashes, arsenic for face lotion . . . probably not belladonna for the eyes, since her pupils look normal . . .* Her skin didn't have the hard, polished pallor of ceruse either. That particular horror had fallen out of fashion, thank the saints. Nasty stuff. The main ingredient is white lead. One of my early patients had been an older woman who insisted on using it to cover age spots. The skin on her face had been peeling and mottled like old paint from the lead poisoning, so of course she'd apply even more ceruse to hide it, and so on. She lived, but her family had needed to take the ceruse away from her. Vanity takes some people strangely.

Lady Anonymous turned to the gentleman next to her, who acquired the expression of someone facing the headsman's axe. Then she paused and turned back to me. "Isn't that dangerous?" she asked.

"The snakes? You need to know how to handle them, that's all." I took a sip of watered wine. Behind her, the man glowed with the joy of a last-minute reprieve. "It's like horses," I said.

Again she started to turn, then curiosity clearly dragged her back against her will. "Horses?"

"People are killed by horses all the time. Bad falls or kicks or whatnot. But we don't think of horses as being dangerous, because people mostly know how to handle them."

Lady Anonymous gazed at me steadily for a moment. "Do you know," she said, "I've never thought of it that way? How intriguing." This time she did turn back to the gentleman on her left. His expression crumpled, a man discovering that the headsman was not out sick after all. I applied myself to the roast beef, wondering whether I'd struck a blow for rational treatment of snakes or simply convinced a random noblewoman that I was a raving lunatic.

When I finished eating, I sat watching the courtiers below. There was so much movement back and forth between tables that I wondered how any of them were actually able to eat. Probably that wasn't the point. Was there a way to politely excuse myself from the table? No, probably not. If I did, everyone would watch me coming down from the high table, and I didn't think I could bear the thought of all those eyes on me.

Fortunately for my nerves, the king rose a moment later and clapped his hands. This seemed to be a general signal for the other diners to get up as well. I hurriedly followed suit. The others descended into the swirl of courtiers, so I did, too. Two walls of the tent had been tied back to catch the cool evening breeze, so I began sidling in that direction. If I could duck outside, I could go back to my pavilion. The garish red walls seemed like a glorious haven now.

Unless someone tries to stab you. Where are your guards?

Oh damnation. Where are *they?* I scanned the tent but couldn't pick out Aaron or Javier. Maybe they were waiting outside. Or were still back at my pavilion.

I had only just stepped around the tent wall and started making my way along the outside of the canvas when I heard a familiar voice on the other side of the fabric and froze.

"He *says* she's a tutor for his daughter," Lady Anonymous was saying, in a tone that indicated she didn't believe it for a second.

"Posh," said another voice. "A tutor, dining at the high table? And riding with him for half the day? She's his mistress."

I'm his what?!

"I don't know," Lady Anonymous said doubtfully. "She's very odd."

"Kings have had odd mistresses before."

The desert is chilly at night, but the breeze was not sufficient to cool the sudden rush of blood in my cheeks. *Oh, sweet Saints, is everyone thinking that?*

"I'd think he could do better," said a third voice archly. "She looks like a lump of dough in vestments."

I went cold, then hot, then cold again.

"Kings have had plain mistresses before, too," said the second voice. "Remember Lady Sorrel?"

"Yes, but King Bastian was *mad,* dear."

I'd heard enough. I bolted for my pavilion, assassins or no assassins, my stomach roiling as if the food really had been poisoned.

I woke up still humiliated. Also sore. Riding for half an hour or so, a few times a week, is not the same as riding all day. When Javier informed me that the king requested my presence at the head of the column again, I asked if I could say no.

He went a bit tight around the lips and glanced toward the distant figure of the king. "Ah . . ."

"In theory yes, in practice, I wouldn't," said Aaron bluntly.

"Right," I said. *It's not that bad,* I told myself. *It's not nearly as awkward as when you were thirteen and you begged Scand for months to attend a real autopsy and, when you did, you had to be sick halfway through.*

My brain made a valid point. The shame I'd felt when I walked back into the operating theater, knowing that everyone had heard me being violently ill behind the curtain . . . no, this could never be as bad as that. I gritted my teeth and followed Javier.

Calm. I was calm. I stared between Ironwood's ears and focused on how calm I was, how easy my breathing was, how relaxed my hands were on the reins.

"Good morning," said the king.

"People think I'm your *mistress*!" I hurled at him calmly.

He looked taken aback for a moment, started to smile, then hurriedly wiped it away. "I see," he said gravely. "I'm sorry, Healer Anja. I hadn't thought of the threat to your reputation."

I exhaled. In the light of day, talking to the king, it seemed foolish that I was worried over what some silly courtiers thought. It wasn't as if they could do anything to me that mattered—at least, not compared to what the king could do if I failed to save his daughter. Also, I had just yelled at the absolute ruler of the country.

"I'm sorry, too, Your Majesty," I said. "I shouldn't have . . ." I waved one hand helplessly. "I wasn't expecting it," I finished weakly.

He smiled. "It's all right. Court gossip can be excruciating if you aren't used to it."

I grunted and went back to staring between Ironwood's ears. They say that you can see ghosts if you stare between the ears of a dog or a cat or a horse. There didn't appear to be any on the road ahead of us. Ghosts are a murky area, theologically speaking. No one is quite sure what Saint they belong to. Each Saint has their chosen people, so some people say that a ghost belongs to whatever Saint claimed them in life, but other people point out that Saint Bird is supposed to carry souls to the afterlife. Does that include ghosts? The jury is still out.

The silence became awkward, then went on so long that it just became the way things were. I certainly was not going to force the king to speak to me. If he wanted to say something, he would. I still had no idea why he kept summoning me up here to ride with him, unless it was to keep people in the train from finding me and offering me money to let his daughter die. (Come to think of it, that would have been far more awkward than this. What do you even say, other than *No, of course not. What's wrong with you?*)

I amused myself by identifying the plants as we rode through the desert, picking out the poisonous ones. *Let's see . . . Creosote bush is toxic to herbivores, but they mostly avoid it anyway . . . Whiteleaf manzanita, that's fine . . . Saint's locust is pretty, but the seeds will kill you deader than a dead thing, and the bark's no great shakes either . . .*

We plodded onward. There is a great deal of plant life in the desert, if you know where to look, but there's a limit to how much is visible from horseback. Mile after mile of gray-green shrubs stretched out around us, the creosote bushes spaced as precisely as if they had been planted, the others tangling around the base of cactus or standing proudly alone. White dust billowed like smoke behind us. Somewhere on the other side of the horizon, there were hills and mountains and other countries and even a sea, but it was hard to believe in such things when you were riding through sand and stone and scrub.

Prickly pear, edible if you cook it right . . . Oh hey, a jumping cholla. That doesn't have to be toxic, it's nothing but spines and hatred. If you imagine a porcupine crossed with a small tree and marinated in the bowels of hell, that's jumping cholla. Fortunately there were none within six feet of the road, or I'd expect at least one person to run afoul of them. The needle-covered pads latch on to cloth or flesh—they aren't picky—and getting the needles out takes a lot of time with the tweezers, during which you're almost guaranteed to get stabbed yourself.

Nothing else presented itself for several miles, until we passed a tiny shaded seep between two jutting rocks. It wasn't large enough to water our horses from, but even the small amount of water from the natural spring meant a sudden riot of plants grew around it. Most of them were harmless enough, but the pale trumpets of white thorn apple hovered over the scene like wicked angels.

Saints, but I hate that stuff. The common thorn apple that grows in the desert is bad enough. It can kill a human or an unwise herbivore quite easily, and it isn't a good death. Racing heart, high temperature, and then you stop urinating, which will kill you a lot quicker than most people realize. (Also the delirium and the screaming and so forth.)

If white thorn apple just did that, I'd have no complaint with it. If you go around eating random plants without knowing what they are, then yes, sooner or later you're going to wind up either very unhappy or very dead. Plants aren't necessarily your friends.

"You're scowling very fiercely," said the king, startling me out of my thoughts. "Not at me, I hope."

"I . . . no, Your Majesty. Of course not." I tried to turn the scowl into a smile, which probably ended up looking ghastly. "I would never scowl at a king."

"Not where he might see you, anyway," the king said dryly. "So what were you scowling at?"

The truth was easiest. I turned and pointed. "That plant there."

"Unlucky plant. What exactly did it do?"

I explained about common thorn apple and the delirium and screaming and lack of urination, while his eyebrows went up. On my other side, Javier made a tiny sound that might have been amusement.

"Saints preserve us," the king said. "What a monster."

"Right," I said. "But this is *white* thorn apple. You hallucinate a bit, and then it puts you to sleep."

"That . . . doesn't sound as bad?"

"Not inherently." I could feel the scowl creeping up again.

The king was right, so far as that went. People had used concoctions that included very small amounts of white thorn apple to assist with surgeries for centuries. Having, for example, your leg amputated tends to burn through the sleepiness remarkably quickly, although I'm sure the hallucinations in that case aren't much fun either.

The problem, as I tried to explain, started when we began getting opium imported from across the southern sea, and while opium is a godsend when dealing with things like leg amputations, some bastard eventually realized that you could mix opium with white thorn apple seeds, and you'd be happy and weightless and watching pretty pictures in the smoke. Unless, of course, you relaxed too much and your heart stopped, and then, if you were very lucky and I wasn't three days away, I *might* be able to yank you back to the land of the living.

The king sighed. "Lotus dens are one of those intractable problems that we face. For some reason, the guard seems ill-equipped to stop them."

Aaron cleared his throat. "Majesty? If I may?"

"You were a city guard once, weren't you?" The king gestured to him. "Speak, by all means."

"They are hard to find, Your Majesty. Compared to drunks, lotus smokers do hardly any property damage, and the dens are much quieter neighbors, but owned by dangerous people. People find it easier to look the other way, if they notice at all. So they can operate on the edges of much better neighborhoods. The guard only hears of them if smokers turn to theft to support their habit."

"One would think that a clever owner would hire guards to prevent that," said the king thoughtfully.

"Some do, Majesty. Which makes neighbors even less likely to report it. And even if they do . . ." Aaron trailed off, suddenly ill at ease.

"And if they do, they find that perhaps the guard in their neighborhood has been paid to look the other way," the king finished. "Who wouldn't want crime to go down on their patch?"

"As you say, Majesty."

I wondered why Aaron was no longer a city guard, and if it was related.

The king grunted. He was quiet for a little while, and I went back to classifying plants. We were passing through an area mostly given over to cactus. Cactus rarely bother being poisonous, though there are occasional exceptions. I eyed a barrel cactus by the side of the road, which had grown large enough to slump sideways. (People always say you can get water from a barrel cactus. This is true enough, but since it gives you diarrhea, it's something of a wash in the hydration department.)

"But you can cure these people?" the king asked abruptly.

"Eh?" I'd lost my place in the conversation and briefly thought he was expecting me to cure a cactus. *Lotus smoke. Right, right.*

"Well . . ." I said, fussing with the reins to buy time, even though Ironwood hadn't so much as twitched. "Sometimes. Not always. And it's not a cure, exactly. I *save* them, but they're still addicted to the smoke."

He nodded. "Is there a cure for that?"

"Time." Opium is another thing we haven't found a cure for. The effects, fortunately, are cumulative rather than instantaneous, so we can still use it to blunt the pain when someone's arm gets sawn off, provided we stop soon enough.

The king sighed. "Time is the thing that Snow may not have," he said. "Though she's lasted this long." It was his turn to stare between his horse's ears. "One of my advisors suggested that if it *is* poison, I should lock her in a windowless room and guard the door so that no one has access to it. Have a cook prepare her food with his own hands and feed half that food to his youngest child."

"It sounds like a good way to give her rickets," I said, before I remembered that I was being tactful.

But the king looked at me with sudden hope in his eyes and said, "Yes! Exactly! And I could not bear the thought of locking my daughter up in a guarded cell for the rest of her days. If she *is* truly dying, regardless of what we do, then it would be monstrous to deny her the sun and the wind and the stars."

"It might work for a little while if it's actually poison," I admitted. "But I'd want to be sure it was first. And if she's lived this long, it seems unlikely that it will suddenly grow worse, unless the poisoner . . . err . . ."

"Sees that we have discovered their work. I know. And I cannot decide if someone is dragging her death out to torment me or if this is simply the best they can do."

"It may be that there is no malice here at all, Your Majesty," I said. "A nurse could be giving her an herbal tonic—oh yes, you would not believe the tonics that I've seen! Made with wolfsbane or sweetened with lead, with the best intentions in the world. Or it may be something she is taking herself, all unknowing."

The king frowned. "How do you mean?"

I made a helpless gesture with my free hand. "Perhaps Snow got hold of some old cosmetics. There are foundations made with white lead, and others made with mercury, to whiten the skin, or cinnabar to provide a blush."

"Cosmetics?" His frown deepened. "Snow is a *child*."

"Young girls are often eager to play at being grown-up," I said. "Did her . . . did the queen use cosmetics?"

The king had to stop and think. "I suppose she could have," he said slowly. "I never thought about it."

No, I thought wearily, *no, you probably didn't. Noblemen notice beauty mostly by its lack. Women know that they are only as powerful as their face, and so they will slather poisons into every wrinkle, merely to keep what little power they have.*

Aloud I said only, "It's possible that Snow acquired some but, being unskilled in the usage, has managed to poison herself in small doses. I would suggest that we search through her belongings, just in case." I grimaced at the thought. It seemed cruel to dig through a sick child's private treasures, particularly if one of them was a reminder of a lost mother.

A mother who tried to cut out her sister's heart. And anyway, it would be much crueler to let her die.

"And this is why I came to you," the king said, smiling wryly. "I would never have thought of cosmetics, and I will wager that the physicians did not either."

Then your physicians were fools. I did not say that, though, because I had the sneaking suspicion that I would prove the biggest fool of all.

CHAPTER 7

At dinner that night, I sat beside an older man who oozed military out of every pore. I was intensely relieved. I didn't know if I could face Lady Anonymous again.

To my surprise and delight, General Matthias proved to be quite a good conversationalist. When I told him that I was a natural history tutor, he fixed me with twinkling gray eyes and said, "And what part of nature do you specialize in, young lady?"

From most other people, I would have resented the title of *young lady,* but he reminded me so much of my late grandfather that I only laughed. "Plants, mostly," I said. "Though I have a great fondness for snakes."

"Snakes!" It was his turn to laugh. "Well, that will certainly wake your students up, won't it? I was on campaign many years ago now, in Mindigal, far northwest of here. Spent most of our time in a swamp, and it was simply lousy with snakes. All kinds, but there were these skinny green ones, as long as a horse, that used to hang down from the trees like vines. I've forgotten the local name now, but we called them 'vine devils.' Those were the worst. The big brown ones that swam everywhere were supposed to be poisonous, but they never gave us any trouble. They just wanted to get away."

"Most snakes are like that," I said. (I didn't bother being pedantic about the difference between venomous and poisonous. If someone screams, *Help, I've been bitten by a poisonous snake!* we all know perfectly well what they mean.) "Probably the green ones were just startled."

"Oh, I don't doubt it." He toasted the absent vine devils with his wine. "I can't imagine I'd be very friendly if I was minding my own business and a pack of young fellows with machetes came barging into my garden. Still, it's not the sort of thing you think of when there's one fastened on to your cheek."

"Oh dear . . ."

He grinned. "No, no, I was too ugly for a snake to want to bite. Saw it happen three or four times to other fellows, though. Still not as bad as the mosquitoes, though. We were all glad to get out of that swamp." He laughed ruefully. "Listen to me rattle on! Is this your first time traveling with the court?"

I nodded glumly.

The general laughed at my expression. "Ridiculous, isn't it?" He gestured with his fork at the crowded lower tables. "I've made better time with a thousand infantrymen in full kit than with this lot. But you're lucky, young lady. Most of them won't be going to Witherleaf at all. I'm stuck with them until we reach Cholla Bay."

This was news to me. I sat up straighter. "They won't?"

"Nah, nah. The king leaves and goes to Witherleaf with just his own staff. Even kings need a break now and again."

"Hear, hear," said the king, on my right. I hadn't realized he'd been listening.

The general grinned at him with a charming lack of formality. "The rest of this lot will head straight to the bay, and the king will meet up with us in a few days, or thereabouts."

I had been delighted at the thought of fewer people around who were speculating that I might be the king's mistress, but that delight was immediately doused. A few days! Was I expected to solve Snow's problem by then? What if I couldn't? If I had to comb through everything she ate and every one of her possessions and eliminate them one by one, it could take weeks. Months, even.

"Ever been to Cholla Bay?" asked the general.

"Eh? Oh. Once, yes." My father had been checking on his warehouse there. Smaller ships can get into the bay, so they mostly carry small high-value goods, like ivory and opium.

"Then you know you're not missing much," he said, and laughed.

I managed a laugh and tried to focus on the conversation, even though my chest was tight with the feeling that I was running out of time before I'd even arrived.

"Dingy little place," said one of the people on the king's right.

"Some parts of it are pleasant enough," someone else argued.

"But even those parts smell like fish."

More laughter. My head hurt.

"Are you feeling all right, my dear?" asked the general.

"I'm fine," I said. What had we been talking about? *Fish. Cholla Bay. Say something.* "There's a species of stonefish there that's so venomous, they're called feedsharks. Because if you step on one, you'll feed yourself to a shark to make the pain stop."

Silence descended on the table like a diver's foot on a stonefish. I closed my mouth on a further dissertation about how they stored venom in glands at the base of their spines.

"Is there a cure?" asked the king, as mildly as if discussing the weather.

"A treatment only." I had to take a gulp of water to keep my voice from cracking. "Hot water and vinegar applied to the wound. Tonic to strengthen the choleric humor. Laudanum for the pain."

And then, the saints bless him, the general came to my rescue. "Now, I don't know about fish, but I tell you, up in Mindigal, they had a frog in the swamp there that would make your whole arm go numb . . ."

The other diners relaxed, and someone else told a story about a scorpion sting that was completely inaccurate, and I pried my fingers from the handle of my cup and fled as soon as I was able.

I was so sore the next morning that Javier had to help me onto my horse. He did so with a commendable lack of conversation and only grunted when I thanked him. I felt as if someone had filled my lower back with angry cement.

I was no longer surprised when I was summoned to the front of the column. Lacking any illusions about my conversational skills,

I wondered why the king was bothering to ride with me at all. Then I looked at the guards around us and behind us, and it finally occurred to me that they were still worried about the hypothetical poisoner having me killed. If you have to protect two people from assassins, it's probably easier to have them both together.

Fortunately the king seemed to realize that I was suffering and didn't require conversation. The general from last night's dinner rode on his other side, and the two of them talked. I clung to the reins and took a surreptitious slug of laudanum when we stopped.

The day lasted forever. I didn't notice when the rest of the cavalcade left us. I just looked back and saw that they were gone. The general had gone, too. Bands of red crawled up the sky in the west and came down the other side as indigo.

The last hour of our ride was almost dreamlike. I was not thinking about poison or assassins or anything else. I wasn't even thinking about how much my legs hurt or how much longer the ride was. I clung to the saddle and fell asleep between Ironwood's strides, only to be jolted awake as each hoof came down.

At some point, we reached Witherleaf. Torches had been lit on either side of the broad brick avenue that led to the front gate. We made our way up it, still on horseback. I could hear horseshoes clicking on the bricks the way that they hadn't on the road. I started to reach for Ironwood's reins, only to discover that I didn't have them. Javier had dismounted and was leading him. I thought about offering to dismount, too, then realized that I didn't know if I could walk.

Massive agaves flanked the avenue, draping stiff leaves across the bricks. They looked like strange sea creatures in the torchlight. Insects circled the flames in a disordered halo, and once I saw a bat swoop down and take one out of the air.

Witherleaf itself loomed before us. Three stories tall, it was a villa in the traditional style, with white stucco walls and a red-tiled roof. Covered balconies studded the upper stories, and I saw the glint of glass doors. The part of me that would always be a merchant's daughter began calculating the cost of so much glass, hit an appallingly high number, and gave up.

The double doors in front had been thrown open, revealing an enormous interior courtyard. Finally we stopped, and Javier helped me down from my horse. I hit the ground and hissed like the chime-adder. My bodyguard stood patiently while I clung to his forearms and my legs asked if I was certain that I wanted to walk after all. Perhaps I could roll along the ground to my room.

There were people there, talking to the king. The only one who made an impression was the housekeeper, who was a tiny, sweet-faced woman with the eyes of a tyrant. Javier stood beside me the whole time, saying nothing.

I was both relieved and oddly bereft to learn that while my guards would be staying at Witherleaf, they would not be standing guard outside my door. Apparently the king felt that such things weren't required here. Instead they would be available if I wanted to ride out into the desert, and would otherwise be taking shifts with the rest of the estate's guards, until it was time for me to return to Four Saints. I devoutly hoped that they wouldn't have time to unpack.

The housekeeper assured me that my equipment chests would be taken to a workroom, and tried to convince me to go directly to my room. That lasted until I explained about my chime-adder, who probably shouldn't stay in my bedroom. Suddenly it was eminently reasonable that I visit the workroom, even at this late hour. I limped down there, trying to pretend that I always walked like I was holding an invisible barrel between my thighs.

It wasn't a bad space. A long room on the first floor, with stone floors instead of tile. I suspect it had originally been used for cheese making or something of the sort. It was cool and dim and had a big table in the middle that would be useful. There were windows, but they were the small kind cut into thick walls that you find in older buildings. The manor house seemed to be built up and around a small core of rooms like this, which were probably original. All the fancy stuff had come later.

I dropped off the adder, made sure she had water, then handed myself back over to the housekeeper. I don't think she approved of guests who carried venomous snakes with them, but she clearly would rather die than criticize one of the king's guests, so we smiled awkwardly at each other, and then she called for a maid.

The maid who showed me to my room had hair that looked as if it was about to devour her head and go in search of other prey. I kept an eye on it as she led me up a wide flight of stairs and along a broad hallway lined with doors. Occasionally the hall would pass under a beautifully tiled arch, for no apparent reason except to show off how many arches the owner could afford.

"And here is your room," the maid said, pushing open the door.

I stepped inside and swore involuntarily.

The maid's eyes went wide. "Is there a problem, mistress?"

"No, no," I said. "I just wasn't expecting anything so . . . err . . . *extravagant*."

"His Majesty said that you were to be treated as an honored guest," said the maid, and dropped a curtsy in my general direction.

Through the door was a room rather larger than the one I had at home, and my father, as I've mentioned before, was *not* a poor man. The floors were tiled in simple red saltillo, but to make up for this restraint, they were covered in the sort of intricate rugs that take years off a weaver's eyesight. The bed was an enormous four-poster, draped with airy silk hangings, and the chest at its foot was so deeply carved that I was surprised it didn't fall apart.

The wall opposite the bed was taken up by an enormous mirror, a good six feet tall and three feet wide, with a gilded frame. I stared at it in mild astonishment. I'd never seen one so large before. Big mirrors are expensive to make.

The maid followed my gaze. "One of the queen's," she said, as if that explained everything.

"The queen's . . . ?"

She nodded. Her hair was making a stealthy play for the cap on her head, and the nod let it gain some ground. "Her Majesty came from Silversand. All the best mirrors come from there. There were dozens of them in her dowry. All the king's estates have them."

It made sense. Silversand is a small kingdom to our west, with abundant minerals and not much else. Our desert is all shrubs and small trees and chaparral, but by the time you get to Silversand, it's nothing but sand and rock. I suppose all that sand is good for making glass.

You'll laugh, but mirrors make me a bit uneasy. They're fine during the day, but I've never liked them at night. I go out of the way not to look into the ones at home after dark. It's not rational and probably doesn't befit a serious scholar, but I just have this instinctive fear that if I look in one, I'll see something moving that shouldn't be. A shape behind me, maybe, or a shadow. Which is ridiculous, of course, because if there's a shape behind me in the mirror, it means that someone is really there, and it's hardly the mirror's fault.

Like I said, it's not rational. I wasn't looking forward to sleeping across from this one, but I could hardly demand that they redecorate the room for me. I walked up to the glass and studied it. Not polished tin, but glass backed with whatever mirrormakers use to reflect light. (Silver is the main ingredient, but the exact formulations are closely guarded secrets. The mirrormaker's circle is no joke. Makers who try to set themselves up outside of circle jurisdiction tend to have accidents. One tried to get my father to carry his work once, and Father had categorically refused. The man later moved unexpectedly, in the middle of the night, without telling anyone where he was going. He left all his equipment behind, too, along with some dark stains. You don't mess with the circle.)

The mirrormakers in Silversand could have taught ours a thing or two. The surface was as clear and smooth as still water. You could sell a mirror of half that size for enough to keep a family fed and housed for a year. A *big* family.

The frame would have been far easier to construct, but was trying to make up for that in sheer baroque enthusiasm. Ornate flowers bloomed at the corners, and leaping rabbits danced along the edges, framed by spirals and curlicues. Saint Rabbit is the patron of fertility and has dominion over the reproductive organs. I wondered if there had been some message in sending such a gift along with a bride or if the woodworker had simply liked rabbits

"Mistress?" the maid said, for what I belatedly realized was the second time.

"Sorry," I said, turning away. "Distracted. I . . . err . . ." I took refuge in honesty. "I'm very tired."

She smiled. "There's a washroom in there"—she pointed to a drape—"and the privy through there"—a small door—"and there's a bathing room through there. If you want a bath, please let us know, and we'll have water heated and brought up."

A bath sounded amazing, but it also seemed like a great extravagance in the desert. The basin in the washroom was generously sized and well supplied with towels, and the pitcher of water was still warm. Someone must have started heating it the moment we arrived. I decided to make do.

"If you need anything else, just ring," the maid said, gesturing to the bellpull. Her lifted arm came into range of the hair, and it leaped for her sleeve. She pushed it back like a deeply resigned animal handler.

"Thank you," I said. "If I need anything, I'll let you know."

She shut the door behind her. I had my robes off before the lock even clicked, scrubbed myself down, and was in bed in less than ten minutes.

In the middle of the night, I got up to use the privy, caught a glimpse of movement out of the corner of my eye, jumped backward, banged

into one of the bedposts, and finally realized that I had seen myself in the mirror. I slumped backward, heart racing. (See, this is why I don't like mirrors.)

I eventually recovered sufficiently to make use of the facilities, which were in a small tiled chamber tucked discreetly into the wall. I was gazing into the middle distance when the thought suddenly occurred to me that by not going to see Snow as soon as we got in, we had given the hypothetical poisoner a dangerous opportunity. (No, I don't know why so many important realizations occur when people are in the privy. For some reason, this topic has gone unexplored by serious scholars, even though the classical mathematician Callixus famously conceived his Third Theorem during the aftereffects of a meal of overspiced beans.)

I tried to think it through. If we assumed that Snow was being slowly poisoned over time, and if they realized that I was here to investigate, would they be driven to a desperate move overnight? A faster poison? A knife?

Oh Saints . . .

My heart, which had finally settled after the mirror incident, began thrumming again. I pressed a hand to my chest.

Think logically, Anja. You can't go racing off with your nightgown hiked up around your hips and your ass hanging out. Snow is bound to have guards. And surely the king would have thought of this?

Sure, the king who thinks that putting a guard on food as it comes from the kitchen is sufficient . . .

Still, what was I going to do? Rush into the bedroom of a girl I hadn't met, babbling about potential assassins? That would certainly go over well. Hell, we still didn't even know if it *was* poison.

For that matter, you're not going to be rushing anywhere right now. Waddling slowly and whimpering a lot, maybe. It was going to take a day or two before I recovered fully from the length of the ride.

I went back to bed, feeling discouraged before I'd even begun.

CHAPTER 8

The next morning, the king introduced me to Snow.

I'd been dreading this part for days. As I said before, I am not particularly good with children, and presumably children who happened to be king's daughters would be even trickier. I had bolted a hasty breakfast brought to my room, but it wasn't sitting very well.

Snow's rooms looked a bit like mine, only larger and filled with people. There were two women wearing maid's clothing and an older woman who was probably a nursemaid or governess or something of the sort. She had a separate bedroom, so everyone was piled into the sitting room. A mirror the same size as mine dominated one wall, and Snow herself was seated in front of it, looking small and pale and tired.

She jumped to her feet when we came in and rushed forward to hug the king. He returned it, ruffling her hair. I looked away, embarrassed. There was such naked affection on his face that it felt like I was intruding merely by observing.

After a moment, the king released her. "Snow, love, this is Healer Anja. She's come to take a look at you."

Snow turned to me. Her expression was polite, but her eyebrows were suspicious. We looked each other up and down.

I knew that she was twelve years old, and I can't tell you if she looked older or younger than that. I am terrible at judging the ages of anyone under twenty. She had hair so pale that it was almost white, and her skin was only a shade darker, so that her eyebrows stood out like scars. Her eyes were faded blue, with circles like bruises underneath, and she was much too thin. When she held out a hand, the bones of her wrists were sharply defined.

There was no question that something was wrong with her. It was my job, I supposed, to find out what. I introduced myself, hoping that the pale green scarf actually did provide an air of authority and that I didn't look as nervous as I felt.

"Are you going to blister my feet?" she asked.

I recoiled. "Saints, no!"

She nodded gravely. "The doctors who were here before bled me," she said. "And purged me, and blistered my feet to draw out the sickness. I don't mind the bleeding, but the blistering was awful." She sounded almost proud of it, now that it was over.

"I promise, nobody will be getting blistered."

The king stepped in at this point. "Healer Anja just needs to examine you," he said. "She's here to make sure that . . . um . . . you're not eating anything that might be making you sick."

"Poison, you mean," said Snow.

The king choked.

Snow fixed her father with the scathing look that young girls do so well. "I'm not *stupid*," she said.

"No," said the king. "Sorry." He coughed. "I didn't want you to worry, love."

Snow hitched up one shoulder in a shrug.

I was deeply relieved that we'd dispensed with euphemisms. "If you'll just sit down," I said, "this won't hurt at all."

I gave the king's daughter a thorough exam, just as I would if she were sitting in the temple's infirmary. I checked her gums, in case there was the blue line that would indicate lead poisoning, and her hair in case it was loose or falling out. Her breath didn't smell suspiciously of garlic, her hands didn't have a noticeable tremor, her balance seemed fine. Her nails weren't overly brittle, she wasn't sensitive to light, and the older woman assured me that her bowels were working fine. Her skin bruised easily—there were yellowing marks everywhere, the sort you'd get from casually banging into a bedpost or doorframe—but wasn't peeling or oddly spotted. Her hair was dull and lank, but so fine that I couldn't be certain if it was caused by illness or simply the wrong soap.

Her teeth were in bad shape. The enamel had eroded in multiple places, and one had been drilled and packed with gold leaf. That must have hurt like a bear, even with laudanum to take the edge off.

"Sometimes I throw up," Snow said. "When I try to eat."

I nodded gravely and wrote this down, while my heart sank lower and lower.

When I finished the exam, the king jerked his head toward the corridor, and I followed him out. I tried to give Snow a reassuring smile as I went, but Saints know if I managed that much.

"Well?" the king said, when the door was closed.

I raked a hand through my hair. "If she's being poisoned—and she might be—I can't tell what it is yet. Her symptoms are too general, and there aren't any that I can point to and say, 'Aha! Arsenic!' Or mercury or lead or what have you. Either it hasn't advanced to the stage where the type of poison is immediately obvious, or it's not one of the common toxins."

Saints curse it. I was really hoping that it would be an easy one.

I was braced for him to berate me—I've had parents do that before, and even though I know it's out of fear for their children, I don't particularly enjoy it—but he simply nodded. "What next?"

"Observation." I looked down at my notebook. "I'll have to spend a few days tracking what she eats and testing anything that seems suspicious. Knowing how it's getting into her system will help narrow it down. And also she can stop eating it, of course."

"You think it's something she's eating?"

"It's the most likely scenario. It's not as if she's a laborer at a ceramic works and breathing in lead dust all day. And the vomiting may be a symptom."

He nodded. "I'll be staying here for four days," he said. "Then I have to go on to the port."

"Yes, of course." Kings couldn't just sit by their daughters' bed-sides, they had to keep doing king things. "If I haven't worked it out by the time you leave, I'll arrange to get a message to you as soon as I know more."

He nodded again. "There's someone else you should meet," he said. "Come with me."

I glanced back at the door to Snow's room. "A moment, Your Majesty . . ."

Royal eyebrows went up in surprise.

I gestured to the door. "I thought I'd tell Snow that, err, it's not bad news . . . ?" *I'd want to know, myself. But maybe you're not supposed to tell children that you don't know what's going on? Oh dear . . .*

"Yes, of course," the king said.

I ducked my head and went back into the room. Snow was sitting in front of the mirror, brushing her hair. She was so pale in the dimness of the room that she practically glowed. It wasn't hard to see how she had gotten her name.

"Snow? I just wanted to tell you that I don't know if it's poison or not, but I *am* going to find out."

"Thank you, Healer Anja." She nodded solemnly to me, then turned away. And then she smiled, a sly, secretive smile. Not a happy smile, but the look of someone who *knows* that they're the smartest person in the room. It was so startling that my first thought was that I was misinterpreting her expression entirely.

If not for the mirror, I wouldn't have seen it at all.

I was still mulling over that odd smile as the king led me along the gallery that overlooked the courtyard. I was vaguely surprised that no footmen appeared to trail after him or rush ahead open-ing doors, but they didn't. Perhaps at Witherleaf the king did not require servants to add to his consequence. *If I were a king, I expect I'd get very tired of being followed around by servants very quickly.*

We went down a set of steps and out onto a wide veranda. Blue ceramic pots stood in little clusters, holding dozens of agaves, some with broad, strappy leaves, some forming tight, spiny balls like giant artichokes. A stout old woman sat at a table among the bristling plants, sipping tea.

"Aunt Sorrel!" the king cried.

Wait, aunt? *The king doesn't have an aunt. All he had was an uncle, and the Demon never actually married.*

She pushed herself upright with the help of a cane and held out her arms. For the second time in an hour, I saw unguarded emotion on the king's face. Whoever this woman was, he cared for her very much.

"Healer Anja," he said, once he had seen the woman settled back in her chair, "this is Madame Sorrel. Aunt, this is Healer Anja. She's an expert on poisons."

Madame Sorrel turned to me and smiled warmly. She likely had never been beautiful, but it seemed as if age had revealed the strength of the bones in her face. She had the fine, pale lines at the corners of her eyes that people get in the desert when they spend years squinting against the sun. "Welcome to Witherleaf," she said. "I realize that you're here for a very unfortunate reason, but I do hope we can make you as comfortable as possible."

She *meant* it, too. That was the surprising thing. I got the impression that she genuinely cared about whether or not I was comfortable here.

"Sit, sit," Sorrel said, gesturing to the chairs. "Randolph, you're working too hard. You have that look."

The king's name was Randolph? Had I known that? I must have, but I'd never given it much thought. Kings are kings for such a long time that you really only need to refer to them as something other than *the king* once they're dead. (Unless you travel, I suppose, and then you can get away with calling them simply the king of your country, or this country, or that country over there.)

Randolph, the king, sat. I took a chair and perched on the edge, feeling awkward.

"You should come here more often," Sorrel said, pouring tea.

The teapot was deceptively simple terra-cotta. No glazes. I accepted a cup of tea with an internal sigh of relief.

"I should," the king said, "but you know how it is."

"Of course," Sorrel said.

She smiled at me. "So, how are you finding Witherleaf so far? I realize that's an unfair question, since you've seen it mostly in the dark, but I'm obligated to ask anyway."

I chuckled. "What I've seen is lovely," I said. "In fact, I'm wondering why it's called 'Witherleaf.' Granted we're out in the desert here, but it still seems much too pleasant for that."

"Ah . . ." Lady Sorrel said, spooning honey into her tea and stirring. "A fine question. Supposedly a king a century or two back—I've forgotten which. A Bartimaeus maybe, but don't ask me what number, they had such a lot of them. You'd think they'd start to crave some variety after a few generations . . . Sorry, what was I saying?"

"One of the Bartimaeuses," I said. "Bartimaeusi?"

Sorrel giggled, sounding suddenly much younger. "Oh, I like that. At any rate, he had married a woman who, by all accounts, was far too much for him, and he eventually exiled her here, saying, 'Let her wither and die out there in the desert!'" She drew herself up and declaimed the words, holding the spoon like a scepter. I caught a glimpse of the king's face, looking fondly amused, as one might well look at an elderly relative, much beloved.

"At any rate," Sorrel said, dropping the spoon back onto the saucer with a *ping*, "this became the estate where kings sent divorced queens and estranged mistresses, and the name stuck."

Estranged . . . mistresses . . .

And then I heard the voice ringing in my ear, sour with gossip: *Kings have had plain mistresses before, too. Remember Lady Sorrel?*

Yes, but King Bastian was mad, dear.

"Saints!" I blurted. "You're the old king's—"

My brain caught up to my mouth then and snapped it shut, but it was too late. King Randolph glared at me. It was the first time he'd glared in my direction, and it felt as if it might sear all the way through me and burn my family by proxy.

"Um," I said. "I'm sorry, that— I didn't mean to—"

I was interrupted by Lady Sorrel's peal of laughter. "Oh, please, don't worry. It's hardly a secret. Randolph, quit glaring at the child like that. It's your fault for not warning her."

The king, to my astonishment, flushed and looked away. "Sorry, Aunt Sorrel."

Aunt. Of course. His uncle's mistress was the closest thing he had to an aunt. It was clear that they were very close.

"I was indeed poor Bastian's mistress," Lady Sorrel said to me. "He wasn't a bad man before his mind went. And after that . . . well." She took a sip of tea. "I did what I could to temper some of his excesses."

"And you were my only friend at court for many years," King Randolph said warmly. "Don't think I've forgotten."

"I was the only one in a position to risk it," Sorrel said. She gazed past both of us, over the gardens, into the desert. "He never forgot he loved me, even when so much else was taken from him."

The long-term effects of mercury poisoning are cruel, and madness is foremost among them. I wondered if Lady Sorrel had not been a target, or if she had simply been less affected. She set her teacup down with barely a tremor. "At any rate," she said, "no one quite knew what to do with me after Bastian died, and Randolph here flatly refused to let them turn me out into the streets, so I came to Witherleaf." She smiled at me, and I could see some of what a young, doomed king might have loved. "Now you must look at my collection of agaves, young lady. I am dreadfully vain about them, and when winter comes, I insist on having the tender ones brought inside where the servants constantly trip over them and wish me to perdition." She rose to her feet, and both the king and I followed suit.

Sorrel was a substantial weight on my arm, and she used her cane to point at the various potted plants that lined the edge of the veranda. "Now, this one is a variety called Silverheart . . . look closely, you can see the white markings at the base of the leaves . . . and this one here is called Whale's Tear, and I was given it by the oddest little man . . ."

I spent an enjoyable morning with Lady Sorrel. The gardens around the villa were quite small, because there was only so much water to spare for them, but they were elegantly designed and shaded into the surrounding desert so gradually that, at first, you hardly realized you had stepped outside them. There were spirit houses in the desert, but not many, and each one was beautifully made. Witherleaf clearly cared for its own, in death as well as life.

I was still recovering from the long ride, but Sorrel moved at a slow amble, which was just about the speed I was capable of.

When I complimented Lady Sorrel on the garden, she laughed. "I've done nothing but enjoy them. The gardeners do all the real work, and they were originally laid out by Randolph's great-grandmother. Her husband sent her here in hopes that she would have the grace to die after it seemed like she'd only have the one child. She outlived him by forty years and had plenty of time to lay out the gardens."

Sorrel pointed out various plants, and I told her which ones could be used to poison someone. (Normally I would have thought this was tactless, given her history, but she *asked*.) The king trailed after us with his hands in his pockets. I wondered if he was bored, then thought that maybe if you were a king, boredom was a novelty, or at least the sort of boredom you'd get following two women meandering slowly through a garden was. Perhaps it was pleasant, if you were a king, to spend a little time when no one wanted anything from you and you didn't have to worry about anything more pressing than avoiding a cactus spine.

At last Sorrel declared that it was time for her afternoon nap. "But you must join us for dinner tonight," she said, pointing her cane at me like a lance. "And come to tea whenever you feel like entertaining a lonely old lady, if you're not too busy saving my god-niece."

"I would be delighted," I said, and meant it. At least about the tea.

There were six of us at dinner that night, and the sole reason that it wasn't awful was because of Lady Sorrel. We were arranged with women on one side of the table and men on the other, so the king was flanked by two male advisors (apparently he was not allowed to stop being king for more than a few hours), and Snow and I sat on opposite sides of Sorrel. She turned to me as soon as the soup was served and said, "We spent all morning talking of poisons. Now tell me about *antidotes*."

I coughed into my napkin. "That's a much more complicated subject, I'm afraid."

One of the king's advisors stopped talking and leaned forward on his elbows. He was a small, energetic man who gave the impression of having just come in from a vigorous run. I'd seen him at the table the past two days on the road, usually gesturing so vigorously that the lace on his sleeves trailed through the sauce. "I've heard that if you are bitten by an adder, you should suck the poison from the wound at once," he said.

"Far be it from me to stop you," I said, "but all that will get you is a mouthful of blood. Better you should wash out the wound."

He laughed and clutched at his heart. "Ack! One of my favorite tales, shot down. I'd always hoped that if I was out riding and one of my companions was bitten, I would leap heroically into action and save their life."

"*Is* there a cure for snakebites?" the king's other advisor asked. He was tall and broad and, compared to his colleague, looked half asleep. There was no lace on his cuffs, and except for the exceptional quality of the fabric, his clothes looked like the sort that any moderately prosperous merchant might wear.

"Not as such. Not something you can take and be perfectly fine afterward." I took a sip of wine. "A great deal depends on the snake and how much venom they secrete. They're as different as humans in a way."

"Healer Anja has a chime-adder in her workshop," the king said.

Everyone was looking at me now. I felt the urge to shrink back in my chair and squelched it. "Chime-adder venom speeds the heart," I explained. "And also hurts like the devil. But distilled, I have managed to make a drug that makes the heart beat harder. I am hoping to expand it into a medicine for people with weak hearts." So much attention was a trifle embarrassing, so I took a rather larger swallow of wine. "As for snakebites, it depends on the type. For a rattleviper, take off any rings you've got on or boots or stockings, if it hit the leg. The swelling is the worst of it. The bite's survivable, but the gangrene won't be, if the blood gets cut off by a ring. For chime-adders, I'd suggest taking laudanum immediately. Slowing the heart may stave off the worst of the effects."

"And if it doesn't, at least it'll hurt less," Lady Sorrel said, and everyone laughed, even Snow.

The conversation circled for a few moments about snakes, as it tended to when the topic came up, and then the king said, "I have read that Emperor Hadrach drank snake venom in wine to build up an immunity."

I shrugged. "It wouldn't help. Anyone can drink snake venom, provided they don't have any ulcers in their mouth or stomach." It's a street performer's trick that you see sometimes, where the performer milks a snake's fangs into a cup, then drinks it while the crowd gasps.

"And what of scorpions, drowned in oil?" the king asked, his lips quirking. "I've heard he ate that, too."

"I cannot swear that it does not work," I said with some asperity. "It is always possible that the emperor had access to a better class of scorpion. But in my experience, it does no good."

"Saints bless us!" Lady Sorrel said. "You tried that?"

"When I first began studying, I tried almost every antidote that had ever been written down. Bezoars, amethysts, a dozen different recipes for theriac . . ."

"And?" asked the energetic advisor.

"And the vast majority were . . ." I tried to find a tactful way to phrase it. "A triumph of enthusiasm over medical knowledge."

The tall advisor laughed so hard at that that the king had to pound him on the back. "You should hire this one as a diplomat," he said, wheezing.

See, Isobel? I can *be tactful.*

"I've heard that unicorn horns can cure poison," Snow piped up, her high voice carrying over the conversation.

"Many classical writers say so," I said. "I'd very much like to test it. Unfortunately I've never been able to find an actual unicorn horn, so I've never been able to find out for myself." (This was also tactful. What usually gets sold as a unicorn horn is taken from scimitar oryx. Oryx are beautiful antelope, but they're no more immune to poison than any ruminant. Actual unicorns seem to be as rare as honest men.)

"So what *does* work, then?" the energetic advisor asked.

I took a moment to admire Lady Sorrel's skill at managing dinner conversation. She had successfully pulled the most reclusive member of the table into talking and gotten everyone else involved, regardless of social status. Sadly, it meant that I had to actually answer the question.

"Every time? Nothing. It depends on how the poison is taken, how strong the patient is, how long the poison has had to work . . ." I spread my hands helplessly.

"What would *you* take if you were poisoned?" the king asked.

"Clay."

"Clay?" His eyebrows slammed together like castle doors.

"Terra sigillata," I said. "The ancients knew it well. I'd also try charcoal—or ground-up toadstones, if I could get them."

"Why those?"

I was beginning to feel as if I were being interrogated for crimes against the crown. "Because most of the roosters survive."

The main course arrived and saved me from having to admit that curing poison is actually mostly guesswork. "Enough of poisons," said Lady Sorrel. "I want to eat my dinner without worrying."

As I bent my head over my food, I caught a glimpse of Snow at the other end of the table, and I wondered what she thought about the adults so blithely discussing a topic that might be killing her.

CHAPTER 9

The next morning, I took full advantage of the bath and presented myself at Snow's door, well scrubbed and professional. Hopefully professional. Professional-esque, anyway. I was staking a lot on those green scarves.

The person who seemed to be in charge of Snow was a tall woman with a long, rabbitlike face. She was smiling warmly, but I got the impression that she had been doing it for so long that it was simply her default expression.

"So, Mistress . . . ?" I raised my eyebrows inquiringly at her.

"Oh please, just call me 'Nurse,'" she said. "Everyone else does."

"Well then, Nurse, if you could write down everything Snow eats in the course of a day, that would be very helpful," I said, proffering a sheet of paper.

The nurse looked down at the paper but made no move to take it. "Oh . . . ah . . ." she said. The smile didn't quite slip, but it frayed a bit at the edges. "I don't know as I'm the best one for that, being so busy and all . . ."

I guessed at once that the woman was uneasy with her letters and revised my plan. "Oh, of course," I said. "It was foolish of me not to realize how busy you are. Why don't I sit here and take notes, and we'll go from there?"

Nurse looked relieved. I looked around, found an overstuffed armchair by the balcony door, and settled in.

The odds were good that I'd have had to do this anyway at some point. Nurse was probably entirely trustworthy, so far as good intentions went, and entirely untrustworthy as far as observations went. She was simply too close to Snow and too used to the daily routine. You'd be amazed the things that people's eyes skip over as unimportant—flypaper, rat poison, a cup of warm milk before bed. (Not that I thought Snow was eating rat poison, but the saints know that I've heard of stranger things.)

If you ever have the opportunity to sit in the corner and observe the morning routine of a twelve-year-old princess, I suggest you do virtually anything else. After about two hours, rat poison was starting to look good. The lives of kings' daughters are exquisitely *dull.*

First, Snow had a long bath. Servants came up with ewers of hot water and poured them into a tub, in a bathing chamber off the main room. The chamber was tiled in pink marble shot with threads of white, and probably I was the only person who thought that it strongly resembled a ham. It was three times the size of the bathing chamber in my room. (Mine also had a connecting door that indicated I was supposed to share it with the next suite over, although that door was bolted and locked. But at least it had mirrored tiles on the walls instead of stone ham.)

I took samples of the bath oil, which was highly unlikely to be poisoned, since Snow would probably be covered in blisters if it were. Then I retired back to the bedroom to wait. The nurse went back and forth, bringing her towels and different soaps and cold water with fruit in it. I interceded to ask where the water and the fruit came from and who had handled it, which flustered her badly. I made notes to track it down later with the cook. Servants came and went, delivering more hot water. I made more notes.

All this might have been less tedious if I'd been able to hold a conversation, but since I wanted everyone to do the things they'd do if someone weren't watching carefully, I did my best to fade into the background. Also, the chair was only just wide enough for my hips, which meant that I couldn't shift my weight at all, which meant that my rear end promptly fell asleep.

Snow emerged from the bath an hour later and sat in front of the fire to dry off. She brushed her hair, one hundred strokes, which she counted aloud. Then she flung herself at the bed and flopped down on it, with a sigh of such world-weariness that it could only have come from someone under twenty. I moved my chair a few inches so that I could watch her through the doorway.

She spent most of the next hour on the bed, staring off into space. Nurse rubbed her back for a bit. Snow eventually sat up, went to the balcony, and sat there instead, staring over the desert. Nurse brought her water. I wrote *Listlessness?* in my notebook.

A little before noon, she came back inside and applied makeup— *See, I told you,* I said to the absent king—then took it off again, then put it back on, slightly differently. She ate pastilles while she did it, so I had to take samples of those and ask where they'd come from.

"The city," Snow said. "They're violet flavored." Her pale eyebrows drew down. "Why, are they poisoned?"

"Probably not," I assured her. "Let me just take a few so that I can check."

She stared first at me, then at the pastilles, then slowly offered me the tin. I took a half dozen and slipped them into an envelope. They were stamped on one side with a little violet flower. I went back to my chair, but she didn't eat any more of them. (This is why I attempt to fade into the background. Who knew what else she wasn't eating because now she was thinking about it? Which was good in the short term, if she stopped taking the poison, but bad if she started eating it again after I'd left.)

One of her maids laid out three different dresses, none of which met Snow's approval. Three more were laid out, one of which was apparently suitable. Then jewelry had to be procured to match the dress, except that a pair of silver eardrops was missing from the box where it was supposed to be. Snow was extremely cutting to the maid who could not locate them.

"Oh dear," Nurse said, interceding. "Perhaps a different set?"

"No. I want the silver ones. There's no point in even wearing this dress if I don't have the right eardrops."

"Now don't take a pet, love," said Nurse. "I'm sure they're just misplaced."

"*I* didn't misplace them," Snow said. "So unless someone's been going through my jewelry when I'm not here . . ." She stared very hard at the unfortunate maid.

"Miss, I wouldn't—"

"*Someone* did."

"Now, now, let's just take another look," Nurse said. "If they're not in the lacquer box here, perhaps they're in another box. You've got plenty of them, after all! And such lovely things. Let's try this one."

"They're not *in* that one," Snow said coldly. The maid wrung her hands, looking as if she were about to be summarily executed. I cringed with sympathetic embarrassment.

"Then perhaps they're in this one, with the clever little kitten on the lid."

"I *hate* that one. I'd never put anything I liked in there." She swatted it aside with the flat of her hand.

My sister Catherine went through a phase in her teens where she was rude to the servants. I think she picked it up from one of her friends. My father got wind of it and promptly gave everyone the week off with pay. "This is skilled labor," he informed us all, "and you will be as courteous as you would be to any other skilled craftsman, or you will do without."

Catherine spent most of the week hiding in her room, which was wise, because neither Isobel nor I was inclined to be charitable. I was used to dressing myself, but the loss of the cook was hard. We lived on sandwiches for the entire week. (The cook and her husband had a very nice vacation in Frithneedle in the nearby mountains and told me all about it afterward.)

Catherine was extremely polite to the servants from then on. But I suppose you're not allowed to do such a thing to a king's daughter. Even if it would probably be good for her.

At last the relevant jewelry was found in another box. "*I'm* going riding with my *father,* the *king,*" Snow announced, and swept out of the room.

Oh, thank the saints. I didn't have to worry about her getting poisoned while in the saddle, certainly not with her father there. I could stand up and walk around until I could feel my left buttock again.

"Right," said Nurse, once Snow had left. "That's at least two hours we've got free. Clara, hang the clothes back up, then go get yourself something to eat." Her voice was suddenly much less fluttery, as if someone had pulled the flounces off a nightgown and left a rather more serviceable garment behind. "Healer Anja, will you join me for lunch and some tea?"

"Oh *Saints,* yes," I said, with real relief.

It was kind of Nurse to invite me to eat with her. My position in the household was still very much in flux. I was not quite a servant and not quite an honored guest. Eating with the king and Lady Sorrel put my rank quite high, but there were ladies-in-waiting in the larger court who could eat with the king and who were treated worse than the lowest scullery maid by the lady they waited on.

This was all important because if I was a servant, the other servants might talk to me, which could be very important—but if I was an honored guest, I could demand things be done in the course of Snow's treatment that a servant couldn't. It was all very awkward, and I hated having to think about it. Nurse's invitation put me on the high-ranked servant side, which was where I'd much rather be.

"So tell me about Snow's illness," I said a few minutes later, my pen poised over my notes. The uneaten plate of sandwiches had been passed over to the maids, and another plate had been sent up as well. "She said there's been some vomiting?"

"Well, yes," Nurse said, "but I didn't think anything of it at first. She always was a bit of a puker as a child." Her lips twisted up. "You know how it is with some children. They get excited, or they forget to eat, or they do eat and then go for a carriage ride immediately afterward . . ."

I nodded. My sister Catherine would always demand sweets at

the market and then be reliably sick on the ride home. I assume she grew out of that eventually, but I simply stopped riding in carriages with her. For all I know, she does it to her husband now.

"And you mustn't think she's doing it deliberately," Nurse added. "I know some girls do—they take these notions in their heads, and it turns into a kind of sickness with them—but Snow was never like that. She *tries* to eat. When it's bad, it might take her an hour to eat a piece of toast, but she'll get it down."

I nodded, writing this down. I really needed to see a bout of this illness in person. So far, Snow had been pale and listless and easily bruised, but that could have been anemia . . . Except that the physicians had ruled out anemia. Damn it.

You hate to wish sickness on anyone, least of all a child, but I had a feeling that seeing it in action was the only way that I was going to get much further at identifying the poison, unless I could waylay it as it was being delivered *and* it was something I could test for.

I finished my sandwich morosely and realized that I'd lost the thread of the conversation.

"Her sister was a taking little thing," Nurse was saying. "I don't say Snow isn't, but of course she can be willful, right enough. But she's a good girl at heart." She gave me a beseeching look.

I had no idea how to answer that. Obviously Snow had been through a great deal and was still suffering the aftereffects. I could be sympathetic to that while still wincing on behalf of the maids.

"A good girl," Nurse repeated, dabbing at her eyes.

Does she think that I won't try to stop her being poisoned simply because she's spoiled? I wondered if I should be offended or not. I thought about saying that I frequently treated criminal addicts, but I had no idea how that would go over. Instead I took another sandwich. Cucumber and watercress, with some kind of spread. It wasn't bad at all. (Hopefully not poisoned, but the poisoner would have to plan to take out the nurse and the maids as well, and that seemed unlikely.)

"If she only had some kind of maternal figure," said Nurse with a deep sigh. "But you know about her mother, of course, and old Nurse, well . . ." She gave a self-deprecating laugh. "Snow got in the habit of ignoring me not long after she left the nursery. I was in charge of Rose. I'm only here now because after the queen . . . you know . . . there wasn't anyone else. And the king asked, of course, so how could I say no?"

"You couldn't," I said dryly, having some experience with that myself.

"Exactly." She shook her head sadly. "If only there was *someone* who could take her in hand . . ."

"Well, the king will probably marry again eventually," I said encouragingly, and helped myself to another sandwich. Tasty, but it must be said, not particularly filling.

"Oh . . . well, yes. But that could take years," Nurse said. "And you know how sensitive girls are at this age . . ."

I did not actually know this. At Snow's age, I had been getting the stomachs of dead hogs delivered from the butcher so that I could see how the internal organs were supposed to look in a healthy animal as opposed to one that had been poisoned. (The cook made a lot of tripe in those days. I think everyone was glad when I turned thirteen and was allowed to witness human autopsies.)

I did not say this out loud either.

"If only there was someone the king trusted, who Snow could look up to . . ."

"Mmm," I said. What was in this spread? Some sort of cheese, of course, but with something else mixed in. I could taste mint and . . . tarragon? "Have you asked Lady Sorrel for advice? She seems very sharp."

"She says that she's too old to deal with spoiled children that she didn't spoil in the first place," said Nurse grimly.

I barked with laughter, tried to cover it, and ended up spraying crumbs into my napkin. Nurse gazed at me, clearly annoyed but too polite to say so. "Sorry," I said, once I'd recovered my voice, if not my dignity. "Of course you already thought of that. I'm afraid

I don't know anyone in court at all, though, so I'm the wrong person to ask."

"I see," she said, a little coldly. Had I gotten crumbs on her, too? Well, it had to be unpleasant, being pulled back into service because your former charge's mother had murdered her. Anyone would be cross in that situation. Still, the sooner I could cure Snow, the sooner I'd be out from under Nurse's feet.

I want to be clear, by the way, that I knew perfectly well what she was suggesting. (Well, fine, I'd figured it out by the second or third repetition, anyway.) I knew how the story was supposed to go. I would meet Snow and my woman's heart would be wrung by the plight of the poor motherless child who had suffered so much, and I would win Snow's affection as I sought desperately to find the cure.

It was a good story. If I succeeded, people would almost certainly be telling some version of it.

The problem was that my heart did not contain a shred of maternal affection anywhere in its chambers, and even if it had, I didn't have the least idea how one dealt with children. They frightened me. I lived in fear that I would say or do something that scarred one for life. (Generally when I say this, some well-meaning soul pops up to tell me that children are actually very resilient and would find what I do fascinating. At that point I have to explain that my *entire job* is deadly poisons and extremely fragile glassware. This usually shuts the conversation down nicely.)

More than that, the story *annoyed* me. If I saved Snow, it would be because I had spent the last twenty years researching every poison known to man and staring into the guts of dead roosters. It wouldn't have anything to do with women's intuition or maternal affection. It wasn't *feelings,* it was *work.*

"Your problem," Healer Michael had said to me once, pouring out a measure of agave liquor, "is that people aren't real to you."

It had been so late that it was early again, and we had actually managed to save someone's life, through no fault of our own. It was a rough one. Charcoal at both ends for nearly six hours, until their breathing evened out and their heart stopped fluttering at every third beat. Then we went back to the temple and drank heavily. It's strange how winning can be more jarring than losing sometimes.

"People are real," I protested. "I'm not a *monster*."

Michael sighed. "Not like that. Look, a patient is a person with a problem, right?"

I took another slug of agave and allowed as how this was so.

"Right. Except that for *you*, a patient is a problem with a person inconveniently attached. If you could just have the problem without the person, you'd be much happier."

There are truths that you can say, drunk, in the small, gray hours of morning, that you can't say at any other time. I grunted as that truth lodged in me like a cactus spine and began working its way inward.

He wasn't wrong. Michael was one of the kindest people I knew, and it's easy to forget that *kind* doesn't mean *stupid*. That was why I wasn't really a healer. A good healer wants to help the person. Whereas what *I* wanted was to solve the problem.

Oh, in the abstract, I wanted to help Snow, of course. I genuinely wanted all my patients to be healthy and happy. I just didn't feel any need to be involved with that beyond solving their current problem.

Even at the very beginning, when Cousin Anthony had been poisoned, my real obsession had been with why there was no cure.

I just want to save people and then have those people go away and, ideally, not take arsenic again. Is that really so much to ask?

"Eh?" I looked up. Nurse had said something, breaking into my woolgathering. I wondered how long I'd been staring into my sandwich and hastily shoved the rest into my mouth.

"I asked if you were finished," she said. "Snow will be back before long, and we need to tidy all this away."

She had told me earlier that Snow took a nap in the afternoons.

I could not quite bear the thought of sitting in a chair, watching the girl sleep for hours on end. "Thank you for lunch," I said politely. "I'll be back tomorrow."

"Yes, of course," Nurse said, and managed a brittle smile.

Halfway back to my room, I had a sudden epiphany—*Blue cheese! That's what's in the spread!*

Now, if I can just figure out what's in the poison so easily . . .

CHAPTER 10

There was another appointment that I had to make and had probably put off for too long already. I went by my workroom to pick up a wicker cage, then went out in search of a doctor and a rooster, in that order.

The villa's doctor was a man named Rinald, who moved with the peculiar choppy grace of people who spend a great deal of time avoiding being kicked by horses. Since a population of fewer than a hundred was not sufficient to employ a doctor full-time, he doubled as the horse leech. I wondered which job he preferred.

"Healer Rinald?" I asked, tapping on the doorframe of the tack room, where he was mixing up a poultice. "May I trouble you?"

He looked up, chuckling. "I don't often get called that. You must be the poison doctor from the city, eh?"

Poison doctor wasn't the phrase I'd have chosen, but I didn't argue. "I'm sorry I didn't come yesterday," I said. "All I can plead is that people kept insisting I be here or there or decide something, and suddenly it was late."

Rinald grinned, showing irregular teeth. "I know how that goes. In truth, Healer, you're the first one of the doctors who's come to see me at all."

"Then the other doctors were fools," I said bluntly. "Also rude, since you don't take someone's patient without the courtesy of addressing them, but mostly fools. Surely you know more about the progression of this illness than anyone who arrived after the fact?"

"I'm only a horse leech," Rinald demurred. "I wouldn't presume to tell a city doctor their business."

"Well, this city doctor is begging you to tell me," I said, taking out my notebook.

He grinned again, but it faded quickly. "Truth is, Healer, I was just as glad to hand it off to someone else. It came up suddenly, and then again it didn't. She was here for a bit with no more trouble than not being able to sleep at night—and who can blame her?—and then the vomiting started. But that nurse of hers said she'd always been a puker, so I didn't think it was anything serious, and it went away the next day. Maybe ten days later, the same thing. Over and over. The gap between episodes got shorter and shorter. But you do get children who'll cast up their stomachs if the wind blows wrong, and at first it was long enough between episodes that it didn't seem like they were related. When I finally realized it was more than that and looked back, it was obvious that it had been going on for months and getting worse."

He took off his hat and fanned himself. I could smell hay and horses from the stable. Ironwood was in there somewhere, getting a good rest after days of work lugging my bones around.

"Truth is," Rinald added, after a moment, "I think it might've been going on before she even got here. I don't know that anybody even thought to notice the early stages. Why would they?"

I stared down at my notes. His account squared with everything I'd learned, though I was glad to hear it from him and not someone too close to Snow to see the larger picture. "Any chance she'd be doing it deliberately?"

Rinald scratched under his hat. "My gut says no," he said finally. "I watched it happen a few times—came up to the house every time she was feeling poorly—and she didn't *do* anything. Just had some tea and a bite of toast, and a minute later . . ." He spread his hands. "And she gets *real* sick each time. I actually worried she was getting antimony somewhere and changed out all the cups and whatnot."

"Damn," I muttered. That was one of the things I'd been planning on trying. Wine in an antimony cup will make you purge everything but your toenails. *Oh well. If it was easy, the king wouldn't have called you in.*

"Thank you," I said, getting to my feet. "This really does help."

Rinald smiled again, though not as widely. "Anything I can help with, you just ask, Healer. I hate the thought of that child wasting away."

"Actually, there's one thing," I said. "Do you know where I can get a rooster?"

The square-jawed man who managed the estate's poultry was in awe of me as the king's physician—or possibly mistress, I didn't want to know—and tried to give me the finest rooster in the pens, a tall black-and-white fellow with a comb as scarlet as a sunset. I would have balked at using such a large rooster anyway, and certainly at such a handsome specimen. (Judging by the number of young chickens with his same coloration, the hens thought highly of him as well.)

After several explanations involving the words *small, tiny,* and *miniature* and eventually hand gestures, the poultryman was talked down to a half-grown bantam cockerel. I would have preferred to use two test subjects, but I had so little material to work with that I was forced to settle on one.

"Sorry," I told the small rooster, lugging him back to my laboratory in a wicker cage. "It's really nothing personal. I'm trying to save a life."

The rooster was not interested in apologies, but was reasonably interested in the violet pastilles. He pecked them a few times to make sure that they were not some kind of weird human trap, then happily devoured the lot. He stretched his neck through the bars of the cage afterward and pecked at the flagstone floor experimentally, in case it, too, was made of food.

I went back to unpacking my lab equipment, keeping a close eye on my test subject. (I use a cage with fitted iron bars on one side so that I can watch in case they do anything interesting, like convulse.)

The floor was not made of food. The rooster tried another section of flagstone.

"Anything?" I said.

This patch of stone was also unsatisfactory. The rooster retired to the back of the cage to sulk.

I carefully decanted the chime-adder into her permanent cage. This was a tricky business and required heavy leather gloves. She rang her tail bells at me in annoyance. She was probably hungry after travel. I hadn't fed her on the road. I was going to have to secure a source of mice. Yet another thing on my list of things to accomplish.

That list was getting sufficiently long that I needed to start crossing things off it. I solved the mouse problem by cornering one of the pages and offering him a bounty on live mice. All the pages were young lads, and if he spread the word to his comrades, I might find myself with more mice than I could handle. I decided, in a fit of recklessness, to charge the king for it.

"For my next trick," I muttered, "I shall inspect the kitchens."

Neither the rooster nor the adder had any opinion of this. I left them to their respective devices and went to see where the food came from.

The kitchens were neat and orderly, with no signs of sloth to be found. The counters were clearly scrubbed nightly, and the staff probably were, too.

It didn't take much time spent lurking in the kitchen doorway to realize that here, too, it would be rather difficult to poison one specific person. The sandwiches were all made up in a bunch, and how would you know that Snow would take a specific one? The soup, likewise, was dished out from a single enormous pot.

On the downside, though, the far wall of the kitchen had two doors that stood open, leading directly to another courtyard and an herb garden that would have made our cook back home weep with envy. Anybody could have strolled into the kitchen. Hell, they might not even have needed to enter the kitchen at all—cuisine in this part of the world involved a lot of sun-dried ingredients, which adorned drying racks scattered around the courtyard, and there were no guards posted to watch them.

Whether guards would be *needed* was up for debate. The ruler of this kitchen had the soft, comfortable shape of a fresh-baked loaf of bread and the savage gaze of a bird of prey. Holding a conversation with her was tricky, because she would break off in midsentence to shout things like, "That's about to boil over! Stir it, you lump!" and "Dip it in egg *first*! What do you expect the flour to stick with, hope and wishes?"

She was more than happy to help me, though, and to my great relief, she didn't take offense at the idea that I was blaming her food for poisoning the king's daughter. "It's a saints-be-damned mystery," she said. "When she started getting sick, I made her food with my own hands and carried the trays up myself—Bruno, you're chopping vegetables, not wood!—and it didn't seem to make a damned bit of difference." She grinned at me abruptly. "And I realize that means I'm the most likely suspect, but I wouldn't know *how* to poison someone. Except with food poisoning, and I'd die of shame if someone took ill out of my kitchen like that." She shook her head. "But nobody else has had more than a bad tummy from overeating, and I can't do anything about *that*."

"I'm not blaming you," I said hurriedly. (She *was* a prime suspect, but I imagined the king had already thought about that.) "But if you ever looked away long enough, someone might slip something in."

"That's what I thought, too," the cook said. "But it's been three months, and I can't believe—Mina, those are supposed to be *symmetrical*. That means the same on both sides. No. Count them again—I can't believe that I wouldn't have spotted someone sneaking something in sooner or later. And I *watched*."

I believed her, too. I wouldn't trust my own opinion of someone's trustworthiness when lives were at stake, but three months was a long time to get away with regularly doctoring the food.

And a crowded room was normally the best place to get away with something like that, but you'd have to move like a frightened fence lizard to get away with it under this woman's nose.

Plus, that put us right back to the question of knowing what, specifically, Snow would eat. When the cook was preparing the food herself, it would be easy, but not any longer. But Snow was still getting worse, not better.

"Do you ever send her up a tray before bed?" I asked. "Cookies or . . . I don't know . . . hot chocolate or something like that?"

To my surprise, she shook her head. "Not since she's been feeling poorly. She didn't eat more than a bite or two for a while, and then the trays started being sent back untouched. I begged her to tell me if there was any treat she wanted me to make, but no matter what I make, she just picks at it."

I thanked her for her time, complimented her sandwiches—she grinned and took a slight bow—and then went back to my room in time to dress for dinner. With the king. Again.

The footman placed a platter of delicate tidbits on the table before us—I had no idea what they were, except colorful and in layers—and another lifted them onto our respective plates. Snow lifted her fork, and I stretched out a hand. "Snow, switch plates with me, please."

She blinked at me. So did everyone else at the table. One of the advisors started to say something, but the king cut across him. "You think . . . ?"

"I don't," I said, "but I want to be sure." For all I knew, the plates had a clear solution of arsenic drizzled on them before being set down.

Lady Sorrel took matters into her own hands by taking Snow's plate and passing it to me. I passed mine back. Snow gave me a thoughtful look, then began to eat. So did everyone else, without notable reluctance. I took a bite of mine. Something in aspic. The layers were flavored with different fruits. It tasted good, even if it was a trifle absurd looking.

The main course was a steaming platter of chicken in a golden sauce. Lady Sorrel took Snow's this time. The energetic advisor turned to the king and said, "Your Majesty, would you like to trade as well?"

By dessert, it had become a game. I swapped my trifle with the king and then with Lady Sorrel. Snow's changed hands three times, to her muffled giggles. The energetic advisor got his own dessert back again and pouted dramatically.

Snow never ate much of any of the dishes, but at least I could be fairly sure that for that one meal, she was safe.

When I arrived at Snow's rooms on the next day, everything was the same as it had been, except that Snow had a cat in her lap and was petting it.

I had honestly never given much thought to the sort of cat that a king's daughter would have as a pet. Something white and fluffy, maybe, with a jeweled collar and a tail like a feather duster.

This cat . . . was not that. It was the shade of dark gray that people call blue, it was short-haired and skinny, and it was missing an eye. Also, it had an expression like it was thinking about disemboweling everyone in the room.

"Have you met my cat?" Snow asked me.

"I have not, no." I inclined my head politely to the cat, who gazed at me in silent contempt. Its one good eye was sulfurous yellow.

"He's just like one back at the palace."

"Is he?" I inched past cat and girl to my chair in the corner.

"Nurse won't let him sleep with me at night," Snow said, clearly aggrieved. "But he *loves* me."

I try not to judge anyone, man or beast, by appearances, but let's just say that I had significant doubts that a cat with that expression loved anything except murder.

"Now Snow, love," Nurse said, "cats are dirty little things. And they steal your breath at night."

"He would *never*. He's the sweetest. Aren't you?" Snow picked up his front half, her hands under his forelegs, and made him dance back and forth. The cat's face indicated not only that murder was on the table, but that the victim had now been selected.

"And he—"

At that moment, the cat decided that he was done. (I didn't blame him, I'd have left as soon as the dancing started.) There was a flurry of motion, too quick for the eye to follow, and then Snow yelped and a gray blur shot past me, out the balcony door, and was gone over the railing before any of the humans could move.

"What did I say?" Nurse scolded. "And now you've got a scratch, and the saints help us if it mortifies. Hatha, get the salve."

"I don't *want* the salve," Snow said sullenly, sounding rather younger than twelve. "It stings."

"It will sting a lot more if those scratches turn putrid and the surgeon has to take your whole hand off."

"That won't happen."

"No, it won't, love, because we're going to wash it and put the good salve on it." Nurse shot me a glance of mute appeal.

I cleared my throat. "It's true," I said. "I knew a man who had to have his foot amputated because of a cat scratch." (This was a lie. I did once know a man who'd had to have his foot amputated because of a cat *bite,* though.)

"There, you see?"

"It turned dark red and black, and swelled up to twice its normal size, which was quite unpleasant, because then his toenails—"

"But none of that is going to happen to *you,*" Nurse said hastily, drowning out my catalog of symptoms. "Because we're going to treat this *right now.*"

Snow stared at me with awed horror. "Did he *die?*"

"Almost."

She was still staring at me over her shoulder when Nurse led her into the bathing room to wash out the scratches. I settled into the chair, took out my notebook, and prepared for a long day of note-taking.

Reviewing my notes in the evening, I felt dejected. Snow's appetite had increased somewhat, stretching to an entire sandwich at lunch and almost half a plate of food at dinner, but that was the only thing of significance. No, Nurse wasn't using any home remedies. Snow sometimes drank peppermint tea for her stomach, but I'd been through the tea, and yep, that was peppermint, all right. My dreams that there might be aconite rolled up in the dried leaves had died before they had even properly started.

I was probably going to have to investigate the kitchens more thoroughly, which I wasn't looking forward to. There are just so *many* things in a kitchen, and the cooks tend to get very annoyed when you confiscate all the spices to run tests. Plus, I still didn't know what exactly I was looking for. Snow's symptoms were all so maddeningly vague. Lead, mercury, arsenic, antimony—I couldn't rule any of them out, nor the possibility of something truly exotic. There is at least one plant that causes wasting illness if you eat the seeds for weeks on end, which seemed like a fine candidate, except that it only grows in harsh cold. Someone could import them, certainly, but you have to eat a *lot* of seeds to get the effect.

This did not make it any easier to know what to watch for.

What I *really* ought to do was go through Snow's belongings, but I kept shying away from that like a horse spotting a snake.

I'd had a friend when I was about sixteen, a broad, colorless girl named Lucia, who blended into the background at parties. I wasn't as good at blending in, but no one was asking me to dance anyway, since by that point, I was a head taller than most of the boys. So I talked to Lucia, who had a sly sense of humor once you got to know her, and we struck up a friendship conducted a few hours at a time, between the strings of bright lanterns above the courtyard and the square red tiles underfoot.

Her mother went through her room at least once a week, convinced that Lucia was hiding something from her. I was never clear on what the woman suspected, exactly. Love letters, Lucia told me, or maybe a boy hiding in the closet. Or money or maps, in case she was going to run away. I got the impression that maybe her mother didn't know either.

We went shopping together once and only once. When we came home, Lucia's mother had held out her hand and snapped her fingers as if ordering a dog, and Lucia had silently handed over her packages. They held the most banal contents imaginable, but her mother dug through them as if she suspected Lucia of smuggling opium. I remember her turning socks inside out, growing more and more frustrated that she wasn't finding anything illicit. It felt obscene, watching her paw through her daughter's things with such bizarrely greedy hope.

Then she turned to me and held out her hand for *my* packages, and I took a step back, my eyebrows shooting up, and said, "Excuse me?"

She must have realized that she'd crossed some line, because she blinked at me like a woman awaking from a stupor, then backed away—but Lucia was never allowed to go anywhere with me again.

"Does she do that every time?" I asked at the next dance, while the favored spun in colorful blurs and the less favored held up the walls or congregated around the drinks table.

"Oh yes," Lucia said calmly. "Every time. She used to pull the ribbons off my hats to make sure that there was nothing hidden under them."

I gaped at her, but Lucia was always very calm.

I imagine she was even calm a few months later, when she vanished without a trace. It wasn't until I ran into her a decade later, while visiting my sister Catherine, that I learned that she had been systematically hiding her pocket money for years, until she had enough to escape to the Convent of Saint Otter, high in the mountains. The sisters will take anyone in return for a suitable donation, and they are notoriously close-lipped.

"Are you happy?" I asked tentatively, unsure of how to respond to this stranger with my old friend's face.

And then she smiled, and it was Lucia's familiar smile, as if we were both sixteen again. "Very, very happy," she said, and I was happy for her, and for a loose end finally tidied away.

Probably there's multiple lessons there, but the one I took away was *Don't rummage through your daughter's things or she might run off and become a nun.*

(Okay, I'm being overly flippant about it. The truth is that Lucia's mother scared me a little. She had *wanted* to find something terrible, if only so that it would justify all her paranoia in retrospect. Even twenty years later, the memory makes me uncomfortable.)

I knew that I was going to have to go through Snow's possessions if I couldn't find another source of poison, and I knew that it was in an infinitely better cause, and I still felt a little ill at the thought.

One more day watching, I decided. *Then I'll get down to work on the spices. Then I'll worry about the rest.*

I put my notes away, cleaned my teeth with sage and salt, then got into bed and blew out the candle. Cool air crept through the gap between the balcony doors, as light-footed and elusive as the one-eyed cat. I pulled the blankets over my shoulders, enjoying the contrast between the warm bed and cool air.

I was nearly asleep when I felt a cold prickle along my scalp and realized that someone was watching me.

I was lying on my side with my back to the balcony. I kept my eyes almost closed, hoping that whoever it was wouldn't notice that I was awake. If it was an assassin, that might make the difference between . . . well, realistically, between dying in the next five seconds or the next five minutes. If they knew that I was awake, surely they'd strike at once.

Still, I'd take the five minutes. There was always a chance that I could roll off the bed and sprint out the door, screaming, before they got me. (Why didn't I start screaming now? Simple, because I hadn't *seen* the assassin. It was possible that I was imagining things, in which case I'd wake the house over nothing. Was I really picking death over embarrassment? Yes. Yes, I was. I am not saying that I was making good choices in that moment.)

I feigned fidgeting in my sleep and moved just enough so that I could see the mirror opposite the bed. My shoulder blades itched, waiting for the knife.

Through slitted eyelids, I studied the mirror. It looked onto an unfamiliar landscape, the humped shapes of furniture gone shadowy and strange. I couldn't see the balcony at this angle, but . . . *There!*

Something glowed white in the mirror. It took a moment to realize that it was the reflection of a face, and worse, it was the face of someone *bending over me.*

I knotted my fingers in the sheets, concentrating on keeping my breathing slow and shallow as I studied it. I couldn't make out any details. It was too dark, and I didn't dare open my eyes more than a fraction. Just that white oval and a suggestion of clothing underneath it, but that was enough to set my heart hammering. It felt as if my whole body must be shaking with every beat.

The face tilted as the assassin cocked their head. I looked in vain for the knife that must be in their hand. *Unless they're going to use poison. That would be ironic, wouldn't it?* Though poison isn't the best weapon for something like this. A needle coated in toxin seems like a good idea, but depending on where it goes in, more or less might actually get into the victim's blood. It could certainly make me very *sick,* of course, and depending on the localized swelling, I might wind up getting sliced open and dying of infection, but that's a risky thing to count on. And there aren't too many sub-stances so potent that a single needle would kill an adult woman my size. They *exist*, but they're extremely expensive. Of course, if you were hiring an assassin, maybe money was no object—

The face moved again. They turned to the side, showing me a glimpse of a pale profile. Moonlight turned their hair the white-blond color of Snow's.

They took a half dozen steps, passing out of my line of sight. I froze, forgetting not to hold my breath. If I moved my head to follow, they'd know I was awake. But if I didn't . . .

Move! I screamed at myself. *Roll off the bed! They're coming for you! Why are you making it easy for them?*

But moving was hard. As long as I stayed still, I was safe in this little bubble of inaction. If I moved, everything would start happening all at once.

That is ridiculous, I told myself crisply. *Move. Now.*

I threw myself sideways, rolled off the bed, and found my legs wrapped up in the blankets. I fell heavily on my forearms, cursing, and tried to fight my way free, rolling to face the foot of the bed where even now . . . even now . . .

There was no one there.

I kicked my legs free and frantically scanned the room, search-ing for the figure that I had *seen*, damn it, I *knew* I had, there was no *question* . . .

Nothing. There was no one else there.

I got to my feet and lit a candle with shaking hands. I looked under the bed but saw only dust bunnies. I yanked open the cur-tain to the little washroom and saw only my own face in the mir-ror. The candle illuminated it from underneath and cast sinister shadows in my eye sockets. I turned away hastily and opened the door to the privy. It, too, was empty.

At last I went to the balcony, looking for a rope or a grappling hook or a ladder—some way that the assassin had climbed up to the second floor. Nothing there either. The house had stucco walls, but

I couldn't imagine anything larger than a gecko climbing them, and they certainly hadn't jumped up from ground level.

I peered over the railing, trying to think. The gibbous moon turned the gardens into a pale boneyard, the hedges dark bands etched across pale earth. Nothing moved. The distance across to the next room's balcony was perhaps eight feet. Could they have leaped to it?

If they had, they were long gone now. There was no trace of anything or anyone, not even a conveniently scuffed footprint on the tiles.

I circled my room two or three more times, arguing with myself over whether I'd really seen what I thought I saw. Could I have dreamed it? It hadn't felt like a dream. That indistinct white face in the mirror . . . could it have been the moon reflecting on something, then drifting slowly out of range?

I hunted for anything on the wall or balcony that would have given the impression of a face, or even a pale blob, but found nothing. I gave up and went to the mirror itself, studying it as if I would see the figure's tracks left on the glass.

The longer I looked, the stranger and more distorted the shadows became. My face looked less and less like it belonged to me, and more like some unkind stranger. *Damn it. I hate mirrors at night, and this is why.*

Yet something was nagging at me, so I didn't turn away, though I tried not to look at myself. I searched the reflected bed-curtain and nightstand and the great humped shadow of the clothes trunk. Indistinct shapes seemed to bleed together until the room might have been carved from a single block of stone, the furniture rooted to the floor, the rugs chiseled carefully into rock.

I closed my eyes and shook my head to clear it, then opened them again. Nothing. Nothing but my own face looking out.

My face.

It dawned on me slowly that the intruder *couldn't* have been looking at me, because if they had been, the back of their head would have been reflected in the glass. Instead, they'd been look-ing at the mirror.

Had they been watching me in it while I was watching them? Had they suspected that I was awake and fled?

It made no sense. Why would you creep into your victim's room and then just . . . not kill them? Unless they hadn't been an assassin at all, but someone . . . what? Staring at my reflection while I slept?

Creepy, but at least not lethal. But are you sure someone was ac-tually there?

I wasn't. The whole encounter was beginning to seem more and more like a dream. Perhaps I had simply woken myself up by fall-ing out of bed.

I sighed. I had to wrestle the blankets back up before I could climb into bed. In the morning, the maids would probably won-der what on earth I had been doing.

Eventually I fell asleep, but I left the candle burning all night long.

CHAPTER 11

I walked into Snow's chambers the next morning, just in time to hear the sound of someone being noisily sick. I followed it past the maids, who were making up the bed with vast resignation, and found Nurse holding Snow's pale hair as the latter was violently ill into a basin.

I did not shout, *Eureka!* but I admit I thought it.

When you are in the business of poisons, you learn quite a lot about vomit. It's not my favorite part of the job, but there you are. I grabbed the basin and took it and its foul-smelling contents off to my workroom.

I will spare you the details of the next few hours, which mostly involved pipettes, reagents, and waiting for liquids to turn blue or precipitate out a yellow sludge or *something*. At the end of it, I leaned back against the scarred table in my workroom and sighed. I'd gotten my wish and witnessed a bout of Snow's illness, and I still wasn't any closer to an answer. I'd run every test I had available on the previous contents of Snow's stomach, and the only result was that my workroom needed a good airing out.

The problem is that there are just so *many* emetics in the world. Arsenic makes you vomit in large doses. You can put wine in a cup of antimony for an hour, and if you drink it, you had best be near the privy. Half the poisonous plants in the world manifest with vomiting. (It's the ones that *don't* that you should really worry about—then you can't get the stuff out of your system and it keeps working on you.)

I couldn't even rule out that she'd been poisoned in such small doses over such a long period of time that her food wouldn't contain a recognizable amount of toxin, even if it was one I could test for. Of course, three months wouldn't usually be enough time to build up something like that . . .

I stopped. The chime-adder rang her bells in the silence.

How did I know it had only been three months?

I had assumed it, because that's what the king thought. Her mother and sister had died, and then Snow got sick, and no one noticed it at first because they thought it was grief. But suppose that it was only three months ago that the symptoms had become *noticeable*?

"I've got to talk to the nurse again," I muttered. Then I looked around at the vomit-stained glassware, thought briefly of what that would smell like after it had a few hours, and shuddered. "First, though, I've got to clean this room up."

"Well, I don't know," Nurse said doubtfully. "She always had a delicate stomach, like I said. There wasn't a point where I noticed that anything changed. Not with her."

There was a hair too much emphasis on the word *her*. I lifted my head from my notes. "Oh?"

Nurse fiddled with the edge of her apron. She was obviously dying to tell me, but she equally obviously didn't want to.

"As a medical matter, it will remain entirely confidential," I said, "unless it becomes necessary to save a life."

It sounded somewhat pompous, but it was clearly what she wanted. She relaxed, picked up her teacup, and said, "Snow hasn't changed. But Rose did."

It took me a moment to remember that Rose was Snow's sister, who had met such a tragic end. "Rose? How do you mean?"

"It was the oddest thing," Nurse said. "Between one day and the next, practically. It was as if she forgot how to do the simplest things. Ask her to button up her coat and she'd have to stop and look at it to see where the buttons were. She was nine years old, and of course no one's terribly graceful at nine, but she turned clumsy overnight." She took a sip of tea. "I didn't think much of it at first, of course. Usually that just means that they're getting some growth on. But then she started getting lost in a castle she'd lived in all her life. It was as if she'd forgotten which way the hallways went."

I frowned down at my notes. Some poisons cause disorientation, of course, but it was also possible that something had gone wrong in Rose's brain. You expect strokes and whatnot in older patients, but that didn't mean it was impossible to get them in young ones.

Nurse was still talking. "And she knew her letters—the king insisted—and then suddenly she didn't. She could hardly read a word, it seemed. She was still just as sweet a child as you could ask for, but she'd been a clever one before, and then . . ." She spread her hands.

"Hmm," I said. Healer Michael might know what would cause those specific symptoms, but I certainly didn't. "What did the physicians say?"

Nurse seemed to shrink into herself. She stared into her empty teacup as if she wanted to crawl inside. "None of them saw her."

"What?" I stared at her. "Why not? Didn't you tell anyone what was happening?"

The teacup trembled just a little. I could see the tendons in the backs of her hands, exposed with age and lined with long blue veins. "Of course I told someone," Nurse said, not meeting my eyes. "I told the queen."

I sat in my workroom and stared at the wall without really seeing it. The rooster pecked around my feet. I'd let him out for a walk around the workroom, figuring that he was probably bored and that if he got unruly, I could just close the shutters so he settled down to roost. At the moment, though, he could probably have smashed half the glassware in the place and I don't know if I'd notice.

It didn't take a trained scholar to put things together. Something had happened to Rose's mind. The nurse had told the queen, and the queen had taken up a knife and killed her daughter. Hard to think that the two weren't related.

She wouldn't be the first woman to kill her own child. They say that poison is a woman's weapon, but in my experience, both sexes are likely to use it when they're trying to be clever. It's just that men also occasionally beat someone to death with a hammer. Women rarely do that. The vast majority of the time, if a woman kills someone, it's their spouse or their child.

"It's odd," Michael had said to me once. "You kill your husband because you're stuck in an abusive relationship and you're afraid, hence the poison. Oh, once in a while you get someone looking for money out of the deal, but it's rarer. But you kill your child because they're part of you."

"Eh?" I had been scrubbing the remains of an autopsy off my hands, as I recall. Even when you use gloves, there's a sort of emotional stench that clings to your skin.

Healer Michael had a look that he got sometimes, the look of a man who understood something too well and would far rather be baffled. "For some women, their children are never really separate people. This woman didn't think of it as murder." He waved his hand toward the door to the autopsy room, with its small, sad occupant.

"Because she thought she owned him," I said bitterly, but Michael was already shaking his head.

"Sometimes, certainly, but not in this case. I spoke with her, you know. She's a sad creature, and she's genuinely confused that this is being treated as murder. In her mind, she was hurting *herself*, not anyone else. If anything, she thought of this as a sort of suicide."

Saints, but I wish you were here, I told Michael inside my head. *You could tell me* why *things are happening, and maybe then I could figure out* how *they're happening.*

For that matter, why had Nurse even told me any of this?

I tried to pretend I was Michael and understood people. She'd told me because she derived something from telling me. All I'd done was say, awkwardly, "It wasn't your fault. You couldn't possibly have known." But she'd seemed satisfied with that, so . . .

Absolution, I thought. *She is looking for absolution that she didn't cause the tragedy.*

Well and good. But there was another tragedy unfolding in slow motion, and that was the one I was here to solve.

Did the dead queen have anything to do with Snow's condition? It seemed unlikely, given that she was, y'know, *dead.* But a woman who stabbed one daughter might not balk at poisoning another one, if she saw them both as an extension of herself, and it was possible that she'd given Snow something, some object, that would slowly kill the girl over months. Possible even that she'd given it to her long before killing Rose.

Or possibly it didn't have anything to do with the dead queen at all, and I was grasping at straws because I couldn't find a damn thing otherwise.

The rooster had completed his circuit of my workroom, made a deposit on the floor, and was now hunkered down in a sunbeam from the window. The light picked out iridescent greens from his otherwise-mangy tail feathers.

"I'm putting this off," I told him, "because I don't want to go through Snow's things. But I guess I don't have a choice, do I?"

Maybe it was because the king was still in residence. Maybe it was the fact that I apologized profusely or that I was so obviously trying to be respectful of her privacy. Regardless, Snow did not argue. I had expected a scene on par with the way she'd insulted the maids, but instead she sat down in the corner and watched. She had a faint, superior smile on her face.

You won't find anything, that smile said.

You're being paranoid and reading too much into a twelve-year-old's smile, I told myself.

With the help of the maids, I went systematically through rows and rows of dresses, checking pockets and trimmings, even taking small swatches of fabric, because there are some dyes that use arsenic for coloring. I checked every jewelry box, every necklace and earring, every lotion and powder. I even carefully snipped a page corner from three different dog-eared books, because everyone's heard the story about pages that poison you when you lick your finger to turn them. (I can't swear it wouldn't work, but I've never heard of it *actually* happening.)

The only time that Snow showed any emotion was when I reached into a drawer and drew out a small silver case, perhaps three inches long. Tarnish had blackened the deeper grooves of a floral pattern, but the edge by the clasp, where your thumb would rub, was worn smooth.

Snow moved then, just a little, as if she had started to rise, then thought better of it. I flicked open the case and found a miniature portrait of a woman inside.

She had a heart-shaped face and hair a shade darker than Snow's. Her eyes were large and gazed at the viewer with disconcerting openness. You could read loneliness in that gaze, but hope curled under it, as if she wished very much for a friend.

"My mother," said Snow. It was the first time that she'd spoken aloud since the process began.

I could see the resemblance. The same shape to the mouth, the same fragile prettiness. I don't know why it surprised me that Snow would have kept a portrait. It certainly didn't surprise me that she'd kept it out of sight.

What did you say at a time like that? What could you say?

"She was very beautiful," I said at last.

Snow's smile slipped. "Yes," she said solemnly. Her eyes were old for a moment, as old as the women pouring ashes into spirit houses, as if she were mourning the loss of a daughter, not a mother. "Yes, she was."

I nodded and closed the case, returning it carefully to its drawer. By the time I finished turning the rooms upside down, Snow's smiling mask was back in place and she was only twelve again.

I took the pile of samples I'd gathered down to the workshop, but I was already fairly sure that there was nothing in them that would bring me any closer to learning how the king's daughter was being poisoned.

The last day passed. I went to bed that night, hoping for an epiphany in my sleep. The ancient philosopher Krathos is said to have dreamed of dividing a bar of bronze and a bar of lead into smaller and smaller pieces, and woke to invent the theory of elemental atoms and molecules.

All I woke up with was a headache.

I stared at the bed-curtain for a few minutes, dread knotting tighter and tighter in my stomach, then sighed, got to my feet, and washed my face. The woman in the mirror had dark circles under her eyes, but otherwise looked remarkably well for someone who felt like I did.

I took five minutes to cover the dark circles with a little makeup, not because I am particularly vain, but because it felt like putting on armor before going to face the enemy.

Not that the king was my enemy. Actually, I rather liked him. He just happened to have the power to break my family without even thinking about it.

When I found him, he was sitting behind a desk, reading papers. Reports, I assume. Being a king probably means you read a lot of reports. (Though it was hard to imagine Bastian the Demon doing that. Had he really cared about how many bushels of grain were being produced in any given province? Maybe he'd had Lady Sorrel read them instead.)

The king looked up. Hope flickered across his face, there and gone, like a lizard on a fence post. My heart sank. I had stayed up until the small hours of the night, trying to find something— anything—but no amount of careful heating or added reagents had turned up anything useful. One of the fabric swatches had yielded the tiniest bit of precipitate, probably indicating a trace of arsenic in the dye, but unless she wore it soaking wet against her skin every day for six months, I didn't see how it could be the cause. I'd tell Nurse to remove it anyway, just in case.

My expression must have told him everything, because the flicker of hope faded. I winced internally. *This man held his younger daughter's body in his arms, and now I have to tell him that I'm no closer to curing the older one.*

I squared my shoulders. Nothing would be gained by dithering. "I know you're riding out today," I said, "and I wanted to update you on my findings, Your Majesty."

He inclined his head. "And what have you found?"

"Not nearly as much as I'd like," I admitted. "I've tested every- thing I can think of . . . clothes, food, lotions . . . even the soap. I'm about to start in on the spices, although I can't figure out how that would affect only her and no one else at Witherleaf."

The king nodded. "Do you think it *is* poison, then?"

I knew I should be calm and reassuring and professional, but what I actually said was "Hell if I know." I stared at one of the walls, registering that it had been tiled to waist height in a shade of blue that was probably meant to be restful. I did not feel restful, and I had my doubts that the king did either.

"Will you keep trying, then?"

I jerked my eyes away from the wall to the king's face. I could read nothing in his expression. We might as well have been talking about bushels of grain.

If I said no, I could go home.

If I said no, I'd be the woman who had failed the king's daughter.

And if I say yes, I'll probably be the woman who failed the king's daughter a month from now.

She wasn't going to die immediately. If I left now, she might go on for quite a long time. Long enough, maybe, for me to fade from memory. Most of the courtiers thought I was either a tutor or a mistress anyway.

It would be sensible to go home. I could tell the king that if it was poison, it was nothing I recognized, and I could suggest that he get an expert to treat Snow. (I *was* an expert, mind you, and I'd put myself against any physician in Four Saints on the subject of poisons, but I would happily swallow my pride if it meant fewer repercussions for my family.)

Which is why I was very surprised to hear myself say, "I'll keep trying. I feel like it must be *something,* but I can't put my finger on it." I snorted. "I'll be honest, it may just be injured pride that I can't figure it out, but I need more time to work on it."

I had forgotten for a moment that I was speaking to a king. How long had it been since I'd added a *Your Majesty?* But he smiled, brief and genuine, and said, "Thank you for not giving up."

I wanted to say that there were no guarantees, but he knew that already. Instead I gave him an awkward curtsy, said, "Travel safe, Your Majesty," and fled.

You absolute numbskull, you could have gone home. This is probably only going to make your eventual failure worse.

"I know, I know," I muttered to myself, startling a glance from a passing servant. "I know."

I still had no proof at all that it was poison. It could still have been some illness that the physicians didn't understand. When had I become convinced that there was an actual cause and that it was something that I could find?

I had nothing. I had tested everything but the walls. And yet I couldn't shake the feeling that I was missing something important.

And I'll bet gold dust against sand grains that Snow knows exactly what it is.

The thought startled me. I've never liked physicians who blame the patient for their illness. It's probably why I work so hard on the lotus addicts. But once the thought had crystallized, I couldn't ignore it.

Something strange was going on in Witherleaf, and it centered around Snow. And Saints help me, if I didn't figure out what it was, curiosity was going to eat me alive.

CHAPTER 12

Two days went by, and Witherleaf settled into a quieter rhythm in the king's absence. There were no more meals in the large dining room. I joined Lady Sorrel for tea instead.

"I am glad you're here," she said to me, a smile creasing the wrinkles on her face. "I get so little company, and I get so depressed after they leave. Worse when it's Randolph. He's grown into such a fine man, but so serious." Her smile faded, and the lines at the corners of her eyes were not all from laughter. "Though how could he not be serious, growing up the way he did?"

"He's a good king," I offered. "Everyone says so."

"I always knew he would be. Even poor mad Bastian knew it, I think." Lady Sorrel shook herself. "But enough of such depressing talk. Tell me something interesting." She perched on the edge of her chair, bird-bright.

"Well," I began, "there's a type of fish found near Cholla Bay called a feedshark . . ."

Tea with Lady Sorrel was the bright spot of the day. Watching Snow was so dull that I was hiding my copy of the latest Red Feather Saga inside my notebook so that I didn't fall asleep. Eventually I gave up, went downstairs, and retested things. I even retested the peppermint tea, on the principle that a dried leaf is much like any other dried leaf, so maybe the smell was covering something. I gave some to the rooster. I drank multiple cups myself. If there was a hidden poison, it was extremely well hidden.

The one-eyed gray cat strolled into my workroom, looked disdainfully at the caged rooster, then leaped up onto the worktable and settled into a comfortable loaf. I rubbed the base of his ears and was rewarded with a ratcheting purr.

"You better be careful," I warned him. "Nurse is ready to make you into a furry hand warmer for scratching Snow."

The cat did not seem particularly concerned about this. He wouldn't make much of a hand warmer anyway. He was going white around the muzzle, and his gray fur, though neatly groomed, was more lead than silver. Even his purr was thin, like honey being scraped over gravel.

"Right," I said, stepping away. "Back to work. Doing . . . whatever the hell it is I do." I stared glumly out the window. At the moment, what I did seemed to be not finding the cure.

"I'm pretty sure it's not arsenic," I told the cat. "And if it's antimony, I have no idea how it's getting to her. I had them change out all the mugs and plates, just in case." Which, of course, they'd done once already.

The cat closed his good eye in a lazy blink.

"It doesn't fit any of the plants I know, and even if she's having an unusual response to one, how is it *getting* to her in the first place? It won't do much good to know what it is if I can't figure out how she's ingesting it." I scowled at the ceiling. Granted, if I could figure out what it was, that would make it much easier to figure out the delivery method, but since I wasn't any closer to figuring out either one, it hardly mattered.

"Hell with it," I muttered. "I'm going to take a walk." I picked the cat up and carried him out of the workshop, then set him down in the corridor and locked the workshop door. (I didn't suspect any of the servants of anything, but somebody here might be a poisoner, and anyway, the chime-adder might spook someone.)

The cat stalked in front of me, looking vaguely offended, until I reached the door to the gardens. He looked at the plants baking in the noonday heat, stopped dead, and began grooming his paw in my general direction.

My favorite garden was a sunken little pocket surrounded by tall desert junipers that had been pruned into a hedge. You approached along the path overlooking it, then took a shallow flight of steps down to a miniature courtyard that held a statue of a woman with a sword and shield. There was no plaque on the statue, and I often wondered who she was.

The junipers provided shade for more delicate flowers and a low bench wrapped in a bougainvillea arbor. I sat down in the shadows. Isobel would have liked this pocket garden, even if the rest would be too spartan for her tastes. Spikes of red adorned the desert hyssop, and hummingbirds buzzed each other furiously for access to the flowers. Tiny bees armored in iridescent green carapaces climbed across white viper-master flowers. Everything was simple and everything was alive.

I must have sat there for nearly half an hour, thinking nothing, when I heard footsteps and voices.

Snow stood at the top of the pocket garden, accompanied by a maid. She gestured, and the maid nodded and trotted away. Snow watched her go for a long moment, then hurried down the steps, looking back and forth, as if she expected someone to be watching her.

Someone *was* watching her, of course, but I was wearing dust-colored robes and sitting in the dappled shadows of the arbor, and her eyes flicked over me without seeing me. I started to stir, thinking to call out, but there was something oddly furtive about her movements that stopped me.

She looked around again, then went behind the statue and leaned down. A moment later she came out again, holding something in her hand. She lifted it as if to look at it more closely, and then, before I realized what was happening, she had taken a bite.

Oh god, what is she eating? "Snow, no!" I cried, lunging to my feet. "Stop!"

The girl spun around, her pale hair flying out in a nimbus around her head. Her eyes went wide at the sight of me barreling toward her. That, perhaps, was not a surprise. What was a surprise was that she hastily took another bite.

"No!" I slid to a halt, grabbing Snow around the waist with one arm and her wrist with my other hand. "What are you eating?"

It was an apple. Snow bit desperately at it, chunks of pale apple flesh falling from the sides of her mouth. I was much stronger, but Snow had a panicky strength to her, and the last thing I wanted to do was hurt her. I managed to pull the girl's arm away from her face, and Snow collapsed, hanging her full weight from my arm and yelling wordlessly.

Oh, blessed Saint Adder, this is it, this must *be it, we've checked everything she's eaten at every meal, this* has *to be it—*

"Where did you *get* this?" I asked, even as I pried the girl's fingers loose.

"Stop it!" wailed Snow. "It's mine—you can't have it—*give it back!*"

Slick with juice, the apple popped free of her grip. I held it up over my head, feeling absurdly as if I was engaged in a game of keep-away with a younger sibling. Snow flailed at me with small fists.

"Snow," I said, in my most reasonable tone, "calm down." (I know, I know, this has never in the history of the world calmed anyone down. I said it anyway. I told you I'm not good with children.)

"*Give it back!*" Snow yelled.

"You know that we have to test all your food for poisons so that you can get better."

"It's not yours! You have no right to take it!" She pummeled me furiously, and, for lack of anything better to do, I did what I had done at twelve when my sister Catherine did the same thing. I put my hand on top of Snow's head and held her at arm's length while she flailed. I felt like the worst sort of bully doing it. Also, I was manhandling the king's daughter, which could have all sorts of repercussions. *But what else can I do? I'm trying to save her life!*

Saints, I wish I was better at this.

"Snow," I said again, while the girl punched ineffectually at the air, "where did you get this?"

"It's mine! You can't have it!"

"Snow . . ." I heaved a sigh and examined the apple, waiting for Snow to wear herself out. It had always taken Catherine a few minutes, too.

It was immediately obvious that this was no ordinary apple. The skin was silvery and so polished that it looked almost metallic, the flesh within as white as bone. I could think of several metals that might give the skin such a shine, none of which would be healthy to ingest. *White arsenic? Antimony? Quicksilver? No, quicksilver usually passes right through, but it could be some other preparation of mercury . . . or the skin could be painted with a solution to give it that look, which might include any number of other things . . .*

Snow had finally fallen into a mutinous silence, cut with sniffles. I released her and the girl stomped a few feet away, arms locked around her middle, refusing to look in my direction.

"Snow," I said, "did someone give you this apple?"

More silence.

"It's very important that you tell me where you got it."

Another pointed sniffle.

"Snow—"

"I hate you," Snow said in a low voice. "You're worse than the doctors were. They bled me and blistered my feet, and it was horrible, but at least they didn't go through everything I owned and see that I don't get a scrap of privacy and have me watched every *minute*—"

I felt suddenly very tired. "Snow, I'm trying to save your life. I know this isn't pleasant, but it's not much fun for me either. The sooner we find out what's causing your symptoms, the sooner you'll be rid of me. Now please tell me where you got this apple."

"Why don't you just chain me up in my room?" Snow spat, and stomped away, her feet crunching on the gravel path of the garden.

Well. That could have gone better.

I thought about following her but decided against it. The confrontation had not gone so swimmingly that I had any desire to repeat it.

A moment later, as I stood there with the apple, one of her maids appeared, holding a parasol. She looked around, puzzled. "Pardon," she said to me, "but have you seen the princess?"

"She went that way," I said, pointing.

The maid grumbled as she passed. "Forgot her parasol and sent me off to fetch it, then wandered off without it, and if she burns to a crisp, it's *me* who'll get the blame . . ."

Clever, I thought, watching the maid leave. *That's one way to get a few moments of privacy. But why would she use that to eat this apple? And why was it so important that she tried to cram as much in her mouth as she could before I got to it?*

It couldn't be the only such thing she'd eaten. But hopefully, with enough tests, I could figure out what was in the apple and if it was the source of all our woes.

And the saints help me if it isn't and I've just manhandled the king's daughter over nothing.

No. This has to be it. I'm sure of it.

Eight hours later, I wasn't quite as sure.

None of my reagents, applied to the peel or the flesh, turned up any sign of poison. Granted that didn't necessarily *mean* anything—there were still many poisons that no one could test for, arsenic among them. Still, it would have been nice if it was easy.

I sighed and cut a quarter of the apple loose, wrapping it in wax paper for later. Then I set about poisoning the rooster.

The rooster was surprisingly wary of the apple. He pecked it once, then shook himself, his neck feathers flaring up, as if it had an unexpected taste. I leaned forward, my pen poised. Was there some odd flavor? Something that alerted him that this apple wasn't quite right?

After a minute or two, nothing had happened except that a blob of ink had fallen on my page. The rooster took a turn around his cage, noticed the apple again, and tried another experimental peck. This time, apparently, it passed muster. He ate up every bit of flesh and then pecked happily at the core. I sat down to watch him and take notes.

By that evening, he was bored by his confinement and had demolished the apple core, but he otherwise seemed healthy. I was ready to tear my hair out by the roots.

For a few glorious moments, I thought that maybe he was getting listless. Then I realized that night had fallen and he was going to sleep. I propped lanterns up near the cage, which woke him up again, but he still wasn't doing anything suspicious, unless you counted trying to repeatedly jam himself between the bars as suspicious.

"It has to be the apple," I told the rooster. "It *has* to be. I've eliminated everything else."

The rooster cocked one suspicious avian eye at me, then went back to trying to fit his body through the bars of his cage.

"It's got to be something cumulative. The dose is so small that it didn't affect you, but it's built up in Snow. That's the only explanation."

The rooster had no opinion about this.

"I suppose she could be eating the seeds . . ." I had set them aside in an envelope. I peered into it now, disconsolate. Apple seeds had long been known to contain prussic acid, but the symptoms were all wrong. "She'd be having rapid breathing and convulsions. And the doctors would probably have noticed that her blood was bright pink."

The rooster had his head stuck through the bars and tried to back up, which ruffled his feathers in a way that he didn't like. He made a hostile sound and tried to turn around without moving his head, which didn't work well at all.

"Prussic acid also doesn't tend to be cumulative. Mostly because people just die of it."

He slapped his body against the bars, decided that he was under attack, and attempted to kick his hypothetical opponent. One of his spurs got stuck in the wickerwork, a clear sign of enemy action, and he kicked wildly until it came free.

I picked up the last quarter of the apple and unwrapped it. The bone-white flesh had turned brown, but the peel still had that otherworldly silver gleam to it. It practically glowed, even in the dim light of the laboratory. I stared at it, willing answers to come.

The rooster managed to extract himself from the bars and began making a hostile *murr-urr-urrrrr* sound at the cage, in case it got any further ideas.

I'd done everything I possibly could with the sample I had. No alchemist or physician could do more. There were no tests I hadn't tried . . . except one.

It might not work. If the dose was cumulative, I might not feel anything. I was a good deal larger than Snow, after all, a plump adult rooster to the girl's half-grown bantam.

But it was just possible that I might feel enough to recognize the substance.

The odds were quite good that it wouldn't be fatal. The rooster was fine, after all, for a value of fine. "Of course, your liver might explode tomorrow," I informed him. The rooster seemed unconcerned by this possibility.

I sighed, noted down the time and the weight of the apple, then popped it into my mouth and chewed.

It tasted . . . cold. Almost like mint, the way it chilled my mouth, but the flavor was nothing like mint. It was apple all the way through, but apple with frost on it, almost painfully crisp, as if I'd bitten into glass instead of fruit. Even after I swallowed, the coldness lingered in my mouth, and I felt each bite going down my throat like ice.

I wrote all of it down, then sat for about ten minutes to see if I was going to die.

When I didn't, I gave the rooster a handful of corn, checked on the chime-adder, then went back to my room to see what would happen next.

I spent the time waiting for the poison to take effect by writing a letter to the king. I wanted to explain to him about Snow and the apple, in case she wrote to him to say I'd attacked her in the garden.

It's surprisingly difficult to compose a letter like that. *Dear Majesty . . .* No, damn it, that probably wasn't right. *Your Majesty, I have discovered . . .* What? The source of the poison? I couldn't be sure that the apple *was* the source.

> *Your Majesty,*
>   *I have made a discovery that I suspect is related to your daughter's condition. I found Snow in the garden eating an unusual fruit that does not grow in this area. She refused to tell me where it came from or how she had acquired it. I fear that . . .*
>
> *That . . .*

I stared at nothing, which in this case included the mirror. The woman reflected in it had her upper lip curled in exasperation.

> *I fear that whoever provided the fruit to her may be the source of the poison. I am currently testing it for contamination.*

That last line was just this side of falsehood. I'd tested it and found nothing. Unless I started to feel results in the next few hours, I would have to admit that the apple had either been harmless or was so cumulative that it would take me weeks to prove anything.

Frustrated, I wadded up the sheet of paper and flung it aside. A streak of gray shot from under the bed and pounced on it. I watched the one-eyed gray cat kick a few times, and then he rolled to his feet and began to stalk off, carrying his prize in his mouth.

"Oh *no*," I said, seized by a sudden vision of the scene that might ensue if my letter was found lying in some distant corner of the manor and somehow got back to Snow. I reached for the cat, who eeled out of the way and bolted for the balcony door.

"Cat, no!" I said, which had about as much effect on the cat as it would have on a goldfish. I lunged after the beast, who skittered sideways toward the wall. I thought I'd lost him, but I got a handful of fur and turned to scoop him up against my chest. I was bent nearly double, though, and the motion overbalanced me.

My head struck the immense mirror, and I fell through into silver.

CHAPTER 13

My first thought was that I had hit my head. It didn't actually hurt, but I rubbed it anyway. Everything had gone oddly dim, as if clouds had obscured the sun. I looked around the room, puzzled by the darkness that obscured the door and the wall and pooled thickly across my writing table.

I took two steps toward my table, half expecting the shadows to evaporate, but they did not. A pewter-gray stain covered the top of the table, as thick as spilled ink. I stretched out my hand to touch the surface and my skin was the proper color, but the wood was not. Nor was the wall behind it, for that matter. In fact, it looked as if a coat of paint had been applied to the desk, wall, floor, and half the chair—but not the other half, which looked perfectly ordinary. The dividing line was as sharp as a ruler: wood grain on one side, flat gray on the other.

I leaned heavily on the chair, suddenly feeling the need for support.

"Concussion," I muttered to myself. Was it odd to diagnose a concussion while having one? *Odd or not, it's exactly the sort of thing that you would do.*

I should probably have gotten help, in case I was about to faint, but the door to my room had also been painted deep gray, and the shadows were even darker there, deepening into a yawning blackness that was not at all comfortable to look at.

I rubbed my head again, feeling for a lump, but couldn't find one.

"I rather like to be held," said a thin, acerbic voice in the vicinity of my elbow, "but I object to being dangled like a wet towel. Either hold me properly or put me down."

I was so startled that I nearly dropped the cat. The cat expressed his displeasure by sinking his claws into my side, twisting around, and climbing upward, until he had settled with his rump in the crook of my arm and his paws on my chest, where he clung like a small, malevolent infant.

"Yes, yes," he said, when I stared at him. "It's a talking cat, oh, how astonishing. In order, then—yes, I'm talking; no, it's not a trick; and I'm sure it's none of *my* business if other cats can talk or choose not to."

Since this actually did dispose of my first three questions, I was left with my mouth hanging open and nothing coming out. After a moment I swallowed hard and said, "I've gone mad."

"That," said the cat, "is also none of my business."

I sat down on the bed with a thump. It, at least, appeared quite normal. The cat thrust his round skull underneath my chin, and I began petting him mechanically. His purr nearly rattled my teeth in my jaw.

"Could I be dreaming?" I asked aloud.

Without pausing his purr, the cat sank a single claw into my shoulder. I let out a yelp and grabbed for his paw, but he had already withdrawn the claw. "No," he said, his voice layering over top of the purr like a thin glaze over cake.

I sat with my arms full of cat while my thoughts stuttered and chased one another in useless circles. *I must have hit my head. Talking cats and shadows on everything—I should go and find someone and tell them that I am hallucinating and to fetch a doctor at once.*

I told myself this very firmly and then did not move. The prospect felt somehow embarrassing, as if it were in very poor taste to hallucinate. *I hate to be a bother,* I thought vaguely, and then, irritably, *A hangnail is a bother. You're hearing cats talk!*

Only the one cat, really . . .

It does not matter how many cats there are! Any nonzero number of talking cats is significant!

Nevertheless, I did not seem to be moving. The cat stretched his head back so that I could attend to the itchy place underneath his chin.

It occurred to me as I scratched that the cat's mouth didn't move when he talked. *No, of course it wouldn't. Cats don't have the right anatomy to actually make human speech. Their lips and throats are all wrong. Whatever he's doing, it's not coming in through my ears.*

"How is it, exactly, that I can hear you talking?" I asked.

"I expect it's because I'm a mirror-cat."

"I see." I considered this from all angles before deciding that I had no idea what he was talking about. "And what is a mirror-cat?"

The cat readjusted himself, setting tiny pinpricks itching along my collarbone. "There was once a kitten," he said, "who had a hole for a right eye." His tail flicked against my wrist. "A man tried to drown the kitten in a pond that reflected the sky and the stars. But a kind woman reached into the pond and grabbed the kitten and pulled him out again." Another flick. "But by chance, she grabbed his reflection and pulled out the kitten who had a hole for a left eye instead. She didn't notice, of course. Humans rarely do."

"And that was you?" I asked, glancing down to make certain that the cat was, indeed, missing his left eye and not his right.

"I did not tell you the story because I think it makes compelling listening." He turned his head so that the empty socket seemed to gaze into my face. "And since I am a mirror-cat and you have gone into the mirror, a number of peculiar things are possible."

"Gone into the mirror?" I looked over at the mirror, baffled, but it looked exactly the same as it always had, except that the shadows behind it were unusually deep. "What do you mean?"

"You're not very observant, are you?" The cat yawned, showing a ribbed pink gullet. "But you're not bad at petting cats, so I suppose some allowances must be made. You fell through the mirror just now, while you were holding me. We're on the other side of the silver now."

"The other side of . . ." I pinched the bridge of my nose. Since this meant that I was no longer petting the cat, his purr trailed off, disgruntled. "This is absurd. Mirrors don't have other sides. They're just glass."

"Windows are just glass," said the cat, "and they manage to have another side."

"Look," I said, "I'll *show* you." I stood up and stalked over to the mirror. "See? It's just a . . ."

And then I stopped because the scene in the mirror was my bedroom, exactly as it should be, but there was no woman and no cat reflected in it.

"Where are our reflections?" I asked, staring into the space that should have held my mirror image and unaccountably didn't.

"I told you, we're on the other side of the silver," said the cat. "Try to pay attention, will you? Things in what we will laughingly call 'the real world' have reflections. We, however, are not in that world, so we don't."

"But it's reflecting the bed and the walls and . . ."

The cat sighed the sigh of the much put-upon. "I didn't plan to educate a human today," he said. "I was going to chase a ball of paper and then have a nap. You had best plan to feed me very well when we return."

"I'll find you a nice saucer of milk," I promised.

"Oh *milk*," said the cat, as if I had suggested he eat sand. "If *that's* all you can do, don't bother."

"Cream?"

"Better. Somewhat." The cat readjusted his grip, managing to sink his claws into the meat of my shoulder in the process. "Now, turn around and look behind you. You see the room, yes?"

"Yes?"

"*That's* the reflection. What you see through the mirror is the actual room."

I turned around twice, trying to get my bearings. I always slept on the right side of the bed, and the room viewed through the mirror had rumpled sheets on that side, and my book lying on the bedside table. But in the room behind me, the book was on the left side and the pillow with the indentation was on the left and . . .

If this is a hallucination, it is an extremely internally consistent one.

"Are you sure I haven't gone mad?" I asked.

"Your questions are remarkably unoriginal. 'Am I mad, is this a dream, oh no, what's going on, why is this happening?'" He gazed off into the distance as if I were no longer worth considering.

Strange as it sounds, this stung a bit. It's one thing to know that a cat holds you in mild contempt, quite another to have it actually insult you in language you understand. I tried to think of a better question.

"Cat," I said slowly, "if someone came into the room right now, would they see *us* in the mirror?"

"Naturally," said the cat. "Assuming they bothered to look, which humans can't be relied upon to do."

"Is this magic?" I asked. I hated to even say the word.

He actually thought about this for a bit, flicking his ears back as if listening to a distant sound. "Yes and no," he said finally. "Mirrors are like blood or bones or oak trees. All the magic is in what is done *with* them."

"I don't believe in magic," I said, aware of how ridiculous it was even as I said it, given that I was having a conversation with a talking cat. *And that* must *be magic, because they are not like parrots, and in a rational world, a cat couldn't make human speech even if it wanted to.*

He jumped down onto the bed, not bothering to pull his claws in. "Then you are being very stupid, even for a human."

"Probably," I admitted. I looked at the mirror again, where there was no cat to be seen, and the dark rectangle around it. "But if this really *is* the mirror, why are so many things painted gray? The real things aren't."

"Work it out for yourself," said the cat. "There's no point educating someone who won't believe in magic when it's already happened to them." He thrust out one hind leg and began cleaning it aggressively. His paw pads were a deep burgundy.

"Sorry," I said. "I didn't mean to offend you."

The cat made a noise that might have been "hmmph!'" though I couldn't tell if it was because he accepted my apology, or didn't accept it, or was simply nipping at the base of his tail in a slightly obscene fashion. I turned back to the mirror, my eye caught by the frame itself. The inside was brilliant gilt, but the outer edges were featureless gray, with only a line of shadow to differentiate them from the dark paint on the wall. When I ran my fingers over the grayness, it felt smooth and cold, but it was the slightly grainy smoothness of a river rock, not the slickness of gilded wood. The line between gold and gray was ruler straight.

It's all so crisp, I thought despairingly. Hitting your head is supposed to make things vague and fuzzy, and this very much wasn't. Nor did it have the disjointed quality of a hallucination. I had experienced those once or twice in the course of my experiments, and none of them had looked anything like this.

The book on the bedside table caught my eye again. *I wonder if the writing inside is mirrored, too?* I picked it up and opened it, but there was no writing at all, only the smooth, cold gray on every page.

I looked over my shoulder at the mirror again, half expecting to see the book there levitating in midair, but it was still sitting on the nightstand.

A thought began to tease at the corner of my mind. I set down the book and walked to the washroom. The curtain fabric was the same color as the wall, but it moved easily under my hand.

When I pulled it back, the alcove was very dark, except for the mirror over the basin, which blazed like a window to some exotic country. Several inches of wall and floor by the door glowed with light, but most of the room lay in shadow. The basin itself had a sharp line drawn across it, white porcelain giving way to feature-less gray.

"Cat," I said, stepping back. "Cat, I've got it! It's gray where the mirror can't see it!" The sheer irrationality of this statement jarred me, so I hastily amended, "Where it can't be reflected in the mirror, I mean."

"You were closer to the truth the first time," said the cat, drop-ping his hind leg, "but yes."

I went to the balcony door and looked out. The sky beyond was a clear, hard blue, but there were small wedges of darkness cut out of it, looking unsettlingly like sharp black teeth. The ground was darker still, a solid bar of shadow lying across the horizon. I turned away quickly and went to the hallway door instead.

On the far side of the door was a deep gray version of the world I knew. I drew back, alarmed. Gray tiles, gray walls, gray railing—all the color of cold charcoal.

"Is it all like this?" I asked the cat, whispering now. There was something unnerving about the corridor. It was too easy to imagine all the doors of the house opening into gray rooms beyond, all the textures flattened down to that strange cold smoothness. "Every-where that isn't reflected?"

"Everywhere I've been," said the cat, just as quietly.

"But the whole *world*?" I pictured the desert outside lying chill and quiet, all the bushes and gnarled trees like black ceramic ver-sions of themselves, stretching down to a blank gray sea. "Does anything . . . anyone . . . live here?"

"Oh yes," said the cat. "Things live here. You don't want to meet them." He leaped down from the bed and approached the mirror. "Time to be getting back."

I followed the cat obediently and reached out to the mirror. I half expected my hand to sink into it like water, but instead my fingertips stopped on the polished surface. "How does this work?"

"Closing your eyes helps," the cat said.

I closed my eyes and reached out again. This time there was no resistance, only a chill, metallic feeling that traveled up my arm. I almost opened my eyes, then had a sudden vision of the glass becoming solid inside my arm and decided that particular experiment could wait until later. I stepped forward, bumping my shoulder on the frame, and then the inside of my skull went thin and silver and I almost stopped (but what if I got stuck?) so I kept walking until my knees bumped into the chest at the foot of the bed.

I opened my eyes. The room looked the same, but the shadows were only shadows, not bands of darkness. When I turned around, my reflection met my eyes, looking flushed and baffled and excited and a little frightened.

I did it. I'm back.

I was in the mirror.

There's a whole world in the mirror. A whole different *world.*

I turned around, went up to the mirror, and closed my eyes. Then I reached out my hand and didn't encounter glass, only that cold metallic feeling again. I pulled my hand back and opened my eyes.

My reflection gazed back at me, looking as stunned and gleeful as I felt.

I dropped onto the bed and found myself laughing with the sheer delight of discovery. If you've never felt this, I don't really know how to explain it. Like a small child surrounded by presents, maybe. Everywhere you look, there's something new to see and get excited about. My chest felt as if it were full of ecstatic bees. *Saints have mercy, there's so much to learn!*

"I'll write a book," I said out loud. "Two books. *Ten* books. Oh, no one's going to believe it, but if I take enough people through—"

"That'll end well," said the cat. "Invite me to the stoning when they decide you're a witch."

This threw a certain amount of cold water on my enthusiasm. "All right, maybe I won't be able to publish. But I can make notes."

"Do what you wish," said the cat, trotting out onto the balcony. He was over the railing with the flip of a gray tail—gone.

Damn it, I had more questions for him. Not that I had any idea what questions to ask, come to that, and the cat had made his opinion of uninteresting questions abundantly clear. Still, I'd probably be able to find him later. *Find a talking cat . . . ?* my brain whispered. *Do you hear yourself?*

I ignored it.

The first question was how safe it was to go through the mirror. If I opened my eyes halfway through, would I get sliced in half? This seemed like a very important point to iron out first. Preferably without losing any parts of my anatomy.

I snatched a quill pen off my desk and approached the mirror. I closed my eyes and slowly extended my hand, the quill in front of me, until I felt the cold, silvery tingle of the mirror on my fingers. I pulled back until it stopped, then opened my eyes.

The quill was sticking out of the mirror. I could see myself and the lower half of the quill reflected, but I couldn't see the rest of it. I tugged experimentally.

It felt as if the quill was stuck in glue. It came out slowly, the individual barbs bending back, then finally popped out. I touched it. It failed to explode or fall apart. This was promising, but probably not enough to risk a limb on. I would hate to learn that, for example, blood didn't flow from one side of the mirror to the other.

But why would it matter if my eyes are open or closed? And how can the mirror tell?

Because it's magic, my brain whispered.

I still didn't believe in magic, but I didn't believe in it a lot less strongly than I had before falling through a mirror. If only I had someone else to help, we could see if their gaze affected it while my eyes were closed.

I thought briefly about summoning Aaron or Javier and asking them to assist me. I was reasonably sure they wouldn't denounce me as a witch.

Fairly sure.

Not actually sure at all.

Saints! I wish Scand were here. My old tutor would have loved this.

Since I couldn't think of a way to answer the question of observation, I shelved it and wondered what to do next. No, that's not quite right—I could think of a thousand things to do; I just didn't know where to *start*.

I looked over at the book on my nightstand, then at the one in the mirror, and realized that the reflected one was turned about ninety degrees. Of course, I'd picked it up and set it down, hadn't I? And now they didn't match.

I looked back and forth again. It was a small thing, but strangely eerie. Mirrors—well—*mirror* things. It's what they *do*. The difference felt like a flaw in the world.

I reached out and turned the real book sideways, then looked back to the mirror.

It was now an exact reflection of the real book.

"Aha!" I could go into the mirror and change a reflected object's position, but if I moved that object in the real world, the reflection reverted back. Or at least, so it seemed.

I spent about ten minutes testing this theory, stepping into the mirror, moving the book, and stepping back out. By the end, I was pretty well convinced.

I was holding the reflected book when I caught a glimpse of movement in the reflected mirror. I jumped back instinctively, pressing myself into the gray area. If someone had come into the room, I really didn't want them to see me cavorting inside the mirror. As the cat had said, that was the sort of thing that got you stoned as a witch.

A moment later, someone walked past me, on both sides of the mirror.

It was one of the housemaids. She crossed the reflected room, holding a basket of sheets under one arm, and began stripping the bed. She didn't seem to notice me. I inched sideways until I could retreat into the deeper alcove of the doorway, but she never looked around, even though I was right there.

Well, of course not. She can't look around unless the real her looks around.

Watching her was unsettling. Since the real woman's back was to the mirror, the reflected woman had no face, only a bare suggestion of features under blank grayness. Bits of her body kept flickering light and dark as she moved. I could hear the rustle of linens, but I wasn't sure if it came from the reflected bed or was being transmitted through the mirror.

When she had finished making the bed, she turned and went toward the washroom, carrying towels. I could tell the exact moment that she stepped out of the mirror's view, because the reflected woman halted. She was solid gray from head to toe, and she stood unmoving with her head bowed over the stack of towels. I watched her for several seconds, and then, like a soap bubble popping out of existence, she vanished.

I'm not too proud to admit that I yelped.

What happened? I wondered. The giddiness I'd been feeling was still there, but it was mixed uncomfortably with alarm. When I'd been very small, my father used to throw me in the air and catch me, while I shrieked in delighted terror. This felt oddly similar.

A beam of light pierced the shadow, and I realized that I could see the maid again, or at least her back half, sticking out of the washroom. The light was coming from the mirror over the washbasin, projecting a band of color and brilliance into the room. She must have opened the curtain there. Had her reflection vanished because it needed to be in another mirror somewhere else?

Do you only ever have one reflection, then? So what happens if there are two mirrors? Or twenty?

I would commit murder for a research partner . . .

The washbasin curtain closed, and the maid flickered out of existence again, then reappeared almost immediately, significantly closer, as if she'd teleported. She walked across the room toward me, half-dark, half-light, like a festival clown. I shrank back as she approached, though she still gave no sign of seeing me.

A moment later, she stepped into shadow, and I waited for her to vanish again.

Except she didn't. She stood silently, her whole body such a smooth gray that it was hard to tell where her clothes left off and skin began. Her head hung down, the basket clutched in one hand, her other arm dangling limply. She should have looked like a statue, but somehow she didn't. The overall impression was of a human standing very, very still.

It was *deeply* creepy.

Hang on . . . if the maid was walking across the room and stepped out of the mirror's range, shouldn't this reflection be in midstride?

She wasn't. She stood with her feet together, which meant that she had moved independently, at least a little, when she reached the shadows.

I took another step back and swallowed hard.

I don't know how long I stood there watching her. It felt like years. I kept waiting for her to disappear, off to reflect in some other glass, but she didn't. Wherever the maid had gone, it had no mirrors.

Saints, maybe she's gone to bed early. That reflection could be here for hours.

I didn't think I could handle hours.

The implications slowly began to sink in. If your reflection stayed beside the last mirror you passed, what happened if you *died*? Was the mirror-world full of shades left behind the dying?

There had been a mirror in my mother's bedroom. If I went through it, would I find her body, wracked with the pains of childbirth, crouched just beyond the frame?

A shudder went through me at the thought. Then I remembered the little hand mirror that I use to see if a patient is still breathing. If that sliver of glass was enough to trap a reflection, then Saint Adder's infirmary must be waist-deep in the dead.

Unless it's just a reflection of their nostrils, I thought, and bit the side of my hand to control what threatened to be hysterical laughter.

"Right," I said, my voice high and flat in my own ears. "I've got to get out of here."

Well. Take stock. How much room was there? Could I inch past the motionless reflection and reach the exit?

She was half blocking the narrow entryway, and there wasn't a great deal of room to get by. I was quite certain that I didn't want to touch her. I kept waiting for her to reach out and grab me. There was no reason to think that she would, but there was no reason to think that she *wouldn't* either.

I pressed myself flat against the wall and wormed my way past, hardly daring to breathe. At one point I had to pass within an inch of her shoulder. I could actually feel the gray chill radiating off her. (Would it have been better or worse if she were warm? I don't know.)

When I was finally out of range, I backed toward the mirror, not taking my eyes off the gray woman until my shoulder hit the cold glass. I closed my eyes and stepped through.

Safely back on this side, I moved to one side and leaned against the wall. It seemed important for some reason that the mirror not be able to see me. Not that the gray woman would necessarily be able to see me, but . . . well, anyway, I was happier against the wall.

It wasn't until my heart had stopped racing that I realized that I was still holding the reflection of the book in my right hand.

CHAPTER 14

"Saints have mercy!" I said aloud, staring at the mirror-book. I'd managed to bring an object back through the mirror. I hadn't expected that. It hadn't even occurred to me to try.

I looked over at the real book. It was still there. In the mirror, the nightstand was empty.

Strange as it may sound, this felt more like magic than entering the mirror had. The world in the mirror was different, foreign, almost dreamlike. This was real and solid and out here in the real world as I knew it.

The mirror-book was no longer partly gray, but it was not quite identical to the real one. There was a silvery sheen to it, not quite reflective, like a thin coat of oil. It also opened on the wrong side. I flipped to a random page, and the letters were indeed backward, which delighted me. The pages themselves had the same sheen, like onionskin. It reminded me of something.

My eyes kept flicking to the mirror, drawn to the gap on the nightstand like a missing tooth. What did it mean, if you could bring things out of the mirror? Books, clearly, would be difficult, given that they were backward, but what about other things? There were always medicines that were in short supply. Suppose you could double them at a stroke?

I leaned against the wall for what must have been a quarter of an hour, my mind racing. *Put a mirror in a granary and you could double food production . . . Reproduce objects like rugs that take so much time and labor to create . . .*

Hell, if I wanted to be crass, bars of gold don't care what direction they face.

The book twitched in my hand.

I would like to say that I set it down calmly, as befitted a price-less object of scientific study. Actually I jumped, squawked, and flung it aside as if it were an insect. A moment later, I realized that it hadn't been a twitch, it had been the book crumbling away.

I watched in dismay as it fell apart. Have you ever seen a log in a fire that has burned completely to ash but retains its shape until you touch it? Then it simply falls apart—and that's what the book did. Bits of silvery grit dripped onto the carpet as the rectangle became an irregular lump, and then the lump itself dissolved. The ash twinkled in the lamplight, then it, too, faded away into nothing.

So much for bars of gold.

Now, why had that happened? Perhaps things from the mirror couldn't exist in our world for very long? It made a kind of sense—not a scholarly, scientific sense, but a wonder-tale sense. There's always a creature who pays you in gold that dissolves when dawn comes.

I told myself that wasn't rational and that I didn't believe in magic. Magic was just a way of waving your hand and saying, *Because I said so*, like an adult who was tired of a child asking, *Why?* You didn't need magic if you were willing to put in the hard work of finding the answer.

Well. I was not the best or brightest student, I was never prone to great leaps of intellect, but I was never afraid of putting in the hard work.

Afraid, ha! I was dying to learn more. However much the maid in the mirror had unsettled me, I wanted to go back. Except . . .

I looked down at my empty hands, where not even a trace of ash remained. Did that mean that if I stayed too long in the mirror-world, I'd turn to dust myself?

I swallowed hard. How long would that take? I'd spent maybe ten minutes in the mirror-world each time. The book had lasted a good fifteen minutes. Would I have more or less time than a book?

How could I even test that without dying?

It occurred to me that I could probably use a rooster, the same as I did for poisons, but that felt wrong. Saving someone's life was one thing. Shoving a bird into an alternate dimension to fall apart into dust while I timed it from outside just didn't feel right. Maybe I could use an inanimate object?

So many thoughts swirled through my head, along with a stomach-clenching fear that I'd only just avoided disintegration, that I did the only thing I could think of to do. I took a nap.

Go ahead and laugh, but intense feelings and intense thinking are exhausting. And frequently when I wake up, my thoughts are clear and I've realized something. I drew the curtains closed, stripped off my robes, and curled up under the blankets, hoping that an hour or two of sleep would clarify the extraordinary events of the last hour.

And in fact, they did. I woke up just as the sun was going down, and remembered that there was someone who knew a great deal about the mirror-world. More than I did, anyway.

I just had to find the cat.

I thought of all the places that a small gray cat could hide at dusk. Then I thought of how I would appear scouring the villa at night, looking for said cat. Then I stared at the ceiling for a few minutes, and then I tugged the bellpull and asked that dinner be sent up to my room.

When the tray arrived, I barely noticed what was on it. I had stopped staring at the ceiling and was now gazing out over the gardens and into the distance, wondering how many mirrors it took to reflect the sky. If someone in the villa had left their hand mirror aimed at the balcony, would that account for one of the wedges of blue I'd seen? Or could it have been someone much farther away? If a mirror at the port was aimed toward Witherleaf, and a mirror here was aimed toward the port, would we provide each place's reflection with blue sky?

Scand would have been the person to talk to. Optics and reflections and the various behaviors of light were his great passion.

He was long retired now, of course, staying on the estate my aunt managed, writing messages for people who weren't comfortable with their letters, and serving as a scribe when my aunt needed something formal drawn up. The rest of the time, he puttered around in his shed, shining light through prisms into rainbows and bouncing them off mirrors and the saints knew what else.

I itched to send him a letter, but I had barely picked up the quill before I set it down again. Of *course* someone was going to be reading my mail. If they'd set guards on my home to keep me from being hired by the king's enemies, they certainly weren't going to let me send letters unsupervised. And anything I wrote would sound as if I had gone utterly mad. At best they might think it was a code of some kind, and then they'd probably arrest Scand.

I was just wondering whether I could ask him to make the long journey here when my stomach lurched and the back of my tongue tensed up in the peculiar way it does when you're about to be violently ill.

I clamped my hand over my mouth and lunged to the privy, where I was, indeed, remarkably ill. Whatever dinner had been, it was determined to vacate the premises.

Clutching the edge of the carved seat, I waited grimly through the next spasm. I hadn't felt nauseated leading up to it. I didn't feel under the weather. Was it possible that I'd been poisoned?

Of course *you've been poisoned, you absolute ninny! You ate that damned apple not three hours ago!*

Saints have mercy, in the excitement of the mirror, I'd nearly forgotten the apple.

The strange, chill apple. The apple with the silvery sheen on its skin. A sheen that looked just like the onionskin gleam on the mirror-book, and a chill that felt almost exactly like the cold prickle when I pushed my hand through the mirror.

Sweet Saint Rabbit, was that apple from the other side of the mirror?

Another spasm wracked my guts. It wasn't pleasant. When that finished, I pressed my sweating forehead against the cool tiled wall. Was this the cause of Snow's illness? It hadn't reacted to my tests, but *would* it?

What if it's just a normal apple, but from the other side?

Could it be that the apple wasn't precisely poison, but reacted badly with food from our world? You were fine until you ate something else, and then you were sick? And the sickness could conceivably taper off, as the apple left your system, until you ate normally for a day, just as Snow did, and then . . . then what? Then she ate another apple?

I didn't have much time to contemplate this before the next round of festivities struck.

When you are in the business of poisons, as I may have said before, you learn quite a lot about vomit. In the course of testing things on myself, I've done it a number of times. (Also, there were several parties in my youth that I prefer not to remember.) There is the quick and efficient ridding yourself of a substance, after which you feel better; the drunken misery where one clings to a spinning chamber pot and prays for death; and the which-end-is-it-going-to-be game of chance that is food poisoning.

And then, of course, there is the kind that practically turns you inside out, trying to shake loose any organs that aren't nailed down. That was what I was experiencing now.

The stomach is sacred to Saint Sheep, although some claim that it's actually sacred to Saint Fish in His Trout aspect. If you're making a pilgrimage to ask for help with an ulcer, you'll probably want to hedge your bets and visit shrines to both. If you're puking your guts out, though, who you pray to is entirely up to you. (If you're drunk, though, you invoke Saint Rabbit, who is the patron of, among other things, debauchery.)

"Saint Trout, have mercy," I begged. "Saint Adder, look kindly upon the health of your . . . your . . ." I blanked out on what I was for a moment. "Faithful. Right. Look kindly upon the health of your faithful."

Look, I never said I was a *good* worshipper.

"I'm not going to die," I told myself. "I'm not. Snow's been eating these for months now. She hasn't died."

Although she could *have built up an immunity over the last three months . . .*

I sighed. I'd been so close to reassuring myself, too.

Why would she keep eating the apples? She must have known that they were making her sick. I could have seen it if it was just an emetic—some people, as Nurse had said, had an illness like that—but surely she'd use something that didn't make you feel as if you were going to puke up your toenails.

Was she *deliberately* poisoning herself?

It seemed utterly absurd, but that didn't mean it wasn't true. People do absurd, irrational things all the time. Hell, Healer Michael had once told me of a case where a woman came in who was clearly in the early stages of hydrophobia, but hadn't been bitten by a dog or a skunk or any of the usual suspects. "And it eventually came out that she had attempted to breastfeed a bat," he said heavily. "Because it was injured and she worried it was hungry."

I'd snorted in horrified amusement. You don't want to laugh at someone who's died such an awful death, but for the love of the saints, what was she *thinking*?

"The point," Michael had said dryly, "is that if you think, 'Surely no one would do that!'—well, someone *will*, and probably they'll be expecting you to fix it."

Snow was so hedged around with guards and servants, though. How was she even getting the apples? It seemed impossible.

But then I remembered that smile I'd caught that very first day, the sly, secret smile in the mirror, and I wondered . . .

And then another, much more immediate thought struck me, and I sat bolt upright.

Chickens can't vomit.

"Oh shit," I muttered, and crawled in the direction of the bellpull.

Aaron and Javier entered my room five minutes later and discovered me crouched on the floor, greenish and shivering, with my hair hanging in damp strands over my face. I had achieved a tentative truce with my innards, but I wasn't sure how long they would keep their end of the bargain.

Aaron's eyes went wide. "Mistress Anja?"

Javier, somewhat more practically, pulled a dressing gown off a hook and wrapped it around me over my nap-rumpled clothes. He sniffed while he did it, clearly trying to see if I was reeking of alcohol, and apparently decided that I wasn't.

I had a wild urge to ask for a hug. It wasn't just the cold. There's something about having been really ill that leaves you feeling wrung out and vulnerable, and I simultaneously wanted to crawl into my bed and never see another human again and to have someone pat me on my shoulder and say, *There, there.*

Sadly, I was pretty sure that you weren't supposed to ask your bodyguards to do that.

"Should we get a healer?" Aaron asked.

I wasn't going to waste words through my bile-ravaged throat to point out that I *was* a healer. "Need to go to my workshop," I rasped instead. "Poison."

Both men went still. Aaron's sympathetic smile vanished. Javier, who spoke so rarely, said, in a voice that was flat and much too calm, "Tell us his name, mistress, and he will die."

That was a strange feeling. I'd never had anyone offer to kill someone for me before. I didn't doubt him at all. Explaining about the apple would take much too long. I shook my head. "Don't know."

My guards swung into action as smoothly as if they escorted retching charges all the time. (Actually, if they had ever been set to guard a drunkard, they probably did have some experience with it.) Javier got my arm over his shoulders and got me to my feet. Aaron grabbed the empty pitcher from the washroom in case I needed to be sick again, and the two of them led me out into the hallway and in the direction of my workroom. Aaron had the lamp from my nightstand and pushed doors open. I had wanted a hug, but being half carried by Javier was not the same thing. I clutched the pitcher for dear life and hoped I wouldn't need it. (The mouth of the pitcher was very narrow, and I did not trust my stomach's aim.)

Somehow, we got to the workroom. Aaron hastily lit the lamps. I imagine they expected me to immediately begin preparing an antidote to the poison. Instead, I fell to my knees in front of the rooster's cage. He was a dark, immobile lump in the back of it. I swung the door open and yanked the dish of corn out, cursing. Had I sentenced him to a horrible death?

(Yes, I know, the whole *point* of the rooster was to test for poisons. I told you I hated doing it, though, and since I already knew the apple was toxic, the rooster's death wasn't necessary. Also, I wouldn't sentence my worst enemy to death by nausea.)

I poked the rooster. "Come on," I muttered. Had he eaten any of the corn? Or had he just gone straight to sleep? "Come on . . ."

"Rrrr-rrr-rrr," the rooster said, the sound of a disgruntled chicken being woken up against his will.

"Um, Mistress Anja?" Aaron said, the sound of a baffled bodyguard watching his charge determinedly poking a chicken.

The rooster's eyes were round, not half-lidded, and his comb was bright. He mostly seemed annoyed. It looked like he hadn't eaten any corn before going to sleep. Chickens pass things quicker than we do. If I gave him a day with only water, maybe the apple would go out of his system.

I got slowly to my feet and put my forearms on the table, leaning heavily against it. Aaron and Javier were both looking at me with the kind of studied impassivity that people get when they think you're about to start raving about whippoorwills stealing your toenails.

"Can you tell us what exactly happened?" Aaron asked, very carefully.

It had occurred to me that the two of them could be very useful in tracking down the source of the apple, regardless of whether it was from the mirror or not. Someone had to be giving it to Snow, right?

Or else she's walking into the mirror and getting it herself.

In which case, maybe they'd see *that* happen and . . . well . . . I'd deal with that if and when it came up.

But why would there be apples in the mirror? There are no apple groves here to reflect. The nearest orchards are back in Four Saints. Though I suppose there might be a barrel down in the cellars . . .

It occurred to me that Aaron and Javier had been staring at me for a rather long time and that I should probably say something. I shoved all thoughts of mirrors down and hoped they'd put the pause down to my illness. "Right," I said. "I'm afraid this was self-inflicted . . ."

I recounted the whole saga, minus the mirrors. At one point Javier fetched me a cup of water from the jug I kept to water the snake and the chicken. Other than that, they just listened.

"And . . . uh . . . that's where we're at," I finished, somewhat anticlimactically.

Aaron said, with marvelous patience, "Are you telling me that you poisoned yourself, then rushed down here in order to save a pet chicken?"

"He's not a pet. He's more of a colleague."

"That's what you said about the snake."

"And I'd rush down here to save her, too." I pulled the dressing gown tighter around myself. "Look, the important thing is that someone is sneaking poisoned apples to Snow."

"Not quite," Javier said, in his deep, solemn voice. "The important thing is that someone is sneaking poisoned apples to Snow *and she is eating them.* Willingly." He looked from my face to Aaron's. "Whoever is doing this, they have clearly convinced her that it is in her own best interests to eat poison."

I nodded glumly. "I can't think that she hasn't connected the apple to the illness. She's not *that* young."

"Could someone have convinced her that the apple is curing her?" Aaron asked.

"Maybe? I don't know. Or it could be like people eating arsenic, and she thinks it's building an immunity to something?" I spread my hands helplessly.

"There must be *some* reason," Aaron said.

"Even if there is, I can't just ask her, since I'm definitely not in her good graces right now. Which reminds me, I have to finish my letter to the king, and Saints know what I'm going to say . . ."

"I can assist you with that," Javier said unexpectedly. "Tomorrow." He no longer had the whippoorwill-and-toenails look, but he seemed to have moved to *you cannot be trusted to care for yourself*, which, under the circumstances, I couldn't argue with.

"We'll help you," Aaron said. "There are only so many times of the day when someone is not watching Snow. We can ask around and watch ourselves."

I nodded. "That would be a *huge* help." I started to say more and caught myself in a jaw-cracking yawn. The exhaustion of the day, both physical and emotional, seemed to crash over me all at once. "And . . . I think I should go lie down."

My guards helped me back up to my room. I halfway wondered if they were going to tuck me into bed, too, but they stopped at the doorway. "Send a page when you require my help with the letter," Javier said. I promised that I would.

I crossed the room, fell down on the bed, and was instantly asleep. Sometime in the night, I woke up long enough to take off my shoes, but that was all.

CHAPTER 15

Morning came on like an unearned hangover. I opened my eyes, closed them again, put my arm over my forehead, and moaned softly.

"Everything'll look easier after a cup of tea," said the maid.

I cracked one eye open again and saw the mass of devouring hair. Was tea preferable to death? Possibly. As a scholar, I was obligated to research the matter. I grunted something.

Tea, fortunately, did not seem to enrage the apple the way dinner had. I drank two cups and decided that since I was alive, I might as well stay that way.

I guiltily asked the maid to have the bath filled, then soaked myself in it until the odor of dried sweat was gone. Even surrounded by the smell of lavender, I couldn't stop thinking about the apple. *How* was Snow getting a mirror-apple? Even if someone was leaving it out for her, why was she eating it? After the night I'd spent, I wasn't sure that I was ever going to eat *food* again, let alone strange apples.

And was her illness really entirely from eating the mirror-apples? Could it all be explained by malnutrition?

I rubbed my temples. I had a dull headache brought on by . . . well, take your pick, really. The tea had erected walls against it, but it was creeping under them like water eroding the foundations.

Well, no help for it. Things to do today. I sat up, reaching for a towel, and my eyes trailed across the small mirrored tiles on the wall.

A figure was standing in the doorway directly behind me.

I whirled around, clutching the washcloth to my chest and sending a flood of water splashing over the side of the tub.

There was no one there.

I stared at the doorway for much longer than necessary to determine that there wasn't anyone standing there. I thought I'd seen someone—the maid?—but the figure, in that half-second glimpse, had looked taller and much paler, though still dark-haired. I looked back to the mirror, then the real doorway again. Both remained resolutely empty.

"You're getting paranoid," I muttered. It was no different than when you are walking around at twilight and a coatrack suddenly becomes a sinister figure. Your mind fills in dozens of details in that half second, until you can almost see the gleam of the knife—and then the moment passes, and the shadows become friendly again, and you realize that you nearly fled in terror from your father's second-best coat.

"Right!" I said, and pushed myself to my feet. Water streamed down my body, and I left wet footprints on the tiles. The desert air did more to dry me than the towel did. I left the bathing room, and the thought crossed my mind that on the other side of the mirrored tiles, a version of me stood motionless and just out of sight, her skin gone to cold gray clay. That she had followed me here across the desert, standing silently for hours, until a mirror snagged my reflection and pulled her close.

It was a strange squirmy thought, like an earthworm wriggling against my hand. "Right," I said again, a little less confidently. "Time to get to work."

The rooster greeted me with an attempted crow. (Young roosters, much like young boys, have to grow into their voices.) It came out as a high-pitched *err-earrrrr-ooooh?* He seemed to realize that it wasn't satisfactory and settled down to sulk.

"You tried, buddy," I said. "I'm just glad you're feeling well." I had managed a small piece of toast, in very slow stages, accompanied by another gallon of tea. The apple was clearly not completely out of my system yet.

I fed the chime-adder—the stable boy had come through so spectacularly that I had had to sneak several mice out to the gardens and release them—and found some willow powder for my headache. Aaron and Javier were following up on the apple, which meant that it was up to me to follow up on the mirror.

I spent the next several hours roaming the villa, looking for the one-eyed cat. It is very likely that the staff's opinion of my sanity dropped significantly in that time. The only person who knew anything about the beast's habits was my faithful stable boy, who said that he sometimes saw the cat walking on the wall around the kitchen courtyard and jumping up on the roof for a nap in a shady patch under the eaves. Unfortunately, the cat wasn't there at the time.

I was eventually reduced to wandering the gardens, calling, "Here kitty, here kitty, here . . . obnoxious kitty who knows exactly what I'm saying, damn it, we *need* to talk . . ." At least one gardener heard me and asked delicately if I should really be out in the sun without a hat.

After all that, I returned to my workshop in despair and found the cat stretched out on his side on my worktable, with the jar of willow powder smashed open on the flagstones underneath.

"You!" I said. "I've been looking for you!"

The cat blinked lazily at me but said nothing. Fear blossomed deep in my gut that he didn't actually talk and I *had* been hallucinating the whole thing, probably because of the apple.

Still, if you find yourself in an upside-down world, all you can do is plow forward and obey the internal logic as best you can. "I accidentally brought a book back from the mirror-world. And then it fell apart into dust."

"Yes," said the cat, "they do that."

He *did* talk. I leaned against the worktable, feeling slightly damp with relief, and shoved down all the questions about *how* he talked, at least for the time being. "Does it work the other way? Am *I* going to dissolve?"

"Real things generally don't dissolve." He sat up and stretched, his body bending into a long fishhook shape. "Always the questions with you. Don't humans ask each other how they've been?"

"You're right," I said, chastened. "I'm sorry. How have you been?"

Another slow stretch, the other way this time. "Well," he said afterward, while I waited impatiently. "I have been *well*." His tail flicked and hit another jar, this one full of one of my reagents. He turned to look at it as if it had personally offended him.

"I think I figured out how I got into the mirror," I told him excitedly. (If you'd told me a week ago that I'd be thrilled to be talking to a cat, I would have suspected you of taking any number of herbal poisons with interesting side effects.) "I ate an apple that came from the other side."

One ear twitched in my direction. "How unwise."

I grabbed a dustpan and set to work cleaning up the broken glass. "I *was* extremely sick last night. Is it likely to do anything else? And will it wear off?"

I looked up from the floor as I said it, so that our faces were briefly level. One golden eye blinked slowly, then he gave a vast, full-body shrug and turned his attention back to the reagent jar.

"But listen," I said, when it became obvious that was the only answer I was getting. "This apple. The book I took out on accident fell apart in fifteen minutes. The apple lasted for hours. Why? What's the difference?"

The cat hooked his paw behind the jar and tapped it a few times, moving it toward the edge of the table.

"Stop that!" I said, snatching it up before he could knock it to the floor. I received an offended look for my rudeness, but nothing more.

"Do you know why?" I asked finally.

Sunbeams through the window gilded the edges of his fur and turned his ears to red stained glass. "Mirrors," he said, after lengthy contemplation, "are strange."

I waited over a minute for a follow-up, which was not forthcoming. "That's it?"

He sat down with his back to me and began to clean one delicate paw.

"You were so helpful the other day," I said, exasperated.

"I *felt* helpful," the cat said. "I don't feel particularly helpful today."

"What if I got you a saucer of cream?"

"Then I would drink it," the cat said, between licks.

"*Then* will you feel more helpful?"

"Unlikely. I am not a dog. I do not perform for treats."

I wanted to tear my hair out. "Then I won't get you any cream."

"In *that* case," said the cat, transferring his attention to the other paw, "it is highly unlikely that I will feel helpful anytime soon."

I gripped the edge of the table and reminded myself that screaming would be counterproductive. "Listen, cat—err—oh *hell*. Do you have a name?"

"I have many names," said the cat.

"Do you have one that you would like me to call you?"

"Mmm." A bit of fur caught under one claw required his attention. "His Gloriousness, God-King of the Deserts, Lord of Rooftops, Kin of Mirrors, Heir to the Mantle of Harar, He Who Treads the Serpent's Tail, Whose Claws Have Scarred the Bark of the Great Tree."

I put my head in my hands. "That . . . is a lot."

He did not dignify this with a response.

"I was thinking of something . . . er . . . shorter. Like Stormy. Or, um, Mouser."

His Gloriousness twisted his head around and gave me a look more venomous than the caged adder.

I leaned against the table. The cat, after a short pause, went back to cleaning his paws. I waited. If he was waiting, he didn't show it.

After about five minutes of this, I realized that I was trying to outwait a cat and gave up. "Your Gloriousness," I said, trying to remember, "God-King of . . . um . . . the Deserts, Lord of . . . Lord of Rooftops . . ."

I got most of the way through my straggling recitation when he stretched and said, "I have occasionally found the name Grayling useful."

Strangling the only being who understands the mirror would be counterproductive. Yes. Very . . . counterproductive. No sense asking why he was like this. He was a cat. If cats were helpful, they'd be dogs.

I had always been more of a dog person.

"Grayling, then," I said.

He curled his tail neatly over his toes and looked up at me with an expression of bland innocence. "Now, I believe that there was some mention of cream?"

The cook did not wish to part with the cream. Despite fierce negotiation, I'm pretty sure that only the aegis of the king's favor allowed me to succeed. The only cows out here were stark, bony creatures with protruding ribs and hip bones, like leather sacks half-full of doorknobs. They lived on things that you'd think were only good for kindling, but they were quite stingy about producing cream.

I returned to find Grayling sitting in front of the rooster's cage. The rooster had his head down, his neck feathers puffed out to make himself look bigger, and was making an extremely hostile noise. The cat gave no sign of fear, but the last inch of his tail was flicking back and forth.

"*Someone,*" he said, "has fed mirror-food to this beast."

"That was me. I was testing the apple for poisons."

"That was . . ." I couldn't tell if he was pausing for effect, or searching for a word. ". . . *unwise.*"

"Oh?"

He'd said that about me eating the apple, too. I was hoping he'd explain himself and add another scrap to my growing store of knowledge, but he didn't. Another inch of tail began to flick.

"Won't it wear off eventually?" I tried.

Grayling sniffed haughtily. "Certainly, if you wait for a year or two."

"I didn't know the apple was from the mirror when I did it," I said apologetically. Inwardly, I was cheering. *It won't wear off right away!* "Does that mean you can talk to him now?"

"No. He's still just a rooster. They aren't bright."

"No, they aren't." I set down the dish of cream. The tiny clink of ceramic on wood was all that was needed. Grayling turned his back on the rooster—who charged the bars in impotent fury—and leaped up onto the table to devour his tribute.

I watched the rooster, who still seemed unharmed by the apple. "Their brains are smaller than their testicles," I said absently.

Grayling paused, his tongue still in the cream. "Come again?"

"Roosters. If you dissect them."

He muttered something that sounded like "figures" and went back to his meal.

He drank it all and licked the dish twice, his small pink tongue scouring away even the memory of cream, then cleaned his whiskers, jumped down from the table, and headed toward the door.

"Will you answer my questions tomorrow?" I asked hopelessly.

"Promises are human inventions," he said pleasantly, and strolled out, tail held high.

I told myself that this was an opportunity. I was, for all I knew, the first person in history to communicate with a nonhuman intelligence. Alongside the mirror, it was an embarrassment of scientific riches. I should be excited. I should be *grateful.* I . . .

Had a feeling that Grayling was going to string me along to get as much cream as possible out of the deal, actually.

"Snakes," I said to thin air, "are much easier."

I walked back to my bedroom as fast as I could without exciting comment.

Despite Grayling's obstinance, he'd told me one very useful fact. (Two, if you counted that the apple's effects would last for a year.) *Real things don't usually dissolve.* Granted, I would have appreciated a little more certainty, but I'd take what I could get, particularly if it meant that I could explore more widely beyond the mirror.

The sheer delight of exploration was so intense that my hands shook as I shoved my pen, penknife, and notebook into my pockets. I felt a pang of guilt at that. I should have been working on how to cure Snow. And yes, if the apple had come from the other side of the mirror, I was following up on that lead, so it *was* work, but it certainly didn't *feel* like it.

I thought briefly about leaving a note, in case something went wrong, but what could I possibly say? It wasn't as if anyone would be able to come after me, except Grayling, who may or may not have been able to read. Even if he could, would he bother? How useful did my cream-wrangling skills make me?

In the end, I didn't leave one, simply because if someone found it, they would assume that I had gone mad. I closed my eyes, took a deep breath, and stepped through into the silver.

The mirrored bedroom looked exactly as it had, fortunately without the frozen shape of the maid. I glanced around once, quickly, then made my way toward the door.

As soon as my candle entered the band of gray, it went out.

I turned to the lamp, planning to relight the candle with it, only to find that the lamp in this world had no flame and gave no light. *Huh. That's odd.*

I went back out, relit the candle with a spill, brought both spill and candle through the silver, and took a step into the gray.

Both flames went out simultaneously.

Realizing that I could get very sidetracked very quickly, I set them both on the table for later consideration and went to see if there was enough light to explore.

The hallway looked exactly as it had before. I paused on the threshold, feeling like a swimmer. My bedroom had been shallow water. Not *safe*, exactly. You could still drown in the shallows, but at least the way out was never far away.

Now I was about to plunge into the depths.

I set my foot on the gray tiles and stepped into the hall.

Nothing terrible happened. I realized I was holding my breath and let it out, laughing at myself. What had I expected? That there were . . . I don't know, pits of spikes lying around, as soon as you got away from the mirror?

I glanced over my shoulder. My room was ablaze with light and color, but as soon as I stepped to the side, it was gone. There was no glow of reflected sunlight on the walls, no hints of color anywhere that I could see.

It was strangely unsettling. You know on some gut level how light works, and when it stops working like it should, your body registers that something is wrong.

Looking over the gallery railing, I could see down to the court-yard, the entire villa as dark as if it had been dipped in coal dust. The long galleries, the archways, the many doorways, all dark and lifeless. No people. Of course, there were no mirrors in the halls—why would there be? They were fragile and expensive things here, if not in faraway Silversand. So no reflections would be caught standing in the halls, waiting like lost children for their owners.

That was probably for the best. The dark halls would not be any less unsettling if there were silent figures standing in them.

They must *dissolve after a while,* I told myself firmly. The alternative did not bear thinking about.

I made my way along the hall to the stairs. The doors were all closed. The archways, with their elaborate patterned tiles, were now dull monochrome. Unless the pattern had been carved or etched into the surface, the far side of the mirror brushed it all away.

From the stairs, I could look up at the sky. It, at least, was still blue, though it seemed dull and faded. I would have expected it to look brighter in contrast to the charcoal villa, but instead it seemed as if the color had been leached away.

There was an angular black scar across the sky, a triangle pointing roughly south. Realistically I knew that it wasn't a presence but an absence, the place where two reflected beams from distant mirrors diverged. But the blackness seemed much more real and solid than the sky itself, and it was hard not to see it as some kind of object. A massive piece of architecture, perhaps, or a freakishly straight-sided mesa looming over the desert.

I looked down to see if it cast a shadow, then realized that I wouldn't be able to tell. There were no truly deep shadows, nor any light sources except the sky. Everything existed in that strange, sculptural light. My hands on the railing had only faint shadows underneath them, and the railing itself had only a slightly darker curve along the bottom.

The staircase itself was surprisingly disorienting. The monotonous color and lack of crisp shadows made it hard to judge the distance between steps. And it was so *quiet*. The scuff of my heels on the steps was the only sound I could hear. This space should have been full of people laughing and talking and working, a bustle of humanity going about its business in the villa. I could not remember the last time I had heard such silence.

I cleared my throat a few times, expecting it to be disproportionately loud, but the noise was thin and small against the vast edifice of silence.

My excitement was rapidly mixing with fear, which did nothing to stop the trembling in my hands. It felt a little like the first time I'd fallen in love. I'd been queasy and trembling and excited then, too.

Hopefully this would work out better.

At the bottom of the stairs, Lady Sorrel's potted agaves stood clustered in one corner. I bent down and touched one of the less spikey ones. The thick leaves felt no different than anything else here. They might as well have been all one with the soil and the pot itself, more like sculptures than anything living.

I took out my penknife and cut a thick leaf free. The inside was gray all the way through. I touched the edge, expecting it to be wet, but it was as cool and dry as the railing or the walls. If I could touch the sky, I imagined it would feel much the same. The blade of the knife, as I put it away, seemed like a world of silvery color.

So the surface isn't just a gray patina, then. It's actually completely made of this mirror-stuff. Huh.

I tucked the leaf into my pocket, wondering how long it would take to fall apart once I brought it back to the real world. Perhaps, like the apple, it would last for hours. Perhaps plants lasted longer than books. Could it be because they were more alive? Maybe. Or maybe, as Grayling had said, *mirrors are strange.*

When I rose to my feet, it turned out that I was still a trifle unsteady from the stairs, and rocked sideways as I tried to rise. I flung out a hand for balance and felt a quick stab of pain. My breath huffed out into the stillness.

Another agave, one of the ones framed in needles, had caught the side of my hand and torn a shallow gouge in the skin. It smarted. I clamped it into my armpit, grumbling. The tiny spot of blood on the needle's tip practically glowed.

Oh well, if that's the worst that happens . . . Where to next? Surface, or dive deeper?

There was only one answer to that, of course.

The possibility that I might meet something dangerous, I put off my mind as much as possible. It might happen. I might die.

And I might have died the first time I dosed myself with arsenic to document the results or the first time I tested my chime-adder drug on myself. Discovery is rarely without risks.

Now on the ground floor, I took the short passage to my workroom. In the real world, these walls were textured plaster, which gave the mirror-walls here a look like concrete or oddly worked stone. It was less unsettling than the courtyard because it might conceivably have existed like this in the real world. I trailed my fingertips along the wall. Not ice-cold, but chill, like a wine cellar or a cave.

My workroom had no mirrors in it, only the faded blue sky visible through cracks in the shutters. It should have been nearly lightless, and yet I could still see everything clearly. Scand would have been beside himself with how light shouldn't behave that way. Saints, but I wished he were here. Not even because I expected him to have any insights, but because I wanted to share this discovery with someone. There's no point in discovering something amazing if you can't grab another person by the forearms and shake each other and yell, *Do you see that!?*

(Grayling didn't count. It's no fun if they just yawn and look bored.)

The rooster's cage was empty, except for a tail feather left on the floor. There was no chime-adder to shake its bells as it moved. Of course, there was no mirror for them to be caught in. The room seemed colder without them, even though I knew that neither one of them particularly cared if I existed. My glassware had become a graphite sculpture, leaving soft but complicated shadows behind it. I drew my fingertip down the curve of the big retort flask, wondering if it was properly hollow or solid all the way through. I wasn't going to break it to find out. Properly blown glassware is expensive. Not expensive like mirrors, but . . .

Glassware.

Wait.

I should have been looking at my reflection in the glass. Distorted, yes, a fish-eye view of my face that mostly meant looking up my own right nostril, but a reflection nonetheless.

Except that there wasn't one.

"It's not *any* reflection," I muttered to myself. "But why? What's the difference?"

The mirrors in my room were glass with a silver backing. If it wasn't the glass, was it the silver?

Where could I find something silver?

In an estate like Witherleaf, silver cutlery was usually kept in the serving pantry. I wasn't sure where that was, so I headed for the kitchen.

As soon as I opened the door, the creeping dread I'd been pushing down rose up and caught me by the throat.

The kitchen was empty, except that it wasn't.

There were no people in it, thankfully. But the tables were covered in knives and cutting boards heaped with gray lemons, the big stewpot hung over the gray logs, and a round splodge of gray dough rose like a mushroom on the side table.

Far more than anywhere else I'd been, this room looked as if the inhabitants had just put down everything they were holding and vanished into thin air.

"Well," I said hoarsely. "I'm probably lucky that the knives aren't levitating in midair." It seemed that gravity still worked, even if on the other side of the mirror, the utensils would all be in use, blades flashing as they chopped.

I went around the central table. My shoulder blades itched as if expecting a blow. Even though there weren't any human reflections standing here, I could almost feel the people around me, as I passed through them like a ghost.

I gave in to nerves and looked over my shoulder. Nothing moved. *See, nothing there.*

. . . Hang on.

There were two balls of dough now. And there were no more whole lemons, only neat halves arranged along the board.

The room *was* changing to match the real world, but apparently it took a while to catch up.

"Ha!" Another puzzle piece falling into place, and my enthusiasm eclipsed my dread again. As above, so below, apparently. (Not that *above* and *below* seemed like the right description, but *as real, so mirror* doesn't exactly roll off the tongue.) Things here matched the real world as well as they could, unless you deliberately manipulated something on this side.

There were two more doors a little farther down the hall. One was a regular pantry. Bins of potatoes and shelves of jars filled most of the available space. There was no way to tell what was in the jars, and I didn't feel like sampling to find out. I took a potato, though. If it turned strange and silvery, I could be absolutely certain that the apple really had come from here, and that it wasn't just a very peculiar variety.

There were no apples in the first pantry. Which said something, though I didn't know what.

The next door opened to the serving pantry. I picked up a pie server and turned it back and forth, but there was no reflection. So either the silverware wasn't real silver, or silver by itself wasn't enough to make an opening from the real world.

Maybe it was the specific combination of silver and glass. Or, depending on how many of Witherleaf's mirrors came from the queen's dowry, it might even be something unique to the mirrors from Silversand.

What bizarre alchemical concoction are they making *over there?*

I wanted to go outside and see how the wider world fared, so I retraced my steps and cut across the courtyard to the terrace. When I opened the door to the short entryway, I was greeted by unexpected spots of light on the wall.

What on earth . . . ?

They looked almost like the sort of dapples you see when sunlight filters through leaves. I reached out my hand, and the light crossed my fingers, bringing unexpected warmth with it.

I had to squint at the opposite wall for a moment. The lack of colors made the shape hard to read. A fish? Maybe? I remembered that there had been something on the wall when I'd come here before, a large piece of artwork. I'd barely glanced at it, scurrying after the king as I was.

It *was* a fish, I decided, a mosaic fish made of dozens of small tiles. I had no idea what the species was, if it was even meant to be a real animal and not, say, a stylized representation of Saint Trout. Most importantly, scattered among the ceramic tiles were chips of mirror the size of my thumbnail.

I stepped into the line of the tiny reflections, suddenly eager for the warmth. Then a thought occurred to me. I closed my eyes and touched a fingertip to one of the tiles. It tingled as it passed through the silver. I pulled it back, just in case someone was at the far end of the hallway. A disembodied finger was bound to cause comment.

So it's not just the one in my room.

I opened the door and stepped through onto the terrace. The sky overhead, however faded, was a welcome expanse of blue.

There was a mirror somewhere on the second floor of the villa that caught part of the gardens and woke them in a riot of color. The terrace itself was gray, with a gray table at the far end, gray chairs, gray tablecloth, gray cup, gray plate. Lady Sorrel's tea, missing only Lady Sorrel herself.

It was the sight of the tablecloth, oddly enough, that made me realize another thing that was missing. There was no *wind* here in the mirror-world. When I'd had tea with Sorrel and the king, a week and several lifetimes ago, there had been a breeze from the desert that stirred the cloth against my legs. It had smelled faintly of creosote and incipient heat.

No wind here. No smells either. The cloth hung in straight folds. Looking over the gardens to where they meshed with the desert, I saw the dark structural shapes of cactus and brush against the equally dark ground. Beyond that, blackness stretched to the horizon.

The sight was chilling. I rubbed my arms and decided that

maybe I'd done enough exploring for the moment. Next time I'd bring warmer clothes.

Besides, I had so many thoughts, and I wanted to write them down before I forgot something important.

I threaded my way back through the villa. My hand was on the cold nonmetal of the doorknob when I heard something behind me.

It was such a familiar sound that if the mirror-world around me had not been so silent, I probably wouldn't have even registered it. A door had closed somewhere in the upper gallery; that was all.

I thought it through, while my pulse spiked inconsiderately. If there was a mirror that faced a door, and someone had opened the door in the real world, then it would open here. If they closed it behind them, it would close here. Granted, I couldn't see any figures standing in the gallery, where they would have been frozen when the door cut off the reflection, but if they'd been going into a room, instead of out, I wouldn't.

Right. Entirely logical. Nothing to be worried about.

Saints, I have to write all this down.

My mirror-bedroom looked no different when I got back to it, and the maid hadn't been in, or if she had, her reflection was now caught in some other mirror. I closed my eyes and stepped through the giant mirror.

When I opened them, Javier was standing five feet away, looking utterly poleaxed, staring straight at me.

CHAPTER 16

The timing could not have been worse. He must have just been coming in the door, in the blind spot left by the mirror. An instant earlier and I'd have seen him, an instant later and he wouldn't have seen me.

If I had the brains that the saints gave an oyster, as my grandmother used to say, I would have been terrified. I would have remembered what the cat had said about being stoned as a witch. I would have immediately started laying the groundwork to convince Javier that he was seeing things, that it was a trick of the light.

But my body was still echoing with the wild enthusiasm of discovery, and when I opened my mouth, what came out was "Saints! Javier, you *have* to see this, it's *incredible!*"

I wouldn't have thought that he could look any more astounded, but he managed. His eyebrows practically touched his hairline. He said, very carefully, "Did you just come out of the mirror?"

"Yes," I said, nodding so vigorously that my hair flopped into my eyes. "There is something very, *very* strange going on with the mirrors here." I waved at it.

Javier took a cautious step forward, then finally looked away from me, to the mirror. "Is it some kind of hidden door?"

"Not exactly. Give me your hand." I reached out and caught his wrist. He resisted for only an instant, then let me take it. Either he trusted me, or he was too stunned to protest.

"Close your eyes," I said. His eyes flicked back to me, then he warily obeyed. I could feel the tension in his muscles as I knit our fingers together. His hand was warm and dry and hard with calluses. Mine was cold and sweaty, and I found a moment to be embarrassed by that, before I closed my eyes and put our hands into the mirror.

His bounced off the glass.

"Wait, *what*?" My eyes snapped open, which accidentally proved that opening my eyes didn't mean my fingers fell off. The side of my hand was inside the silver, tingling with cold, but Javier's knuckles lay against the mirror's surface. He opened his eyes, too, to see my hand submerged in the mirror as if it were water.

"What," he said, quite calmly, "in the *hell*."

"Oh, damn it," I said, pulling back out. "I can't bring you through." I knew that I could bring physical objects from the real world—I wasn't naked on the other side of the mirror, so my clothes obviously transferred—but apparently living things were different. "It's because of the apple. The one I ate yesterday. I tripped and fell into the mirror."

"You've lost your mind," Javier said, "or I have."

"No, no. Well, that's what I thought, too." It appeared that Grayling had been right, that *was* unoriginal.

"Am I dreaming? Or hallucinating?"

Fine, all right, the cat probably had a reason for being so snide. I decided not to mention Grayling right away. Javier was having a hard enough time without adding a talking cat to the mix. "No, I thought *that,* too, but this is real. It's really happening. The mirror is *weird*."

His throat worked as he swallowed. "Is this witchcraft, then?"

"I don't believe in witchcraft," I said primly. "There's always an explanation if you're willing to study it." I paused, then admitted, "I grant you, the explanation on this one is taking me a while."

He shot me a glance, quick and sharp as a pinprick, and I realized belatedly that the question had really been *are you a witch?* I didn't know if my answer had been correct or not. It was too late to turn back now, though. I was almost manic with the need to share my discovery.

Damn it, I have to get him through the mirror. Then he'll under-stand, I'm sure of it.

In order to pass through the mirror, I'd eaten a mirror-apple. Did it have to be the apple, though? Grayling had said something about feeding the rooster mirror-food, which might mean that any food would work, as long as it was from the other side.

"Here," I said, reaching into my pocket. "We can fix this, I think. You just have to eat this."

"You want me . . . to eat . . . a *raw potato*?"

"I suppose we could cook it," I said doubtfully. Heat destroys a lot of substances, but could it really destroy being from the other side of the mirror?

"It's a *potato*," he said again.

"It's a *mirror*-potato! Look!" Its passage through the glass had rendered it pale tan, not silver, but a strange iridescence still shimmered over its skin.

Javier took the tuber from me, with the expression of a man who had stormed the gates of heaven and discovered a public privy on the far side. "Are you sure about this?"

"Of course I'm sure. Who ever heard of an iridescent potato?"

He made a noise somewhere between a grunt and a sigh. "Okay, that's . . . fair. Somehow." He pulled out his belt knife and carved off a slice. The potato flesh was chalk white, just like the apple had been.

"Err—" A thought occurred to me. "There's a chance that if you eat it, you'll be sick tonight. Like I was. It passes, though? I had toast this morning."

"This has *got* to be a dream," Javier said, almost to himself. He popped the potato into his mouth and chewed.

"What does it taste like?" I asked, leaning forward.

An expression of bafflement crossed his face. "It tastes . . . *cold*."

"Yes! Exactly! Like mint or wintergreen, except not like that at all, right?"

"No. But also yes." He pinched the bridge of his nose as if warding off a headache. "And this is poisoned?"

"I don't think it's *actually* poisoned. I think it's just that the mirror-food doesn't combine well with real food. That's my current guess, anyway. I didn't get sick until I ate something, and then you saw what that was like last night." Another thought suddenly occurred to me. "Hang on, why are you in my room now?"

"I came to help with the letter," he said. "When you didn't answer the door, I was afraid that you'd taken ill again. I thought I'd just glance inside, and then you stepped out of the mirror."

"Right, the letter." I'd nearly forgotten. *In fairness, it's not like you haven't had some distractions.* "Thank you."

He grunted. I assumed the strategic word mines were starting to run low.

"Now close your eyes and let's see if this works."

It was probably a measure of how thoroughly confused Javier was that he let me take his hand and lead him to the mirror again. There was a very slight resistance as I pulled him through, as if the surface went briefly spongy, and then I was through and he was stumbling over the lip of the mirror after me.

I caught him before he could fall face-first onto the floor. He regained his footing, mumbling an automatic apology, and stared at the colorless walls. "What . . . ? *How* . . . ?"

To give Javier credit, he accepted things much more quickly than I had. I tried to explain everything I'd figured out about the gray, and by the time I reached the end, he was nodding slowly. Possibly, he was quicker on the uptake than I was, or maybe he was simply chalking the whole thing up to magic. I suppose it's easier to accept things if you don't know they're impossible.

"Isn't it *amazing*?" I said, when I'd run out of explanation. Then I giggled. It was a perfectly normal giggle for a scholar who's just discovered something fantastic, but it was a bit more maniacal than the average person was used to. I clamped my hand over my mouth and hoped he hadn't noticed.

Javier did the same back-and-forth prowl of the bedroom that I had, before finally going to the door. "Is it just this room?"

"Oh no. There's more. In fact, I think it might be the whole world." I could feel the giggle trying to start up again and squelched it firmly. "Open the door and look."

I crowded into the entryway behind him, so I was close enough to see his neck muscles tighten as he looked into the lightless hall. "That," he said, "is *not* right."

"Isn't it creepy?" I asked delightedly.

He looked at me over his shoulder. "You are far too excited about this."

"Well, *yeah*." I waved my hands wildly, probably conveying nothing except unfocused enthusiasm. "Nobody's ever discovered anything like this before. We're like explorers who suddenly found a new continent. Except most continents already have people on them, so even more so."

Javier frowned. "And there are no people here?"

"Ah . . . not exactly. Sometimes there are reflections of people, but it's not quite the same." I tried to explain about the reflections freezing in place, while his head tilted to one side like a confused dog.

He continued staring at me for some time after I finished, then finally said, "Are they dangerous?"

"I don't *think* so?" Remembering how my skin had crawled when confronted with the maid's reflection, I shrugged helplessly. "They don't seem to *do* anything."

Movement caught the corner of my eye. I had barely begun to turn when Javier put himself between me and whatever it was, one hand on his sword hilt, as reflexive as breathing.

A servant was coming out of a room two doors down. The hall was briefly splashed with light, then he turned and closed the door behind him. Three-quarters of the way through, he stopped, one hand still on the doorknob, and sagged in place, cut off from the mirror that animated him.

"There!" I said. "That's one."

Javier was braver than I was. He walked up to the reflection and studied it, peering into the gray face. Then, carefully, he reached out a fingertip and poked the servant in the shoulder.

I held my breath. Logically, nothing should happen. It wasn't a person, it was just that the mirror took a little while to catch up to reality. There wasn't a mind there to retaliate. Logically.

At that moment, caught between ebullience and terror, logic seemed like a very flimsy shield. If the reflection had suddenly woken, spoken, grabbed Javier's hand, bitten his face off, anything—well, I'd have been shocked, but not actually *surprised*.

Nothing happened. *Score one for logic.*

"And he will stay like this?" Javier said. "For how long?"

"I don't know," I admitted. "He'll disappear if he gets reflected somewhere else. I haven't watched one long enough to see if they fade away eventually. I don't know if the mirror just doesn't work fast enough to keep up with moving things or if there's something special about living things. Well, living animal–type things. Plants show up just fine, but that might just be because they're so much slower. Although—"

The servant winked out. There was nothing so dramatic as a flash of light, even though it felt like there should have been. *Maybe there was a flash of gray. Would we even be able to tell?*

Javier bit back a curse and took a step backward, as if teleportation might be contagious.

"I think that means he found another mirror," I said.

The lines around his mouth deepened. "Is it any mirror here, then?"

I shrugged helplessly. "I don't know. Every one I've seen so far? The maid told me a lot of them came from Silversand, so it may only be those specific mirrors. I haven't had a chance to really look at anything but the ones in my bedroom and privy. I'd feel weird walking into other people's rooms to look at their mirrors, even if it wasn't in the real world. It feels like spying."

"Can you step through any one of them?"

"I think so? I haven't been able to test it. I can put my fingers through smaller mirrors, and it seems likely that they're back in the real world, but I couldn't exactly fit my entire body through them."

His frown turned to a scowl. "If so, it would be an extraordinary tool for an assassin."

I blinked. "I hadn't thought of that."

He went back to the railing and leaned against it, looking down into the silent courtyard.

I joined him, the rail a cold bar across my elbows. "But isn't it amazing?"

Javier looked at me, then away, a smile ghosting across his lips. Even that lit up his face and made him briefly handsome. "Yes," he admitted. "It's pretty amazing."

I could feel myself beaming.

After a long moment, he asked, "Do you really think the whole world is in here? If we walked to Four Saints, would we find the whole city empty like this?"

Empty except for gray people clustered around the mirrors, I thought, but didn't say. "I think it's likely."

"Couldn't it just be this building?" I detected a plaintive note in his voice. As calm as Javier seemed, apparently the idea of an entire mirror-world was a lot to take in.

"Afraid not. I went outside earlier, and the desert's there."

"And it looks like . . . ?" He swept his arm in a broad arc, indicating the cold, gray galleries. "All of it?"

"Yeah. And there's the apple, too."

"Eh?"

"The apple had to come from somewhere. I didn't find any in the kitchen, so where did Snow get it?"

"Maybe one of the people in the king's retinue brought an apple here and she got hold of it somehow?" He shrugged. "If all mirror-food has the same effect, then it could have been anything, couldn't it? A mirror-sandwich would work just as well."

"Y-e-e-e-s . . ." I said slowly. He wasn't wrong, exactly, but I had a feeling there was more to it than that. Gut feelings aren't very scientific, but they're often the result of a lot of observations that you don't know that you're making, so I wasn't ready to discount mine entirely. Still, I didn't have any way to argue the point.

Javier lapsed back into brooding silence for a few moments, then seemed to come to some decision. "I'm on shift in half an hour," he said. "How can we find out if an assassin could come through any mirror in the villa?"

"Oh, that's easy," I said. "We'll test it in my washroom." I pushed open the door to my mirror-bedroom and waved in the direction of the washroom. "I'll go out into the real world. You put your hand through the mirror in there, and if it comes through, I'll see it, and we'll know it works."

He nodded. I stepped out of the silver and was slightly relieved to see that no one else had turned up in the interim. Explaining everything to Javier was draining, and he didn't seem nearly as thrilled by it as I was.

I heaved a sigh. *Nobody's ever excited by the right things,* I thought mournfully.

Javier's reflection was already in the washroom mirror. I turned and looked over my shoulder involuntarily, even though I knew he wouldn't be there. The reflex was just too strong. Like just this morning, when I had taken a bath and seen someone, and turned—

Except there wasn't anyone there that time. It was a trick of the light. Not everything you see out of the corner of your eye is real.

I stepped to one side so my mirror-self wouldn't be blocking the looking glass on the other side. If Javier had to jostle my gray shadow reflection out of the way in the mirror-world, I wasn't sure what would happen to me here. One experiment at a time.

He reached toward the mirror, and for a moment nothing happened. I pointed to my face and closed my eyes. I opened them again in time to see him close his eyes and push his hand forward.

His fingers emerged from the glass.

"It worked!" I said. I reached out and clasped his hand, giving it a quick squeeze.

His eyes snapped open again. An expression crossed his face for just a moment, but long enough for me to drop his hand as if I'd been burned.

Disgust. It had been pure, lip-curling disgust. He hid it quickly, pulling his hand back, but I'd seen enough. Through the mirror, Javier had looked like a man standing knee-deep in pig shit.

What the hell was that? I squeezed his hand, I didn't kiss it. It was friendly, that was all.

I mean, yes, fine, I had been excited to share the mirror-world with him. And sure, it's hard to stay stiff and professional with someone who has draped a bathrobe around you while you're sick and who immediately jumps between you and a perceived threat. And maybe I was secretly glad that it had been Javier who found me out, because he kept his mouth shut and, let's face it, wasn't bad looking. But I'd barely moved to the *oh, hmm, you're interesting, aren't you?* stage of attraction. I wasn't expecting him to fall to his knees and swear undying fealty to me. I would have been horribly embarrassed if he had. But he didn't need to look so revolted that I'd touched him.

Javier emerged from the main mirror a moment later. "It worked, then," he said.

I nodded coolly, not trusting myself to speak.

He was holding one hand up, palm cupped. "I found something odd on the floor," he said. "I think it may be from the real world."

Surprise loosened my voice. "Oh? What is it?"

"I'm not sure." He reached out and decanted the object into my hand. I made sure that our fingers didn't touch, and then I saw what it was and stopped thinking about that at all.

It was small and white, and I recognized it immediately.

It was a violet pastille.

I sat down on the bed with a thump. "Snow," I said numbly. "She's been here." My memory skittered through the last few days like an insect, before settling on the night that I'd sensed an intruder in the room and seen a pale figure watching me. And—shit—I'd even thought that their hair was pale, like Snow's, hadn't I? I'd blamed it on the moonlight, but the reason it had been that color was because it had been Snow all along.

Which meant, of course, that she'd seen my undignified tumble out of bed and the saints knew what else. She could have been watching me at any time. Hell, she'd been watching me for so long, at one point, that she'd actually brought a *snack*. She could even be—

Get a hold of yourself. She can't be there right now, because Javier was just in the mirror. Yes, all right, it's a little unsettling . . . a lot unsettling . . . to realize that a twelve-year-old has been staring at you at night, but there's no need to panic.

"Anja?"

I blinked up at him. "She's been watching me. She's been coming in here and watching me through the mirror."

Javier absorbed this information, then reached out and gripped my shoulder. Despite my earlier misgivings, the solidity of that grip reassured me. "We can fix this."

"Can we?"

I could cover the mirrors, but presumably anyone could just reach through and push the fabric aside. I'd either have to move to a room with no mirrors at all, which might not be all that easy in a house outfitted by the princess of a mirror-making kingdom, or sleep in my workroom.

Javier cocked his head, gazing into the distance while he thought. "You said that things you change in there stay changed, right? If you move something, it stays moved?" I nodded. "So if you lock a door, it should stay locked, correct?"

This was true. If I hadn't been too busy feeling mortified, I'd have realized it myself. "Of course. I'll just go lock the door. You're right, I'm just . . ." I put a hand to my face. My cheeks were hot. "It's. Um. Upsetting. To realize you've been spied on."

Javier nodded. He helped me through the mirror as courteously as if it were simply a high step, then watched while I closed the chamber door and locked it. "Hopefully that will stop her."

I grunted.

"She can only be coming through at night," he offered, as we returned to the real world. "During the day, she is surrounded by an army of maids."

This was true, and it raised the question of where she'd gotten the apple in the first place. I mentioned this to Javier, who shrugged. "Whoever it was could have simply left it inside the mirror in a place where she could pick it up, correct? If it was somewhere out of the way, perhaps around a corner, she would only have to reach a hand through."

"Right," I said. "They don't have to be left in the real world, do they?"

He grunted, then glanced toward the balcony. "It's getting late. I need to report for duty. You should stay out of the mirror until I can return."

"What? Why?"

"It could be dangerous."

I folded my arms, annoyed. "I've been in and out of it dozens of times since I found it." Which was an exaggeration, but close enough. "I know more about it than you do."

"It could still be dangerous."

"How? There aren't even any real people there. Except Snow, and I think I can take her."

"Snow and whoever is poisoning her."

I ran into his words like a kitten into a wall. Right. The poisoner. Them.

Until he'd said something, they hadn't been *real* in my head. They were a placeholder, an idea you read about, like the hypothetical patient who takes the hypothetical poison and suffers the hypothetical symptoms. I knew that someone must be getting the mirror-food to Snow, but since I knew nothing about them, I had filed them mentally into the same box. It hadn't occurred to me that they could be out and about in the mirror-world the same way that I was, and if they encountered me, they might have a very good reason to wish me harm.

". . . Huh," I said.

Javier had the decency not to look smug. "On the bright side," he said, "if we can catch sight of them in there, we'll know who it is."

I wasn't quite willing to yield all access to the mirror-world. "If I do go in, I'll stay in this room," I said.

He clearly wanted to argue the point, but then glanced at the balcony again—or rather, I suppose, at the position of the sun—and sighed. "Fine."

"Are you going to tell Aaron?"

"What? Saints, no!" He seemed startled by the suggestion. "I love Aaron like a brother, but he could no more keep a secret than he could fly. And the fewer people who know about this, the better. Now I really must go. I'll come back as soon as I'm off shift—no, damn it, that's at midnight. I'll come back tomorrow."

He gave me a very slight bow, and went off to report for whatever it was that bodyguards did when they didn't have a body to guard. And I stared at the pastille in my hand and thought about Snow watching me and shivered.

CHAPTER 17

In the end, I didn't go back into the mirror after all. Instead I draped a sheet over it and a towel over the one in the washroom. When the maid brought me a dinner tray, both she and her hair took a long look at the covering, then carefully ignored it.

I went to bed early, but even though I was exhausted, sleep eluded me. I kept opening my eyes, looking to see if the sheet had been moved aside. It hadn't, but that didn't stop me from checking.

When I wasn't worrying about being watched, I was brooding on the look that Javier had given me. There was no question that I'd mistaken it. His lip had actually curled back in disgust, and for a man who doled out his expressions the way a miser doled out coins, that said a lot.

It must have been the bit where he half carried me around while I was sweaty and limp and retching. This struck me as unfair. *I was hardly at my best, but it's not like I make a* habit *of poisoning myself.*

Well . . .

Okay, I do poison myself, but not all that often. Once or twice a year. Once a season at most. And he's never had to deal with it before. He's only seen me limp and retching the one time. (Sweaty, fine. We were in a desert, after all. But it's not like I don't wash regularly.)

Anyway, when he gave me that look, I was standing upright and hadn't vomited once. So there.

I rolled over, hugging a pillow against my chest. Fine. Maybe it was me. Or maybe he just didn't like women. I hadn't gotten that impression, but some people are subtle. (I hadn't realized that about Scand until after I'd fallen wildly and inappropriately in love with him at age fifteen. He immediately went to my father in stark terror, and then Father had explained to me about the birds and the bees and, more specifically, the bees who preferred the company of other bees. I was horribly embarrassed and hid in my room for a week, until a new shipment of books arrived and I got over it.)

Even if Javier preferred men, though, I'd just squeezed his hand to let him know it had come through. You'd have to *work* to read desire into that.

I was just about to start another round of pointless brooding when something landed on the bed with a soft thump.

I shot upright, ready to run. A quick glance at the mirror showed that the sheet was still over it, but they might have snuck through and put it back, and what if—

"Jumpy, aren't we?" said the cat.

My breath went out in a whoosh. "Oh. It's you."

"No need to sound quite so thrilled."

"Do you need something?"

"No."

"Then why are you here?"

"Your bed," Grayling said, with a pointed glance at the pillows, "is warm."

". . . ah."

He waited until I'd lain back down, then strolled up the length of the bed, examined my sleeping position, then pushed at my arm repeatedly with one paw until I'd moved it to his liking.

"You could just *tell* me what you want moved," I grumbled. His claws weren't all the way in, and the pinpricks itched.

"Too much talk before bed gives you ear mites," he informed me, and curled up in a ball practically in my armpit.

"Do humans even get ear mites?"

"Keep talking and you'll find out."

He was small and soft and very warm. I lay there, slightly uncomfortable, my neck crooked and my arm itching from his claws, and felt, despite everything, grudgingly privileged.

I fell asleep not long after he did, and I didn't even dream.

In the morning, with Javier presumably still asleep, I decided to pursue knowledge a different way. A way that would likely involve cream.

I didn't delude myself that one night spent snuggled up against my arm was going to change Grayling's behavior. I've known too many cats. Nevertheless, I had an idea.

When I was young, my father had tried to teach me the merchant's art of bargaining, and while it dealt largely with understanding people, which meant I took to it like a duck to arsenic, I did remember a few things. "Anja-bear," he said once, "there's a certain kind of person who needs to be smarter than you. It's mostly men, but I've known a few women like that, too. What you do is say something you know is wrong so that they can correct you. That makes them feel smug and in control of the situation." He'd winked at me. "*Then* you take them for everything they're worth."

It was possible that human psychology wouldn't work on a cat, but I suspected that this might. Cats all know they're smarter than you are, and they're smug as hell about it. (This is not to say that there aren't kind and loyal and humble cats out there. There probably are. I'm just saying that even the nicest cat in the world thinks it's funny when you fall down the stairs.)

I went down to my workroom, left the door open, and began washing the glasswork, a chore I'd been putting off because the very fine tubes require some time spent with a small wad of sponge soaked in alcohol, on the end of a bit of wire. About halfway through this process, the rooster made a hostile noise, and the cat landed on the table with a soft thump.

"Hello, Grayling," I said.

He rolled over on his back and wiggled invitingly. The fur on his underside looked as soft and fluffy as a storm cloud.

"Oh no," I said. "Don't even try it. I know it's a trap."

The cat tilted his head sideways, still upside down, and flicked his tail. "Trap?" he said, sounding affronted. "How is it a trap?"

"Because if I go to pet your belly, you disembowel my arm."

The single yellow eye narrowed. "Did I *ask* you to pet my belly? I'm quite certain I didn't."

"You rolled over and wiggled!"

"That," said the cat, rolling to his feet, "was an invitation to wrestle. You're misinterpreting it, then blaming me because I didn't go along with your misinterpretation. Typical." The tip of his tail continued to shiver. "If you think that a chime-adder ringing its tail is a sign of affection, whose fault is it when you get bitten?"

I stared at the ceiling for a moment, annoyed. The cat was right. Damn it. How embarrassing. "Sorry," I said, a bit gruffly. "You're right."

This seemed to mollify him. "Have you come to badger me with more questions, then?"

This was rich, given that *he'd* been the one to come into *my* workroom, but I didn't want to start off arguing. "No, no," I said. "I think I'm getting the hang of things."

"Are you, then?" he asked, in a tone that implied I was wandering naked in the desert without a map.

"I think so. Though the first time I saw someone's reflection just standing there, to one side of the mirror, it gave me a hell of a turn. Just that horrible mirror color all over." I went back to scrubbing the glassware, watching the cat out of the corner of my eye. "Though I suppose they bleed if you cut them, same as the rest of us."

"They do not," said Grayling. I noticed with some satisfaction that his tail had stopped twitching. "If you cut one, they'd be solid mirror-stuff all the way through."

"Really!" (I had been pretty sure this was the case, of course, after my test on the plant.) "So they aren't really alive, then?"

"Alive," said Grayling, "is complicated." He turned his paw over and inspected the burgundy pads. "What you ought to worry about is *awake*."

"Awake?" I started to ask what he meant, then remembered my father's advice. *Let him correct you.* "Those reflections didn't look like they were asleep."

"They were not asleep, but neither were they awake." Grayling nibbled at a claw. "You'll know if you meet a waking one."

"Will I?"

"Oh yes."

Without knowing more, I couldn't come up with a statement for him to correct, so I went directly for a question. "Are they dangerous, then?"

"Are humans dangerous?"

I snorted.

Grayling stretched, clearly amused. "There's your answer, then. I don't suppose you have any cream?"

"I don't suppose that I do. I could probably manage a bit of fish, though." I set the glass tube down in the sink where he probably couldn't knock it onto the floor. I suspected we'd come to the end of the discussion, but maybe I could get one more question in. "Do you have any idea why someone would be feeding mirror-food to a human child?"

Grayling inspected his paw again.

I put my hands on my hips.

The cat cocked his head in my direction and gave a small, piteous mew. "I'm sorry," he said. "I seem to be faint with hunger."

"Answer the question and I'll fix that."

"Ugh." He flicked his tail in annoyance. "I am not a dog performing for a treat."

"No, you're a heartless monster being bribed."

This seemed to please him, as I'd rather suspected it would. "You're certain that there's no cream?"

"The cook will make rugs out of both of our hides if I come asking for more." I reached out a hand toward him. He shoved his head nonchalantly under my fingers, and I scratched at the base of his ears, feeling the small round skull vibrate with a purr. Strange that a brain that size could hold something that talked and thought as well as a human. I really hoped that it was because he was a mirror-cat and that all cats weren't like this. It's one thing to know that your pets are judging you, but it's quite another to know that they're doing it on the same level a human might.

(I wondered if Grayling, being a mirror-cat, was made of the gray mirror-stuff himself. But the only way that I could test that would be to cut him, and I didn't see any way that would end well for either of us.)

"So why would someone feed mirror-food to Snow?"

The purr stuttered briefly. "Those who eat mirror-food gain some . . . abilities. You've seen them yourself."

"The ability to go in and out of the mirror?"

"Among others."

Others? I racked my brain, trying to think of another ability.

Grayling pulled back from my fingers. "So hungry . . ." he said, and gave another piteous mew.

I rolled my eyes. "Fine. Wait here."

I took myself off to the kitchen, where the cook parted cheerfully enough with a bit of fish. It was brought in from the coast in a light brine to keep it fresh for three days of travel. I watched her quick hands slice off a piece, remembering the strangely empty kitchen on the other side of the mirror, imagining what I'd see if I were standing there now. The fish, first whole, then sliced into bits. If I moved a piece of it, it would stay moved on the other side. She used the side of her knife to sweep the cut pieces onto a small plate. *Now, if I had turned one of the pieces sideways, say, but it was still in the path of the knife, would it go onto the plate?* I suspected that it would, but I wasn't sure. If I returned the potato that Javier had eaten part of, it wouldn't just hover in midair as the rest of the potatoes were taken away around it.

An idea struck me, as I pictured the potato. *Those who eat mirror-food gain some abilities. You've seen it yourself.*

And I had told him about the book, how it had fallen to dust in my hands . . .

"Grayling!" I called, bursting into the workroom. "Is one of the powers taking things *out* of the mirror-world?"

"Hmmm," said the cat. "For a human, you're not *completely* hopeless." He eyed the saucer full of fish. "If you expect me to stand up and beg, though, I shall revise my opinion."

"No, no." I set the dish down on the table, and he sniffed haughtily at the fish, as if he weren't going to fall on it and devour it. "But that doesn't make sense! If you can get into the mirror and get mirror-food, why not just bring things out yourself? Why use Snow?"

"Why, indeed," muttered the cat, face-first in the fish.

I leaned against the table, thinking. "It must be something that Snow could get at that they can't. Like . . . um . . ." I racked my brain. "Maybe they want Snow to steal something for them? The crown jewels?"

Grayling snorted into his fish.

"Okay, probably not the crown jewels. Do we even *have* crown jewels? But maybe something like that?" I tried to picture a situation where Snow specifically being able to bring something out of the mirror would be important. All I could think of was Javier talking about assassins. If she pulled a dagger out of a mirror at a critical moment . . .

I listened to the tinny rasp of the cat's tongue against the saucer. "Could they be hoping to use Snow to *kill* someone?"

The rasp paused for a moment.

"It's something *like* that, isn't it?"

Grayling finished licking the saucer for any stray memories of fish, then checked his whiskers over for the same thing.

"Grayling?"

"Mmm?"

"If Snow is going to murder someone, you have to tell me."

He gave me a look somewhere between pity and contempt. "In fact, I do not. I never have to speak to you again if I don't wish to."

It was hard to imagine that this was the same animal who had snuggled up under my arm and purred. "But we're talking about people's *lives*! Saints, what if she killed the *king*?"

"A man who has never, to my knowledge, fed me." He hopped down from the table, then paused and gave me a wry look. "Don't fluster yourself so. Your human princess is not going to go stabbing people anytime soon. Unlike her mother."

He sauntered out. I stared down at my basin of glassware, my mind awhirl. *Was* Snow being set up as an unlikely assassin? Did the cat actually know something, or was he just enjoying toying with me in between free meals?

For that matter, was Grayling actually a cat? He acted like one, but cats don't talk and they certainly don't talk in your head. I had mostly managed to shove that to one side, figuring that as I came to understand the mirror-world, I'd understand the mirror-cat as well, but that hadn't happened yet.

"Saints," I muttered. "Maybe it really *is* magic."

Even saying that made me feel dirty. I picked up the sponge and jabbed it into a tube again, watching the built-up grime scrape away from the sides. When it was finally clean and I held it up to the light, I discovered that a gray cat hair had somehow gotten wedged inside.

Javier found me in the workroom, milking the chime-adder's venom.

"Please don't get too close," I said calmly. At home, I locked the door to my workroom when I did this, but there was no lock on the inside of the door here.

Javier froze. I couldn't take my eyes off the snake long enough to see his expression, but if it was anything like other people I knew, it registered horror, then confusion, then reluctant fascination, usually in that order.

The chime-adder, who had her fangs embedded in a piece of cloth, was mostly registering annoyance, judging by the angry carillon of bells. I held a polished wood stick against the roof of her mouth, pushing gently against the fangs while venom ran down and dripped into the funnel I'd positioned below. (Well, most of it got into the funnel, anyway. There's always a little that ends up on your hands or the cloth or the tabletop, because liquids are like that.)

"Is that . . . ? Are you . . . ?" Javier stopped and tried again. "Is that *poison*?"

"Yep." (Like I said, there is really no point in being pedantic about venom versus poison in practice.) "I do this once a month or so."

"Isn't that dangerous?"

"Oh no, it doesn't hurt her at all. She just doesn't like having her head held. I mean, who would, really?"

"I meant for *you*," said Javier. I didn't have to see his expression—I could hear it in his voice.

"Oh. Yes, but I'm good at it."

"I see."

I finished with the snake, unhooked her from the cloth, and put her back in her cage, dropping the lid on quickly. "There you go, sweetheart. There'll be a nice mouse for you in a day or two."

Javier's face was a study in baffled stoicism. He shook his head slowly while I sealed up the tube of venom, which was already starting to crystallize in the air. "How deadly is that there?"

"This?" I held up the tube. "You could drink it and be perfectly safe, so long as you don't have an ulcer. A needle dipped into it and inserted into your flesh would give you some nasty swelling around the site—and it would hurt like the devil—but it certainly won't kill a healthy individual. As much venom as is in this tube . . ." I held it up and did some quick calculations in my head. "If you could inject it the way that the chime-adders do, it'd kill two, maybe three people. By pouring it into a fresh wound, I expect you could kill one person, or at least give them the worst day of their lives."

His eyebrows were going up.

"Don't worry," I said hastily, putting the tube away, "the adult snakes rarely pour all their venom into a bite. It's not worth it when it takes so long to produce."

"Good to know," he said faintly, as I washed my hands.

"How are you feeling?" I asked. He was standing upright and not retching or moaning the way that I had after eating the mirror-apple, but since guards are presumably trained to stand upright without retching, I couldn't be sure.

"A little queasy," he admitted. "I skipped dinner. And breakfast. I'm running on tea at the moment."

"That should pass soon." I'd tackled my breakfast with great enthusiasm, and the rooster was eating normally as well. "So . . ."

"So."

"Now what?"

Javier rubbed the back of his neck. "We need to write the letter to the king," he said. "Then I'd like to go through the mirror and walk the perimeter of the villa. Maybe it doesn't actually extend all that far."

"Sure," I said. "And if it does go as far as the rest of the world?"

"Then I suppose we'll deal with that. If assassins can come out of mirrors, no one here may be safe."

"Assuming that the assassins *know* about the mirrors. I can't imagine many people do. Someone would have written a paper about it by now."

He gave me a look. I gave it right back. Eventually Javier sighed, and his shoulders slumped a little. "I could barely sleep," he admitted, "thinking of all the terrible things that someone could use this power for. You could bring an entire invasion force straight into the heart of someone's city, unless they had an army stationed on both sides of the mirror. This could change the entire world."

"Only if the world finds out about it," I said, determined to stay cheerful. "And it's not like crossing the mountains gets any easier inside the mirror."

"Crossing the desert does, though," he said gloomily. "If it doesn't get hot there, you'd need so much less water. You could just set up mirrors at each watering hole."

"They'd have to be awfully big mirrors, if you're planning on getting an army through."

"There's that." He brightened a little. "I've never seen mirrors any bigger than the ones here, and a horse probably wouldn't fit through these."

"And feeding them the mirror-food would be dicey." Horses can't vomit any more than chickens can, and their digestion is so fragile that I'm sometimes amazed they don't catch fire and explode.

"Right." Javier nodded. "Letter, then let's check the mirror. If nothing else, if our poisoner is using the mirrors to get around unseen, they may have left some sign."

Javier proved skilled at letter writing, by which I mean that he crossed out most of what I'd written. "You're making a report," he said, "not trying to impress a courtier. I've reported to King Randolph before."

The final letter simply read:

> *Your Majesty—*
>   *Discovered the poison. Trying to track down the delivery method. Will write as soon as I know more.*
>   *—Healer Anja*

"Really?" I said, looking down at the message, which was so terse as to border on rude.

"Trust me," said Javier, already heating up the sealing wax.

I do trust him, I thought, as I sealed the letter. Even if I was still somewhat offended by the look he'd given me earlier, I didn't think for a moment that he was going to denounce me as a witch. And I had no reason to doubt his skill or dedication as a bodyguard either.

Granted, the fact that he could also pass into the mirror meant that he'd probably wind up on the pyre next to me, which didn't hurt.

He checked his weapons and nodded to me. Then we both stepped into the silver.

CHAPTER 18

The mirror-door was still locked, which made me feel slightly better about things. Granted there was nothing I could do about the balcony, but I couldn't see Snow managing the acrobatics required to get up there.

We headed outside to the gardens. "I'd like to check the place where I found Snow with the apple," I said. Javier grunted. I wondered how many words he was allotted a week and whether he had been going into a deficit with all the talking I'd been demanding.

A sharp dividing line of color ran down the middle of the gardens. I wondered whose mirror was causing it. A bedroom on the second floor, as far as I could tell. Maybe it was Snow's. Regardless, it threw a wedge of light a long way across the world.

As we approached the boundary, I saw something odd about the garden path. It looked like there was a small gray rise, maybe three inches tall, at the edge of the reflection. *Is that a threshold? That's not there in the real world . . .*

Then we got closer, and I stopped so abruptly that Javier ran into my shoulder.

"Oh, *yuck,*" I said.

It was made of insects. Drifted up against the edge like sand, their reflections had flown or crawled out of the gaze of the mirror and then stopped. I saw beetles and moths, crane flies and mosquitoes, butterflies with scalloped wings, all of them jumbled together in a chitinous pile of gray.

(I'm not afraid of bugs, let me be clear. I have administered both scorpion and centipede venom to myself to document the effects. I have even worked through my fear of spiders. But the effect of the whole pile, lying motionless, was both unnerving and sad.)

Javier took his belt knife and hooked it under the curved tail of a hairy desert scorpion, lifting it up. It dangled there like a strange piece of jewelry, apparently dead.

No, not dead. Not awake, according to Grayling. Whatever that means.

They were densest on the path, probably because the flying insects used the gap between trees, but there were bodies all along the mirror edge. Not just insects either. I saw a swallow belly down on the ground, wings outstretched, tail a sharp scissor shape against the dirt. The area nearest the flowering sage was littered with frozen hummingbirds.

Even knowing that they weren't dead, that they were just mirror-stuff, not real birds, I still found it a tragic sight. I reached down and picked one up. What would happen if I stepped into the light? Would it come alive for a brief moment and take flight from my hand?

I stretched my hand out into the beam of light, and the hummingbird turned brilliant. Green feathers bloomed along its back, and its head lit up with a hundred shades of iridescent pink. I almost gasped at the sight.

But that was all that happened. It still lay limply in my hand, the sharp needle of its beak stretched out across my palm. I carefully folded down its wings, but it didn't react, or move, or breathe.

Of course. It's just a reflection without its creator. It can't do anything on its own. Except . . . I'd brought the book through the mirror, hadn't I? And it had been a real book on the real side, at least for a few minutes. Would the hummingbird be real, too?

I took out a handkerchief and wrapped it carefully before putting it in my pocket. I had to know. Purely scientific curiosity, I told myself. It had nothing to do with how sad the stiff little reflections were, how cold and gray when they should be living jewels.

And there are just so many of them.

I forced myself to think objectively. Of course there'd be a great many of them. How often would insects wander into a reflection out in the desert? In fact, given that the mirrors had been installed at least thirteen years ago, when the king had brought his bride to Witherleaf for her honeymoon, that meant . . .

"They dissolve eventually," I said out loud. "They *must*. This proves it."

Javier looked from his scorpion to me and back again. "You're going to have to explain that one to me."

"Look. There's a couple of inches of insects here, right? But how many insects fly through here every day? Their bodies would drop right here. This is, what, a week's worth of accumulation? Maybe less? Do you know how many bugs there are in the desert?"

"I suspect you're going to tell me."

"A *lot*." I nodded my head furiously, hoping to somehow impress the sheer quantity on him. "*So* many. This might only be one night's worth. But the mirrors have been here for years, right? So there should be . . . I don't know . . . drifts of dead bugs as high as your head."

". . . Vivid," he said, setting down his scorpion.

"So that means that the reflections should eventually disintegrate!" I beamed at him.

"That's good?" asked Javier.

"Well, if you don't like the thought of dead people standing around mirrors for all eternity."

He went a little green. I gave him a moment to recover himself, then stepped over the line of color.

There was nothing much of interest in the gardens, other than the unsettling drift of insects. The little pocket garden where I had found Snow had a line of mirrored tiles behind the statue of the woman, which split around her into two fans of color. They were about five inches on a side, but so subtly placed that I hadn't noticed them in the real world. I wondered how many other mirrors were hidden around the villa. I might have passed one a dozen times a day and never even noticed.

Javier studied the area closely, looking for signs that someone had been here recently, but if they had, they had not been accommodating enough to leave any tracks.

"The apple was probably tucked up behind the statue," I said. "No one would have noticed it there, and she could have just reached through and picked it up."

"We could break the mirrors," Javier suggested. "But that will almost certainly put the poisoner on their guard."

He looked at me expectantly, and I realized that I was supposed to decide. *Me? Why? I distill things and dose people with charcoal, I don't run spy campaigns.* But of course Javier was my bodyguard, and by some bizarre alchemy, having a bodyguard meant that you were nominally in charge of them, as long as you didn't try to send them away.

"I have no idea what we should do," I said. "I've never done anything like this before."

Oddly, that didn't seem to bother him. He nodded. "You can't unbreak a mirror," he said. "We'll leave it for now and do it later if we must."

I nodded. There was an ache in my chest, and I didn't know why. It felt a little like fear.

We left the garden and continued on our circuit of the villa. Off to the left, I could just make out the barn that held the non-cream-producing cattle. It occurred to me that if I went down the road to the barn, all the stalls would be empty.

Unless there are cow reflections left standing around. But how often do cows encounter a mirror?

Javier passed with little more than a glance. "Too many people coming and going," he said, when I looked at him askance. "You'd be gambling that no one would ever have a mirror on them when they went out to the stables and that they wouldn't happen to notice that the reflections didn't match up. It's possible, and we can check it later, but *I* wouldn't do it."

"Where would you hide out?" I asked, slightly amused. "If you were a diabolical poisoner."

"If I had a base of operations on this side, I would want it to be somewhere that no one would wander through on accident. So either concealed outside or in a private room inside."

"I'd think inside would be more likely," I said, as we resumed trudging around the perimeter.

"It is, but I want to rule this out before we go opening random doors."

We kept going. There was a low embankment on the southeast side of the villa, where the ground had been leveled before building. I followed Javier up, watching my footing. Mirror-stones turned as easily underfoot as real ones.

"What the hell is *that*?" Javier stopped so abruptly that I nearly ran into his back.

"What? What are you . . ." My voice dried up. One more step up the embankment and I saw what he saw.

A few years ago, my father had gone out to inspect a quarry that someone was trying to sell him, and I'd gone with him. Five or six miles out of town, there was a small city of tents, and then a vast crater hewn out of the earth, hundreds of yards across, with a single road spiraling down into the pit. I remember standing on the quarry's edge and thinking how strange it was, how obviously man-made, not like canyon walls at all.

The pit at our feet was not as wide as the quarry had been, but much deeper. The desert simply fell away into steep walls that went down and down for . . . well, for a long way. The mirror-walls might have been stone, but they were the same featureless gray as everything else, and I didn't trust my ability to distinguish depth. I definitely wasn't going to jump in, anyway.

My first thought was that I couldn't possibly have missed something this size. My second was that I hadn't looked out any windows on this side of the villa, so why would I have seen it at all?

"I take it this isn't here in the real world?" I asked.

"It is not."

"Ah."

The pit was roughly circular, and I thought it was about a hundred feet across. There was no spiral road, but nevertheless, I couldn't shake the memory of the quarry. "Someone had to make this," I said. "Otherwise it would have just filled back in to match the real world. I think." I started to lean out over it, and Javier's arm was in front of me like a bar.

"Please don't do that."

"I'm not going to fall in."

He closed his eyes briefly. "Please. For my nerves."

"Well. If it's for your nerves . . ." I stepped back.

We slowly skirted the edge of the pit. It was farther around than I'd expected. The ground was solid underfoot, but I nudged a small stone toward the lip. It rattled against the wall as it fell, skittering downward, but the muffling silence of the mirror-world meant that we couldn't hear it hit the bottom.

I saw what looked like scratch marks cut into the walls, though it was so hard to tell in that unrelieved gray. Quarry marks, maybe?

"There are holes in the sides," Javier said, pointing. I followed his gaze and realized that he was right. What I'd written off as un-evenness in the stone were actually openings. Caves? Tunnels? It was impossible to tell how far back they went. I picked up another pebble and tried to toss it into one, but the angle was completely wrong, and while I might be able to get an arrow across the pit, I certainly couldn't throw a stone that far.

"Perhaps we don't want to throw rocks into the mysterious hole in the unnatural mirror-world?" said Javier.

"More nerves?"

"They're a trifle unsteady today."

"Can't imagine why."

We stared into the pit some more. It did not suddenly begin to make sense. I had the feeling that we were both hoping the other one would suggest some course of action other than staring into the hole. Neither of us did.

"Well?" I said finally.

Javier grunted.

"Do you think our poisoner dug this?" Once I said it aloud, it sounded laughable.

"An army would take weeks to dig that," Javier said. "And they don't have an army. I hope."

I scanned the desert, as if an army might have been camped next door, and we'd simply overlooked it. Nothing materialized. Toward the villa, I could see the palo verde trees that lined the approach. The trunks should have been smooth and green. I looked down at myself just to see colors. The tan robes that Isobel had mocked as drab seemed as vivid as a sunset.

"This place could drive you mad if you let it," I said.

He looked toward me, clearly surprised. (Not nearly as surprised as I was, to be honest.) "What happened to 'isn't this amazing'?"

"It's taking a beating," I admitted. "If it weren't for the poisoner, I'd still be excited. But here is this astounding new world, and instead of being able to take the time to study it and figure out the rules, we're fighting against someone who's poisoning a child to get what they want. Whatever the hell *that* is." I pulled my robes more tightly around myself against the cold.

Javier was silent for a moment, then reached out and gripped my shoulder briefly, the same way Aaron had when I'd lost the lotus-smoke patient at the temple. "I'm sorry. It must feel like something important has been taken from you."

He was right. It felt exactly like that, and I somehow hadn't realized it until he said something. This ache in my chest was *loss*. I felt a prickle at my eyelids and squelched it ruthlessly. "It's fine," I said, when I was sure that my voice would come out steady. "I'm sure the first person who discovered the ocean was upset when he learned about sharks, too."

"Well, we're not getting closer to catching our shark standing here looking at this hole," Javier said. He helped me down from the embankment when the rocks slid under my sandals. "Let's go back and figure out what to do next."

There were several newly frozen servants in the hall as we made our way back to my rooms. We both gave them a wide berth. You couldn't tell if their eyes were open or closed until you were so close that you could make out the line of gray eyelid on gray eye. It made it feel as if we were being watched, even though I knew we weren't.

"When this is over," I remarked, "I'm going to make sure there's not a single life-sized sculpture anywhere on my father's estates. I may lobby to have them removed from the city, in fact."

"You'll have my support," Javier said, opening the door. He went through first, looking around, then pronounced it clear. I wondered idly what he'd do if he found Snow lurking inside.

The mirror was also clear. Javier went through, then nodded to me. I stepped through and . . .

Something snatched at my back. For a moment it felt like a hand grabbing my robes, and I smothered a cry, stumbling forward. The fabric pulled taut around my legs.

Javier was already at my side. "You're hung up on something." He put his face and shoulder into the mirror, and I felt a different tug, then he withdrew, looking baffled. "You're *not* hung up on something. You'd better take a look."

I told my racing heart to settle down and turned back myself. The cause of his bafflement became clear. Part of my robes were just . . . stuck? They hit the surface of the mirror and went no farther. I grabbed a handful of fabric and pulled until it became clear that I would tear it before it would go through the silver.

Is the apple wearing off? No, of course not, my clothes didn't eat the apple. This isn't even the same set I was wearing.

. . . Wait, is there something in my pocket?

I had to step backward through the mirror to get everything disentangled, then dipped my hand into my pocket and pulled out a handkerchief-wrapped bundle. For a moment I couldn't think what it was, then I remembered the hummingbird. I unwrapped it carefully, afraid that trying to pull it through had damaged the delicate lace of its bones. It looked unharmed, but it still lay limp and lifeless in my hands. I put it against the silver, and it was exactly like when I'd tried to bring Javier through before he ate mirror-food. My fingers went through, the bird did not. It would be crushed to paste against the glass rather than cross over.

"But you can take things *out*," I said, baffled. "It's going *into* the mirror that's the problem, isn't it? I brought a book through before. And the potato."

"The bird's alive," Javier suggested, joining me on the far side of the mirror.

"So are potatoes. You can plant them and grow another potato. And even the apples have seeds that are alive."

Javier lifted his hands in a helpless shrug. "Maybe they're a different kind of alive?"

I tried to pass the hummingbird through the silver again, and then again. There was a strange tension to it somehow. I had the irrational feeling that I was doing it wrong, that if I somehow pushed the correct way, the tiny body would go through the glass. I pressed, leaning forward, shifted a little to one side, following that tension . . . just a little closer . . .

Suddenly it was as if I were trying to hold something heavy at the fullest extension of my arm. That fragile body, which weighed no more than a breath, felt a hundred times denser than lead. My muscles began to tremble with the strain of holding it, but I kept pushing, feeling as if something were being *drawn* up out of me, not just energy but something real and physical. I could feel it sliding out of my body. If I had looked down and seen myself gutted and my intestines dragged painlessly through the mirror, I would have been horrified but not surprised.

"Anja?"

Sweat popped out on my forehead, but it was *working*, I was sure it was working, the mirror was thinning, more like glue than glass now, and if I just . . . kept . . . pushing . . .

"Anja!"

Strong arms locked around me, and Javier pulled me away from the mirror. I tried to struggle, but my muscles wouldn't obey. I felt as limp and drained as if I'd been running.

"What were you *doing*?" Javier looked utterly horrified. "Whatever it was, don't do that again!"

I blinked up at him. I kept getting hugs that didn't count. This one *definitely* didn't since he seemed to be holding me up. I locked my fingers on the edge of his coat, trying not to fall. My head throbbed. "What happened?" I asked. "I was trying to push the bird through, and then . . . I thought if I could just do it the *right* way, it would work, but it was so hard . . ."

"You started to turn gray." His face was only a few inches away, brown eyes searching my face with alarm. I could see the line between his eyes, gone deeper with concern.

Concern? About me?

Don't read too much into it. He's your bodyguard, that's all. If you die, it'll be a professional failure.

But he was so very close. If someone walked in, it would look like we were about to kiss, if they didn't know I felt so dreadful, and that apparently he was disgusted by me.

Okay, kissing was probably out of the question.

"I do feel woozy," I admitted.

"*No*," he said, with some force. "I mean you were turning gray *like the mirror*."

I stared up at him, no longer thinking about kissing at all. "*What?*"

He shook his head. "Come on. I want to get you out of here."

I left the hummingbird on my desk, out of the way, but where there was still a tiny bit of reflection to keep it colorful. Getting through the mirror together was difficult, but only because it wasn't wide enough to fit two humans. I slid through the silver as easily as ever.

Once we were out, I sat down on the bed, winded just from the walk. Javier grabbed my hands and turned them over, peering at them as intensely as a palm reader. "No gray," he said, even though

I could see it for myself. "Your hands went first." He looked at me, his brow furrowed, and I think he would have ordered me to strip if he could. Which was either tragic or hilarious, when you got down to it.

"I'll check later," I promised. "I think I need to lie down."

"I don't want you to be here alone. What if it starts to happen again?"

"What would you be able to do if it does?" I pointed out, quite reasonably.

The intensity of his scowl surprised me. His face fell quite naturally into it, the lines bracketing his mouth deepening into canyons. I wondered what his life had been like in the palace guard, to cause such lines.

"I have no idea," he admitted. "Damn. I hate it when you're right."

"Sorry." I flopped on my back across the bed. "I just really need a nap. Right now."

I remember him taking my sandals off and me muttering some kind of thanks, and then I was dead to all the world.

When I woke up, the sun had begun to sink. I sat up in bed, my head pounding. My mouth felt as dry as the desert outside.

"Saints. I feel hungover," I muttered, scrubbing at my face. I'd slept in my clothes, which didn't help.

"You look hungover," Javier said mercilessly. "Drink some water." He handed me a mug. The water was tepid, but slid down my throat like silk.

"Thank you. Wait . . . what are you doing here?" I squinted at him over the rim. "I thought you were leaving."

"I didn't. Obviously."

"Aren't you supposed to be on guard duty?"

"I'm your guard. This is my duty. The captain's been informed." He snorted. "The nightly patrols here are basically to justify the expense of having guards and to keep any of them from getting too drunk on shift. Well, and to watch for fires."

"Oh." I drank more water. My eyes felt gritty. (That's caused by your tears evaporating while you sleep, incidentally. Tears are salty, so when your eyes dry out, tiny salt crystals get left behind. Bodies are so marvelously revolting.)

"Should I send for some dinner?" Javier asked.

"*Saints,* no." The thought of food was appalling. This really was exactly like a hangover.

I felt human enough to get to the privy, then went to the washroom. A little water splashed on my face revived me about as much as I was going to be revived. The face in the mirror looked better than it had the night I'd eaten the apple, but there were bodies pulled out of rivers that looked better than that, so that wasn't saying much.

My braid was a dead loss. You could only call it a braid because there was no reason I'd have three angry snakes in a mating ball on the back of my head. I pulled out the ribbon and sat down on the bed, combing through it with my fingers.

"So what do we do now?" I asked.

Javier grimaced. "I was about to ask you that."

"You're the expert military person."

"My military days are long behind me. Being a palace guard is just a lot of standing around." He folded his arms, obviously deep in thought. I gazed out the balcony doors at the sky, pretending to also be thinking, but mostly just admiring the sunset. There's a saying about *red sky at night, shepherd's delight,* but it doesn't really work here, since the sunsets are almost always red. I suppose if there were a storm, you wouldn't see the red, though.

"Have you tried confronting Snow?" Javier asked.

"Kings' daughters get the same sunsets as the rest of us," I informed him.

"What in the name of Saint Sheep's sullen eyeballs are you talking about?"

"I . . ." I put a hand to my forehead. "I think I'm more tired than I thought, actually. Never mind. Confront Snow how?"

"Tell her you know about the mirror and the apples," Javier said. "If you're interrogating someone, showing them that you already know something about it makes them more likely to let something drop. They don't want to be caught in a lie."

"Interrogating someone? I thought you said that your job was just standing around."

"Sometimes I stood around interrogation rooms. The point still stands."

"Right." I went back to work re-braiding my hair. "So I tell Snow I know about the mirror and apples and hope she mentions the name of the person who's doing this." I grimaced. "I do not like plans that rely on my skill at verbal manipulation."

"They're not going to let *me* talk to her," Javier pointed out. "Being the healer's bodyguard does not convey the same authority as being the healer."

I groaned. He was right. I didn't like that he was right, but the world had a bad habit of not taking my likes and dislikes into account. "Right. I'll do that. Tomorrow."

I realized at that point that my braid was badly off-center, muttered to myself, and unbraided it. I had only just started again when Javier sighed and said, "May I?"

"Sure," I said, with absolutely no idea what he was talking about. He stood up and patted the seat of the chair. I sat down in it, still confused, and he picked up the mass of my hair and began to braid it.

Oh.

Oh, that was *nice*.

I'd never had a man braid my hair before. He wasn't running his fingers through it in an erotic fashion or anything—he was, if anything, ruthlessly competent as he scraped it back—but I could feel my scalp tingling in a way that made my toes curl.

Oh Saints, I do not need another fetish right now. I particularly did not need one centered on a man who had looked at me like I was a piece of salmon left out in the sun for too long.

I was a little surprised he was even willing to touch me, given that, but it was possible that competence had overridden disgust. *I should not be aroused by a man who is disgusted by me.* I told my sanguine humors this. They laughed at me.

I tried to distract myself by talking. "Thirty-five years old, and I still haven't mastered braiding my own hair."

He grunted.

I carried on. "You're good at this."

"Two younger sisters."

"Ah. I didn't know that."

"No reason you should."

"Still. You know all about my family."

"I'm a bodyguard. It's part of my job."

"Yes, but you're more than a bodyguard now. You're my . . . err . . ." I tried to think of the appropriate term. Fortunately his fingers were away from my scalp now, plaiting the hair, and coherent thought had gotten a bit easier. "Partner in crime?"

He grunted again.

"Co-conspirator?" Grunt. "Fellow victim of circumstance?"

Javier sighed, patted my shoulder as if I were a horse whose mane he'd braided, and stepped back. "That ought to hold for a bit."

"Thank you." I ran my hand down it. It was much better than my attempts had been, and all it had cost me was a deeply inconvenient and misplaced arousal. I made another attempt to distract myself. "So we've both got younger sisters, then."

"Seems that way." I thought for a moment that he was done, but then he added, "And a younger brother. I was the oldest."

"Me too. Though I never braided my sisters' hair. Our mother did Isobel's, and Catherine used to shriek when anyone waved a hairbrush in her general direction."

"My mother died when I was seven."

"This is why I don't make small talk," I muttered, half to myself. Javier snorted. "I'm sorry," I said.

"It's fine. That was a very long time ago. But that's why I learned to braid hair."

I wondered if it was also why he'd joined the military, to send money back home. I did not think this was a good time to ask. "Thank you," I said, touching the tight weave of my hair.

Javier frowned. "Do you think you'll be okay?"

"I'm fine. I feel like hell, but I'm fine." (Also, there still wasn't a damn thing he could do if I wasn't, but that would probably only lead to more discussion.) I got to my feet.

Javier gave me a brooding look. An actual brooding look, not the dramatic reflecting-on-personal-woe-to-be-interesting kind. That one only looks good on poets. This one made him look thoughtful and a little stern and altogether too handsome for a man in my bedroom whom I couldn't do a damn thing about. "I'll check on you tomorrow," he said, as I opened the door to let him out.

"I'll try not to be dead," I promised him, and closed the door.

CHAPTER 19

In the morning, I was not dead. In fact, I woke up at dawn, probably because I'd slept for half the day yesterday. There was a furry weight against my back. "Grayling?" I asked.

"No, it's one of the other cats."

"I haven't *seen* any other cats."

"They're down in the stables, catching mice." He sat up and yawned. "Why are you awake at this hour? I thought you were a sensible sort of human."

I told him about my experiment trying to bring the bird through the mirror. He was unimpressed. "What did you expect would happen? Living things are hard."

"Potatoes are alive."

There are few things in life more disdainful than a one-eyed cat. I could actually feel my hair withering under the force of his stare. "*Potatoes,*" he said at last, "do not make *gods.*"

I was not expecting this argument and so responded with an articulate "huh?"

Grayling leaped off the bed and stalked into the mirror, tail twitching. Since very few cats enjoy being chased, I went to the privy instead.

Potatoes don't make gods. Hmm. That implied that the living things that didn't pass through *did* make gods. Which meant that the ability to make a god was somehow essential to whether an object could pass through a mirror, which meant . . . I had no idea what that meant.

We don't actually have gods in my country, as you may have noticed, just saints. The story goes that our gods were pitiless and cruel, and in despair, humanity began to pray instead to the beasts of heaven, to Rabbit and Bird, Adder and Toad, and all the rest. The beasts of heaven rose up in their numbers and slew the pitiless gods, and since those days, we have called only upon the saints.

In fairness to Grayling, there was not a Saint Potato. If you wanted a good crop, you called upon the Saint of Bees. (Not Saint Bee, because this saint is not singular the way the others are.) Did this mean that bees were capable of making gods? What kind of god would a bee make? I pictured tiny evangelists standing outside a hive, preaching the gospel of bees. *Hmm, maybe Grayling has a point. How would a potato preach to the other potatoes? You just don't get that many missionaries among root vegetables.*

All of which was mythologically interesting, but not terribly useful. I splashed water on my face. Maybe there was a humor associated with god making and the mirror version was deficient in it? Or *wasn't* deficient in it, and the presence of that humor meant that it couldn't pass through? A mirror-humor, say. Anti-sanguine.

Or maybe Grayling was messing with me because I'd woken him up early.

I made my way down to the kitchen, where the staff was already awake and baking, and begged some cold meat and cheese. As I went, I looked around for mirrors. I'd overlooked the ones in the pocket garden, so what else had I overlooked?

The only ones I found seemed innocuous enough. A band of mirrored tiles no wider than my thumb ran across the top of an alcove in one of the hallways. No one could possibly fit through that. Though perhaps they could pass something through. Like a dagger, or a message.

It was in a thoughtful frame of mind that I went out into the garden to watch the desert come awake. A hummingbird zipped past, focused on the red sage flowers, and I wondered if he was the real-world version of the one I'd carried away.

I sat there for perhaps an hour, soaking in nature's glory and putting off confronting Snow. Then I went to speak to Rinald, the horse leech, to ask about an herb I'd seen and put off confronting

Snow. Then I went to the workroom, fed the chime-adder, let the rooster wander around, and finally couldn't invent any more ways to waste time and went to confront Snow.

Getting Snow alone to talk to her was easier than I'd expected. Nurse had planted herself alongside Snow, clearly planning to be present, but I cleared my throat and said that I had a question or two of an . . . ah . . . delicate nature, and perhaps she could make sure none of the maids were listening?

I could practically see the fire in her eyes when she thought of the way gossip spread, and she ushered us out to the balcony and went back inside, loudly ordering various girls to fetch things, clean things, and take things away.

Snow went to the railing, then looked back at me with a questioning half smile. "Yes?"

I had been hoping all morning that I'd have an idea about how to approach a twelve-year-old girl about her activities in a bizarre secondary world inside the mirror. Unfortunately nothing had come to me, so I fell back on Javier's advice.

"I know about the mirror."

Snow inhaled sharply. I waited to see if there was anything she wanted to say, but she turned and stared out over the desert, her face expressionless.

"I know you were watching me. And I know that it's mirror-food that's making you ill."

She still didn't look at me, but red lines bloomed around her knuckles as she gripped the railing.

"Snow," I said, gentling my voice as much as I could, "I'm not angry you were spying on me. Well, I was upset at first, but I got over it." I really didn't want to lie to her. I was still grateful to the herbwife telling me the truth about poison all those years ago. "But if you keep eating mirror-food, you'll get sicker and sicker. What you're doing is dangerous."

The sharp, explosive sound that came from her throat held more disdain than words ever could. She finally turned to look at me. "Do you think I *want* to eat it?"

I had to fight my instinct to take a step back. The look in her eyes was of a small, cornered thing turning to bite. "Err . . . well . . ."

"Tell me where she's keeping my sister, and I'll never touch an apple again."

"Your sister?" I repeated inanely.

"Rose," Snow said, in the talking-to-stupid-adults tone that I knew so well from my own childhood.

"But Rose is dead," I said, because Isobel was right about my tactfulness. I started cursing myself before the last word was even completely out of my mouth. "I'm sorry—"

"You don't understand *anything*," Snow said, her voice as cold and intense as a driving rain. She turned on her heel and stalked away into her bedroom, slamming the door behind her. Nurse and the maids watched her go, then turned, practically in unison, to look at me. Nurse's expression had turned hard as glass. She had trusted me, and I'd upset her charge.

"Right," I muttered. "That went well." The path to the door, past looks both curious and accusing, seemed to take hours. I mumbled something about coming back later and slunk out.

Well. Now what?

Tell me where she's keeping my sister, and I'll never touch an apple again. What did that mean? Rose *was* dead. Snow had to know that. Was this some kind of delusion born of grief? And who was the *she* that Snow was referring to?

I'd hoped to get more answers, and now I had even more questions. What did Rose have to do with any of this? And *keeping her*? Did she think that someone had kidnapped Rose instead of murdering her?

It wouldn't be the first time that grief had led to someone making up elaborate fantasies about their loved ones secretly being alive. I found an alcove with a bench and sat down with my head in my hands. *I am not equipped to deal with things like this. This needs someone who understands minds. I just do poisons.*

Healer Michael, I wish you were here. You could handle the emotional part.

I rubbed my temples wearily. Well. Healer Michael wasn't here. And at least now I was sure that Snow understood she was poisoning herself but thought she was doing it for a reason. *That's progress? Maybe?*

I'd talk to Javier. Maybe he'd be better with kids. Hell, maybe he *had* kids. And he could help me write the letter to the king saying all this, and surely the king could afford the very best healers for broken minds . . . but if I tried to write anything about the mirror-world in the letter, the king was going to send healers after me, not Snow.

Oh Saints, what am I supposed to do now?

I couldn't tell the king the full truth, obviously. I'd do Snow no good if I got locked up in an asylum. If I were gone, that would leave this mysterious *she* free rein.

Well, at least we've figured that much out. Whoever is bringing Snow mirror-food is female. That has to narrow it down.

A servant girl walked down the hall and gave a quick, startled smile when she saw me. I watched her walk away. Surely she was too young to be poisoning the king's daughter, and why would she even want to? For that matter, I had no proof that the poisoner was anyone staying at Witherleaf, or at least, not staying in the real world. For all I knew, they could have come from elsewhere and were living in the mirror-villa, watching us through the reflections.

I jumped up, suddenly paranoid. There were the small mirrored tiles that I'd seen here and there, but how many *hadn't* I found? Javier had mentioned assassins, but what about spies?

For that matter, Snow herself had been spying on me, and while she hadn't done anything, it was still . . . well, it was *weird*. Even if Javier was being paranoid about the assassin thing, there are just not that many situations where I want to be watched in my sleep by a twelve-year-old girl.

Actually, being spied on while I was awake wasn't that much better.

Calm down, I told myself firmly. *You're panicking, and that never helps anything. You know there can't be mirrors in the main hallways because you'd have seen the colors when you went through the mirror-villa.*

That was true. There were incidental mirrors in some of the smaller passageways, but it seemed like there were more in the garden than inside the villa itself. That only left the ones in my room and, of course, the tiles in my bathroom.

Was there something I could do to prevent anyone from using those? Locking the door should help at night, in theory, but what about the rest of the time?

What I really needed was some way to check if there was anyone around me in the mirror-world. Which was easier said than done, of course.

How could I watch what happened in the mirror-world? There were only a few mirrors on the estate that I could actually fit through. Lugging one of those around with me didn't seem workable. (What was I going to do, have Javier and Aaron follow me around, carrying it between the two of them? It'd get broken before the first hour was up, and we could kiss any hope of keeping things subtle goodbye.)

Although . . .

I tapped my finger against my lips. I didn't need to *walk* through it, I just had to be able to *see* through it. That only required a mirror large enough to put my face through and open my eyes. It didn't even have to fit over my entire head—if it was mobile, I could literally just turn in a circle and see if Snow's reflection suddenly popped up.

I turned around, retraced my steps, and went downstairs to ask the housekeeper if I could borrow a hand mirror.

The hand mirror was easily acquired. Unlike the big, dramatic mirrors from Silversand, this was a plain wooden frame with a handle and a small square set into it. The maker's mark was from Four Saints, which was oddly comforting. I went to my room and dropped the hand mirror on the nightstand for later use, then sat down at the desk and tried to figure out what I was going to do now.

Sadly, I hadn't had any great epiphanies when I heard a light knock at the door.

I jumped up and stepped into the mirror. Even if it was just the maid, I didn't have the energy for a conversation right then. If it was Nurse coming to ask what exactly I'd said to her charge, then I *really* didn't have the energy.

The familiar cold tingle washed over me as I passed through the silver. A moment later, the maid with the carnivorous hair entered the room. (She had told me her name that first night, and I promptly forgot it in the haze of exhaustion. Then I'd been distracted by a lot of other things, and now it would be too awkward to ask.)

I sagged against the wall, relieved, then straightened up hastily, rubbing my arms against the cold. I *had* to remember to bring a coat next time, or they'd find me frozen to death on the . . . hmm, actually they wouldn't find me, would they? I'd just be bones quietly decaying in a corner of the mirror-world, unless Javier came through and dragged my bones back to the real world.

I wondered how many missing people who seemed to have vanished off the face of the earth had found their way through the silver instead?

What a happy thought. I'm so glad that I had it.

The maid straightened up, fluffed the pillows, and turned her attention to the nightstand. I watched the half-and-half gray re-flection reach out and pick something up in her hands.

Everything suddenly went ghostly. I don't know how else to de-scribe it. The section of the room in the band of mirror-light went strangely insubstantial. Objects sprouted haloes that doubled and tripled their sizes, like visual echoes. And the maid . . .

Half of her, unseeing, turned the object this way and that, ap-parently admiring it. The other half, the gray half, began to shud-der and jitter back and forth. Something erupted from the back of her head, a band of flesh like a sharp-edged tumor, and then another one beside it and another, and then she turned even fur-ther and her face broke into two pieces that slid along each other until one eye was half an inch above the other one, and then one of those pieces broke and she had three eyes and then it broke again and again—

The maid tossed the mirror onto the bed and went to get fresh towels.

The haloes faded from around the mirror-furniture, though it took a moment. The mirror-woman didn't snap back so quickly. Her reflection dragged to the edge of the mirror, out of the light, then stood shuddering in the grayness, a tragic and monstrous figure with a dozen faces layered over her head like a succession of blocky-edged masks. She swept her head slowly from side to side, her neck sagging under the weight, and lifted an arm with a dozen hands to touch it.

I had stopped breathing some time ago. *Why . . . ? How . . . ?*

The mirror. She picked up the mirror *on your nightstand and an-gled it to catch the other mirror's reflection.*

We had done it a hundred times as kids, though our mirrors were much smaller than the enormous one on the wall. You held two mirrors at just the right angle and saw yourself reflected in-finitely, the angle changing just a fraction every time, and when you moved, a thousand versions of yourself moved with you.

Except that there was only one world inside the silver, and one reflection breaking into a thousand versions of herself, and the mirror-world tried to keep up, splitting that reflection into more and more selves, like a piece of meat cut into thinner and thinner slices . . .

The woman vanished, presumably as the real one changed out the towels in the washroom. But not *all* of her vanished this time. I jumped back, startled, as the bands of eyes and hands and fractions of a face calved away from emptiness and crashed to the floor.

I expected them to turn to dust, the way that mirror-stuff did in the real world. But they lay on the ground like slabs of clay from a frustrated sculptor, and then the hands reached out and went creeping over the floor, dragging sections of arm behind them. The faces lay tumbled across each other, in a pile that blinked and twitched and moved, the corners of mouths working madly as if in pain.

Two hands met in the center of the floor. They circled each other, then hooked their thumbs together and stood up on their fingers, swaying against each other like drunken spiders. Together they lurched across the floor, their gait growing rapidly more confident, until they reached the pile of broken faces. Half a mouth, attached to a cheekbone and a single eye, bit on to one's fingertip. The spidery hands stopped, then began twisting and turning, until they could heave the half face up between them. The gray eye blinked.

No. No, that is not right. *That should* not *be a thing that happens.* I backed up, looking around wildly for something to climb on, as if I were a silly child frightened by a stray mouse.

Something touched my foot. I looked down and saw another of the hands up against my sandal, the fingers feeling blindly across my toes, as if trying to figure out where they were and what they might be touching.

It was too much. I let out a horrified squawk and kicked it away. The hand dropped to the floor like a deformed spider, the fingers still flexing as it fell. I did not stay around to see if it survived the fall, but scrambled and leaped over the flailing mirror-stuff and lunged out of the mirror so fast that I didn't remember to close my eyes.

"Oh, Miss Anja!" The maid came out of the washroom, her arms full of towels. "I didn't hear you come in. I'm just finishing up." She smiled at me, while her hair eagerly enveloped one of the hand towels.

"I just got in," I said, breathing heavily through my nose.

She paused, her smile fading. "Are you all right? You seem out of breath."

I just watched you split into pieces, and those pieces are still crawling around on the floor half an inch of glass away. One of your hands just tried to latch on to me. And I can't explain any of this to you because I'll sound completely crazy.

"I'm fine," I said, clearing my throat. My voice came out almost normal. "Everything's fine."

CHAPTER 20

"A mirror-geld," Grayling said. "A small one, by the sound of it. The parts will all fuse together if you leave it long enough."

To give the cat credit where it was due, he hadn't played games when I'd come running for him. I'd spotted him in the shadow of the roof and hissed his name and he came down immediately, alerted by some note of panic in my voice. I met him behind the courtyard wall, frantically whispering what I'd seen.

"You didn't warn me about those!"

Grayling rolled his good eye. "I would think that *anyone* with sense would know not to get between two mirrors."

"No, we don't." I thought of those games we'd played as children and shuddered. How many mirror-gelds had my sisters and I created? Had our faces all landed together in a twitching pile, our hands crawling unheeded along the bedroom floor? We'd done it for a lot longer than the maid had. The sheer mass of splintered reflections must have been enormous.

Hell, one time Isobel had flipped up her skirt and mooned the mirror, and we'd laughed until Catherine threw up. I didn't know whether to laugh hysterically at the thought of her bare ass on the pile of fragmented body parts, or maybe just throw up myself.

And these things melded together somehow? I imagined the hands I'd seen lurching along, dragging hundreds of faces behind. Hundreds of *our* faces.

"It was horrible," I whispered, trying to keep my voice low enough that the kitchen staff wouldn't hear. "How long before they stop moving?"

Grayling gave me an almost pitying look. "What makes you think they stop?" he asked, and with a flick of his tail, he was gone over the wall.

I had arranged to meet Javier in the garden, in an open area as far from listening ears as possible. The hummingbirds had retired and hawkmoths had taken their place at the flowers. The sky overhead was a blaze of copper and blood.

I looked up from a hawkmoth to see *two* figures walking toward me. Javier and . . . Aaron? *What? Why? Did he tell Aaron after all?* If he had, I was going to be rather annoyed that he hadn't talked to me about it first.

"Hello, Healer Anja," Aaron said, grinning broadly.

Javier caught my eye and gave a tiny negative shake. *Ah. I see.*

"So, is it your turn to play bodyguard instead?" I asked, hoping that I wasn't contradicting anything Javier had said earlier.

"No, I just came along to see what Javier was doing. Do you really *need* a bodyguard out here?" Aaron glanced around the garden, clearly noting the total lack of assassins.

"Not a bodyguard, exactly, but I like to have someone on hand in case something gets me."

". . . gets you?"

I had him now. Sometimes being me has its advantages. "There are a great many venomous things in the desert," I said. "A great many. Chime-adders, diamond rattlevipers, the desert coral snake, and the beaded lizard—I don't actually expect to see that last, since they're mostly found farther west, and we're too far south for timber rattlevipers—and that's just the reptiles. Then there's the scorpions, both the big ones, which aren't terribly venomous, and the little bark scorpions that will make you regret you've ever been born. And that doesn't get into the desert centipedes, which—"

"Saints, don't mention the centipedes." Aaron shuddered the-atrically. "There was one as long as my hand in my shoe once. My foot swelled up like a melon."

"—plus sundry other insects, like assassin bugs, which would love a garden like this." I stood up from the rock I'd been sitting on and brushed my skirt off. "And of course there's the spiders, including two varieties of widow and—"

"I retract the question," said Aaron, holding up both hands. "And I will now retract myself, because my skin is crawling. Javier, if you survive the horrors of nature, I'll see you later."

Javier grunted. I tried to look disappointed. Aaron retreated, shaking his head.

"That was neatly done," Javier said, once the other guard was out of earshot. "I tried to dissuade him, but he was bored and wanted to stir something up."

"Stir something up?"

Javier coughed and found a nearby bush fascinating. It was an-telope milkweed, which genuinely is fascinating—you can make a poultice that reduces the swelling of snakebites—but I suspected that wasn't the reason. "He, uh, is wondering if we, uh . . ."

He trailed off. "'We, uh'?" I prompted.

"Bodyguards and their charges spend a great deal of time in close quarters," Javier said, still staring at the milkweed. "It's, uh, something of a cliché that some of them will . . . uh."

"*Ohhh.*" I could feel a blush starting. Aaron thought that? Shouldn't Javier have set him straight? "*That* kind of . . . uh. But of course you and I aren't . . . uhh-ing. At all."

"Right," said Javier. "No uh."

"Right. Glad we cleared that up."

Javier cleared his throat. "How did speaking with Snow go?"

I drew a blank. "Snow?"

"This morning?"

"Oh. That." My conversation with Snow had been an age of the earth ago, in a time when I didn't know about mirror-gelds. "Um.

Badly, I think." I recounted what she'd said. Javier leaned against a waist-high stone and listened.

"'Tell me where she's keeping my sister'?" he repeated, after I had finished. "What does that mean?"

"Either she's convinced herself that her sister is still alive, or someone else has convinced her of that, or . . . I don't know." Snow had not struck me as particularly delusional, but it's not like you can tell from the outside. Plus, she was *twelve*. "Maybe something to do with souls? Surely they would have put her ashes in a spirit house."

"I know they did," said Javier. "I was part of the funeral procession."

"You were?"

"They turned out most of the palace guard for it. And there was someone stationed there for a month, to keep anyone from stealing ashes."

I grimaced. Disgusting, but of course there was always someone. "I suppose it could be something convoluted related to that. But we still don't know who 'her' is. Anyway, look, that's not the most important thing . . ."

I told him about the mirror-geld, leaving out only the bits about Grayling. I was going to have to tell him, I knew that, but it sounded so utterly unbelievable that I was hoping Grayling would be present for the conversation so that my bodyguard didn't think I'd cracked under the strain.

When I had finished, Javier said, "Huh!" almost explosively. He looked curious more than horrified. (Yes, I was conscious of the irony.) "Are the parts still there?"

"I haven't looked."

He slid off the stone. "Then we should do that."

The mirror-geld was gone. Javier even looked under the bed and behind the towels. I sagged against the wall in relief. "They must have fallen apart," he said. "I don't know where else they could have gone. And the door's still locked, so they didn't leave that way."

It hadn't occurred to me that the horribly animated severed limbs could perhaps work a doorknob. I thanked him for the mental image.

"All part of my job." One corner of his mouth crooked up, and I wondered that I'd ever thought him humorless. Or possibly he was like most of the healers I knew and his humor grew in proportion to the direness of the situation. Certainly the amount he talked did.

"Could they have gone over the balcony?" I asked.

"You tell me."

The railing had balustrades holding it up; it wasn't a solid piece. I supposed the hands could have crawled there. I shuddered at the thought and was glad when Javier went through the doors first.

The mirror-desert was even grimmer at sunset. The red sky, cut with black, gave the scene a dreadful quality, like looking down into some bleak, forgotten hell. If the mirror-stuff had reflected even a little of the red, I think it might have been less disturbing. Then it would have just looked like weather. The stark gray under that blaze of bloody light was so clearly unnatural that it dragged at the eyes, while the mind struggled to make sense of it and failed.

There were no severed limbs and faces lying on the ground below, which was a relief, and also not something that I'd ever had to worry about before. Maybe they *had* just dissolved. It was entirely possible that Grayling would just run when he saw them, the same way that I had, and he was too . . . too *cat* to admit that he didn't know what happened afterward.

We turned away from the red sky in mutual unspoken agreement.

"We'll have to start checking the other rooms soon," Javier said. "The poisoner's bound to be in there somewhere."

"Tomorrow, then." He didn't press me to do it tonight, and I was grateful, and slightly resentful for being grateful. I knew he was humoring me because he hadn't seen the mirror-geld and had no idea just how horrific they'd been.

We parted at the door. I took shameful advantage of my status as a guest, had the tub filled with hot water, and soaked in it while reading the Red Feather Saga. The heroine's cousin had just found a secret door in the house seized by her evil uncle when he'd stolen her inheritance. She was making what I felt was an excessive fuss about it being full of spiderwebs. *Spiders, feh. You should see mirror-gelds.*

Grayling was already on the bed when I got in. He flicked an ear at me but didn't open his eye. "I know, I know," I said, contorting myself so that I didn't disturb him. For a small cat, he took up an ungodly amount of space. "Ear mites. Good night."

I think he said, "Good night," but I was mostly asleep by then, so it's possible I dreamed it.

"Oh dear . . ." Lady Sorrel tutted at me during lunch the next day. "You've gotten quite a sunburn."

I had? I had been avoiding the mirrors so determinedly that I hadn't noticed. I pressed a fingertip into my forearm and watched the mark turn bright white against red. All that roaming around looking for cats had clearly taken its toll.

"I've got a lotion that works wonders," Sorrel said. "Come with me."

Her private rooms were exactly like I would have expected, had I given the matter any thought. Richly colored fabric lay on every surface, rag rugs covered the floors, and the seats were so deeply upholstered that when I sat in one, I sank down at least an inch. The furniture seemed to be mostly dark wood, but I caught only glimpses of chair legs and footboards under piles of fabric. The only exception was an armoire that looked large enough to sleep three, provided they were all good friends.

"Now, let's see . . ." Sorrel said, going to a small sideboard while

I craned my neck, taking in the colors. She picked up a small jar, unstoppered it, sniffed, and put it back down. "Not that one . . . not that one . . ."

The sideboard was covered in little jars and bottles, like a vanity table. Except there was no mirror.

In fact, looking around, I couldn't see a single mirror anywhere. And now that I looked at it, that fall of cloth against the wall wasn't a hanging; it was clearly covering something tall and rectangular.

She turned back to me with a smile on her face, and I blurted out, "There aren't any mirrors in here."

Her smile fixed in place like a butterfly pinned to a card. "Ah," she said. "No."

I stared at her, this pleasant, charming woman who had been the mistress to a royal madman. Could *she* be the person that Snow had been talking about? It made no sense, but I'd given up on people making sense. And she was here and Snow would trust her. But why would she want to poison a twelve-year-old girl?

Revenge for Bastian's death? Or maybe the mercury got to her, too, and she went mad in a much colder way?

Or maybe she *actually poisoned* him, *and now she's . . . I don't know, keeping her hand in?*

I studied the ranks of bottles and vials on the vanity. If I hadn't known about the apple, I'd be very suspicious right now. Granted, Lady Sorrel didn't fit my idea of a black widow—not nearly enough husbands—but she might have her own motives that I knew nothing about.

Oblivious to my thoughts, she sank down into a chair opposite mine, the lotion bottle forgotten in her hand. "Bastian never liked them," she said. "Sometimes he thought that his enemies were watching him through mirrors. It was the poison talking, of course." She made a small, aimless gesture with her free hand. "Even after he was gone, I didn't feel like surrounding myself with them. I used a little polished tin thing for checking my makeup.

Then, of course, Randolph married and had his honeymoon here, and she brought all those mirrors as a gift . . ."

"There are a lot of mirrors here," I said cautiously.

"So many. It showed how wealthy the bride's family was. And the queen loved mirrors. She'd have had them up on every wall if she could. I'm told you can hardly turn a corner in the palace without meeting yourself coming and going."

Damn it, I didn't want to suspect her. I *liked* her. More than anyone here, except maybe Aaron and Javier.

"The servants think that it's vanity," Lady Sorrel said, with a laugh that was both amused and unutterably weary. "They think that I'm afraid that if I have mirrors about me, I'll suddenly realize that I'm old. As if I couldn't tell without that." She lifted a hand like the claw of some great bird, the knuckles ridged and the tips swollen around the nail, then let it drop again. "Though you do forget sometimes, I admit. In my head, you see, I'm the same person that I always was. I see old friends and think, 'But how did that happen? How did *they* get so old?'"

I smiled at that. Sorrel smiled back, then her smile faded. "I don't know. Perhaps I'm going as mad as poor Bastian. But the mirrors in this house feel dangerous now."

"Dangerous?" I asked. How much did she know? Was this a warning or a confession?

"Mmm." Lady Sorrel turned the bottle over in her hands. Her hands trembled, but her grip was still sure. "Perhaps all mirrors could be dangerous. Most of them aren't, I imagine. These, though . . ." She gestured toward the shape with the cloth hung over it. "I haven't trusted them since before the queen died."

"What do you think is wrong with them?"

She studied me for a long, long moment, and I actually saw the moment that she decided she'd said too much. "Nothing, I'm sure. An old woman's fancies. Perhaps I really am afraid of growing old and I'm trying to pretend I'm not." She rose to her feet and handed me the bottle. "Use that on your skin twice a day, my dear, and maybe by the time you're my age, you won't end up quite as wrinkled as I am."

I thanked her and left, my stomach already beginning to knot with dread.

"Lady Sorrel?" Javier asked. He sounded like he was about to protest, then reconsidered. "Well. I suppose it's possible."

"The timing fits," I said gloomily. "Damn it, I liked her. And *don't* tell me that bad people often go out of their way to be likable, because I *know* that, and it doesn't make it any less awful."

"By those standards, you're definitely a good person," Javier muttered.

"Thanks." I wanted to glare at him, but I didn't, because it wasn't his fault he'd been assigned as a bodyguard to someone with all the grace and tact of a charging water buffalo. He was stuck with me. However much I feared the king's displeasure, the royal guard had to have it much worse. I settled for scowling at my shoes.

We were in the open part of the gardens again. Cicadas screamed overhead, and locust trees cast filamented shadows across the ground. I sat on the bench, and Javier stood beside me. To a distant observer, we were healer and bodyguard, nothing more. Certainly not two people discussing sedition against the lady of the manor.

Leather creaked as Javier shifted his feet. "I'm sorry," he said finally. "I shouldn't have said that."

"It's fine," I said wearily. "I know what I'm like."

"You're not unlikable, though. You're just blunt. And stubborn. And you want to be right."

I sighed. "You sound like my sister. She used to say that once I knew I was right about something, I'd club people over the head with it rather than let it go."

"You're dedicated to the truth. That's not a bad thing. And you're passionate about lots of things."

"That doesn't help." I shook my head. "It turns out that very few people want to listen to a treatise on the long-term effects of lead poisoning whenever they pick up a bottle of sweetened wine."

"I wouldn't mind."

I looked up, startled. He was looking at me intently, and I felt a flush start to creep along my skin. I had to remind myself that this was the same man who had given me a look of such disgust only a day or two ago.

A bird whistled overhead—*whit-wheeet!*—and startled us both. I looked away hurriedly, and Javier tried to pretend that he hadn't just grabbed for the hilt of his sword.

"Anyway," I said, clearing my throat. "Do you really think Lady Sorrel could be the one behind all this?"

Javier shrugged helplessly. "I've never actually spoken with her. I'm attached to the king's household, and normally I go where he goes. I can tell you that everyone who works here thinks highly of her, but that doesn't mean anything. If *I* was going to be evil, I'd treat the staff very, very well."

I tried to picture Javier being evil and couldn't quite manage it. I suppose there are evil people who are solid and reliable and even-tempered, but either you don't meet a lot of them, or they hide being evil remarkably well. Either way, I imagine they pay their staff quite handsomely.

"How can we figure it out?" I asked. "I suppose I could ask Snow, but I'm not sure she'd tell me."

"We could search her rooms in the mirror," Javier suggested. "See if there's anything incriminating. If she's got a bushel of ap-ples hidden there, for example."

"That's a good idea." I rubbed my forehead. "Saints. What do we tell the king if it does turn out to be her? Will he even believe us?"

A frown creased the edges of Javier's mouth. "We'd have to show him the mirror-world."

The heaviness of his tone surprised me. "I thought we'd have to do that anyway?"

Javier was silent for a moment too long.

"You don't think we should tell him," I said.

He didn't meet my eyes. "I keep thinking how dangerous this could be. As soon as they figure out how, everyone will be making as many mirrors as they can. It'll become an arms race. And everything—everyone—will need twice as many guards so that they can be stationed in the mirror-world as well. We'd be opening another battlefront across the entire world." He rubbed a hand over his scalp and looked suddenly old, not merely a man in his late thirties but ancient, with the weight of history looming over him. "King Randolph is a good man and a good king, but what if this gets in the hands of someone like Bastian the Demon?"

The sun was high overhead, but the thought made my skin prickle with cold. "It would get in hands like that eventually," I admitted. "There would be no way to keep it secret. Not when we'd be stationing guards inside mirrors."

"Exactly. If we tell the king, we have to realize that we're telling the world."

"It might only work with mirrors from Silversand?" I asked plaintively.

"Then Silversand becomes the target of every army on earth."

Cicadas whined their long descending note. I could see heat shimmers on the horizon, blurring the distant farms.

"We used to talk about it," I said slowly, "my tutor, Scand, and I. If you discovered a poison that could kill hundreds of people all at once, something you could put in a well or a waterway, say, would it be better to tell everyone so that people could try to find a cure, or to tell no one so that evil people couldn't use it, but risk someone else discovering it later?"

"What did you decide?"

I pressed my lips together. "When I was sixteen, I wanted to tell everyone. I thought that we could solve everything just by piling more knowledge on it. Now . . ." I leaned back and studied the hard turquoise bowl of the sky. "I would only share the knowledge if I had already found the cure, I think. Cures are . . . not easy to find." *And I am surprised that Saint Bird does not send lightning to strike me down for the sheer depth of that understatement.*

"What's the cure for this?" Javier asked.

"Break all the mirrors, I suppose. Or at least make sure none of them are large enough for a person to fit through. Who'd have human-sized mirrors after this?"

He was already shaking his head. "Someone could still get in if they had a set of properly sized mirrors with them. You get a long narrow mirror, pass it through the existing mirror, set it down, pass the next one through the first one, and so on until it's big enough to fit through. Any mirror bigger than your hand ought to work."

He was right, of course. Mirror glass was, what, a quarter inch thick? If someone hung a four-inch mirror on the wall, all you needed was a mirror three inches tall and three feet long. Slide that through and you could put a mirror three feet tall and six feet long through that, and then an assassin could walk through as easy as you please.

"Hell, all you'd need would be a mirror bigger than the point of a crossbow bolt, come to that," Javier added.

I winced. He'd thought it through, more than I had. Even though I'd long since had the belief that I was the smartest person in the room knocked out of me, it was humbling. "You're right," I said. It hurt that he was right. I'd known that I couldn't publish, but I had always planned to tell Scand, at least.

"Three can keep a secret," I said heavily, "if two of them are dead. And we're past three already."

"And one of them's a twelve-year-old royal heiress. I know." Javier shook his head. "And we don't know how many people the poisoner's told. Lady Sorrel—if it *is* Lady Sorrel—could have dozens of people working for her."

"To say nothing of who discovered it in the first place. It might all be moot." I worried at the end of my braid with my fingernails.

"Saint Adder's mercy, I'm not cut out for this. I putter around my workroom and shove charcoal down throats and occasionally up asses. This is all . . ." I made helpless gestures with my hands, trying to encompass the size of everything and the size of me in proportion.

Javier snorted. "You think *you're* not cut out for this? I'm a mere guard."

"There's nothing *mere* about you," I shot back.

An indescribable expression crossed his face, and then he was holding my eyes again, a little bit too long.

Saints, this is not *the time. Not with everything else going on. And anyway, you hardly know the man.*

I knew him before I fell through the mirror, I argued with myself. That felt like it had been years ago. In fact, it had only been, what, three, four days?

If this goes on for a full week, I may drop dead of sheer anxiety.

"Well," said Javier, finally breaking away, "we should, uh, probably go investigate Lady Sorrel's chambers and see if we can find anything incriminating."

"Right." It was good to have the next step to focus on, a simple task, not the whole tapestry of who knew about the mirrors and how much the world would change if more people found out. "Let's get that out of the way."

CHAPTER 21

The coolness of the mirror-world was a shock after the heat of the day. I unbolted my door and reached for the doorknob, but Javier stepped in front of me. "There's a chance she's out there now."

"She's what, seventy? I think I can probably fend her off."

"Can you fend off a poisoned knife?"

"Can you?"

He tapped the quilted armor surcoat that he had donned. "Cloth will bind a knife like you wouldn't believe. Besides, this is what I'm *for*."

I grumbled but let him go first. He opened the door, slipped outside, then gestured to me, something complicated with two fingers. I assumed it meant it was safe to exit, though it could have meant anything up to *I have decided that I would like curry for dinner*. I followed.

We were halfway to the stairs when a door opened across the courtyard and a gray figure stepped out of it. I watched the reflection close the door, and stand frozen.

"Begin in Lady Sorrel's rooms?" Javier asked.

"Yes, I . . . wait . . ." The gray figure had begun to walk along the hallway perpendicular to us. With no mirror in sight.

I grabbed Javier's wrist. "That one's moving!"

Javier's head jerked around, and he stared at the gray figure. It was a man, and though it was hard to tell in the gray-on-gray twilight of the mirror, I didn't think he was wearing a servant's livery. One of the guards, perhaps?

Another door opened to our left, much closer. Javier spun around, drawing his sword. It was another man, and this one seemed to actually be wearing armor.

The gray man closed the door and began walking toward us. Javier put himself between me and the newcomer, sword held up between us. "I thought you said they didn't move!" he hissed.

"None of the others did!"

The first gray man turned the far corner and came down the hallway toward us as well. They both had a steady, measured gait that was somehow more frightening than if they had been charging.

"Maybe we should get out of the way?" I said. "I don't know why they're still there without a mirror, but maybe they're going to another mirror? If we just step to one side . . ."

The armored one drew his sword.

". . . Or not."

Javier said something short, sharp, and sexually explicit. I darted toward the nearest door, two down from my own room— *Please, Saints, let it be unlocked! . . . Oh blessed Saint Adder, thank you!*—and yanked it open.

Javier leaped through the doorway after me and slammed it practically in the armored man's face. I heard him fumble with the lock, then ram the bolt home, just as a fist descended on the other side.

Knock. Knock.

I looked around the room. It was clearly another guest room, though not quite so large as the one I was in. There were dustcovers on the furniture, though, so it appeared unoccupied.

Knock. Knock. The door actually rattled in the frame that time. The narrow metal bolt seemed terribly puny.

"Is there a way out?" Javier had his shoulder against the door, holding it in place.

"Balcony, if we want to break both legs. Unless . . . *Aha!*" I yanked a dustcover away from the wall, revealing a standing mirror. It wasn't nearly as large as mine, maybe four feet tall by eighteen inches wide, but it looked onto a sunlit world that looked like salvation.

Knock. Knock. Knock. The armored man's fist struck like hammerblows against the wood. Every one knocked Javier back an inch.

"Go, go!" my bodyguard said. I could hear wood splintering. "I'm right behind you!"

I went. I had to duck and turn sideways, and I felt my ass scrape against the frame, but I was through.

Whereupon the dustcover from the real world fell over me, and I flailed like a bird trapped in a windowsill, trying to get it off.

Javier ran into me, full tilt. I fell down. He fell down. The dustcover fell over both of us. Something whacked me in the ribs, and I realized he still had his sword out. Thankfully it had just been the flat, or an already bad day would have gotten a great deal worse.

"Stop moving," I ordered, clutching at the edge of the sheet that I found near my knees. I tried to yank it loose, with minimal success.

In the mirror, the armored man looked down at the two of us lying sprawled on the floor in the real world. His face was cold and chiseled stone, and then he smiled.

None of the other reflections had had any expression. Seeing this one felt very, very wrong.

He reached out a hand to the mirror. Javier swore and got the sword up over me. *He can't come through—he's just a reflection—this isn't how it works—*

The gray figure tapped one finger against the glass, and there it stopped. He was wearing gauntlets. Sound didn't carry to this side of the mirror, but I could imagine what steel would sound like against glass.

Tap. Tap. Tap. Still with that unnerving smile. His eyes were blank, but his head was tilted down, so I was certain he was looking at us. I swallowed convulsively.

The door to the room opened. The reflection stepped back. Javier lurched toward the sound, sword up to meet this new threat.

The hair with a maid attached stood in the doorway, her mouth an O of surprise. She was carrying a feather duster.

I looked back at the mirror, but the reflection was gone. And I was lying on the ground, on a sheet, extremely rumpled, partly underneath my equally rumpled bodyguard.

The maid's eyes traveled over the two of us. "Hullo, Javier," she said. "Miss."

There is a level of blush beyond which human capillaries simply won't hold any more blood. I lay under my bodyguard and wished for a vasoconstrictor.

Javier closed his eyes. "Hello, Eloise."

Huh. Her name is Eloise. Good to know.

Eloise put the feather duster on her shoulder, where her hair promptly engulfed it. "We air these rooms out once a week so they don't get musty," she said.

"Very good," I said. *Ergot. Ergot's a vasoconstrictor. You get the hallucinations, though, so that won't work. Damn.*

"I tripped," said Javier. "And . . . err . . . Healer Anja tried to catch me. And we fell. On the floor."

Arsenic might work; you get the white complexion out of it.

"Uh-huh," said Eloise. "Do you want me to bring some sheets for the bed in here, then?"

Yes, definitely arsenic. Several pounds ought to do it.

"That will not be necessary," I said, with what shreds of dignity I could muster under the circumstances. "Please don't be so clumsy again in the future, sir."

He scrambled off me and extended a hand to help me up. "Certainly not, Healer Anja."

"And put away your sword."

"Yes, Healer Anja."

Eloise nodded. "I'll come back later, then," she said, and stepped out. The door shut behind her.

My neck snapped around toward the mirror so fast that I felt a vertebra pop, but there was no figure in the mirror except our own.

We retreated to my room. I passed a servant on the way and felt myself flushing again, even though there was absolutely no reason to be embarrassed about walking somewhere with my guard. Up until five minutes ago, I hadn't worried that anyone other than Aaron would think anything salacious was going on. Now everyone in the villa would think so by daybreak.

Oh hey, I wonder if they're going to think that I'm cheating on the king?

Once we got to my room, I started laughing. I couldn't help it. All the fear and embarrassment and adrenaline came out in a hyena-like cackle, and Javier jumped like a spooked horse, which made me laugh harder until I collapsed in a chair, and I finally managed to gasp out, "They're going to think I'm cheating on the *king*!" and his eyes went big and round as saucers, and then he started laughing, too.

It was one of those laughs where if you meet each other's eyes, you start up again, and that sets them off, so it took a good five minutes all told until we finally settled. I wiped tears from my cheeks, resolutely not looking in Javier's direction. "Saints," I said hoarsely, feeling wrung out. "I needed that. Oh, we're in such a mess, aren't we?"

"Yeah," he said. "Yeah." I heard him get up and risked a glance in his direction. He poured some water from the pitcher on the table and drank it down, then leaned against one of the bedposts. He caught me looking in his direction and lifted the cup in an abbreviated salute.

"So some of them can walk around," I said, leaning back in the chair, "and they didn't seem friendly."

"Not friendly at all. Though I can understand their position."

"Eh? What position?"

"How would *you* react if two strangers suddenly appeared in the middle of your house?"

"Uh . . . well, I'd assume my father had brought some of his colleagues home and ask their names?"

Javier sighed through his nose, which is not quite the same as a snort but shares some common ground. "For someone who studies poisons professionally, you are remarkably trusting."

I rolled my eyes. "It's worked for thirty-five years. It's not like I'm royalty. No one wants to kill me. Why would they?"

"Has your father never ruined a business rival?"

"Well . . ."

"And have you never given testimony in a poisoning case?"

"Errr . . ."

"Or saved someone the poisoner very much did not want saved?"

"When you put it like *that,* I'm surprised I haven't been murdered already."

"That makes two of us." His tone was so bland that I eyed him suspiciously. "At any rate," he continued, "it's also possible that we were observed previously, marked as outsiders, and they were waiting to kill or capture us."

"Which still doesn't get to the matter of why they were alive and moving in the first place," I pointed out. "I'd think it was someone from our side wearing mirror-armor, but I saw the one's eyes." The memory of that flat charcoal gaze made me shudder.

"I don't think they came from the villa originally," Javier said, surprising me.

"What? How can you tell?"

"They weren't dressed like our guards. And the one who almost caught us was wearing metal armor." I must have looked blank, because he made a sweeping gesture down his body. "Look. The king's guard generally wears quilted gambesons like this, yes?"

I nodded.

"Because you don't wear metal in the desert, unless you want to cook yourself alive. But those guards are. And that armor was fitted, so wherever he came from, he was used to wearing it."

"I bow to your expertise," I said. "So they came from somewhere else, and either they came through the mirror or they carried armor with them and put it on here."

"So there should be a real armored man somewhere around here," Javier said. "But I certainly haven't seen one."

I massaged my temples. "What if there isn't a real one?"

"Doesn't there have to be? Reflections don't come from nowhere."

"No, but I think they might be awake," I said.

A line formed between his eyes. *"Awake?* What do you mean by that?"

I sighed. There was no help for it; I was going to have to explain about Grayling. "Okay," I said, carefully watching a corner of the ceiling in case it might have useful advice. It did not. "This is going to sound utterly mad. I wanted you to . . . err . . . accept the mirror-world before I tried to explain this part."

The line deepened into a chasm that threatened to draw in the eyebrows. "Explain what part?"

"Someone told me that I had to watch out for reflections that were awake."

"Someone—you mean someone else *knows*?" His voice rose on the last word. *"Who!?"*

"Well . . . when I fell through the first time, I wasn't exactly alone . . ."

To Javier's credit, he listened to my story without scoffing, though his eyebrows escaped the chasm and began creeping up his forehead instead.

When I finally finished, he gazed at me steadily for an uncomfortable length of time, then said, "You're right. It sounds utterly mad."

"I know that."

"Cats don't talk."

"I know that, too."

"So this Grayling's obviously not a cat."

I paused with my mouth hanging open. That was not where I had expected the conversation to go. "Um . . . I'm pretty sure he's not a dog?"

Javier pinched the bridge of his nose. "I *mean*, he's clearly a shape-shifter or a sorcerer or something like that. Not a cat."

"What are you talking about? Shape-shifters don't exist."

"Neither do talking cats. Neither do otherworlds inside the mirror. But here we are anyway."

I scowled at him. Here we were again. "You're talking about magic. I don't believe in that. It may be that eating the mirror-food provides the body with a fifth humor. And like a lock and a key, only those with the fifth humor can pass through the mirror." I had been working on this theory in the back of my mind, and it was definitely not ready for public consumption yet. "In any event, I am sure there is a completely reasonable explanation."

"Yes," he said, with exaggerated patience, "and the reasonable explanation is that it's *magic*."

"So maybe Grayling's a magic talking cat! If we're going to start using magic to explain things, why not that, too?"

I was bitter and annoyed, and I sounded like it, and it only helped a little when Javier stopped, thought, and finally said, "Okay. I have to give you that one."

The problem was that I didn't know how Grayling worked, and I hadn't been trying to figure it out. Granted, I had a lot on my mind. But the mirror-world was so alien and fascinating that I'd mostly been trying to get information *from* Grayling, not *about* him.

Also, let's be honest, he was a bit of a bastard.

"*Anyway,*" I said, "I'll introduce you as soon as he shows up again. Whenever that is."

"You can't find him?"

"Cats don't come when they're called." I held up a hand. "At one point, he said something about some reflections being awake. I didn't follow up on it because I was still trying to figure out if I was going to turn to dust if I spent too long on the other side. But a reflection that moves and apparently thinks . . . that's got to be what he meant."

Javier grunted. After a minute he said, "If it's awake and moving around, what happens if the original walks in front of a mirror?"

"That . . . is a very good question, actually. I suppose the reflection would get yanked back to that mirror?"

"So if you were using a reflection of yourself to guard something, you'd have to be careful not to walk in front of any more mirrors."

"Assuming that you know your reflection is walking around without you and you *want* that to be happening. We still don't know how or why the reflections wake up, though." I thought of my reflection wandering around the villa without me and got a nasty little shiver along my spine.

"If this reflection's original is working with our poisoner, he wouldn't want to be too far away, I imagine. Otherwise, if he accidentally reflected in a mirror, his reflection would have to walk all the way back here. So either he's in the villa, or camped out in the desert nearby, or . . ." He trailed off.

"Or being fanatically careful about mirrors coming near him."

My mind flashed to the covered mirror in Lady Sorrel's rooms. What had she said? *Bastian never liked them. Sometimes he thought that his enemies were watching him through mirrors.*

No, no, that had been decades ago. Surely that wouldn't have any bearing on what was happening with Snow.

Surely.

Unless Lady Sorrel was using her reflection to creep around the villa *now* and avoiding mirrors was essential . . .

I rubbed my temples. "And we can't check for signs on the other side of the mirror without having armed men after us."

"That's about the size of it."

The silence dragged like a stick through mud. "So . . ." Javier began.

". . . What do we do now?" I finished.

He grunted. So did I.

"I'm going to go see what weapons we've got available," he said finally. "And try to squash the rumors."

"Godspeed," I said. "I'm going to take a nap."

I did not get my nap. Javier was gone for perhaps five minutes when there was a pounding on the door. I yelped and jumped sideways, picturing the armored figure hammering the door open, but then I heard a voice call, "Healer! Healer!" through the wood and realized that it was one of Snow's maids.

Oh Saints, please don't let someone have been injured and they're expecting me to fix it . . . I've done enough dissections that I don't mind blood and internal organs, but I'm generally not expected to put the bits back when I'm done with them. I opened the door with trepidation.

"Healer," said the maid, panting. She'd obviously run, probably from Snow's rooms. "It's the princess. She's sick. Really sick this time. Nurse sent me. Please."

"Oh hell," I said, and snatched up my bag from where it sat next to the desk. I hadn't expected to encounter any emergencies, but old habits die hard, and I'd set it out anyway. The maid made a grateful face as I swept by her and pounded down the hallway toward Snow's suite.

The sounds of retching greeted me the moment I entered the room. Snow was kneeling in the bathing room with Nurse holding back her hair.

The older woman's expression when she saw me was complicated—half hope, half suspicion. I'd upset Snow the last time I was here, but the king trusted me, but, but, but. I went to my knees next to Snow and felt her forehead. She was clammy with sweat and her hands shook on the bowl.

Shit. I knew what questions I wanted to ask, and I also knew that Snow would never answer them with Nurse there.

"Nurse," I said, never taking my eyes off the king's daughter, "I need you to bring me a pitcher of water. Not the one in the room. I want you to go to the pantry, pick one at random, go to the well, and have someone pull up a bucket of water. Don't take your eyes off them while they do it. Don't let the pitcher out of your hands, before or after you fill it. Then bring it up here, and do not set it down until you're back."

Nurse gaped at me. "You don't think . . . ?"

"I don't know," I lied. "But this is the only way I can be absolutely certain that it will be safe, and I don't want to put anything into her system that has even a chance of being poisoned."

Nurse straightened her back and nodded to me. "I shall, Healer," she said, and swept out of the bathing room.

A frightened maid was standing nearby with an armload of towels.

"Don't hover," I snapped at her. "Go and build up the fire in the other room."

That disposed of both potential eavesdroppers. Snow was watching me with haggard amusement. I knew that she knew what I was doing, even if no one else did.

Another spasm wracked her. A moment later, she began to shudder, not quite the same way as before. Her hands fell off the basin, and her back arched. I reached for her, holding her upright, and felt the tremors of her muscles. Then she went limp for a long moment, just long enough for me to panic, then shook herself and bent over the basin again.

Shit. Was that a convulsion? A small one, perhaps. Oddly, she didn't seem to have noticed it. I smoothed back her hair. Her neck was so delicate, the skin so soft that I was almost afraid to touch it. It was easy to forget that she was only twelve, and then moments like this brought it crashing back.

"How many did you eat?" I asked quietly.

She turned her head to look at me. "Two," she said, just as quietly. "Down to the core." I could not tell if she was gloating or confessing. A little of both, I think.

"Two!" Even assuming that she was building up a tolerance, I could not imagine it.

"I can handle two," she said softly. "I did it once before."

"*Why?*"

Snow looked away.

I took a deep breath and tried to calm myself. Saints, how I wanted to be the sort of person who could hold out their hand and say, *I don't know what the problem is, but I promise I'll solve it with you.* Someone who radiated trustworthiness, someone that Snow would believe. Someone like Healer Michael.

But I was only myself, and if we were relying on my skill with people to save Snow, she would be dead in the ground before too much longer.

Instead, I told her the truth. Plain and unvarnished. "Much more of this, and you *will* die. Something will rupture in your throat and you'll drown in your own blood. I can't imagine that's what you want."

She shrugged, looking down at the basin.

"Please. Tell me what's wrong and I'll try to fix it."

Nothing.

"*Who* is making you do this?" I asked. "Is it Lady Sorrel?"

Snow looked up at that, genuinely startled. "*Sorrel?*" she said, sounding twelve again, talking to an adult who had just said something unbelievable. "How would that even work?" Her shoulders shook, though whether from a laugh or an oncoming spasm, I couldn't tell.

"Who is it, then?" I asked hopelessly. My only theory, destroyed.

Snow slumped against me. I looked down, startled, realizing that her face was now only inches from my ear.

"The queen," she breathed.

Oh Saints. Maybe there isn't anyone else. Maybe she really has just gone delusional with grief. I took a deep breath. "Snow, the queen is dead."

"The queen is dead," she echoed. That sly, unhappy smile crept across her face again. She knew things I didn't, even if they brought her no joy. "Long live the Queen," she added, and bent forward over the basin.

CHAPTER 22

I left Nurse giving Snow sips of carefully guarded water and re-treated to my room, feeling as if I'd been beaten with hammers.

Two apples! Saints.

At least I knew now that it wasn't Lady Sorrel. That was a good thing. Except that now, apparently my suspect was a woman who'd been dead for months. Could she have given Snow orders before she died? Was Snow still obeying them, even now?

Could the queen have known about the mirrors?

She came from Silversand, and she brought the mirrors with her. Their primary industry is mirrormaking. If anyone was going to find out . . .

Did that mean the rulers of Silversand knew? They weren't our enemies, but Javier was right to be afraid of that knowledge in the hands of . . . well, of *anyone,* really.

I gave up, summoned Eloise, and sent her to find Javier. She gave me a look that I didn't want to analyze too closely. "Miss . . . you know that men need a bit to recover after . . ."

I put my head in my hands. "Just . . . please tell him I need to speak to him."

When he arrived half an hour later, he didn't look terribly pleased. I suspected that word of our supposed affair had spread. "Don't tell me," he said. "Something else has gone wrong now, hasn't it?" He pinched the bridge of his nose wearily. "I should just staple myself to your back. Every time I leave you alone, some-thing else happens."

I told him about Snow. At the end of it, he still didn't look pleased, but he'd sunk into a chair and was staring at the ceiling while he did it.

"Now what do we do?" I asked him hopelessly.

He shook his head. "What would you do if you could?"

"If I could? Lock Snow in a room with no mirrors, one door, and the two of us as door guards." I smiled mirthlessly. "Though the king was specifically opposed to that."

"If she gets much sicker, they'll let you do just about anything," he said grimly.

"If she gets much sicker, nothing I do will matter. Convulsions. Shit. It's the beginning of the end. If she keeps going . . ." I rested my forehead on my fist against the bedpost. "The king would let us lock her up if we told him about the mirrors. But then he'd know about the mirrors. But if we *don't* do it, Snow will die unless we can figure this out, preferably yesterday."

Javier grunted. It was the grunt that meant agreement, or at least acknowledgment, so I kept going. "This is like one of those horrible philosophy questions. Do you sacrifice one person to potentially save thousands?" I huffed a laugh. "I always thought that was such an easy question, too. *Obviously* you sacrificed the one person. It turns out it's a lot harder when you're going to watch the person die."

"And now?"

I stared at the ceiling. We couldn't tell the king. We'd have to find another way. I wasn't willing to give Snow up for lost. If need be, I'd kidnap her and take her out in the desert myself, away from any sort of mirror.

I relayed this plan to Javier, who pinched the bridge of his nose. "I want to tell you that's a terrible idea."

"No, it's fine, it *is* a terrible idea."

An hour later, sadly, we had no better ideas. The sun had set, and Javier finally got to his feet and gave me a narrow-eyed look. "Is it safe for me to go back to the barracks, or is something else going to happen as soon as I leave?"

"You could stay here, if you're that worried," I said waspishly, then realized what I'd said. I could feel blood rushing into my cheeks. "I don't mean it like that. I mean . . . you know what I mean."

"No *uh*," he said agreeably. Damn it, it wasn't fair that he had to be reliable and brave, did he have to have a sense of humor, too?

"Definitely no uh." The tips of my ears felt hot. "I'll see you tomorrow. Maybe if we sleep on it, we'll think of a better idea than kidnapping."

His sigh seemed to come from his toes. "I hope so. Because if this goes on much longer, Saints help me, I'll be helping you do it."

I slept that night with the mirror covered, and I woke feeling, if not optimistic, at least slightly less doomed than I had the night before. I'd write a letter to the king and tell him that no, Snow really did need to be locked in a tower somewhere. I'd make up an allergy to mirrors. Some people were allergic to silver, after all, and nobody outside the guild knew what chemicals were going into the things. Javier could help me write the letter.

I went down to my workroom in a better frame of mind and spent a pleasant hour puttering around, doing all the small tasks that had needed doing for days but which I'd been putting off. I let the rooster out to roam around and tossed a little parched corn down to give him something to do. "Not much longer now, buddy," I told him. "You're probably out of danger. Which I suppose means you'll have to come home with me, or else you'll end up in the stewpot."

Naturally that was when someone knocked. "Healer Anja!" a voice called through the door.

"What is it?" I called back.

A pause, then another knock. "Healer Anja?"

Damn it all to hell. I scooped up the rooster so he wouldn't bolt when I opened the door, and tucked him firmly under my arm. He radiated resignation.

I pulled the door open and saw . . . no one. *What?*

I took a step forward, into the hall, looked left, looked right, caught a glimpse of a body and a chair, and then someone dropped a mirror on my head.

The cold wash of silver went through me like a line of ice water. The rooster squawked in alarm. Something crashed. I looked down to see that I was standing in a radiating pile of shards. By the look of the frame, it hadn't been a terribly large mirror, but they'd angled it perfectly.

"What?" I said, as the rooster flailed in my arms. "Why—?"

The scrape of a boot on the tiles was the only warning I had. I looked up, saw the guard from before, saw that he had a sword out, and threw the rooster directly into his face.

Much is made about the aggression of roosters toward people, but I've always felt that was a sign of poor husbandry. If a rooster attacks humans, you eat him. This solves the problem nicely, and you get a chicken dinner out of it. It also removes them from the gene pool, so the next generation of roosters will often be rather more pleasant. Most roosters go their whole lives without ever lifting a claw against a human under normal circumstances.

The key words there, however, are *normal circumstances*. Being flung into someone's face is not normal. The rooster went feetfirst, leading with his spurs, which were quite impressive for a beast his age. His claws hit the ornate open mouth guard, one got tangled, and in panic, he began beating the mirror-man's head with his wings.

The guard let out a yell. (Anyone would, really. I hadn't heard them make a noise before, but I decided this wasn't the time to dwell on it.) He had a sword, but there are some circumstances where having a sword works against you, and one of those is when the enemy is quite small and attached to your head. Unable to attack the bird without stabbing himself in the face, he dropped the sword and began flailing.

I did not stick around to see the outcome. I tore past him, down the hall, into the central courtyard, and ran up the stairs. Someone had apparently decided that I needed to go back to the mirror-world, and I did not want to find out why. I heard shouts behind me—shouts plural—and felt an intense pang of guilt for the rooster. *Sorry, buddy. I'm not fast, so I needed the distraction. I will make an offering to Saint Bird for you.*

I made the top of the stairs with a stitch in my side and ran for my room. I yanked the door open, thought, *Wait, wasn't that supposed to be locked?* and skidded inside.

And stopped. And stared.

My mirror had been shattered. It lay in a hundred pieces, throwing fragmented stars of color across the ceiling and walls. I took a numb step forward. How had this happened? You couldn't break the mirror from this side, could you? So someone must have done it in the real world, but why?

The same reason they dropped a mirror over your head. To trap you here. And you walked right into the room.

I spun around, but it was too late. Cold mirror-stuff arms closed over me, clamping my arms to my sides like a vise.

"*Hey!*" I yelled, struggling. I'm not a small woman, as I've said before, and I managed a couple of good kicks, then a hard stomp on the instep. My captor yelped, and his grip loosened a little, but before I could take advantage of that, another figure stepped into view.

It was the armored man, and he had his sword again. He put the point up to my face until my eyes crossed looking down it.

"Ah," I said, and swallowed hard. There was a feather stuck in the helmet's mouth guard, and several long scratches in his dark gray flesh. My rooster had given his best, and I'd squandered it like a fool.

"Come with us, Healer Anja," the armored man said. His voice sounded strangely flat, as if it was coming from some place without echoes. "Your presence is requested by the Queen."

CHAPTER 23

My captors brought me down the hallway, to the pair of suites reserved for the king and queen. Another waking reflection stood in front of them, a woman this time, opening the doors as we approached. The armored man was at my side, his sword still out, holding my elbow in one mailed hand. The one still nursing a sore foot was prodding me along with the point of a sword in my back.

We stepped through the double doors. "Healer Anja, Your Majesty," said the armored man, in his flat, distant voice.

On the king's side, this had been a waiting room of sorts, longer than it was wide, with several comfortable couches. On this side, there were no couches, only a single chair at the far end. As close to a throne room as one could manage, given the circumstances.

In the chair sat the Queen.

She was wearing a scarlet dress that stood out like blood on burnt ground, and her skin was shockingly white. Her eyes looked black. As I went closer, driven by the sword prodding the small of my back, I realized that they were mirror-stuff gray. So was her hair.

Snow sat at her feet, leaning against the Queen's legs.

Oh, I thought, and so many things were suddenly falling into place that I couldn't grasp them all at once. *Oh. I see now.*

"Healer Anja," said the Queen. Her voice had the same flat quality as my captor's. "Snow has told me so much about you."

I didn't answer. My eyes were flicking from Snow's face to the Queen's and back, seeing the resemblance, remembering the little portrait of the sweet-faced chestnut-haired woman in Snow's room.

The queen is dead, I'd said to Snow, and I hadn't been wrong. But the queen's reflection, by some terrible alchemy, lived on.

Five paces from the chair, my guard pulled back on my elbow, and I stopped. I could already feel the bruises forming under his fingertips.

"You did well, pet," said the Mirror Queen, stroking Snow's hair. She wore white gloves. Snow turned her face a little, into her mother's leg. Her mother's reflection's leg. *Oh Saints, what have I gotten myself into?*

"Nothing to say?" the Mirror Queen asked. Her lips were very red.

"Ceruse," I said.

She seemed faintly nonplussed. "What?"

"You're wearing ceruse. But not mixed with egg white, because there's no cracking." I licked dry lips. "I assume it's to cover the mirror-gray color. But everyone knows that it's dangerous now, so you must not have to worry about lead poisoning."

A line formed between her eyes. "After all the time you've spent chasing your tail through my realm, all you can talk about is my makeup?"

The gauntlet dug a little deeper. I lifted my chin. "I don't know what else to say, Your Majesty."

Those red lips curved upward. "Aren't you going to beg for your life?"

I considered this. "Sure, if it'll do any good. Will it?"

"No, but it might be amusing."

There really wasn't anything to say to that. I studied Snow instead. Her face was expressionless, but her eyes were screwed tightly closed.

"I have to go back," she said in a small, childish voice. "They'll come looking soon. I had to lock myself in the bathroom, and Nurse will think I drowned."

"Yes, of course." The Mirror Queen bent down, and for a moment, their hair mingled, white and gray together. She kissed Snow on top of her head, and Snow bounced to her feet.

"Tell me, pet," said the Mirror Queen, "do you think you can put the healer's reflection through the mirror?"

Snow scowled, studying me like a buyer at a slaughterhouse. "Too big," she said. "Even Lady Sorrel's still too big. But maybe soon."

"I know you're trying, pet. Just keep eating your apples." The Mirror Queen nodded graciously, and Snow scampered away. I heard the door close behind me, and the Mirror Queen's smile grew wider and lost some edge of restraint that I hadn't realized was there.

"Is that why you're feeding her the apples?" I asked. "Because you think it'll help her push things through the mirror?"

"Oh, it does," the Mirror Queen said. "She's already done some quite extraordinary things." She tapped one gloved finger against her lips. "Of course, it would be helpful to have you as well. A healer appointed by the king has so much *leeway,* doesn't she?"

Not enough to matter, apparently. I grunted. Javier would have been proud of that grunt.

"I suppose I'll just have to settle for the old lady who runs the place."

"Mmm." I looked down at my feet and wiggled my toes in my sandals, trying not to show my alarm. If Lady Sorrel was under her control, she'd have a great deal of power with the king. Would she tell him about the mirrors? It would be ironic if Javier and I had worked so hard to keep anyone from learning the secret and then the poisoner told him outright.

I wonder how she's controlling the reflections. Bribery? Some kind of power she has?

The Mirror Queen sighed. "I don't get much new conversation here, you know. I was hoping you'd provide more."

"Fine. Why aren't you dead?"

Her smile grew into a predatory thing, revealing black teeth and gums. People say smiles like that are catlike, but I couldn't imagine a bigger contrast than scruffy Grayling and the Mirror Queen. "You still haven't figured it out, have you?"

"Apparently not."

She posed. It was very clearly a pose, very considered—a woman enjoying her audience. "Shall I tell you a story, Healer?"

I shrugged.

"There was a woman," the Mirror Queen began, "once upon a time . . ."

I wished that I had the nerve to demand to sit, but the guard's hand on my arm wasn't letting go. I listened.

"There was a woman, once upon a time, who loved her own reflection. I think perhaps she was a very lonely girl, and so she made her reflection into a companion and spoke to her and imagined the girl in the mirror speaking back. Children do such things, and mostly they grow out of it." The Mirror Queen's red lips thinned a little. "This one did not, and her parents cared only that she was alive and might be married to advantage someday. Her womb was useful to them; her mind was not. Perhaps she knew that, because she did not stop speaking to her reflection. When she grew up, the woman in the mirror grew with her, always agreeing, always present, and the woman's love for her grew greater and greater. In the end, she would not take her meals unless she was in front of the mirror, and she would not sleep unless her reflection slept as well."

"That seems inconvenient," I offered.

"It was terribly dangerous," said the Mirror Queen, "although she didn't know it. Occasional, incidental contact, it does little enough harm. But the woman gave her reflection too much attention, too much emotion, day in and day out. When she married, for a little while, it might have been different. She loved her husband, and he was kind to her, but he was a king first and a husband second, and he was often busy. So she turned back to her old familiar friend in the mirror." Dark teeth flashed again, shocking against the ceruse skin. "Everyone around her thought that she was a little mad, of course."

I could picture it all too clearly. A lonely young woman in the throes of an obsession that drove away anyone who might befriend her. If not for Scand and my sisters, I might have walked the same path myself. By the grace of Saint Adder, I had been able to turn my obsession into something useful. The dead queen had not been so lucky.

The living Queen was still speaking. "And then one day, the woman cut herself, only a little, only a nick, and her hand shook, and the smallest drop landed on the lips of the woman in the mirror."

She paused then, striking another pose, her gloved hands spread on one knee. I had a feeling that I wanted to know the rest of the story, so I gave her what she clearly wanted. "And what happened then?"

"It was the most incredible thing. Her reflection woke up."

You'll know if you meet a waking one, Grayling had told me, with extraordinary understatement. It seemed unlikely that a single drop of blood on glass had actually been the cause, but perhaps there was some other mechanism at work.

Or maybe it really is magic, and you don't know as much as you think you do.

"She woke up?" I prompted.

"Oh yes. Most of the mirror-folk are no more awake than your shadow at your heels. But *she* woke, and she learned, and bit by bit, she began to covet what the woman had and she did not. She began to resent the words that the woman said for her. It was not enough that the reflection had no voice, but to be forced to parrot every insipid thought that entered the woman's head . . . oh, she grew to hate that most desperately of all." The Mirror Queen's eyes had narrowed, and while she was still performing, there was an echo of dark emotion underneath. If I'd doubted that this was a story about herself and the dead queen, I didn't now.

"It took some time to make a plan and to put it into action. In the end, she wrote notes to the woman and left them in the mirror for her to find. The woman was delighted, of course. Her only friend was alive and wanted to speak with her? She could barely contain her joy. So the reflection taught her the way through the mirror and brought her to the other side."

I had the feeling that a lot was being glossed over there, but I didn't want to interrupt the Mirror Queen when she was in mid-flow.

"The reflection confronted the woman there, in the mirror. Not that it was much of a confrontation. The woman was weak and rather silly. How could she have been anything else, given how she'd been raised? But her reflection was strong and hungry, and she wanted the world on the far side of the silver, the world full of warmth, the world that goes on even when there is nothing to reflect it." She sat back in her chair and very deliberately struck another pose. "What do you think, Healer? Can you blame the reflection for coveting what the woman had and she did not?"

"No." I think I would have answered that way even if I hadn't been held in place by a large man with a sword. "No, I can understand that. You wanted to take her place on the other side, didn't you?"

"Can you blame me?"

And the more mirror-food Snow ate, the more she could bring back from the mirror. That was how the Mirror Queen had planned to take the real queen's place. I tried a different tack. "No. But what you're doing is killing Snow. Her body can't take much more of this."

The Mirror Queen made a careless gesture. "She's managed before. Children are stronger than you think."

"A child is already dead."

The Queen's lip rose in a soundless snarl, an ugly look that she smoothed away almost immediately. "That weak, stupid little woman. Who would have thought she had it in her?"

"Please," I said, knowing the words were useless. "Please stop using Snow. I'm sure there's some other way."

She scoffed. "Do you think we haven't seen you poking around here, trying to figure out how everything works? I *let* you do that. I thought you might discover something I'd missed, but no. I made those experiments years ago, and far more besides. I have done things you can't even imagine. And now I am doing what I must."

"I could help you—" I began, but the Mirror Queen was already shaking her head.

"You could, but you won't. Do you think I'm a fool, Healer Anja? The moment I let you go, you'd keep yourself out of the mirror, and Snow with you."

I had no answer for that, because she wasn't wrong.

The Mirror Queen nodded. "Fortunately, I have a use for you on this side, Healer Anja. Guards, take her away."

CHAPTER 24

The guards walked me down to the lower levels, to the servants' quarters, and selected a door. I saw a shiny bolt attached over the outside, a bit of striking real-world color over mirror-stuff. The one in front opened the door, and the one behind prodded me with the sword again.

I took two steps through the doorway and let out a scream that they could probably hear in Four Saints.

A centipede made of hands and fractured faces scuttled from the corner of the room toward the bed, running on dozens of individual fingers. Eyes blinked wildly from the thing's back, and most of a face opened its mouth in a silent shriek.

"*M-mirror-geld!*" I squawked, frozen in place, as it ran beneath the bed.

The armored guard sighed, pushed me aside, and got down on one knee to peer under the bed. He nodded, pulled out his own sword, and made a quick stabbing motion, then dragged the blade out with the mirror-geld impaled on it. It writhed and squirmed, halves of mouths grimacing in apparent agony.

I shrank away as he approached, and he smirked and waved the creature at me, driving me away from the door and farther into the room. The finger legs were held in more mouths, teeth biting into the stumps, with lips that twisted in place. One opened, and the finger it held fell to the floor, making me squawk again.

The guard stomped twice on the severed finger, reducing it to a smear of gray paste, then stalked out, still carrying his grisly prize. The door slammed behind him, and I heard the scrape of the bolt being thrown.

I threw myself at the door in a panic. It rattled slightly. I did it again. It rattled again.

Calm down. Think. The mirror-geld's gone. The bolt isn't going anywhere.

I took several deep breaths and tried to calm my racing heart. No mirror-geld. That was good. I was a prisoner. That was less good. Panicking wouldn't help either way.

Think like a chime-adder. Cool. Quiet. Snakes aren't really coldblooded, they simply adapt to their surroundings. You have to adapt to yours, that's all.

The room itself was small, with a simple bed, a wardrobe, a washbasin, and a chamber pot. It took me a moment to nerve myself up to open the wardrobe, which was empty of both mirror-gelds and useful items.

And then, of course, there was the door. By my calculations, I would have worn my shoulder down to bone long before I damaged the wood enough to get through.

This must be an unused room. Otherwise the owner's things would be here. Maybe that's why they chose it as a cell.

They hadn't searched me. I patted down my pockets and found my penknife, my notebook, and a flat, cloth-wrapped bundle. *The mirror!*

I pulled it out with shaking hands. Would it work here? Could you use a mirror *inside* the mirror? What would happen?

When I was thirteen and doing my first experiments with flasks and burners, Scand had said that any chemistry experiment has three outcomes. "Either what you want happens, nothing happens, or it explodes."

(As it turned out, there was a fourth option, namely 'it turns into a tarry black sludge and ruins a test tube,' but Scand had claimed that was just a subset of nothing happening.)

"Right," I muttered. "Three outcomes." Either nothing happened, or I'd have a working mirror, which I could put my hand through and hopefully unlock the door, or . . .

The thrashing limbs of the mirror-geld filled my brain. *Right. What you want happens, nothing happens, or you explode.*

I gritted my teeth and yanked the wrappings off.

Absolutely nothing happened.

No light. No blaze of color. On the bright side, no dozen extra faces falling off my head.

I looked into it and saw my own reflection looking back. I touched the surface, and it was only cool glass.

. . . Huh.

Wait, if my reflection is in this *mirror, but* I'm *in the mirror-world, does that mean there's another mirror-world past this one? And another past that and another past that?*

When we'd stood between two mirrors as kids, was that infinite line of reflections bouncing back and forth a vision onto infinite silvery worlds? Had we made mirror-gelds not just here, but in each one? Or would I have to take two mirrors into this world and stand between them to make a mirror-geld in the next?

I took a deep breath, rewrapped the mirror, and put it away. This wasn't helping, and I was getting a headache from contemplating too much infinity. Better I should see if I could unscrew the door hinges with my penknife.

As it turned out, no. I managed to strip the screwhead nicely, whereupon I did what I'd been wanting to do for hours now, and burst into tears.

There was no light. There was no dark. Time passed, presumably, but I had no way to measure it. All I could do was sit on the edge of the bed and get colder and colder. The obnoxious thing was that it *wasn't* actually that cold. It was miles away from freezing. But the mirror-stuff didn't ever warm up; it just pulled the heat out of you, hour after hour. And without any water, you'd be amazed how fast you die of exposure, even above freezing.

There was water, after a fashion. The basin was full of dark, oily mirror-water. Sooner or later I'd be thirsty enough to drink it. It probably wouldn't kill me. If the Queen had wanted me dead, she could just have had her guards kill me.

It's not as if she has to worry about how to dispose of my body. Everyone will think I've vanished without a trace, except maybe Javier. I sighed. Blessed Saint Adder, Javier. When he couldn't find me, he'd know I'd gone into the mirror, even though I'd said I wouldn't. Would he guess I'd had a reason? Would he come after me?

A small, treacherous hope bloomed at the thought, which was immediately crushed by the large boot of guilt. One man against however many guards the Queen had? I'd only seen three, but she could have dozens stashed in out-of-the-way rooms. We hadn't gotten anywhere near searching the guard barracks or the barns just down the road.

I took off my outer robe and folded it to sit on, in hopes that the heat would leach away a little more slowly. Normally if you want to stay warm, you want some kind of platform, so you have a layer of air in between your bedding and the ground. But when the blankets might as well *be* the ground, that didn't help much.

What I really need is a hammock made of real fabric. Then if I had enough real layers, I could probably survive for quite some time. So all I need is a large piece of real fabric and two anchor points . . . Hmm, I could probably use the bedposts, if I had something to tie it off with . . .

And while I'm wishing for things, I would like a battering ram to knock the door down.

I sat. When I got too cold, I stood up and walked around, swinging my arms, trying to generate heat. I wondered if I'd survive a night of sleep.

I was doing another circuit of the room when the door opened and they shoved Javier through.

I let out a squawk. The door slammed. Javier fell onto his knees, then his face.

"Javier!" I dropped next to him. "You're here! But what *happened*?"

He groaned. "Worst charge," he mumbled, still facedown. "Gonna staple myself to you." He tried to prop himself up on one forearm and hissed. One eye was already swelling shut.

"Look, it wasn't intentional."

"Yeah." He took a deep, wincing breath. "Saw the broken mirror. Figured something happened."

"Someone decided they wanted me back over here and dropped a mirror over my head." I slid my arm under his. "If you can get up, I can get you onto the bed."

"Fine . . . I'm fine . . ."

Judging by the hissing through his teeth, he was not actually fine, but I managed to haul him up onto the bed, where he fell on his back. "Ahhh . . . that's better. Saints." He put a hand to his black eye. "I chopped one of them in the leg. They weren't happy. There was some kicking."

I began unlacing his jacket. He looked down and managed a weak smile. "First you get me in bed, and now you start undressing me . . ."

"Checking your ribs," I told him tartly. "If one's broken, you could puncture a lung." (Mind you, if one was broken, there wasn't a damn thing I could do about it. You were supposed to bind ribs tight, I think? Not for the first time, I regretted that I hadn't paid more attention to medicine that didn't involve poison.)

There were marks darkening across his body, but none of the ribs moved weirdly when I touched them. That seemed good? Maybe?

"It was mostly the kidneys," he said. "I'll be pissing blood for a while."

I grimaced. That sounded bad. Also completely beyond my ability to fix. "I have no idea what to do about that," I admitted.

"Not much," he said. "The cold sheets feel good. Just give me a minute."

"Take your time. We're not going anywhere."

He squinted at the door. "Where are we?"

"Maid's room."

"Can we break down the door?"

"No." I couldn't, and I was pretty sure Javier shouldn't be slamming into doors with potentially damaged ribs. "The hinges aren't coming unscrewed anytime soon either."

He grunted. It was the resigned *well, shit* grunt. That seemed to pretty well cover the situation.

I fussed with my outer robe and Javier's padded jacket, trying to make something for him to lie on so that he didn't keep losing heat to the mattress. Also, if I was fussing over that, I wasn't thinking about the fact that Javier had come after me and now he was probably going to die along with me. All because he'd walked in on me being careless with the mirror.

No, I definitely didn't want to think about that. If I did, I might start crying again, and that would be utterly humiliating, so I *wasn't* going to do it, and that was *final*.

"Anja?" said Javier. "Anja, it's all right. I'm not going to die of this. I've been hurt a lot worse. I'll be fine. Don't cry."

"I'm not crying," I informed him, my voice thick with tears. "I never cry in front of strangers."

"I'm not a stranger," he pointed out, quite unfairly reasonably.

"Yes, but you shouldn't *be* here. The king made you, and I know how you feel about me, and this is all my fault." I couldn't stop the sob at the end of the sentence, so I turned away and bit the side of my hand so I didn't wail like an infant.

Blessed Saint Adder, was this man doomed to be present at every humiliating moment of my life? *Retching and sick and sobbing . . . Maybe I can get explosive diarrhea and round out the set.*

I took a deep breath and shook myself mentally. My chime-adder wouldn't do this. Chime-adders were slow and calm and deliberate, and as patient as the grave. Utterly unhampered by sentiment. If our souls come back in other bodies, as some followers of Saint Bird believe, I really hoped that next time, I'd get to be a chime-adder.

I wiped my eyes, feeling a little more centered, and then Javier said, "You know how I feel about you?" and blew that all to hell.

"I saw how you looked at me through the mirror, that first day," I said dully, carefully not looking at him. "You were utterly revolted when I took your hand. I'm sure you forgot I could see you. It's not how we expect mirrors to work."

The silence on the other side of the bed got very loud. I scrubbed my sleeve across my cheeks, feeling the brocade scratch against puffy skin. "Look, it's fine. How you feel is how you feel. You've been completely professional the whole time regardless. I shouldn't have said anything. I'm just sorry you got dragged into this."

"I was revolted," said Javier carefully, "because when you took my hand, your reflection reached out on *my* side and actually shoved its fingers *through* my wrist. I could feel each one going into my skin and passing through the layers of meat and then hitting the bone. It didn't hurt, but it felt disgusting."

". . . Oh."

My sister Catherine had hit me on the side of the face with a bowl once. (It wasn't intentional, she was getting it down from the shelf and didn't see me, and I stepped right into it.) What I remember is a bright flash in my vision and then a moment when the whole world slewed sideways and then snapped back into the proper configuration.

This was like that, only without the flash or the headache. I felt the world shift around me. Javier hadn't been looking at me at all. Why had I believed that he was?

Because it was easy. Because it was what the voice of despair whispered all the time, whenever my guard slipped enough to listen. I was too big, too loud, cared too intensely about things that no one else did. Of course he'd find me revolting. Some days I found myself revolting.

"Have you been thinking that all this time?"

I blinked. "Ah—what?"

"That I thought that about you."

"All *what* time?" I muttered. "It's been what, four days?" Granted, those four days had felt like forty years, but still.

I heard a long sigh from behind me and turned around. He had propped himself up slightly, his arms folded rakishly behind his head. "Is this why you're always so grumpy with me?"

"No! Well . . . maybe a little. But mostly I'm just like that. Mostly."

"Uh-huh." He grinned. Javier actually *grinned*. I'd never seen such a broad expression on his face. "Meanwhile, I've spent the last four days assuming you resented being shackled with a guard who wasn't nearly as clever as you."

"What? No! You're plenty clever. And you know all sorts of things about . . . I don't know . . . this kind of thing. Tracking people and dealing with people with swords and all."

His face fell like a rooster launched off a cliff. "For all the good it's done us, since we're currently prisoners of a woman we didn't realize existed."

"I wish I knew how the Queen was still alive, when the real one's dead. I mean, she told me how she 'woke up,' but it sounded like a fairy tale."

"After all this, you don't believe in fairy tales?"

I scowled. "She thinks a drop of blood on the mirror is what woke her up. How is that possible?"

"I'm here because of a bite of potato. How is *that* possible?"

I grunted, because I didn't have an answer. It turned out that grunts were very useful. I'd picked that up from Javier. Eventually we'd probably just be grunting at each other instead of talking. It was a shame that we were going to die, because I would have liked to see that.

Just face it. You're more than half in love with him already.

I was. I'd been fighting it, but it was hopeless and I *knew* it was hopeless, and my head was full of too many things, full of Rose and Snow and the dead queen and the living reflection, and this was the worst possible time to think about love, but here I was thinking about it anyway.

That's humans for you, I suppose. In dreadful danger, with the weight of the world crushing us down, we'll somehow still find ourselves thinking, *I wonder if he likes me?*

I didn't know if that was a great virtue or a mortal failing. Both, maybe. I was pretty sure I knew what Grayling would say about it, anyway.

If I blurted out something like, *By the way, I'm falling in love with you,* there was a chance that Javier would reciprocate. There was also another, much larger chance that I'd just have succeeded in making the last hours of our lives incredibly awkward. Tough call.

Okay, if the guards come back and it looks like they're about to stab us, I'll say it. Then it'll only be an awkward few seconds, and hopefully I'll be dwelling on my upcoming death too hard to be embarrassed.

This seemed like a solid plan. I nodded to myself, pleased, and then something hit the door with a scrabbling thud that sounded like a mountain falling.

SKREEEEE-*thump!*

Both Javier and I jumped. My spine hit the wall, and he actually managed to sit up.

SKREEEEE-*thump!*

It sounded like something was trying to climb up the door, then falling back down. "Oh Saints," I whispered. "Not another mirror-geld, please not another mirror-geld . . ."

SKREEEE . . . eee . . . eee . . . *click!*

Thump.

And then, a thin, cranky voice that didn't quite arrive by the ears said, "Bolts are a stone bitch to work if you don't have thumbs. Don't make me deal with the doorknob, too."

CHAPTER 25

"Grayling!" I yanked the door open, and he strolled in, tail held high, as if he staged single-pawed rescues every day. I went to one knee next to him. "I will get you *so much* fish."

"Yes, you will." He gave my knee a proprietary cheek swipe.

"This is the cat you were talking about?" Javier asked.

"Good to know my reputation precedes me."

Man and cat stared at each other. "You can't be a cat," Javier said finally. "Cats aren't smart enough to talk."

Grayling cocked an ear at me. "Who's this tower of wit?"

"Grayling, this is my friend Javier. Javier, this is my friend Grayling. Could we save the discussion of comparative intelligence until we're *out* of here?"

"That's probably wise," Javier said. "But how did you get past the guards? Shouldn't they have heard that?"

"There aren't any," Grayling said. "Haven't you figured it out, Mister Cats-Aren't-Smart? She's only got four servants in total, and one's her maid. One guard is with her at all times, one does a patrol . . ."

"And I made sure the third one isn't walking anywhere soon," Javier said. "So we're just a stop on the patrol."

"Precisely. Now, we have about four minutes until he's back within earshot, so I am leaving. You can come with me or not, as you like." He strolled back out the door. We hurried after him. Javier shot the bolt on the door so that if the guard didn't check, there'd be no reason to think we'd escaped.

I looked down the hall to the landing and winced at the thought of trying to sneak out past the patrolling guard. Grayling was almost mirror-gray himself, but Javier and I stood out like rabid dogs at a wedding reception.

To my relief, Grayling led us to another servant's room instead, across the hall and one up. There was a bolt on this one as well, but it wasn't locked. We scooted inside, and I was astonished to see *actual* blankets on the bed, an entire nest of them in shades of dull blue and brown, thick enough to ward off the cold. "Someone was here?" I whispered.

"It can't be Snow," Javier said. "I don't know how she's getting away from her maids as often as she is."

This squared with my thoughts. For someone so hedged about with watchers, she was certainly skilled at escaping them, but actually sleeping here?

"Did you think Snow was the first?" Grayling asked. "She started with someone else. An old woman, a little dotty, who trusted the image of the Queen in the mirror." His voice was light and bored, but his tail flicked as he spoke. "There were so many mirrors in the king's palace that even an old servant woman had one. And the queen's reflection needed someone to carry her apples through to this world."

He leaped onto the washstand and leaned over, his tongue flicking out. I saw an inch of water in the basin—real water!— and lunged for it as if . . . well, as if I'd spent most of a day without any water.

It tasted like ambrosia. I didn't even mind that Grayling had been drinking out of it.

"Quiet," Grayling said, lifting his dripping chin from the water. "Guard's coming."

We fell silent. Javier pressed his eye to the crack between door and jamb and watched. I strained my ears and heard the click of bootheels coming . . . pausing . . . then going back the other way, just as my heart had begun to sink.

"Give him five minutes," Grayling said, his thin voice sunken to a whisper (and how did that work, when his mouth didn't move and it seemed to be in our heads?). "Then we'll go."

"Why are there so few of them?" Javier asked, after a lengthy pause.

"Waking them up isn't as easy as all that."

I frowned. "How *does* she wake them up?"

"Blood from the vein," said the cat.

We both stared at him. "What?" I said. "How would that . . . ? It's just *blood*."

"They don't bleed when you cut them," Javier volunteered. "It's all just solid black inside. The one guard didn't fall down until I'd chopped off enough of his calf that it couldn't hold him up."

"Yes, but . . ." I put my hand to my forehead. "Blood isn't *magic*. It's just a fluid in your body, like urine or bile."

"Blood is exactly as magic as mirrors," Grayling said. "I wouldn't begin to speculate about urine or bile."

"Maybe it's the nutrients," I muttered. "Could you use a strong broth instead?"

Claws swiped my ankle, and I yelped. "I do not like to repeat myself," said the cat. "I particularly do not like to repeat myself for *humans*. It is blood from the vein that wakes a reflection, not bile or broth."

"Sorry," I said. "You're the expert." I certainly hated it when amateurs walked in and started giving me their opinion on how I could cure rabies with two quarts of brandy and a raw onion. (The recipes varied wildly, but there was always alcohol and always, *always* an onion.) Here I was doing it to Grayling. "I didn't mean to be rude. I'm just so confused."

"Hmmph." He looked up at me from one golden eye, exactly like an old man looking over his glasses. "Very well. The Mirror Queen, awakened, had an idea of how to wake the others. But for that she needed blood. And once she had Snow and the queen, she no longer needed the old woman to bring things back and forth through the mirror. So she overpowered her and drew her blood to wake the first of her personal guard, then imprisoned her in the mirror-world to keep bleeding her as needed."

His thin voice grew thinner and sharp as a papercut. "She was no one, and nobody missed her. Except an old one-eyed cat that she'd pulled out of a pond once." He turned his head and began savagely grooming his shoulder, not looking at either of us.

"Oh, Saints. Grayling . . ." I reached out a hand to him, then pulled it back, reading the warning signs. "I'm so sorry."

"That's *why* I tried to keep you fools from wandering about in here in the first place. If the Queen catches you, she'll bleed you dry to wake more reflections. But no, humans know better. Humans *always* know better." His tail lashed twice.

"If you'd told me why—" I started to say.

"You'd have listened? You'd have stayed out of the mirror completely? You wouldn't have said, 'Oh no, we have to save the little mewling human kitten, so let's go through the mirror and meet the Queen and see if we can talk things out'?"

I opened my mouth and closed it again.

"That's what I thought," Grayling said.

The Mirror Queen wanted to bleed me to wake up reflections? I pictured it, being trapped in the mirror-world, dragged out occasionally so they could milk my wrist the way I milked the chime-adder's fangs . . . *Dear sweet Saints.* I shuddered.

"She has more guards back in the city," Grayling added. "Or else I would have broken my human out there. But she could only take so many with her across the desert."

"Did you follow the Queen here?" Javier asked. "From Four Saints?"

"Didn't have much choice, did I?" Another tail lash. "Cold and hard and dry, the whole way, and the only water what I stole from their horses. *She* bled for each of those horses, too. The Queen had been going slowly, because there was only so much blood left in the old woman's body, but she woke five horses in a single night to follow Snow here." He shook his head, his ears flat against his skull. "The Queen brought the woman here, hoping she'd regain her strength, but it was too late. She died waking Sorrel's reflection, and the guards threw the body in the pit outside."

"I'm sorry," I said again.

"I should have checked the stables," Javier said. "If we'd seen the horses, we'd have known something was happening. I shouldn't have put it off."

Grayling rolled his good eye. "If I'd known I was going to set off such a spate of apologies, I'd never have said anything. The past is as dead as yesterday's dinner. Now let's get moving, shall we?"

Grayling assured us that the guard's usual circuit took him out the front door to check the pit, then around the garden and back through. He strolled out the door with his tail up, while Javier and I slunk after.

"What *is* that pit?" I asked.

"Mirror-geld work," Grayling said. His tail fluffed a little as he spoke.

"There was one hiding in the cell earlier," I said. "One of the guards killed it."

"They like hidden places," the cat said, "and no, he didn't. You can't kill them, only disassemble them for a time. This world is rotten with them."

I shuddered, remembering the way the one had squirmed on the end of the sword.

We reached the end of the hallway. The courtyard was empty. Javier scanned it, then nodded, and we went forward. "We'll have to find another mirror," I said. "The one in the empty room we used before should work—"

And then the guard who had been sitting on the third floor above our heads, invisible until we were actually in the courtyard, shouted, "*Intruders!*"

Javier swore. I heard the front door slam and the sound of running footsteps. *Oh, of course, they'd put the injured guard up high so he could raise the alarm, that makes sense . . .*

Grayling vanished, a gray-on-gray streak. "Go, go!" said Javier, shoving me toward the nearest door. I opened it, and he flung himself after, slamming the door. There was a thick metal bolt on the inside of this one, to my surprise. *Who has bolts like that in the villa?*

Then I took a few steps down the short entryway, and the room opened up, and I knew.

The room was almost completely dark gray, like all the rooms, except for one thing. A single blanket thrown over a chair, woven in brilliant turquoise and scarlet and gold, blazing like the sun against the mirror-gray.

Lady Sorrel's rooms. Of course. I could easily imagine why someone with her past would want the ability to lock out the world sometimes. Snow must have stolen the blanket at some point and brought it back here.

I heard the bolt shoot home. A moment later, blows hammered ineffectually on the other side of the door. "That'll hold him for a while," said Javier with satisfaction. "He'll have to go out and up through the garden door. Once he's gone, we can—"

The blanket moved.

Gray on gray hides a multitude of things. Even old women tucked under blankets. Lady Sorrel's reflection rose to her feet, pulling the colorful blanket more tightly around herself. "My goodness," she said, cocking her head to one side. "Do I know either of you?"

"Uh. No. I'm afraid not, Lady Sorrel." *Oh Saints, she's awake. Blessed Saint Adder, I don't want to fight her.* "You know us—err—over there." I gestured toward the covered mirror.

Javier followed my gesture, inhaled sharply, and darted toward it. He yanked the dustcover off, revealing—

Nothing.

An empty rectangular frame stood against the wall. He stuck

one hand through it anyway, as if hoping there might be a mirror hidden within, then cursed softly.

"I'm afraid I got rid of that years ago," Lady Sorrel's reflection said apologetically. "I never liked mirrors. And no, the irony's not lost on me." She pursed her lips, her wrinkles rearranging themselves in the cold sculptural light. "Let me guess, you're on the run from that awful woman who calls herself the Queen, aren't you?"

"Yes?" I said uncertainly, grappling with the notion that one of the awakened reflections was not on the Mirror Queen's side.

Mirror Sorrel nodded. "Dreadful, isn't she? My Randolph would certainly never have married *her,* let me tell you!"

"But didn't she wake you up?"

The reflection sniffed. "Yes, by pouring blood down my throat! Can you *imagine?* And then has the nerve to tell me that she wants me to take the place of the *other* me out there, by methods I shudder to contemplate, so I can dance to her tune, thank you *very* much." She rolled her eyes. "I told her to go away while I thought about it, and she hasn't bothered me since. Though little Snow was kind enough to bring this for me." She ran her hand down the blanket fondly.

"Sorry," I said, "can you go back—what were those methods you shudder to contemplate?"

"I hardly like to say," she said. "Incidentally, young man, there's a secret stair behind the wardrobe. I've never had to use it, but I believe it comes out somewhere in the wine cellars."

"I'd really like to know what she said," I said, while Javier grabbed the wardrobe and began tugging it away from the wall. "It could be important."

"Mmm." Mirror Sorrel pressed her lips together. "She said that I'd be eating the other Sorrel's heart. My 'rival's heart' is how she put it. And she didn't even ask if I would, she *told* me that I'd be doing it. I think not." She sniffed again. "I don't know if that's murder or suicide, but I want no part of it."

"Oh," I said weakly, while more things jostled into place inside my head. *To wake up, drink blood from the real world. To exist in the real world without fading away, eat your opposite's heart.* It made horrible fairy-tale sense. And what would you do, to live outside the mirror, in the color and warmth, instead of the mirror's eternal cold and gray?

I was honest enough to admit that if I were a reflection, woken by the Queen, I might look on the real world with enough envy that I would think one woman's death was a small price to pay. Maybe that was how the Queen held her subjects, with the promise that they would someday eat their counterpart's heart and be free of the mirror-world forever.

But the Queen had figured without the will of Lady Sorrel's reflection.

"You are very—ethical," I said. "And strong."

"Never could abide organ meats anyway. Now go! They'll be pounding on the garden door soon enough."

"Will you be all right?" Javier asked.

"We're remarkably hard to kill over here," Mirror Sorrel said, lifting a dark gray hand. I started to ask about that, but Javier had my arm and was tugging me toward the doorway behind the wardrobe.

The door was concealed in the wainscoting, so we had to drop to our hands and knees to enter, but once inside, it was a cramped but walkable passage, ending in a flight of stairs. Javier pulled the wardrobe back against the wall as far as he could and closed up the door. We went down the stairs hunched over, trying not to bang our heads on the ceiling.

"What a remarkable woman," Javier said softly.

"On both sides of the mirror."

The stairs hit a landing and a hairpin turn. This must have been a servant's stair once, in the original building.

"So how does eating someone's heart fit in with your theory of humors, not magic?" asked Javier.

I tried not to bristle. It was a good question. "The heart is the seat of the sanguine humor. Perhaps the mirror-folk are lacking in the sanguine humors, which is why blood awakens them. A whole heart might strengthen them enough to pass through."

"Makes sense."

It was my turn to grunt. It was a good theory, but it didn't explain a few key facts, like why Mirror Sorrel would have to eat her counterpart's heart specifically. Scand would have been poking holes in it like no one's business.

Javier's next question was the one that took me by surprise. "Do you think Snow is real?"

"I . . . don't know. No, the mirror-food makes her sick, so I *think* she is real? And if she wasn't, she'd have had to eat . . . her own . . . heart . . ."

She was cutting our daughter's heart out.

Ask Rose to button up her coat and she'd have to stop and look at it to see where the buttons were . . . Then she started getting lost in a castle she'd lived in all her life. It was as if she'd forgotten which way the hallways went . . .

"Oh hell," I said. "Princess Snow is real. But her sister Rose wasn't."

CHAPTER 26

It made sense. It made awful sense. If the real Rose had gone through the mirror, the Mirror Queen could easily have captured her, cut out her heart, and fed it to her reflection. I wondered what had motivated her. Was it an experiment to see if it would work? Surely the Mirror Queen had tested it beforehand. I'd have been feeding mirror-roosters their own hearts for weeks before I tried it on anything bigger, but I had no reason to think that the Mirror Queen was terribly rigorous about experiment design. Perhaps she'd simply wanted a cohort on the other side.

Hell, maybe it had been maternal affection. Perhaps the Mirror Queen wanted her children to have that world full of light and warmth just as much as she wanted it for herself.

Regardless, the mirror-Rose had gone through into our world to take her counterpart's place, but everything would have been backward. Buttons, hallways, letters . . . An adult might be able to hide that, but not a nine-year-old child.

And then Nurse told the queen. Our queen, on this side. And she must have realized at once what had happened. That her own daughter had been replaced by this simulacrum from the other side.

There are plenty of stories of changelings out there, and they're generally used to explain why a child is suddenly behaving badly, or getting sick, or acting peculiar. *It can't be* my *child. My child is normal and healthy, so* this one *must be a stranger.*

Poor dead queen. The first person in history to believe that her child was replaced by a doppelganger and actually be correct.

I wondered why she'd tried to cut out mirror-Rose's heart. A twisted sense of justice? A desperate belief that maybe if she could get the heart out, she could feed it to Rose's body and wake her again?

It must have been far too late for that. The real Rose was probably in a shallow grave somewhere near the mirror-palace. Both Roses lost, killed by their mothers from the other side of the silver.

I explained this to Javier, who listened gravely. "Have I missed anything?" I asked, when I was done. I was hoping that maybe there was some place where my theory unraveled, something that proved it was only a monstrous flight of fancy, not cold truth.

"One thing."

"Yes?"

"We're here." Javier waved to a door set low in the wall.

"Oh, thank the saints." I pressed back against the wall and let him go by me. He pulled the door open with a squeak of hinges—I winced at the sound—and then let out a curse.

The door was apparently as well hidden on the far side as it was at the top. So well hidden, in fact, that someone had stacked barrels against it. All we could see was curved wood and a metal stave.

Javier tried to push it out of the way and got exactly nowhere. "There are too many of them," he said grimly. He started to lie down on the stairs to push with his legs, but I had images of his abused ribs on stone and stopped him.

"I'll try it. And if you say I'm not strong enough, I will punch you in the kidneys."

"Wouldn't dream of it."

Unfortunately it didn't matter that I was bigger than most women. I could have been muscled like a blacksmith and that barrel wouldn't have moved. By the angle of the curve, it was one of the big wine casks, and there were probably two or three more stacked on top and alongside.

In the Red Feather Saga, the secret passages always come out somewhere convenient. I was beginning to suspect that the dialogue wasn't the only thing that was unrealistic.

"Do we go back?" I asked.

Javier pulled a face. "I guess it's that or try to kick the barrel open. And then the next one that falls on top of it, and the next one after that."

"That seems like it would take a lot of work," I said doubtfully.

"But who's going to be waiting for us at the top? I doubt Lady Sorrel can convince them we simply vanished into thin air."

With fine dramatic timing, there was a thud from the distant top of the stairwell. We both looked up.

"Well," I said. "That doesn't—*eerk!*"

There was a scraping noise from the wall, and before my ears had finished registering it, hands grabbed me and yanked me backward. A *lot* of hands. My first disjointed thought was that there must be at least five people holding me and where had they come from? I was carried ten feet back along a passageway, my feet no longer touching the ground.

"Anja!" Javier came pounding after me, his eyes wide. Over his shoulder, I saw something gray come scuttling down from the ceiling, where it had been nearly invisible. It touched something on the wall, and there was another scraping noise as the opening to the secret stair closed up.

The hands set me down. Javier grabbed me and pulled me to him, one hand slapping at the absence of a sword at his side. He swore. I turned and looked at my kidnapper, already half knowing what I'd see.

It was a mirror-geld. Dozens of times larger than the one I'd seen before, a thicket of arms and grasping hands. The ones at the bottom had palms flat against the ground, like feet. The passage we were in was only about four feet wide, but it was at least twelve feet high, and the mirror-geld more than filled it. It looked squashed against the sides, and I saw more hands braced against the walls.

"Oh. Shit," Javier said, forming each word clearly and distinctly.

The wall of hands parted vertically, like mandibles opening, revealing dozens of faces. Only a few were intact. The rest had been pieced inexpertly together, broken mouths fitted against bridgeless noses, skewed and mismatched eyes, all of them wedged against each other like bits of shattered pottery reassembled by a madman.

With horrifying synchronicity, every face squinted down at us.

"There's another one behind us," I said. I had gone past terror into a kind of frozen calm. I was dead. I was utterly and unbelievably dead. The arsenic was drunk, the hemlock eaten. There was no point in screaming about it now. All I could muster was a vague regret that my family wouldn't have ashes to put in the spirit house.

"That's . . . that's one of the things you talked about," Javier said. "Before."

"Yes."

"I didn't realize."

"It wasn't this big."

"It's going to eat us, isn't it?" Javier asked, sounding as calm as I felt.

"Yeah, it is." Our hands found each other and gripped tight.

The small, scuttling mirror-geld went by, clinging to the wall above our heads. We both ducked instinctively. I say *small,* but it was easily as long as I was tall. It had feet like a gecko, if geckos had human hands instead of toes. Each hand spread its fingers, digging into irregularities in the stone.

It occurred to me that Javier had *seen* the mirror-geld grab me, and yet he'd run toward it, not back. With no time to think, he'd still run toward a monstrous horror to save me.

How could you not love a man like that?

The mirror-geld raised its hands in a wave, folding some inward like an insect's legs. We flinched back. But each inward hand only raised an index finger and held it over a face's lips.

Quiet? It wants us to be quiet? But why—

Footsteps clattered down the secret stair. I heard the sound of something knocking on wood, and the head of the Queen's guard said, "What the devil?"

Oh. That's why.

We stood there in absolute silence, Javier, the mirror-gelds, and I. They didn't seem to breathe, and we tried not to. There were two guards, judging by the sounds, and every time one moved, it sounded as if they were standing directly behind me.

Whatever's between us isn't actually stone. Plaster, maybe. I suppose that's the beauty of the mirror-stuff, it all looks the same.

Finally a disgusted voice said, "Well, they didn't get out this way," followed by footsteps going up, followed by silence.

All of us sagged with relief, even the big mirror-geld. The arms lowered, and the faces relaxed, their eyelids drooping.

Then it drew itself up, putting its hand-feet more firmly under it, and began to move backward. It made beckoning gestures with a dozen arms as it went.

I looked at Javier. He looked at me. We had uttered some variant of *now what do we do?* so many times that neither of us needed to say it out loud.

"No idea," he said.

"Me neither."

We followed the mirror-geld, but we didn't let go of each other's hands.

The passage widened gradually as we walked, its edges becoming softer and more organic looking, a tunnel rather than a hallway. The mirror-geld widened as well, and I realized just how compressed it had been. It slumped downward and out to the sides, forming a shape rather like a caterpillar, if a caterpillar were nine feet tall and six feet wide. The hands that enclosed the faces were overhung by a bulky mass of mirror-flesh, seamed together in a patchwork of undifferentiated flesh, studded with dozens of eyes. It looked like a head of sorts, although Saint Adder only knew if it kept a brain there or if it even needed a brain. *And how would it get a brain anyway? You'd have to take one out and hold it up between two mirrors, wouldn't you?*

(Granted, I'd removed brains before, in the course of dissections, but I didn't go waving them at mirrors afterward.)

It must have taken years to grow to that size, if it was only made of parts that fell off between two mirrors. And the fact that the individual bits *hadn't* dissolved meant . . . what? That they were fundamentally different than a regular reflection? That they stayed alive if there were enough of them squished together? That the process somehow woke them up?

It seemed unlikely that I was going to stay alive long enough to find the answer.

Whenever we slowed, the hands would beckon again. At one point, we reached a cross tunnel, and the mirror-geld held up its arms crossed at the wrists and shook its gigantic head back and forth in exaggerated warning. I could feel Javier thinking about bolting, and gripped his hand more tightly.

"I'm not sure it's going to eat us," I said. "It could have picked us both up and dragged us out if that's what it wanted."

"I don't trust it."

"I'm not suggesting we do. But it's bigger and faster and a lot stronger, so I suggest we do what it says for now."

He grunt-sighed. We kept walking.

The tunnel opened abruptly into a much larger passage, wide enough for a team of draft horses. The mirror-geld backed into it, waving us forward. I looked to my right—and saw a scrap of blue.

"Oh Saints," I whispered. "It's the sky. It's brought us out."

Javier looked as baffled as I felt. "But *why*?"

"I don't know. Maybe it doesn't like the Queen?" The Queen's guards *had* killed the small mirror-geld. Was that the reason?

Did they really kill it, though? It wasn't dead, just squirming around on the end of a sword. Looking at the big mirror-geld, it did not look like a thing that would die so easily, or at all. Maybe if you had a few dozen barrels of flaming pitch or a lake full of aqua regia?

The mirror-geld waved us forward again. Swallowing hard, we walked toward the tunnel mouth, past the creature's side. Its very . . . very . . . long side. Looking back along it, I guessed the mirror-geld was at least forty feet long.

Forty feet isn't so bad, I told myself, to stave off the bubble of panic that was starting to rise up again. *There are ordinary animals that big. Whales. Kraken. A couple of sharks. That one fish. With the fins and the weird things coming off its head.*

Trying to remember the name of the fish got me to the tunnel mouth. The faded blue of the sky, even with the dark notches taken out of it, was the most amazing thing I had ever seen. I took a shuddering breath, found that I was, for some reason, near tears, and told myself firmly to stop that nonsense right now.

Unfortunately, the sky was a lot farther away than normal, because the tunnel mouth opened directly onto the side of the giant pit.

"Fifty or sixty feet to the top," said Javier glumly. "Can you climb that far?"

It was sweet of him to ask, when we both knew the answer. "Can you?"

He eyed the smooth gray stone. "I don't know. Maybe."

"It's a long fall down for a maybe."

The mirror-geld shuffled up beside us on its hand-feet, and we pressed against the far wall to give it room. The atavistic horror of its appearance hadn't gone away. I forced myself to study it, the way I'd once forced myself to study spiders. Eventually the spiders had resolved into beautiful alien jewels, inlaid with rose and tan and dusty gold. Something I could admire, even if I had no desire to touch one.

The mirror-geld resisted such treatment. No matter how I looked, it remained a gigantic wall of fragmented flesh, studded with blinking eyes and patchwork faces. I wondered how it assembled itself.

Assuming that the bits all stuck together, did it just build outward, layering new bits on top of old ones? Were there hundreds of faces walled away inside it, still moving?

When the maid Eloise had stood between two mirrors and the parts had fallen off, it seemed as if they had sought each other out, the hands crawling toward the broken faces. Assuming they *wanted* to be together, did that mean that small mirror-gelds wanted to merge into bigger ones, like this? Or was it some kind of cannibalism of the weak by the strong?

More importantly, how many mirror-gelds like this *were* there? There had been multiple tunnel mouths in the pit. Had they all been dug out by this one, or was it one of many?

The mirror-geld swung its overhanging head in our direction and extended two arms. When we did nothing but stare at it, it made grabbing gestures with the hands.

"Does it want something?" asked Javier softly.

"It did save us. Maybe it thinks it deserves payment?" I rummaged through my pockets. What could I possibly offer a creature like this? What did it want?

My fingers closed over the wrapped mirror.

Oh Saints. This is either a brilliant idea or a breathtakingly stupid one. Still, if there was a time for sane and normal ideas, we were long past it. I pulled the mirror out, unwrapped it, and held it out.

The mirror-geld pulled back a little, as if in surprise, then stretched out both hands. I set the mirror on its palms, careful not to touch that chill gray flesh, then held my breath. *Mirrors have power in this place. Mirrors are why it exists.*

I guess now we find out if it's happy with its existence.

The mirror-geld lifted the hand mirror to the wall of faces and gazed into it, tilting it back and forth. "Are you sure that was a good idea?" Javier asked in an undertone.

"I'm not sure about anything right now." I watched the thing's faces, hoping for some clue as to whether we should be celebrating or running.

And then the dozens of mouths began to smile. Awkwardly, one side often unmatched to the other, but smile nonetheless. Eyes crinkled at the corners. The mirror-geld lowered the mirror, and then it went down on its many elbows and *bowed* to us, or as close as it could manage.

"Oh, blessed Saint Adder," I said, exhaling.

The mirror was passed from one hand to another, down the mirror-geld's length, until I lost sight of it. I wondered if it had some pouch to store it in or if it had a hoard at the other end of the tunnel, like a dragon. Then, still smiling, it stretched two hands out to me again.

My heart sank. "I don't have anything else," I told it. "I'm sorry."

The mirror-geld swayed. It took me a moment to realize that it was trying to shake its enormous head. It pointed dozens of fingers at me—at us—and then at the palms of the two outstretched hands.

"Uh," I said.

"Does it want to shake hands?" Javier asked.

"Your guess is as good as mine."

He squared his shoulders. "Right." Before I could move to stop him, he'd put out his own hand and walked toward the mirror-geld.

It took both of his hands in his own and gripped his wrists. More hands shot out and seized his ankles. *Oh Saints, it's got him!* I thought, then scoffed at myself. The mirror-geld had had us all along.

But it did not eat him or rend him limb from limb or any of the horrors I was imagining. It lifted his feet up and slid more hands underneath, then moved one up and stretched out another hand a little higher. He stepped up onto it, and the mirror-geld lifted his other foot up, and offered another hand, higher up its body.

It's making itself into a staircase. Is it trying to help us get out of the pit?

The hands beckoned to me, and I went forward. Cool gray fingers gripped mine, and I felt it seize my feet and lift them. I stepped up onto the next hand. It gave a little under my weight, and my stomach clenched with dread, but the hand gripped my foot, and then the mirror-geld began to move.

It came out of the tunnel mouth, length after length, lifting itself up like the chime-adder pulling back to strike. It swayed as it crawled, and I closed my eyes, clutching at the hands that held me.

It can't possibly reach the top. It's big, but not that big. Is it going to crawl up? Can it do that?

But it did not. The mirror-geld stood, half reared, and then sounds began to come out of it, both familiar and unfamiliar at once.

They were the sounds of hands clapping and fingers snapping. Percussive sounds. Certainly it had no shortage of hands to make them. But then the sounds began to smear together and to modulate into something uncomfortably like speech. It was no language that a human could ever speak, but it had the right cadence, the rise and fall and pause of words strung together.

"What's it doing?" Javier called down to me.

"How should I know?" I yelled back, and then, contradicting myself immediately, "I think it's talking to someone?"

"I was afraid you were going to say that."

I craned my neck over my shoulder, looking for movement. And there it was, off to my right, another bulky body coming out of another nearby hole. It had the same caterpillar-millipede shape as our mirror-geld, but it seemed smaller.

More clapping and snapping noises rang out, some of them from the newcomer. *Newcomers.* I could hear another one behind and above me, and another lower down. I closed my eyes, but that didn't make it any better, so I opened them again and stared fixedly at the gray hands in front of me.

A wall of mirror-flesh slid by in my periphery. A moment later, the hands began handing me up again. I looked up and saw a second mirror-geld hanging out of a tunnel. It reached its hands out to me, and the first mirror-geld heaved me up into its arms, patting my feet as it released me. Then it was up and up again, and then a third mirror-geld, or maybe the first one, had moved into position. Each one could only get us about ten feet, since they had to keep the bulk of their bodies in the holes to balance the rest, but there were a lot of them. At least five, I think. Five isn't a lot when it's grains of rice, but a great deal when it's bites of hemlock or forty-foot monsters. I was past panic again. The mirror-gelds were helping us. Friendly nightmares. I had no idea what to do with that. It didn't make my skin crawl any less. Did that make me ungrateful? I was grateful to the spider that spun her web in the corner of the chicken pen, catching the flies that liked to concentrate there, but even now, I didn't much want to touch her. Unlike the spider, the mirror-gelds were clearly intelligent in some fashion. Father had said many times that you never judge people by how they look, but he meant things like cleft lips and goiters, not hundreds of arms pasted together in a composite abomination. Still, the same principle applied. I told myself I was a bad person.

So what else is new?

Maybe I could get used to the mirror-gelds if I had enough time. It was starting to seem like I might have enough time on the climb out of the pit. Surely we had been doing this for hours. My arms were very tired, but it didn't seem to matter. The hands pulled and tugged me upward, even when I was no longer moving on my own.

And then, quite suddenly, the hand that grabbed me was warm and tanned and encased in a dark blue sleeve. Javier pulled me up onto actual solid ground, even if it was the wrong color. My legs immediately tried to give out, and he grabbed me around the waist to hold me up. Another hug that didn't count. I blinked up at him and thought, *Shit, I'm in love with you,* but what I said was "Oarfish."

Whatever he was expecting, it wasn't that. "Say again?"

"It's an oarfish. The long fish with the things on its head. I was trying to remember . . . You know what? Never mind."

"Are you hysterical?" asked Javier with interest.

"What? No!"

"It wasn't an insult. After that little jaunt, most people would be."

"Well, I'm not. Anyway, who talks about oarfish when they're hysterical?"

"Oh, I can think of at least one person . . ."

I glared at him, but my heart wasn't in it. It's not as if he was wrong.

A massive shape heaved itself up onto the edge of the pit, then over. I thought maybe it was our mirror-geld, the first one. It shook itself, rather like a dog coming out of water, except that hands flailed instead of hair.

"Excuse me," I said, "but I have a couple of questions?"

Javier put a hand over his face and sighed. The mirror-geld tilted its head, still doglike. *Right. Think of it like a dog. A very strange* dog. *The size of a house.* "When someone is reflected between mirrors, and the bits fall off, and they . . . um . . . glom on to each other . . . are those bits like the person who got reflected?"

It cocked its head back the other way.

I tried again. "I mean, do they have the personality and memories? Are there thousands of fragments of *me* running around in the mirrors back home?"

A dozen hands flipped back and forth in an equivocal gesture, then held up their fingers a little space apart.

"Sort of? A little bit?"

The mirror-geld nodded ponderously. Half the hands pointed to itself, and the other half stretched out an arm span apart, holding up their hands.

"You're very big?" I tried.

Another nod. It pointed to me, made the small motion again, then back to itself and the large motion again.

"I'm small . . . you're big . . . uh . . . oh! The bits that came from me are a tiny part of something the size of you?"

Several hands clapped in delight as it wagged its head up and down.

I felt myself grinning. This might be a nightmare, but it was at least an interesting nightmare. "But the little tiny ones, are they more of a person?"

A nod, accompanied by equivocal gestures.

"They are, but it's complicated?"

Nod.

"Do you think you'll be playing twenty questions in mime for a while, or shall we start trying to find our way back home?" asked Javier.

"Mime, I think," I said. "This is important. I wish I knew sign language . . . no, *it* probably wouldn't know it, so that wouldn't work." I raised my voice. "The little ones, how intelligent are they?" I was thinking of the mirror-geld that the Queen's guard had stabbed. Had that been a sentient being?

It made the gesture for *small* again, then tried something more complicated. Two hands held low and tapping across the ground, then lifted up and clasped together. Then it hugged all its arms tightly to itself and looked at me expectantly.

"Um . . . do you mean us? Rescuing us?"

The mirror-geld shook its head, then made the same set of gestures again, then again.

"Uh . . . running . . . scurrying . . . like insects? You eat insects? No? You *collect* insects?"

It looked at me as if it thought my brains were a small gesture and shook its head.

"I know people who collect insects," I muttered defensively.

"I think it's saying that the little mirror-gelds combine together," Javier said. "Then maybe they join up to the big one here?"

The mirror-geld pointed to him, nodding, and clapped its hands in evident delight. I tried not to feel jealous.

"So the bigger you are, the smarter you get?"

It combined a nod and a shrug, which I suspected meant that it was more complicated than that, but that I wasn't too far off. Maybe there was some kind of upper limit to how big a mirror-geld could be, and the big ones had reached it. Or maybe there was just a limit to how smart a mirror-geld could be. I wondered how smart that was. For all I knew, this creature pantomiming at me was a genius far beyond human intellect.

"I wonder if it can read?" I mused. Of course, there'd be no point to it here in the mirror-world, where the writing would be gray on gray, but if I brought regular paper over, maybe it could communicate more effectively—

"I hate to interrupt," said Javier, "but the guards are bound to come by eventually, and this may not be the time."

"Oh. Right."

"Think we could get up there?" Javier asked, pointing up.

The third-story balconies on this side of the villa opened onto rooms for somewhat-less-honored guests, or for the servants of more honored guests, depending on occupancy. Those rooms would certainly have mirrors, if not so large as the ones in the second-floor rooms. I had no idea if they would be big enough to fit through, but it was worth a try.

"If our large friend here can help us climb, maybe."

I started to mime what we wanted to the mirror-geld, but it reared up and placed itself against the villa wall. The thumping of many hands taking its weight shook the building, and I winced. If the guards didn't know where we were before, they did now.

Javier was already climbing hand over hand up the creature's body. I joined him.

Halfway up, I heard a shout. I looked down, and saw the head of the Queen's guard standing a good distance away, staring at us. My heart began thumping, and then I laughed out loud at myself. What was he going to do? Try to chop the mirror-geld to bits with his sword? It would be like trying to cut apart a hillside.

To give him credit, he tried. He lunged at the mirror-geld and hacked his sword down into its back. It thrashed in soundless agony, and I closed my eyes in terror as the hands holding me swayed back and forth.

When I opened them again, the lower half of the mirror-geld had twisted, and dozens of hands were slapping at the guard, trying to pull his sword away.

He can't possibly win. This thing is the size of a dozen elephants.

Evidently he had the same thought, because he backed toward the door, then turned and ran. A moment later I was over the railing, and the mirror-geld hung there like an exhausted caterpillar.

"I'm sorry you're hurt. Thank you," I said. "I don't know why you helped us, but *thank you.*"

A shrug rippled through it.

Then Javier grabbed my wrist and pulled me inside the room. "Quick," he said. "Before he gets here."

There was a mirror on the vanity, throwing a beam of light through the room. It was maybe two feet by eighteen inches, which was a flagrant display of wealth for glorified servant's quarters. It didn't look large enough to fit me, but I didn't care. I stepped onto the chair, got my head and one shoulder through, and dragged myself out the rest of the way, my hips scraping the sides.

I tumbled headfirst onto the floor, acquiring what would probably be some spectacular bruises, but the tiles were *warm*, gloriously warm. I wanted to stretch out and roll around on them.

The mirror gave birth to Javier a moment later, and it did look uncomfortably like birth. He did the same headfirst tumble I had, but managed to turn it into a shoulder roll and landed on his back with a thump. His breath hissed between his teeth, and I remembered the ribs. "You've got to go to a healer," I said. "I mean the real healer, not me."

"Yeah," he said. "And tell everyone we haven't died or run off."

"That too."

Neither of us moved. It was so warm, and there was so much color. Sunlight streamed through the thin slats in the shutters, and the tiles were red and orange with flecks of black, and the walls were white, and I wished that I could breathe in the colors or eat them or something.

"Look at us go," I said, after a while.

"We do seem to be moving awfully quickly." He groaned. "Enough, or we're both going to fall asleep."

"Sleep is everything I want in life." I pushed myself to my elbows and looked over at him. He looked exhausted and disheveled, and I had a strong desire to kiss him. All I'd have to do was roll to one side and . . . *Slow down. There's a large gap between* doesn't find you repulsive *and kissing.*

I tried to think unromantic thoughts. Fortunately one came immediately to mind. "Do you think Grayling made it out okay?"

"I'd be very surprised if he didn't. He's awfully smart for a . . ." Javier paused, then shook his head. "No, I still don't think he's a cat."

I flailed my arms at him, and he changed the subject. "We need to get our story straight. People will have realized that we're missing. You've been gone for at least a day, and I didn't show up for duty last night."

"Right. No rest for the wicked." I pushed all thoughts of kissing aside and sat up. "So, what supposedly happened? Did I fall in an old well or something?"

"You were kidnapped by the poisoner," Javier suggested, "and taken out into the desert. Hours away. You don't think you could find it again."

"How'd you find it?"

"I caught sight of them off in the distance and recognized you. I thought it was something innocuous, like gathering herbs, so I just went out to meet you. Then I realized you had a sack over your head."

"Oh, did I? How'd you recognize me with the sack?"

Javier gave me a look. "Please. I'd know you anywhere."

"Really?"

He looked away hurriedly. Was that a flush? Blessed Saint Adder, it was. Maybe kissing wasn't completely out of the question after all.

"Anyway, I gave chase and found where they took you, then fought them off and ran away with you."

I grinned. "How many of them did you fight? A dozen?"

"Two," he said sternly. "We're trying to make this story plausible."

"What if the guards ask you to lead them to the poisoner's camp?"

"I will be mysteriously unable to find it again. I was too busy not being seen, and everything here looks alike."

"Fair. Did we meet the poisoner?"

"Probably, but I didn't get a good look at him."

"And I had the sack over my head." I considered this. "Not too bad. If anyone starts to grill me, I'll just burst into tears."

Javier gave me a wary look. "Can you do that on command?"

"Usually? No. Right now? I'm so tired that I'm going to start crying if someone looks at me funny." I groaned and hauled myself to my feet. "Which is a bad thing, because the very first person we should talk to is Snow."

The maids gaped at us as we burst into Snow's quarters. Nurse's mouth fell open, but she immediately positioned herself between us and her charge. I briefly wondered why, then realized that Javier had never come here with me before. A strange man charging into the princess's quarters would have been bad enough, but a quick glance in the mirror showed that I looked like I'd been dragged backward through a cactus. My braid had failed hours ago, my clothes were rumpled, and I had hollows under my eyes as deep as Cholla Bay.

"*Healer Anja?*" Nurse said. "What are you—"

"I wasn't really going to do it!" Snow cried, backing toward the balcony doors.

Her voice sounded like breaking glass. It was enough to throw

Nurse into confusion, and that was enough for me to stride past. She tried to get in my way again, and Javier stepped between us. She actually bounced off his chest and backed up with a startled cry.

I left Javier to do what he did best and went after Snow. Behind me, I heard *"What is the meaning of this?"* but Nurse's heart didn't seem to be in it.

Snow had backed past the double doors and was looking about wildly for somewhere to run. The only option was over the balcony, and I closed the gap hastily to make sure she didn't try. "It's fine," I said. "Snow, it's fine. It will be okay." It was not actually fine, and I couldn't see how it would be okay, but sometimes the words matter less than breaking someone's panic.

Snow stared up at me. "I wasn't going to do it," she whispered. "I told her I couldn't."

"I know." I held up both hands. "I'm not angry. It's okay." Actually, on some level, I was unutterably furious, but I could work through that sometime in the future when lives weren't hanging in balance. It didn't matter anyway, because Snow's disbelief was obvious.

"Tell me about your sister, Rose."

Snow looked away, her lips pressed together. I took a deep breath and gripped the railing. *Tell them something wrong so they can correct you.* I hoped it worked as well on Snow as it did on Grayling. "Fine. I'll talk, and we'll see if I'm right. You've known the Queen in the mirror for a long time now. You eat the apples that—what, allow you to manipulate the mirror-world better? Something like that?—so that you can bring living mirror-things through. Mirror-people to replace real people, ideally."

Snow remained stubbornly silent.

"Your mother knew about the mirror, of course. I imagine you saw what she was doing and stole an apple—"

"I did *not*!" Snow burst out. "Mother *gave* it to me!"

I looked out into the desert so that Snow couldn't see my smile. *Gotcha.* "Very well. She gave you the apple and took you through the mirror, I imagine. And you met your sister's reflection there, didn't you? A little girl just like Rose. A waking reflection who could talk to you. And you started trying to bring her through."

Snow's shoulders slumped. "I wanted her to play with my Rose," she whispered. "She was always bothering me to play with her, and I thought maybe if she had someone else . . ."

I nodded. "I have two younger sisters. I remember what it was like. They never leave you alone, even when you have something important to do."

Snow nodded furiously. I wondered if the whole situation could have been averted if there had been more children Rose's age around. *No, probably not. Some tragedies are like landslides, and once they're up to speed, there's no diverting them.* "So you worked out that if you ate enough mirror-food, you could bring the other Rose through. But not for very long, right?"

"Not at first. I got better at it, but it still wasn't for very long. Twenty, thirty minutes. They used to play at being twins, and sometimes they'd play tricks on Nurse. Rosie—the other Rose— would go into a room and then turn to dust, and then Rose would come up behind Nurse while she was looking."

"Not at first . . ." I repeated. "But then Rosie could stay out longer, couldn't she? All of a sudden?"

Snow nodded. "Because Rose was in the mirror, I think? Rose had an accident and hit her head, and mirror-mother was taking care of her. But she needs quiet, and they can't move her while she gets better. So Rosie came out to pretend to be Rose so that no one would wonder where she went."

So that was the story the Mirror Queen had told her. Clever. I closed my eyes and damned the woman to the deepest hell Saint Badger could dig.

"But then Mother . . . with the knife . . ." Snow took a deep breath. "Now she and Rosie are gone, and Rose is all I have left. But mirror-mother won't let me *see* her!" Her voice grew thinner as she talked, stretching like a tendon about to snap. "She keeps saying that if I just eat enough apples to bring other people through, she'll make everything right. And I looked and looked, and I couldn't find Rose, and now I'm stuck out here while she's back home at the palace. I just want to *see* her. She's my *sister*."

"Snow . . ." Healer Michael would have had a gentle way to do it, a kind way. The only way I knew was to drop the truth like an anvil in a millpond. "Snow, reflections can only stay in the real world if they've eaten the real person's heart. Rose is dead. The Mirror Queen killed her so that her reflection—Rosie—could stay out here."

Snow stared at me for a long, long moment, then flushed suddenly red, so red that her eyebrows stood out as starkly white as her eyes. "Her h-heart?"

I nodded. "The Mirror Queen found out how."

"But I *saw* her!" Snow wrung her hands together. "I saw Rose! She was alive!"

I inhaled sharply. Had my theory been wrong? Had I just traumatized the hell out of a child for no reason? "Where did you see her? It's very important."

"In mirror-mother's bedroom. She was asleep in bed, though, and I didn't get to tell her I was sorry and hoped she got better soon."

"When?"

"I . . ." Snow's throat worked. "Right after mirror-mother said she'd had an accident. She told me not to tell my mother, that Rose would get in trouble because she wasn't supposed to be in the mirror by herself."

So the Mirror Queen cut out a child's heart, fed it to her twin, then cleaned her up and put her in her own bed so she could parade the corpse in front of the child's sister. And people think I'm *cold-blooded.* "Snow," I said, "I'm afraid that . . . well . . . that probably wasn't . . . I mean, Rose wasn't . . ."

Something died in Snow's eyes, something I recognized only

by its sudden absence. "She was dead, wasn't she," said the king's daughter, in a flat, final voice.

Part of me said that I was the adult and should invent some comforting lie. I ignored it. "I think she probably was. I'm sorry."

Snow swallowed hard, then turned and rushed directly at me. I started to step back, but she flung her arms around my waist, buried her face in my midriff, and began to sob.

Oh shit. I had lifted my hands out of the way instinctively. Now I lowered one and patted her on the back, saying, "Um . . . there, there. It's okay." It wasn't okay, it would never be okay, but what else could I say? I knew what it was like to have younger sisters you loved. I could well imagine the weight of guilt that had driven Snow to keep serving the Mirror Queen in the hope of someday seeing Rose again.

The queen—the real queen—hadn't realized that Rosie had taken Rose's place until Nurse told her about how she'd changed. Then she'd realized quickly enough. She must have known how such things happened. I wondered how *she'd* learned. It didn't seem like the Mirror Queen would casually drop *by the way, I've been feeding hearts to reflections to see what happens* into conversation, but the saints only knew what kind of twisted relationship the woman had had with her reflection.

Nurse, seeing that Snow had broken down, made another determined effort to get past Javier. I was just as glad to hand her over to someone who could make the proper soothing noises. Once the transfer was complete, I knelt down beside Snow and said softly, "Snow, listen to me."

One watery blue eye blinked at me from the shelter of Nurse's gown. I patted Snow's back again. "I'm sorry. But it can be over now. It can all be over. Don't go back in. Don't eat any more of those apples. As long as you don't go back, she has no power on this side. Do you understand?"

Snow choked something out. I couldn't decipher it, but Nurse, clearly shocked, said, "Now, now, dear, we don't say things like that. You don't want to do anything nasty like that."

"I *do*," Snow declared, yanking herself free. "I'll kill her! I *will*! She lied to me, and she . . . she . . ."

"The worst thing you can do to her is stay here," I said. The saints only knew what Nurse was making of the conversation. "Then she'll have nothing. Just stay out and she loses. Forever. Can you do that for me?"

Snow shuddered, but nodded. "But she . . . oh, *Rose* . . ."

Nurse swept her up in her arms again, and Javier and I went quietly away, leaving Snow to her long-deferred grief.

CHAPTER 27

The captain of the guard was an amiable man with a face like an elderly bloodhound. His duties mostly consisted of breaking up fights between visiting servants and making sure no one got too drunk. There were fewer than a hundred people at the villa, after all. Kidnapping was an astounding break in his day, and judging by his face, he didn't know whether to be excited or horrified.

I had demanded that Javier go to the healer first, and he had said that you reported in to your commander first and that we'd already strained that by going to Snow. We compromised on me yelling, "Rinald!" as we passed the stable, and he appeared a moment later and began stripping Javier's shirt off him while he gave his report.

The bruises that had just been starting when I'd examined him were starting to turn spectacular colors now. I couldn't believe he'd been climbing with his ribs in that state. Rinald let out an appreciative whistle, and the captain stopped mid-word and stared.

After a minute, he recovered and said, "I'm going to guess you engaged the enemy, then."

Javier made a self-deprecating gesture at himself. "The enemy beat me bloody, sir. Three against one. But not quite as bad as they thought they did, and they threw me in with the healer here, so once they were gone, I managed to secure our escape."

The captain's bloodhound jowls trembled as he shook his head. "You did the right thing, man. Can you lead us back there? All . . . well . . . four of us?" I could tell by the deepening wrinkles that he didn't think much of their odds, but presumably he had to do *something*.

"We'll roust a few lads from the stables," Rinald put in. "Can only horse eight, but that should even the odds a bit."

This did not make the captain look much happier, but he nodded. I was suddenly glad that there wasn't an actual camp for them to stumble across.

"I'll be honest, sir, I don't know," Javier said. "I can try, but I was following them, not looking for landmarks, and I'm a city boy. But I'll do my best."

"If they were smart, they'd clear out as soon as they knew you escaped," the captain said. "But maybe we'll get lucky. Healer Anja, did you get a look at any of them?"

I shook my head. "Just heard their voices. I might know them again if I heard them, but I can't swear to it." If being a healer has taught me anything, it's that memory is desperately fallible, so that wouldn't raise any eyebrows.

"Right. Well, guardsman, it sounds like you performed above and beyond the call of duty. I could wish you'd gone for backup, but . . . well, I understand why you didn't, all things considered."

"I would have if I'd had more than a few seconds," Javier promised. "There's a reason we usually work in pairs."

"Right." The captain rubbed his hands over his face. "Healer Anja, let me extend my deepest and profoundest apologies. This should never have happened. This never *has* happened. If I'd thought for an instant that there might be a chance of someone being snatched, I'd have written to the king himself to demand more men."

I felt a stab of guilt. The poor man was probably worried about what had been his retirement post. "No, no, Captain. There was nothing you could have done. I don't doubt that they'd been biding their time since the king left. No one had any reason to believe that matters would escalate like that." Which was true, more or less. Witherleaf's safety lay in its remoteness and the fact that everyone knew everyone else and an outsider would stick out like a sore thumb. "I'll tell the king that to his face if he asks."

That did ease one of the creases in the bloodhound face. The captain nodded, tapped the table, then rose to his feet. "Rinald?"

"Nothing broken," Rinald said, in deep disgust, "though not for lack of trying. Your man here has bones like an ox. I'm binding those ribs, though. And if we do find these miscreants, you are not to engage them, you hear?" He leveled a finger at Javier. "You've done quite enough of that."

"Yes, Healer Rinald," said Javier meekly.

"You're never that obedient with *me*," I muttered.

"Healer Rinald doesn't get into trouble every time I leave him alone for five minutes."

I rolled my eyes and left them to their preparations. I didn't envy Javier a long ride on horseback, but our story seemed to have gone off without a hitch, and I could feel nothing but intense relief.

I limped back to my room, feeling like laundry that had been dropped on the floor wet and had dried out into some fantastically wrinkled shape. Eloise had already bespoken a bath, and she clucked over the bruises on my arm. They were a nasty shade in the shape of fingers with a tight grip, but I was pleased, since it sold the story better.

"It's shocking is what it is," Eloise told me, while her hair made inroads on one of the towels. "We'll be murdered in our beds next."

"Saints, I hope not. I intend to spend a lot of time in my bed in the near future."

She put her hands on her hips. "Are *you* all right? Truly? They didn't . . . ah . . . take any liberties?"

Damnation, we hadn't thought our story through that far. "Other than the sack on my head and dragging me along, no. I don't think they were interested in that. I think they just wanted to know if I'd figured out what was wrong with Snow and, if so, to make sure I didn't tell anyone about it."

"Have you?"

"Have I what?"

"Figured out what's wrong with Her Highness."

"Oh. Uh. Not exactly. I've got a pretty good idea, though." I sank deeper into the water, until I was up to my chin. "If we can just get through the next few days, I think everything will be fine."

And it was fine.

For about three days.

Javier came back from his wild goose chase stiff but in good humor. "I think the captain was relieved we didn't find them," he told me. "We decided they must have run off." Patrols were organized, pulling in half the people at Witherleaf, but of course they didn't see anybody. I felt even more guilty for putting so many people to so much work, but since the alternatives were much worse, I squelched it. Lady Sorrel actually came to see me and made a fuss, which was horribly awkward. The shame over having suspected her of being the poisoner made me want to writhe in my chair, and I couldn't even begin to think about her other self, all alone in the villa except for her enemies.

Another side effect of our adventure was that Rinald put Javier on extremely light duty, so Aaron shadowed my every step for three days. I didn't feel like I could protest, under the circumstances, so I went out and gathered herbs and tried to pump him for information about his partner. This might have been more successful if Aaron weren't demanding to know the identity of every insect he saw and how venomous it was likely to be.

Well, I had no one to blame but myself.

I desperately wanted to talk to Javier about what had happened— the mirror-geld and Grayling and everything else—but without the excuse of him guarding me, I didn't have any chance. Even when I went to check on him in the barracks, telling myself that I was a healer and healers got to do that, we weren't alone, so all we could do was give each other meaningful looks.

"Rinald says I can get back to work soon," Javier said. His black eye had achieved its full magnificence and was starting to fade.

I wanted to say something about how I would be glad to have him back and that it had felt strange without him, but what I blurted out was "I miss you."

"Anja—" he said, but I was already stammering out something about needing to go check on Snow and fled.

"Javier's fine, you know," Aaron told me, as we walked up to the villa.

"What?"

He gave me a sidelong look. "There's nothing wrong with him. No real reason that he hasn't married. Hard to invite women home when you live in the palace barracks, though. And not so many women interested in what passes for married housing up there."

Married? I temporarily lost all power of speech.

"He thinks highly of you."

I grunted.

"Saints, you even sound like him."

It was with some relief that we reached the villa and I saw one of Snow's maids come running. "*There* you are," she gasped out. "Do *you* know where Snow is?"

The villa was in an uproar. As far as I could tell, nobody had seen Snow for at least an hour, and panic was starting to set in. Maids scurried about like mice, checking and rechecking closets and privies and all sorts of places that a twelve-year-old could possibly conceal herself.

I checked my room. To no one's surprise, she wasn't there. She wasn't in my workroom either, or in the pocket garden where I'd seen her eat the apple. I had a pretty good idea where she was, but with Aaron on my heels, I couldn't follow. I joined the kitchen staff in staring down the well.

"She probably wouldn't fit down there," the cook said dubiously.

"Had a dead rat down there last year," said one of the scullions.

"A girl's a lot bigger than a rat."

"It was a big rat . . ."

Aaron was called away to help search the grounds. I thought that meant that I was getting away without a guard, but to my surprise—and mild mortification—Javier came limping into the kitchen courtyard and made a beeline for me.

"Oh . . . ah . . . hello," I mumbled.

"I am provisionally returned to duty," he said. "As long as I don't get into any wrestling matches with any kidnappers."

Our eyes met, and even through my embarrassment, I could muster some humor at the situation.

"Let's . . . err . . . check the workroom again," I suggested. We left the kitchen staff to their discussion of the relative sizes of girl versus rodent and retreated somewhere we could talk without being heard.

"You know where she's gone," I murmured.

"Almost certainly. But why?"

I shook my head helplessly. "I don't know. Or how she got there. According to the maids, she was right there in her room, and she can't have jumped through in front of them."

Javier frowned. "Let's check her room. It's possible she just wanted some time to herself."

"I hope that's all it was."

Snow's room was the villa in miniature, full of people running around, looking into the closet and under the bed as if she'd somehow been invisible the previous dozen times.

"She'll turn up," Nurse said, a tower of calm amidst the chaos. She didn't look terribly pleased to see either of us, but given what had happened the last time, I couldn't blame her. "She slips out sometimes, but she wouldn't just run off."

"When did you last see her?" Javier asked.

"Ah—well—"

"She was using the necessary," one of the maids spoke up, pointing to the privy door. "But she didn't come out, and when I opened it, she wasn't there no more." She had an East Counties accent that thickened on every word, until by the end, there wasn't an *r* to be found.

"She must have slipped out when you weren't looking," said Nurse sternly.

I swung open the door to the privy. Two things struck me simultaneously:

The first was that someone had hung a mirror on the back of the door, which was profoundly bizarre. Who wanted to watch themselves crap? It was tall and rather thin, and I couldn't have fit through it, but someone as skinny as Snow . . . Yeah. I knew exactly where she'd gone.

The second thing that struck me was that the floor was littered with apple cores.

I bent down slowly and picked one up. The remaining fragments of skin were silvery. The flesh beneath had only just begun to brown.

A shadow blocked the light. Javier looked down at me, and his eyes looked like I felt. "How many?" he asked.

"Five," I said.

His grunt sounded like a man taking a mortal wound. "What was she doing?"

I stood. My heart was thudding as if I'd taken a dose of adder venom. "Enough to push an adult through. She's gone to kill the Mirror Queen."

CHAPTER 28

"Kill her?" Javier asked, as I threw things into my medical bag that would probably do no good at all. "Won't pushing her through the mirror mean she's alive over here?"

I shook my head. "Not without the heart. She'll fall to dust, like all reflections do, but she can't come back. There's no one on this side to cast her reflection again. She'll just be gone."

It was clever, in its way. I wouldn't have thought of it, but clearly Snow had. Fortunately I'd given up counting the number of times I'd been outwitted by a twelve-year-old in the last week. It would have been too depressing.

Five apples. She might last until she took a drink or ate real food, but not long after that. Hell, I wasn't sure she'd last even that long. She'd had a convulsion after two, albeit a mild one. Five . . .

There was no cure for any of it, but I packed my medical bag as if there might be. The broken glass had been cleaned from my mirror, so we went up to the empty room on the second floor, pretending to be looking for Snow there, and went through the silver.

It was quiet again, deceptively quiet, as it always was. We were still outnumbered. I'd had an idea, for what little it was worth. The mirror-gelds seemed well inclined toward us. Perhaps that would stretch a little further. Or I'd offer them as many mirrors as they wanted and hope that tipped the balance.

Before we'd stepped through, I'd sent Javier to the stables while I packed. He'd come back with his sword and a rope. Once mirror-side, we tied it to the balcony and went down. (I will spare you the details of me going down a rope. It was horrible, I burned my hands and laid down red lines on my thighs, it probably would have hurt less if I'd just jumped, etc.)

We hurried to the mirror-geld pit, and I knelt on the edge. I didn't want to shout loudly enough to be heard inside, but I needed to summon the mirror-gelds, so I wound up yelling as softly as possible. "Hello? It's me! I need your help again! Hello?"

There was a horribly long silence, and I was starting to think we should hide somewhere for fear of the guard patrolling, when I saw a gray head poking out of one of the holes. It turned and writhed upward, clinging to the wall, and trained a hundred blank eyes on me. Not ours. This one seemed to collect eyes without faces attached.

I lifted one hand and waved, which felt ridiculous. It stared at me for a while longer, then waved back with one arm out of dozens, and went back down into its hole.

Damn it. Had it just been saying hello? Did it realize I needed to talk to another one? I cupped my hands around my mouth, preparing to yell again, when I heard snapping and muted applause. A moment later, our mirror-geld (and wasn't *that* a thing to be thinking?) crawled out of its tunnel and came scurrying up the wall toward us.

"Hi," I said, when it had its head over the edge. "I, uh, need a favor. Another favor."

It held out a dozen pairs of arms, palms up.

I chose to take that as an inquiry. "The Mirror Queen—um, that's the bad woman here. I don't know if you know her—"

The mirror-geld's nod was sharp and furious. Its many mouths dragged down at their mismatched corners in anger.

"Right. She's stolen a child from the other world. Well, it's complicated. But she's been using this child as her link to the other world, and . . ." Oh hell, did the mirror-gelds even know there *was* another world? No, I had to assume they did; we were out of time and had been for at least two hours. "And we'd like her back."

The mirror-geld cocked its head to one side. If it had been a human, it would have been thinking. Saints, I'd been halfway hoping that it was a rescuer of humans in need and would leap at the chance, but maybe not.

Javier spoke up abruptly. "The swords the guards are carrying come from our world. If she has this child, she'll be able to get more and wake more soldiers to use them."

The mirror-geld reared back a little, and the angry faces grew even worse. Those with teeth began to gnash them. It *definitely* didn't like that. I remembered how the guard's sword had chopped into its side. Maybe real metal did more damage than mirror-metal somehow?

It turned then, gave a single emphatic snap into the pit, and crawled up over the edge and toward the front of the villa. I blinked. I'd been hoping it would wait outside a balcony, maybe as some kind of escape plan, but this was different.

This looked like it was going to war.

It made an imperious gesture at the double doors, and we hastened to open them. There was no guard, which I was grateful for, but which had me worried. The mirror-geld gestured to us to go forward. Javier drew his sword and entered the villa. I followed, then looked back over my shoulder.

The mirror-geld began to squash itself down, then went wriggling forward. Hands and faces began to extrude through the doorway, length after length, like malformed living clay.

I had to look away. It's not polite to be sickened by people who are doing you a favor.

Javier paused just before entering the courtyard. "There's a good chance the sentry will see us once we enter," he whispered.

I nodded. The mirror-geld couldn't nod, since it was crammed into a tiny space, but it made shooing gestures. We obeyed.

Javier was about three steps into the courtyard when the voice from the third floor shouted, "What the— *Intruders!*"

The mirror-geld surged forward. I heard the snap of side tables being reduced to matchsticks and the crunch of paintings dragged from the walls. Then I heard a quiet, heartfelt, "Oh, fuck," from overhead and the sentry began shouting, "Mirror-geld! *Mirror-geld!*"

We ran up the stairs, but apparently not fast enough, because hands picked us up from behind, and our monstrous ally carried us up as fast as a horse could trot. It grabbed the railing in a dozen places to pull itself up, and at least one place splintered, but that didn't slow it. That much flesh in motion had a horrible inexorable quality to it, like a landslide somehow thundering *up* a hill. I had the nasty feeling that if the hands dropped me, I'd be crushed before it was even able to stop.

"There!" I said, pointing toward the Mirror Queen's chambers. It, too, had double doors, but they were smaller than the ones out front, and I had no idea how small the mirror-geld could make itself. Had we brought the creature all the way here, only for it to be unable to join us?

"We can open it . . ." I began, ". . . or not," as the creature ripped the doors off their hinges.

Five people stared up at us, their mouths open in shock. Two guards, one servant, the Mirror Queen—and Snow.

"Snow!" I shouted. "Snow, you . . ." And there I stopped, because I had been so focused on finding her that I had no idea how to continue. The Mirror Queen wasn't holding her prisoner. She wasn't shackled to a wall or pinned by the guards. She was standing next to the Queen, looking as shocked as everyone else.

Had I been wrong about why she was here?

Gray hands pushed us into the room, and the bulk of the mirror-geld hit the doors with a sound like raw meat being thrown on a board. Only part of it fit. Cracks appeared in the gray, running up toward the ceiling, and gray plaster dust rained down from the ceiling like ash.

"*What* is the meaning of this?" shouted the Mirror Queen, drawing herself up. Even with the strange muffling of the mirror, it was a very impressive shout, with just the right amount of rage and *what are you doing here, you grubby peasant* scorn. Evil she might be, but the Mirror Queen was royalty to her fingertips.

Unfortunately for her, when a hundred gray hands are clawing their way through the door and the walls are shaking, shouting doesn't actually do much. Her maid shrieked and bolted. Sensibly. The guards, less sensibly, drew their swords and charged toward the mirror-geld, though it must be said, they didn't charge particularly fast.

My only plan was to get to Snow before she collapsed. She was still upright, so maybe I had time to get the charcoal into her after all. I dodged around the guards, which only partially worked. One of the two broke away to stop me.

However relieved he was to be facing a human, not the mirror-geld, he had reckoned without my bodyguard. Javier leaped between us, and the enemy's sword slid off his with a snarl of steel. I hesitated, almost fatally, thinking of Javier's ribs.

"Go, *go!*" he snapped, retreating before a flurry of blows. "I'll hold him!"

Hold him he did. The guard undoubtedly wanted to follow me, but Javier offered him a choice between me and keeping his head, and he sensibly opted for the latter. I shot a glance past them and saw the second guard, the big one in armor, slashing at the mirror-geld. Gray hands littered the floor, but their loss didn't seem to be slowing the creature down. It hit the wall with another foundation-shaking thump.

"Stop," said the Queen. Her voice cut through the sounds of battle like broken glass through flesh. Everything parted around it. Even the mirror-geld froze, though its severed hands twitched and crawled about the floor nonetheless.

The Mirror Queen's skin was arsenic white, and her dress was as red as the drop of blood that slid slowly down Snow's neck, from the point of the dagger pressed against the girl's throat.

Too slow. This whole time, I'd been too slow. Both Snow and the Mirror Queen had been one step ahead of me, and now I couldn't even cross a single room in time.

"Now," said the Mirror Queen quite calmly, "you are all going to leave here. At once."

I knew—I *knew*—that she had to be bluffing. Snow was the linchpin to all her plans. Without her, the Queen wouldn't even be able to get apples back through the mirror to entrap more victims.

Knowing that someone is bluffing turns out not to matter much when they've got a knife to someone's throat.

"Let her go and we'll leave," said Javier.

"This is not a negotiation," the Mirror Queen informed him. Another drop of blood slid lazily downward. Snow's eyes were half-closed. I wondered if she was about to faint.

Five apples. She's probably going to die anyway. You know *that.*

I knew it. I still couldn't move.

Javier set down his sword and took a step forward, his hands spread. "You don't want to do this," he said.

I was trying to watch both him and the Mirror Queen, so it took me a moment to notice that beyond them, the mirror-geld was gesturing. Even the guard who had been fighting it had turned to watch the scene unfolding, so I was the only one to see its hands moving.

It pointed to me, to the Mirror Queen, to something in its hand. Then again. I couldn't tell what it was carrying at first, a small object of some sort. Then it turned it, and I caught a glimpse of reflected color and realized that it was holding the mirror.

Me. Queen. Mirror.

Javier took another step forward. The Mirror Queen's gray fingers tangled in Snow's hair. "Not another step, guardsman."

Me. Queen. Mirror.

"If you kill her, you'll lose your link to the real world," Javier said.

"What makes you think I only have one?"

I slowly reached into my bag. The saints bless my father and

Healer Michael for impressing the value of organization on me. I knew exactly what I wanted and exactly where it was.

Javier tried another tactic. "She's only a child."

"Her mother killed my child. Only fair, don't you think?" The Mirror Queen pulled Snow's head back by the hair. Snow let out a faint moan.

I pulled out the tiny square of mirror that I used to see if a patient was still breathing. I had no idea if this would work, or even what working would look like, but we were out of options.

If you caught someone between two mirrors in the real world, their reflection fell apart and became a mirror-geld. What would happen if you did the same thing on *this* side?

I didn't know. Whatever it was, it couldn't happen very often, because to get a mirror on this side—a true mirror, not a window back to our world—you had to carry one with you through the silver.

Which I had. Twice now.

The mirror-geld stretched out a hand, nearly at the ceiling, with its mirror in it. I turned mine in my hand, hoping I could match the angle and hoping even harder that the mirror-geld knew what it was doing.

"Enough talking," the Mirror Queen said. "Either you start walking toward the door and take your monstrosity with you, or your king finds himself childless."

I cleared my throat. "He's got an older son, actually."

The Queen said, "What?"

Javier said, "What?"

Both of them looked at me. Under other circumstances, their identical expressions would have been comical. I knew that expression quite well. It was the one that said, *Anja, is this really the time to have this conversation?*

"Prince Gunther," I said. "I believe he's currently attached to the court of Tohni."

The mirror-geld's arm moved back and forth, trying to get the correct angle. *Please, Saints, let this work.* We were only going to get one shot at . . . at whatever this was. I swallowed. "Tohni's a fascinating place. They have a poisonous bird there. It's the only known one in the world."

"Guardsman," said the Mirror Queen, "I suggest you take your idiot and leave. *Now.*"

"It's a type of parrot who eats cocklebur seeds, and the poison seems to transfer to its feathers, so if you handle it, you break out in a ra—"

The mirror-geld stretched a final inch and turned its mirror just so. It reflected off the one in my hand and caught the Queen between us. For a moment, she extended to infinity.

Her white face erupted. Cliffs of gray mirror-stuff extruded from the side of her head, and she cried out in evident agony. Her hands sprouted dozens of extra fingers, and the red dress acquired a monstrous weight of gray sleeves.

The myriad reflections began to calve off her at once. Unlike the incident I had witnessed before, there was nothing solid underneath. When the mirror-stuff fell away, it took part of her skull with it. One dark eye blinked from the floor, and what remained of her head looked like a half-eaten apple, bites taken out, leaving a bloodless void behind.

Snow, with astonishing presence of mind, jerked away from the dagger and slapped at the Mirror Queen's hands. Fingers fell to the floor like grisly rain.

The Mirror Queen staggered back, out of the narrow band of reflection, and the grotesque doubling stopped. The mirror-stuff growths shrank and snapped back into place, but the damage had already been done. She tried to reach for Snow, but only thin slivers remained of her hands. She lifted them before her single eye and cried out, turned, and ran.

Of all of us in the room, Snow was the only one who wasn't frozen in silent horror. The Mirror Queen bolted through the door in the wall with the king's daughter hot on her heels. That was enough to jar me out of my paralysis. I ran for the door and hit it at the same time as Javier.

The room beyond was dominated by the largest mirror the king's wife had brought to Witherleaf. A blast of light and color filled the room, and against it, the broken Mirror Queen looked even more monstrous. I could see daylight through her head. Nothing that looked like that should be moving around.

The Mirror Queen staggered to a halt, turning as if at bay. Her mouth was perfectly intact, the red lips parting as she panted, revealing a blackened tongue.

Snow rammed into her midsection, shoulder first, driving her back toward the mirror's surface.

Snow was only twelve and already half dead of poison, and the Mirror Queen, though torn apart, was still far stronger. But the Mirror Queen took half a step back to brace herself, and there was a small gray cat exactly in back of her ankle, and she went over backward and struck the mirror.

For an instant both she and Snow hung there, as if suspended against the surface. Charcoal shadows ran up Snow's arms and across her face, and I understood what Javier must have seen when I tried to push the bird through the mirror. We both cried out and tried to step forward, but then the gray vanished and the Mirror Queen fell through and Snow fell through on top of her.

By the time we reached the other side of the silver, Snow lay unconscious on the floor, and of the Mirror Queen, there was only sparkling gray dust, and then no longer even that.

CHAPTER 29

"Is she . . . ?"

Javier didn't have to finish the sentence. I was already on my knees, holding the mirror under Snow's nose.

Several ages of the earth passed, and then it fogged. I sat back on my heels and exhaled. "Not yet. Help me get her onto a bed." I looked around the bedchamber that belonged to a dead queen. Everything lay under dustcovers, like the ghosts of furniture. "Maybe not here."

Aaron happened to be coming up the hallway at just that moment, intent on his flirtation with Eloise. They were both treated to the queen's door being kicked open and Javier emerging with the princess in his arms.

"You found her!" Eloise said. "But what happened?"

"Shit," said Aaron, taking in the way Snow's head lolled over Javier's arm. "Is she . . . ?"

"Not yet," I repeated. "Get Rinald. *Now*."

Aaron spun on his heel and ran down the staircase. Eloise darted ahead, flung open a door, and said, "This one's being aired."

The room was a duplicate of mine, down to the enormous mirror. There were more dustcovers, but the mattress was covered in sprigs of lavender. Javier laid Snow down in a cloud of fragrance. The off-white canvas mattress cover was darker than her skin and made her look even paler by comparison. If you were a poetic soul, maybe you'd say she looked like a princess in an enchanted slumber. To me, she mostly just looked dead.

"What can I do?" Eloise asked.

"Get some water," I said. I didn't know that I was going to need any water, but it's the task I always order family members to do.

Eloise nodded. Her hair, perhaps aware of the solemnity of the occasion, was hiding behind her neck. "Do you need a sheet torn into strips?"

I stared at her, baffled. "What?"

"Birthing," murmured Javier in my ear.

"Oh!" Blessed Saint Adder, of course. Most people were used to healing involving a lot of blood. "No, it's not that kind of thing. Just water."

She fled. Javier looked at me. "What do you need?"

"I don't know yet." I curled my fingers around Snow's wrist, trying to feel a pulse, but there was nothing. Not that it meant anything. Finding a wrist pulse in children can be nearly impossible. I tried her throat and then finally just rested my ear against her chest.

When Rinald arrived, panting from the run, that was the pose he found me in. He put his hands on his knees, doubling over, and managed to gasp out, "Is she . . . ?"

"Not yet," I said. Saints, maybe Grayling was right about humans. We did all ask the same questions. "Listen."

He took my place, his ear against Snow's chest. I knew what he was hearing—terrifying silence, finally broken by a thump, then another long silence.

"Saint Sheep's shit," Rinald growled. "Uh—begging your pardon, Healer—"

"No, that about sums it up." I rubbed my face. "She took a massive dose of the poison. The smaller dose causes intense vomiting, but this . . ."

"No convulsions," said Rinald, sitting up. He lifted one arm and let it drop. "No stiffness."

I nodded. "It's not arsenic. I still don't know the exact nature of the compound." I was already digging through my bag. "We'll start by inducing vomiting. Then we'll see if we can get some charcoal in her."

Eloise arrived with water, and I took it with heartfelt thanks and set to work.

Forty-five minutes later, Snow still wasn't dead, but we'd acquired an audience. Aaron stationed himself at the door. The only person who came through was Lady Sorrel, who, for a wonder, did not ask if she was dead. She looked the situation over and asked, "Is there anything the house can provide that will make your lives easier right now?"

"A stiff drink," muttered Rinald.

Lady Sorrel turned her head and barked an order.

Rinald flushed. "Didn't actually mean . . ."

"I am told that brandy is medicinal," Sorrel said calmly. "Anything else?"

I shook my head. "Eloise, are you tired yet?"

The maid, who had been tirelessly cleaning up the mess left by our treatment, shook her head. "I'm here for the long haul, Healer."

I felt an unexpected pang of gratitude. I barely knew Eloise, beyond the fact that she was very good at what she did, but she was familiar where most of the staff was not. I needed that familiarity right now. "Thank you. Javier?"

He shook his head.

Sorrel nodded. "Inform me if there is anything else that can be done. And now I shall get out of your way." She swept out again. The thought came to me in passing that she would probably enjoy the company of the Sorrel in the mirror.

Snow wasn't dead, but she was cold. We'd piled blankets around her but had to leave her chest free so that we could track her heartbeat. I didn't know how much it was helping. I didn't know how much *anything* was helping. We'd managed to get the remains of the apples from her system and put charcoal in at both ends, with no notable change. I was starting to suspect that this wasn't actually from the poison so much as it was from the effort required to push the Mirror Queen through the mirror. I had slept for hours after failing to bring a bird the size of my thumb through the silver. It was hardly surprising that someone the size of the Mirror Queen would induce a coma. Charcoal wasn't going to help with that.

Rinald had come to a similar conclusion, even without knowing about the mirror. "Almost reminds me of a laudanum overdose," he said, scratching the back of his neck. "Only thing to do is wait and see if she wakes up."

"Laudanum overdose," I said blankly.

"Saw it a few times," Rinald said. And then, very quietly, so that only the four of us could hear, he added, "It's not a bad way to go. She's not in any pain."

"Laudanum," I said again. A thought, terrible in its possibility, had come to me. It hung suspended in the middle of my mind, fearful and glorious as a god. "Presents almost like lotus smoke . . ."

Javier met my eyes.

"Do I dare?" I asked him. "It almost never works. It could kill her."

"Is she dying now?" Javier asked.

Rinald sighed. The sun was setting outside, and the shadows were deepening all the worry lines on the horse leech's face. For a moment I could see how he would look when he was old. "Yeah," he said. "She probably is."

Javier's eyes never left my face. "Do it," he said.

That was what I needed to hear. I might have stood and dithered all night otherwise. Eloise went around lighting more lamps, and I went to my bag and pulled out the vial of chime-adder venom.

My hands knew what they were doing. I let them do it. The rest of me prayed as intensely as I had ever prayed in my life. *Blessed Saint Adder, Coiled One, let me save this one life. This girl is dying because she killed a great evil. Please.*

Down at the root, it was the same prayer I prayed over all my patients, addicts and princesses alike. *Please let this work.*

"What is that?" Rinald asked.

"Distilled chime-adder venom," I said. "It strengthens the heart. Hold her head for me."

Snow was so small that it was hard to get the tube into her nose at all. Rinald helped and didn't argue. I suppose he'd dosed horses the same way. I took a deep breath, put my mouth over the end, and blew.

Was there a reaction? The faintest twitch? Was I seeing things just because I wanted to see them?

"Now what?" Rinald asked.

"Now we wait," I said. My voice shook a little, and Javier gripped my shoulder and I wanted to lean into him and cry because this was it, the very last throw of the dice, and I was staking everything on something I'd concocted, something that no other physician had ever prescribed. Harkelion had never written a word about it. If it failed—and it almost always failed—how would I explain it to the king?

Javier tugged gently on my shoulder and I turned and he put his arms around me. It nearly undid me. I pressed my face against the hollow of his throat and thought, *Finally, a hug that counts.* I almost laughed at that, but I was on the fine edge of hysteria, and I knew if I started to laugh, I wouldn't stop.

I stood in the circle of Javier's arms for what felt like a long time. His chest was warm and solid and hard-muscled. As long as neither of us moved, maybe time would stop passing and Snow wouldn't die and I wouldn't have killed her.

Rinald cleared his throat, and Javier released me. Reluctantly, I thought, or maybe that was only the hope talking. The stupid, treacherous hope. It's the hope that wrecks you.

"Is she . . . ?" I asked, because Grayling had been right about almost everything.

Rinald shook his head. "Not yet. In fact, listen."

I laid my head down on Snow's chest.

Silence, and then . . . a beat. And another one, with less time between them. Still not very strong, but closer together.

I sat up. Was that the faintest flush on Snow's cheeks?

It might not mean anything. It could be the last rally before she dies. Don't hope. Don't hope.

Eloise reached out and took my hand. Her fingers were warm. Mine were cold and sweaty, I'm sure. Before I could apologize, she had a warm towel and was wiping my fingers clean, as calmly as if I were an end table that something had spilled on.

"Thank you," I said hoarsely. "You'd be a good nurse."

"I'd hate it," she said.

"Not as much as I hate being a healer right now."

Rinald gave a choking laugh at that. Eloise smiled, and her hair ate the towel.

Rinald and I took turns listening to Snow's heartbeat. Poison doctor and horse leech. I would not have traded him for all the physicians in Four Saints.

I don't know how long it took—not that long, I think, even if it felt like hours. Rinald straightened and nodded to me. The sound under my ear was stronger, faster, almost normal. I bit my lip. *Don't hope. Don't hope.*

"I think it's working," Rinald said.

"Shit. I was trying not to hope."

"Here goes nothing," he muttered, and rubbed his knuckles over Snow's sternum. Javier winced. It's extremely painful. It also works. I reached out and clutched Javier's hand.

Snow's eyelids fluttered and she moaned.

The cheer that all four of us let out was as hoarse and croaking as toad song. Aaron jerked upright from where he leaned against the doorframe. "Is she . . . ?"

I peeled back one of Snow's eyelids, and her pupil contracted. She moaned again, and one hand came up a little way off the bed.

"She's alive," I said.

Aaron let out a whoop, charged into the room, picked Eloise up, and spun her around. She laughed delightedly and flung her arms around his neck.

"Blessed Saint Adder—" I began, and then Javier kissed me.

It was a good kiss. It was warm and solid, and then I think he realized what he was doing and started to pull away, so I opened my mouth and wedged a foot between his, fully intending to trip him and follow him down to the floor if needed. At that point, he got the message and slid his hand up the back of my neck, under my braid, and things proceeded quite nicely until the sound of Aaron braying like a hyena intruded into our awareness and we pulled apart.

"Ah," I said, wiping my mouth.

"Uh," Javier said.

Aaron slapped us both on the back, which staggered me a bit.

"We shouldn't celebrate too soon," I said, in a fine case of closing the door after the horses had burned down the rest of the barn. "This might not last."

Rinald gave me wry look. Aaron tried to look sheepish and failed. Javier grunted.

"You lot should go to bed," Rinald said. "It's late."

"It's just as late for you as for me," I pointed out.

"Yeah, but I didn't drag Snow back from hell by the heel. Or wherever you found her." He gave me another look, this one much too thoughtful. I had a suspicion that Rinald and I would have to have a long talk in the near future.

I started to protest, but a jaw-cracking yawn stole most of it. "Right," I said. "You'll wake me if anything changes?"

"You'll know as soon as I do."

If I was a good healer, I'd probably refuse to leave my patient. But I'm not a good healer, I'm a good problem solver, and the problem with Snow attached was as close to being solved as I could get. I left Rinald to it.

Javier followed me into my room without either of us even

thinking about it. We'd spent the last week in such close quarters that it was almost a reflex now. Except that when I turned around and looked at him, he looked back, and there was something in his eyes like a distant flame, and suddenly it didn't seem like reflex anymore.

I was suddenly intensely aware of the bed. That it existed. That it was right there, behind me. That it was big enough for two people.

That I was so goddamn tired that if the Saint of Rabbits had appeared and blessed us both with libido beyond human comprehension, I still couldn't have done a damn thing about it.

I opened my mouth to say something and lost it to another massive yawn. Javier grunted.

"Hold on," I demanded. "Was that a *preemptive* grunt?"

He grunted again, but there was a definite smile lurking at the edges of his mouth.

"So," I said. "*Now* what do we do?"

"Oh Saints, not that again!"

I snickered.

Javier ran a hand over the top of his head. "I . . . uh. That is . . ." He glanced toward the bed, then quickly away, as if the sight had burned him. "I don't want to go back to the barracks," he said. "In case something changes with Snow. Or the Mirror Queen isn't really dead. Or those mirror-gelds come pouring through the mirror, demanding payment. Or something I haven't thought of goes wrong." He squared his shoulders. "I should. Uh. Go bed down in another room, maybe."

"You could stay here," I said.

He met my eyes and held them. "I could."

I thought long and hard about Isobel telling me to be tactful. But Isobel was what she was, and I was what I was, and if thirty-odd years and a lot of poison hadn't changed that, I might as well embrace it. *Tact is overrated anyway. And if I started being tactful now, he'd probably die of shock.*

"I'm exhausted," I said. "And I'm going to fall asleep standing up in a minute. But I wouldn't mind falling asleep in the same bed as you."

I expected a grunt, but instead I got a smile. A surprisingly shy smile for a man carrying a sword.

"Yeah," he said. "I wouldn't mind that either."

CHAPTER 30

I woke up with something warm and alive against my back, and said muzzily, "Grayling? Izzat you . . . ?"

"No," Javier said, "but I could try to get him if you like."

Shock fired my muscles, and I sat up, suddenly wide awake. "Oh my god. Javier? You're here?"

He was stretched out full length next to me. I'd been on my side, and he'd had one arm flung over my waist and the other stretched out under the pillow. The lazy smile on his face was slowly being replaced by a worried frown.

"Um," he said. "I can leave if you'd like."

"No!" I practically yelled it.

He blinked at me a few times, but then the smile came back and grew wider.

"Sorry," I said. "I was just startled. I didn't expect . . . uh . . ." I looked down at myself. I was wearing a perfectly respectable nightgown. Javier was wearing breeches. *Just* breeches.

"There hasn't been any *uh*," he said.

I swallowed a few times and reminded myself that I was done with trying to be tactful. Then I met his eyes squarely and said, "Would you like there to be?"

For the record, it is not easy to make love to a man with badly bruised ribs.

Afterward, we lay around with the hazy smiles of people who had just *uhhh*-ed. "I would like to try that again," I said, "when

I'm not afraid that you'll puncture a lung if you get too enthusiastic."

"This seems like an excellent plan." He idly stroked his fingertips over my wrist, right where the skin was more sensitive, and I shivered. He made a noise, a furry sort of chuckle deep in his chest, and I decided that I wanted to hear that noise again, preferably as soon as possible.

We lounged for a bit, while the sun streamed in through the glass doors. "I should close the curtains before it gets hot," I said.

"Good idea."

Neither of us moved. I gazed at the fabric hanging over the bed. "I'd like to say something, but I'm afraid I'll ruin this."

He rolled to face me, that familiar line forming between his eyes. "That sounds serious."

"I don't want to ruin this."

"Neither do I."

"If what I say is stupid, will you just forget I said anything?"

He considered. "I suppose it depends on what it is. If it's 'I wish you were Aaron,' I'm afraid I'm not going to get over—"

The pillow took him in the face, and he fell back, laughing. I found an undamaged length of rib cage and poked him in it. "Obviously it's not that."

He grunted. "I think you're just going to have to say it."

I stared at the ceiling and summoned my courage. I didn't look at him. I didn't think I could get through this if I looked at him. "When I thought we were going to die, in the mirror, I wanted to tell you that I was in love with you, but then I thought that it would make everything awkward."

Javier grunted again. The silence drew out until I thought I was going to keel over, and then he said, "It wouldn't have."

"What?"

"It wouldn't have made things awkward." He joined me in contemplating the ceiling.

I felt my brow furrowing as I tried to parse that. "What do you mean?"

"Oh," he said, as if it were nothing of import, "I've been completely mad for you since you dragged me into the mirror."

"*What?*"

He reached over and took my hand, interlacing our fingers. "You were so excited. You tried to show me everything at once, and your eyes lit up, and you were just so fascinated by everything. Gets a man thinking what it would be like to have you look at *him* that way." He cleared his throat. "Anyway, I thought you knew."

"No! I thought I repulsed you."

"Dead and merciless gods," Javier said, and dragged me down into a kiss that proved that whatever else he was, he was definitely not repulsed.

When we finally broke apart, I slumped back against the sheets, feeling positively wrung out. "Well. Glad that's cleared up. But why didn't you *say* something?"

"Didn't want you to think I was a fortune hunter."

I opened my mouth and then closed it again. *Oh.* In the last few days, my family's wealth hadn't seemed terribly important, given the mirrors and the poison and a lot of other things that money couldn't fix. But if you were a guardsman, living in the palace barracks . . . Yes, all right, I understood. "I doubt a fortune hunter would run *toward* a mirror-geld."

"Not a smart one, anyway."

I propped myself up on one elbow. "I should probably go back and thank them. Bring them mirrors or something . . . Do you think Grayling got out okay?"

"I'm sure he did. And I still don't think he's a cat," Javier said.

"Why not? Because he can talk?"

"Yes. No." Javier frowned. "Would a cat really follow someone across the desert like that? A dog, sure. But a cat?"

"Cats can be loyal," I argued.

"Yes, but they're fundamentally lazy."

"Loyalty had nothing to do with it," said a thin voice from under the bed. "She was my person. *Mine.* No one else had the right to interfere. And I wasn't done with her yet."

In a human, that sentiment would have been horrifying. In a cat . . . yeah, I couldn't say I was surprised. "I'm glad you made it out," I said, trying not to think about the fact that he might have been there during the . . . uh.

Grayling emerged from under the bed. There was a dust bunny stuck to his tail. "Please. As if that was ever in doubt."

"So did you get what you wanted?" I asked.

"Vengeance, yes. I could do with more cream." He finally noticed the dust bunny and, with immense dignity, removed it from his tail. Between licks, he added, "I cannot believe you involved *mirror-gelds.* Revolting creatures."

"They saved our lives," I protested. "And they were very helpful."

"Which does not alter the fact that they're revolting."

"Are there a lot of them?" I asked.

"Thousands, I imagine. You get them wherever there are two mirrors together. They dig tunnels under the world and click to one another in the dark." Grayling gave a delicate shudder.

"I thought I might bring them some paper and see if we could communicate."

"Of *course* you did." The cat rolled his good eye. "It's just the sort of thing you'd do." He got to his feet and stalked toward the washroom. Over his shoulder, he said, "The Queen's guards took the horses and fled, incidentally. So, if you decide to go back, you ought to be safe enough."

He vanished through the curtain. I heard a soft thump, as of paws landing on the edge of the basin, and then the non-sound of a cat sliding through the silver.

"There's no way that's a cat," Javier said.

"Don't start."

He glanced over at me, and a wicked grin lit up his face. "So . . . now what do we do?"

I glared at him, which only made his grin wider. "You're lucky I don't—"

Now, I want you to assume that was about to be a truly excellent threat, a threat laden with both menace and literary allusion, cleverly worded but so hyperbolic as to be obviously joking. I'm sure I would have come up with something along those lines, anyway. Unfortunately, before this masterpiece could pass my lips, the door banged open, and Aaron yelled, "Snow's awake!"

Aaron saw rather more of me in the next few seconds than he'd probably expected, but that was his own fault. Certainly by the time I had yanked on my clothes, he had turned around and was staring fixedly at the (now-closed) door. I shoved past him and barreled down the hall to the sickroom.

Rinald beamed at me as I came in. I dropped to my knees next to the bed. Snow still looked wan, but she turned her head to look at me. "Did it work?" she asked hoarsely, glancing past me at Rinald.

"You did it," I told her, knowing she'd understand.

She closed her eyes, an expression of unutterable relief crossing her face. "Then it's over."

I took her hand. It was cold, but the pulse in her wrist was strong again. "You just have to focus on getting better. I suspect it'll be easier now."

She gave a soft huff of a laugh. After a moment, she said, "I think I'm hungry? I haven't been hungry in a long time."

"I suspect the cook will be thrilled to hear that." I got to my feet. "I'll have her send you up a tray."

The king's daughter smiled, and I slipped out of the room, then slumped against the wall. It felt as if I'd been holding my breath ever since the king had walked into my stillroom.

"*Is* it over?" Javier asked.

"Mostly. She's Rinald's patient now. He'll do a much better job than I would." I had never been one to stand around and oversee a recovery. That takes patience and caring and a certain sort of temperament that I absolutely do not possess. Should you happen to be dying and have a choice between me and a cactus to nurse you, the cactus will likely be less prickly and do a better job. "I suppose we should write a letter to the king." I wondered what on earth to tell him. Probably not that killing his wife had been a tragic misunderstanding. I winced at the thought. No, not that. It would be enough to tell him that Snow would get better now. Maybe that would ease some of the lines in the king's . . . in Randolph's face.

Probably there would be rewards and signs of royal favor. The thought was exhausting, but I'd probably be able to deal with it in a few days, or off-load it onto my father, who would know how to handle royal favor gracefully.

But there was still one thing I had to do first.

"Where are we going?" asked Javier, as we climbed the steps to the third floor.

"To confront the Mirror Queen's accomplice."

"I thought that was Snow."

"So did I, at first."

I stopped before a particular door and knocked. The door opened immediately, as if the occupant had been expecting me.

"Ah," said Nurse. "I knew you'd get here eventually."

CHAPTER 31

"Come have a seat," Nurse said, waving us toward chairs. Her room was smaller than mine, but it had a neat little sitting area.

We sat. Nurse perched on the edge of her own chair. When we'd first met, I'd thought of her as rabbitlike, but now she reminded me of a bird.

A surprisingly large number of birds will attack snakes to drive them out of their territory. Snakes eat eggs and baby birds, so it makes sense, but that's still always struck me as a terrible kind of courage in a tiny ball of feather and bone.

"I suppose you know why we're here," I said.

Nurse smiled a little. "I have a fairly good idea, but suppose you tell me?"

I couldn't blame her. No sense in incriminating herself if it turned out that I'd only come to ask about the weather. "You were working for the Mirror Queen," I said.

Javier gave a startled grunt, but Nurse ducked her head like a child caught at mischief. "I suppose one of the servants saw me carrying that mirror?"

I shook my head. "No, actually. I assumed it must have been Snow. It wasn't until later that it occurred to me that she probably wasn't strong enough and certainly not tall enough to drop a mirror that size over my head. That would take an adult. A fairly tall adult. Even then, I wasn't sure. It was Javier who put me on the right track."

"I did?"

"He did?"

"You said that you didn't know how Snow kept slipping out when she had all those people watching her. At the time, I just thought, 'Eh, twelve-year-olds are slippery.' But they aren't. Not to that extent, anyway. Unless somebody is helping them. Somebody who could order the maids out of the room or send them off on errands."

"She didn't know," Nurse said. "She's a clever child, but not as clever as she thinks."

"That makes two of us," I said dryly. "Because there's no way that she could have gotten sick so frequently without someone watching every morsel of food that went in her mouth. And who better to do that than her devoted Nurse?"

"I had no choice," Nurse said. "You know that."

"I don't, actually. Why were you letting her poison herself?" I kept my voice light and calm, despite a strong urge to shake the woman until her teeth rattled.

Nurse gave me an incredulous look. "Because she'd die without it! Haven't you figured that out?"

I gaped at her. *"What?"*

"She's a mirror-child. If she didn't eat mirror-food, she'd waste away to nothing. It was hard enough on her as it is, before you people started coming in, prattling about illness and poisons."

"But she isn't," I said. I *knew* she wasn't. What lies had the Mirror Queen told Nurse? "She's from here. It was Rosie who . . ."

Something clicked inside my head. It wasn't the last piece of the puzzle—probably I'd never get the last pieces, since they were all too scattered now—but it was enough. "Saints. You were helping the Mirror Queen because you felt guilty that Rosie died."

Nurse's composure cracked, and she wiped at her eyes. "It was my fault. I told the queen—I didn't know about the mirrors then—and she killed them. I nearly killed myself. But then *she* came to me in the mirror. I thought I was going mad. And she held up a note, a backward note." She wiped her eyes again. "I've never been easy with my letters, so it took me forever to read it."

"What did it say?" Javier asked.

Nurse gulped. "It said, 'My child is dead.'" She pulled out a handkerchief with trembling hands. "She knew it was my fault. I thought she was the dead queen's ghost haunting me at first, but she explained. The real Snow was dead, too—the queen had killed her first, poor mite—but she sent *her* daughter over here to take her place. And since Rosie was stabbed in front of the mirror, the Queen in the mirror, she had to . . . she was only a reflection, she couldn't stop it . . . so she murdered the real Rose with her own hands . . . I *had* to help her." Nurse looked at me with eyes like broken glass. "Two children were already dead because of me. But I could save this Snow."

She broke down and buried her face in her hands.

I looked at Javier helplessly. I wanted to say, *Now what do we do?* but that had become a joke, and this was not a joke, this was a woman crushed under the weight of guilt for something that had never been her fault to begin with. Javier clearly had no answers, because he was gazing at Nurse with horrified pity.

The Mirror Queen had wrapped Nurse up in a chain of lies and regrets that I couldn't even begin to unpack. I didn't even try. "The Mirror Queen is dead," I said bluntly. "Did you ever go through the mirror yourself?"

Nurse looked up, her face as crumpled as the handkerchief. She looked confused. "Go through how? It was *her* magic that did it."

"Right." *Thank the saints, we don't have to figure out how to stop her from talking. If she tries, they'll assume she's gone mad with grief.* I hated to sentence her to such a fate, but damned if I knew what else to do.

Nurse buried her face in the handkerchief again, her shoulders shaking.

"Snow will be fine," I said. "She's . . . err . . . adapted to the food on this side. The mirror-food was just slowing it down, so she could still go . . . errr . . . home."

The silent sobs slowed. "Truly?" whispered Nurse. "She'll truly be all right?"

"Truly. I . . . err . . . tested some samples." (What samples and what I'd possibly test for, I had no idea, but the point was to re-assure her with the mystique of a healer doing Important Healer Things. It works sometimes, and it was working now, thankfully.)

She whispered a prayer of thanks and pressed the wreckage of the handkerchief against her mouth. After a moment, she said, "Maybe it's for the best. That poor woman. She never got over any of it. Maybe she's happier now."

"I'm sure she is," I said. I wasn't sure if she was talking about the Mirror Queen or the real one, and I decided it didn't matter. I rose to my feet before she could ask any inconvenient questions. "I think, perhaps, it's best if Snow—this Snow—makes a clean break with the past. You should go home. I'll make it right with the king."

Nurse swallowed hard but nodded. Probably she thought that I could make trouble for her. Probably she was right, though I had no intention of doing so. "I'll pack tonight," she said. "The supply wagon comes tomorrow. I can ride out on it." She straightened up a little, and some of the tension in her face eased as she realized that I had no intention of denouncing her. "Yes. I'll be glad to go. I miss my family. And I'm so tired."

"You deserve a rest," I said firmly, and we showed ourselves out.

"Are you sure about this?" Javier asked in an undertone. "She did drop a mirror over your head so you'd be captured."

"I doubt she knew anything about the blood or the hearts. And what am I going to do? Demand restitution?" I was fairly sure that Nurse received a royal pension and wasn't in poverty. I was also sure that a single chest of goods from one of my father's ships was worth more than she saw in a year. "I don't think she's going to do it again."

He nodded slowly. "So now what do we do?"

I snorted. "We wait for the king to arrive, shower us with praise, then get the hell out of here and go home."

"I suppose you'll go back to being a healer."

"I suppose you'll go back to being a guard?"

He grunted. After a moment, he said, "I may be done with guard duty. I'm too old for this. You've seen my ribs."

"Yeah." We had made our way, without really thinking about it, down to the garden, to the stone bench where we'd met so often. There was a gardener working in the distance, but we were well out of earshot.

"You know," I said, sitting down, "sometimes healers go into pretty rough neighborhoods."

"I've seen some of those neighborhoods. It fills me with dread that you'd go galloping through one without an army at your back."

"I never gallop," I said, with dignity. "But it had occurred to me that maybe a bodyguard wouldn't be a bad thing."

"Had it, now?" He raised one eyebrow.

"They might have to stay at the house. Or at least near it. I could get called out at any time of day or night." I shrugged. "Of course, you're done with guard duty. Maybe I'll ask Aaron—"

"You will do *no such thing*," Javier growled, and kissed me, while hummingbirds buzzed furiously around us both.

CHAPTER 32

The mirror-desert was gray on gray, with the sky a soft blue over-head. I shifted my basket to my hip as I climbed the steps to where Lady Sorrel sat.

"I didn't expect to see you again," she said.

I sat the basket down. "Are you alone here?"

"It seems so. That dreadful woman is gone, and her guards have all gone running away." She sniffed haughtily. "Not that they were good company anyway. But they might have left me one of the horses."

"You might talk to the mirror-gelds," I suggested. "If you get lonely. They're . . . um . . . intelligent. Sort of."

She tilted her head and looked up at me skeptically, the exact same way that her counterpart did. That her eyes were solid gray did not lessen the effect at all. "And what, young lady, is a mirror-geld?"

I sat down on the cold chair beside her. "That's a very good question . . ."

After she'd listened to my explanation, such as it was, Lady Sorrel said, "*Huh.* They sound fascinating. Horrible, but fascinating. Well. If I get lonely, perhaps I'll go talk to them." She gazed at the reflected patch of garden a while longer, then said abruptly, "I don't mind this. You'd think I would, but I find whole days go by while I just sit and watch the hummingbirds. And at night there are moths. It's very peaceful." She pursed her lips. "Not much of my life was peaceful, you know. Not for many years. This feels like a rest, at last."

I nodded. "I brought you something, in case you get cold." I flipped open the basket and pulled out a stack of blankets in the most brilliant colors I had been able to find.

A smile spread across her wrinkled charcoal face. "You're a good girl," she said, and patted my hand. "Come back anytime."

After Sorrel, there was only one loose end left. I sat on a bench against the villa wall, where the bougainvillea had grown into a shaded arbor. The shadows lay light and gray along the wall. One of those shadows had a single golden eye.

"Grayling?" I asked quietly, after we'd sat together for a little time.

A thin sigh rippled through my head. He stretched. "More questions, I suppose?"

"Not this time. Or at least, not yet. First I have an answer for you."

"How novel." He examined his claws, found one imperfect, and began nibbling at the point.

"I couldn't figure out how the first person had gone through the mirror," I said. "The Mirror Queen couldn't put anything through. The real queen ate a mirror-apple, but someone had to have brought it back with them in the first place. You said the old woman brought the apples through before the Mirror Queen imprisoned her. But how did she get through?"

The cat stopped even pretending to groom himself and watched me, his tail curled around his hindquarters, as neat as an onyx carving of a cat.

"She would have had to eat something from the mirror first herself. It was a chain with no beginning."

"Perhaps it was magic," said Grayling.

"Actually, I'm pretty sure it was cat hair." I had found little gray hairs all over my robes, impossible to brush off. "It gets in everything. I found one inside my distilling equipment. Sooner or later, it was bound to get into her food. Then . . . what? I suppose she passed by a mirror one day, when the Mirror Queen was watching. You knew that the rooster had eaten mirror-food, so there must be some way to tell."

"You glow," Grayling said quietly. "Like fox fire."

I nodded. A thrasher called from somewhere nearby, *whit-wheet!* The petals of the bougainvillea glowed like fire, even the ones that had fallen and lay dusted like sparks along the path.

"It wasn't revenge, was it? You were the first link in the chain."

"Many things can be true." Grayling closed his eye in a slow blink. "Don't delude yourself. I am not a dog, to feel shame, nor a human to feel responsibility. I am a cat. What I feel is something you will never know. At best, you might call it 'tidiness.' The fur of two worlds was ruffled and needed to be groomed down again."

"*Are* you a cat?" I asked. "Really?"

He was silent for so long that I thought he wasn't going to answer. Just as I started to speak again, he said, "I am more a cat than I am anything else."

Both my eyebrows went up.

He made a thin scoffing sound. "Did you never hear the old tales? The wolf and the fox and the mare that speak to the hero. Did you never wonder where they came from or why they were so much smarter than any other beast?"

"No," I admitted. "I never did. I think probably I have missed some things, by not listening to fairy tales."

It cost me a great deal to say that. I wondered if it was more or less than it had cost Grayling to admit that he had been partly responsible for the Mirror Queen.

"There may be hope for you yet, Healer Anja." It was the first time Grayling had ever used my name. I felt as if I had been given a great compliment, yet I had no idea how to respond.

He stood and stretched again, slow and luxurious, every claw extended and biting into the dust under the arbor. "Speaking of beasts," he said, "you may want to take one last trip through the mirror. That ridiculous rooster of yours has been huddled in the coop in your workroom for days, and he's nearly out of water."

I shot to my feet. "Saints! *Really?*"

"Mmm." He leaped up and landed easily on top of the wall.

"You and the snake and that guardsman of yours are going back to your city, are you not?"

"As soon as the king gets here. You could come with us, if you wanted."

He tilted his head, looking down at me. His eye glowed like fire, and a strange little shiver went over my skin. The thought came to me that the parts of Grayling that weren't very much like a cat also weren't like anything I knew or understood. I licked suddenly dry lips and said, "It seems like the beasts in fairy tales might get lonely, being so different."

"A mirror-cat is never lonely," Grayling said.

I shrugged. "If you feel like doing me any more favors, there's still an old woman on the other side of the silver. I'd feel better if I knew someone was looking out for her." I paused. "Of course, you're not a dog, so you probably don't do things like that."

Grayling gave me a look that said he knew very well what I was doing. "Humans," he said. "Always *wanting* things. Perhaps I'll wander that way. I make no promises."

"I wouldn't expect you to."

"Until we meet again, Healer Anja." Then he was gone, and the last I saw was the flick of a gray tail tip vanishing over the wall.

The world came slowly back into existence around me. I heard the thrasher calling again, and the fallen bougainvillea petals continued to glow, if less brightly than a cat's eye.

There isn't a Saint Cat. The story goes that when all the beasts of heaven banded together and overthrew the pitiless gods, the cat was nowhere to be found. He had been down on earth, and when the beasts asked him why he hadn't joined the battle, he laughed and told them that no cat anywhere came when he was called.

I wondered where that forgotten beast of heaven would be now. I suppose that wasn't very scientific of me.

I sighed. One thing scientists *do* know is that there are mysteries that will never be solved in our lifetimes. Perhaps not for a thousand lifetimes to come. Scand always said that was part of the point. What good is life, if there's nothing left to discover? And I had the mirror-gelds to investigate still. I was on fire with curiosity to know more about them, strange as they might be.

And there was Javier, of course. Maybe it wouldn't work out. Maybe we'd find that if we weren't fighting for our lives, we didn't have much to say to each other.

Maybe we'd be happy beyond our wildest dreams.

I went to collect my rooster, my snake, and my love, and to discover what happened after that.

ACKNOWLEDGMENTS

A little over a decade ago, I went out to lunch with some friends at a strip mall that included a PetSmart, and after lunch, I went by to look at the cats up for adoption. I had recently lost my intensely beloved cat Ben and I was feeling his absence acutely, but I wasn't really looking for a new cat yet. But kittens are always cute, so I thought I'd look.

There were no kittens. There was, however, a lean gray cat, the type that gets called Russian blue even if they're just plain old domestic shorthairs. He had one eye. The other was not gone, but literally never existed in the first place. The eyelid opened onto blank red flesh.

He looked regal and bored and diabolical. His name was listed as Prince Sergio. I stared at him for a while, then went away.

Next week we had lunch at the same mall—this was a regular occurrence—and I went back, assuming that Prince Sergio would have been snapped up by now. He had not. I stared at him awhile longer. I went away.

The next week, he was still there.

After about six weeks of this, I went in and asked for adoption paperwork. At that point I learned that the prince had, in fact, been up for adoption for over a year. He was so unadoptable that he had been taken off rotation, and was only at the Petsmart because his foster carer was moving house and needed the cats out of the way for the duration.

Why was he unadoptable? Was he bad with other cats? People? Dogs? Furniture? Litter boxes? No, he was fine with all of them. People were just creeped out by the blank red eye socket. He had been found living at a motel in Virginia, where he would sneak into the rooms while the maids cleaned up so that he could sleep on the beds. Somebody had dumped him, again, probably because of the eye.

Infuriated at the perfidy of humans, I took him home. While his name was eventually shortened to Sergei, he was just as imperious and demanding and regal as he looked. He was also terrifyingly intelligent. He taught himself to use the toilet, which was extremely startling. (The urge to apologize when you walk in on someone on the toilet, incidentally, does not change even if they're a different species.) He was an escape artist and loved nothing more than to bolt out the door, have a human chase him, then stroll nonchalantly back. He occasionally urinated in the dog's food dish when she annoyed him. We had to move the magnetic knife strip out of his reach because he learned to flick them at the feet of anyone in the kitchen who was not paying sufficient attention to his needs.

But he also loved my husband dearly, enjoyed being carried around like a small, malevolent tree sloth, and wanted to be the little spoon at night.

(I am writing all this in past tense because it is a sad truth that books have longer lifespans than cats. Nevertheless, at the time of this writing, Sergei is still alive, coming up on sixteen, and made mostly of bone and sinew and insolence. And while talking cats in fantasy is a cliché, when the story called for a cryptic mentor, I was completely unable to resist.)

As for the rest of the book—well, years ago now, (though long after Sergei's adoption) I read a wonderful book called *The Artifice of Beauty* by Sally Pointer and immediately thought, "Oh, I *gotta* write a book about this." And I did, and the book was called *Paladin's Grace* and mostly it's about perfume, but poison did come up.

In the course of researching that book, I read another wonderful book called *The Royal Art of Poison* by Eleanor Herman and thought, "Oh, I *gotta* write a book about this."

This is basically my creative process in a nutshell. (I have not quite figured out the fantasy romance that resolves around medieval sewer design, but I'll get there.) So *Hemlock* came about mostly because I read a lot of nonfiction about poison, but also because I find mirrors at night deeply creepy and because I have a one-eyed gray cat who believes that he is a god.

No book is written without help, of course. Thanks go to my editor Lindsey Hall and the whole awesome staff at Tor, to my agent Helen, who somehow keeps selling the books when my pitch is "Ok, so it's like Snow White, except forget Snow, the important thing is the mirror and the poisoned apple, right?", and to my readers, who somehow stay with me when I write book after book that bears very little resemblance to the thing I wrote last time.

Thanks also to my mom, who is awesome, and despite the fact that I keep writing books with wicked mothers, I swear it's no reflection on you!

And as always, my husband Kevin, who reads these things when I'm still feeling my way through the book and convinced that I am the worst writer in the history of the world, and who makes sure the cat litter gets changed before Sergei decides to destroy us all.

T. Kingfisher
Edgewood, New Mexico
2025

ABOUT THE AUTHOR

JR Blackwell

T. KINGFISHER writes fantasy, horror, and occasional oddities, including *Nettle & Bone*, *Thornhedge*, *A Sorceress Comes to Call*, *Swordheart*, *What Moves the Dead*, and *A House With Good Bones*. Under a pen name, she also writes bestselling children's books. She lives in New Mexico with her husband, dog, and cats that almost certainly do not talk.